PERCEPTION

CLUB DESTINY

By Nicole Edwards

The Walkers

Alluring Indulgence
Kaleb
Zane
Travis
Holidays with The Walker Brothers
Ethan
Braydon
Sawyer
Brendon

The Walkers of Coyote Ridge
Curtis
Jared
Hard to Hold
Hard to Handle
Beau
Rex
A Coyote Ridge Christmas
Mack
Kaden & Keegan

Brantley Walker: Off the Books
All In
Without A Trace
Hide & Seek

PERCEPTION

CLUB DESTINY

NICOLE EDWARDS

NICOLE EDWARDS LIMITED
A dba of SL Independent Publishing, LLC
PO Box 1086
Pflugerville, Texas 78691

PERCEPTION
Club Destiny, 8
Nicole Edwards

COVER DETAILS:

Image: © Gabriel Moisa | 123rf.com
Design: © Nicole Edwards Limited

INTERIOR DETAILS:

Formatting: Nicole Edwards Limited
Editing: Blue Otter Editing | www.BlueOtterEditing.com

IDENTIFIERS:

ISBN: (ebook) 978-1-939786-20-3 | (paperback) 978-1-939786-19-7

BISAC: FICTION / Romance / General

To my family.
Thank you for putting up with me and my crazy schedule.
I love you.

Dear reader,

First and foremost, the books that I write are fiction. They are not intended in any way to be a reflection of real life. In Perception, you will find mild BDSM practiced. This book is not intended to be hardcore BDSM by any means. I did a lot of research for this book, and I thank all of the wonderful people who have helped me through this. I will be the first to admit that I am not an expert. I have used creative liberties at times. But one thing I can assure you of is that all scenes within this book are safe, sane, and consensual, as they should be.

Much Love,

~Nicole

Per·cep·tion \pər-ˈsep-shən\

noun - physical sensation interpreted in the
light of experience

PROLOGUE

Nine years ago…

XANDER EXITED THE ELEVATOR ON THE THIRD floor after a painfully long ride in what could easily be referred to as a death trap. Seriously, getting to the third floor shouldn't have taken that long. What the hell?

As he stepped out into the dimly lit area, he glanced around at the well-kept yet drastically outdated furnishings of a small, two-room office. Not only was it drab and dark, it had a musty smell, like there was a water leak somewhere that had never been fixed.

Why in the hell did anyone work in a place like this? He wasn't sure what he had been expecting, but this certainly wasn't it.

Less than impressed, he tried to pretend not to notice. He was there to meet one of his closest friends, Shane Gibson, who had been raving about a real estate agent who was rapidly making a name for herself. He wasn't going in for a design consultation. Thank God.

Based on the office that this up-and-comer worked out of, Xander was having difficulty seeing her success, but he hadn't met her yet, so he refrained from passing judgment.

Xander had no idea how Shane had come to meet Mercedes Bryant, the Realtor who clearly needed a new office, but he didn't necessarily need to know, either. He was in the market for property; his friend believed she could assist him. Nothing else really mattered.

According to Shane, Mercedes specialized in commercial properties, and she'd been referred to as aggressive and emphatic. Based on her office building, Xander was inclined to believe that *wet behind the ears* could probably be added to the list of adjectives used to describe her.

Following the sound of voices coming from the only other room in the place, Xander stopped just outside of the open door and waited for them to acknowledge him.

"What's up, man?" Shane greeted him pleasantly when he looked over from his seat across from an incredibly beautiful woman. "Xander Boone, I'd like you to meet Mercedes Bryant."

Xander ignored the strange smirk on the man's lips.

"Very nice to meet you, Mercedes," Xander greeted the well-dressed woman, who rose from her chair and walked around her desk as he entered the office. A few steps into the small room, he was standing directly in front of her, extending his hand out for her to shake. "Shane," he tacked on with a nod of his head toward his friend.

No, Xander wasn't at all impressed with her choice of offices, but he certainly approved of Mercedes's appearance. Dressed in a pair of black slacks, a crisp white shirt with the top two buttons left undone, her shiny black hair pulled back in a tight ponytail while small gems twinkled in her ears, the woman exuded professionalism. Not to mention sex appeal.

So maybe she looked like she worked for the FBI with the fact that she lacked any color in her wardrobe, but he had to admit that the contrast between that white shirt and her black hair was striking. And her eyes. An intense gray that seemed to peruse slowly over him, leaving a trail of heat in their wake.

When Mercedes took his hand, he swore he felt an electrical current shoot through his arm. Her grip was firm and confident, her hand soft and smooth. An incredible combination, if you asked him.

There was no denying he was physically attracted to the woman.

"Likewise," she responded in a smoky tone that Xander's entire body responded to.

"Xander's looking to purchase that overhauled warehouse you were telling me about," Shane stated after clearing his throat.

"I wouldn't go that far just yet." He glanced over at Shane and then back to Mercedes. "However, I'd like to take a look at it, if you don't mind," Xander added as he continued to watch her.

"Do you have time now?" Mercedes asked, surprising him.

"I do. Shall I follow you?"

"No, I'll drive. That way we can talk on the way."

"I've, uh … got a meeting to run to," Shane interrupted, his eyes darting between the two of them. "But I'll catch up with you later," he told Mercedes, his hand gently touching her arm. "And *you*," he said to Xander, "I'll talk to you this afternoon."

Xander nodded to Shane, not saying a word.

A minute later, Xander was following Mercedes out into the brilliant morning sunshine. Had he not been so drawn to the woman leading the way, he might've noticed there wasn't a single cloud in the sky. But as it was, he was mesmerized by the way the sun shone off of her black hair, giving it a vibrant blue tint.

As they made their way over to the fancy black BMW sitting in the parking lot, Xander did his best to keep his eyes focused on where they were going, but he couldn't seem to look away from her.

Shitty office. Nice clothes. Expensive car.

The combination confused him.

"Shane told me you're a property developer," Mercedes said, glancing over her shoulder as she continued to walk, her heels clicking on the eroded asphalt of the parking lot.

"I dabble here and there," he answered ruefully. He did more than that, but he didn't feel the need to explain himself.

Busted.

There was no doubt she'd just noticed he was staring at her ass. If it bothered her in the least, he couldn't tell.

"Yes, that's what I've heard," she said with a mischievous smirk.

He liked her already.

When Mercedes unlocked the doors to the small car using the key fob she clutched tightly in her hand, Xander climbed inside, ducking so that he didn't hit his head on the roof. He hated little cars. With a passion.

"How do you know Shane?" he asked as she got situated, buckling her seat belt. Xander was attempting to do the same. Attempt was a rather loose interpretation of it, too. As it was, he had to hunch over, crook his head sideways and then reach for the buckle without looking down. Damn little cars.

"I met him a couple of months ago. I'm in the market to rent a new office building. I called on a listing, and he answered the phone," she told him as she started the car, put it in reverse, and began backing out of the parking space.

Xander knew Shane was following in Xander's footsteps as far as property development went, but Shane was starting out slow. He was interested in residential, not so much commercial. The man had recently purchased a couple of buildings and was looking to rent them as office space. Xander, on the other hand, had taken the fast track in both commercial development as well as venture capital investments, and he attributed his success to his aggressiveness.

"This place is not doing it for you anymore?" he asked, nodding toward the building they were passing as she headed out of the parking lot.

Mercedes glanced over at him, pinning him in place with her stare. "Everyone has to start somewhere, Mr. Boone."

True.

"I'm sorry, I wasn't implying—"

"Yes, you were." She laughed gruffly. "And I happen to agree. But I *did* have to start somewhere."

When Mercedes turned her attention back on the road, Xander fought the urge to squirm in his seat. Definitely time to change the subject.

"Tell me more about the warehouse. Shane didn't know much. Just that it's somewhere close to a hundred thousand square feet. True?"

"Yes, give or take a few." She drove the same way that she walked, with sexy precision. He found himself transfixed by the way her hand maneuvered the stick shift. "The building went up in 1967 and has seen quite a few tenants over the years. The current owner's been leasing it out for approximately fifteen years now. The asking price is two point four mil."

Mercedes glanced over at him briefly, and he had to wonder whether she was checking his reaction to the price. If she was waiting for something, she wasn't going to get it. The price was incredibly low, even he knew that much.

"What did the last tenant use it for?" he asked.

"From what I understand, it was used as a call center."

Xander intended to lease the building out as soon as he acquired it. Maybe he'd hang on to it for a few years, then let it go for the right price. He knew without a doubt that he could get a tenant in there rather quickly, but he decided to question Mercedes. "If I need to find a tenant, can you handle that, as well?"

"I can't," she told him matter-of-factly. "However, I do have a friend who can get me the name of a good leasing agent. I'll get more information, and I'll make an introduction."

Xander definitely liked her. She wasn't just looking to pass him along to someone else. And maybe that was because he was ready to purchase a two-million-dollar property, and she was more interested in the commission. He didn't know for sure. But he did get the feeling that he could trust her to follow through.

A solid fifteen minutes later, Mercedes was pulling through an electronic gate that had seen better days. It was rusted and hanging by the hinges on one side, and Xander didn't doubt that it was out of commission, which explained why it had been propped open.

He noted the eight-foot stone wall that ran around the perimeter of the parking area and then back around behind the building. Interesting. They were in a light industrial area, but he knew the crime rate wasn't high because he'd done some preliminary research. He figured the original owner must've thought the wall added something.

Aside from making it look like a prison, it didn't hold any appeal whatsoever.

But Xander wasn't going to say anything. He didn't give a shit if the place was surrounded by land mines. The price was right, and if the building wasn't going to fall in on itself, he knew it'd be a damn good investment.

And at this point, that was all that mattered.

MERCEDES PULLED INTO ONE OF THE PARTIALLY striped parking spots near the front doors of the vacant building. She was doing her best to focus on the road and not on the intimidating man crammed in her car.

She had struggled to hold in her laugh when he somehow managed to squeeze his gigantic body into her small car. And then again when he somehow managed to get the seat belt on. No wonder he'd offered to follow her. Then again, he had been a good sport, because if she'd been in his shoes, she wouldn't have attempted to fold herself into such a small space. As it was, his neck was at an odd angle.

Definitely a good sport.

But despite his discomfort, they had made it. Thank God. She was about to get a chance to breathe fresh air, rather than the subtle, sultry scent of what she could only assume was expensive cologne. The man smelled amazing, but she damn sure didn't want him to know she thought so.

Xander Boone was everything Shane had described him as being. Tall, confident, straightforward. And blunt, as she'd learned by his less-than-discreet reference to the dilapidated building she currently worked out of. Too bad Shane hadn't bothered to add that Xander was also ruggedly handsome and a tad on the intimidating side.

Not that she was going to let the last bother her. She could hold her own.

Climbing out of the car, she headed to the glass doors. Using the key she'd had to pick up that morning, she gained entrance and held the door open for Xander. To her surprise, he merely glared at her, placing his hand above her head and holding the door open.

"Ladies first," he told her with a grin that gave her a glimpse of straight white teeth.

"Thank you," she answered, trying not to smile back at him and failing.

Once inside, Mercedes did her best to stay out of his way. There wasn't much she could show him, and he wouldn't have to go far to see everything. The warehouse was huge, without a lot of walls. Not to mention in desperate need of some cosmetic surgery.

That was an easy fix, and if what Shane had told her was true, Xander wouldn't be bothered by a few blemishes.

So, she stood back, watching him move around the warehouse.

She was drawn to him, just as she had been when he'd stepped through her office door. But she'd realized after one glimpse that she shouldn't be drawn to him. They were too much alike.

Just that morning, while she had waited for Xander to arrive, she'd dared to ask Shane a little more about the mystery client who was coming to see her.

"He's a Dom," Shane had told her.

Interesting. "Does he belong to the same club you do?" she had inquired, hoping to sound casual. Shane had informed her that he was a member of Kink, an opulent BDSM club she'd heard about but had never visited.

Mercedes belonged to a club, but she hadn't bothered to mention that to Shane. She'd been surprised to find out Shane was a Dom in the first place, and still hadn't produced the nerve to question him more even though she was intrigued.

"Yeah. He's the one who got me in there."

Yep, that's about all she'd learned about Xander Boone. Well, other than what the Google search had offered her. He wasn't just a Dom. He was a rich Dom. A very successful, rich Dom.

Which meant he was off-limits.

And that was a good thing, because the man's charisma was palpable, and when he turned those sexy, moss-green eyes on her, had she been any other woman, she might've swooned.

She wasn't the swooning type.

"I want to know how serious the owner is to sell," Xander stated firmly as he made his way toward her. "There're quite a few things that have to be done to this place to get it up to code."

Okay, so the man definitely wasn't new to this.

"I can ask."

"I prefer to tell," he told her as he approached. "I'll list out the issues, because I do want to make an offer. I assure you, it'll be fair."

Mercedes nodded her head as she watched him. Yes, she certainly could see his dominating personality. It was prominent, yet somehow not terribly overbearing. If that were even the right word to use to describe a man who stood at least six and a half feet tall and was built like the defensive line of a football team. The whole freaking line.

"So what do you say? We'll go back to your office and get things started?"

Although he'd kindly phrased it as a question, Mercedes got the distinct impression that he was informing her, not asking.

Mercedes was speechless.

For the first time in her entire life, she didn't know what to say. And that was saying something, because not only was she a damn good real estate agent, she was also a formidable Domme.

One who, from this moment on, knew she could easily like this man.

As a friend. And nothing more.

CHAPTER ONE

Soft opening of Devotion…
Tuesday

XANDER BOONE COULDN'T TAKE HIS EYES OFF of the dazzling blonde walking through the door of the private room he had reserved at Devotion. The beauty he was currently eyeing was none other than Samantha McCoy, the alluring wife of Logan McCoy, a man Xander considered a friend and potentially a future business partner.

Tonight at the soft opening of Devotion, just like almost any night, from what he'd heard, Logan's wife had certainly garnered some attention. Xander's was no exception. He might not know her all that well, aside from what her husband had mentioned, but Samantha had a way about her that drew people. It was in her eyes.

Considering she'd set her sights on him specifically, according to Logan, Xander knew she was making an honest effort to get his attention.

It had worked.

Then again, thanks to his conversation with Logan, Xander had been expecting it. Since he was always interested in shaking things up a little, he had committed to playing along, hence the reason they were there.

Making no attempt to conceal his appreciation for Samantha's physical appeal, Xander continued to eye her as she made her way closer.

He offered the hint of a smile when she tentatively walked into the room, allowing the door to close behind her as she stared up at him. There was curiosity gleaming in her celadon-green eyes, along with what he sensed was something akin to nervousness as she glanced down to the toy in his hand and then back up to meet his gaze.

Mission accomplished.

Sure, Xander had purposely untucked and unbuttoned his shirt and carried the mini-flogger with him to answer the door, but that was for effect. Mostly. He wanted to see her reaction, and he got exactly what he was expecting. Samantha was walking into a situation that she was not all that familiar with, but he'd already known that thanks to his conversation with Logan.

Sue him for wanting to have a little fun with her.

As Sam and Logan moved slowly into the room, Xander continued to study her, his eyes perusing her lean, slight build. There was no denying the fact that the woman was gorgeous, with her long blonde hair, glowing green eyes, and tons of curves. However, the way she carried herself — strong and confident, despite her reluctance to the situation — was far more enticing than her mere physical beauty.

Xander was immensely drawn to a woman's inner strength. More so than any physical characteristic. In fact, it was a prerequisite of his.

And he'd met a number of submissives who didn't quite understand the concept. He'd played with many who were under the incorrect notion that a Dom was looking for a woman who would just roll over and submit.

They were wrong. Dead wrong.

At least as far as Xander was concerned.

The stronger a woman was, the more he admired her. Regardless of if she would easily submit or not.

Looking at Samantha now, Xander noticed the way she was clinging to Logan, holding on as though he were her lifeline. In his opinion, her response to his presence was somewhat deceiving in the sense that it gave the distinct impression she was unaware of what might happen tonight. But from what Xander knew of her, he wasn't fooled. Samantha McCoy was anything but oblivious.

Xander'd had the pleasure of talking to Logan on more than one occasion about this scenario specifically, and the little adventure they were about to embark upon had been in the works for a couple of weeks, ever since they'd had a definite date determined for the opening of Devotion.

His first impression of Sam? Quite the opposite of what he'd seen of her tonight, he'd have to say. During his first and only encounter with her outside of the club, he'd pegged her for all business, all the time. But then he'd seen her with Logan a few minutes ago in the hallway, and she'd definitely been getting down to business, but not the way Xander had figured her to.

Seeing her standing there, her hands gripping the iron rails that surrounded the second floor with Logan's hand hidden beneath her skirt, had been gratifying. If he'd had any concerns about what she wanted, he was eased somewhat by seeing her pleasured by her husband right there for anyone and everyone to see.

She had certainly passed his initial test.

Nodding his head toward the opposite side of the dimly lit room, Xander urged Logan and Samantha farther inside. Since Logan was already up to speed on how this session would go, Xander didn't feel the need to give him guidance. Watching as Logan took Sam's hand and led her over to the lone chair that sat in a corner on the opposite side, he waited.

Knowing that he didn't have time to waste, as soon as Sam had her back to him, Xander tossed the small flogger away and moved to the other side of the room to retrieve the one he intended to use.

His hand had barely wrapped around the braided handle before his slacks were getting a tad uncomfortable. Just the thought of what was about to happen had his cock rigid and anxious.

Knowing that he wouldn't be able to pay attention to Samantha and do what he needed to do, Xander turned his full attention back to the woman who'd been his main focus for the last few hours. Mercedes Bryant. The mouth-watering woman standing on the opposite side of the room.

Xander wouldn't deny the fact that there were plenty of beautiful women in the world; he'd had the pleasure of being with plenty himself. But truth be told, not a single woman held a candle to Mercedes. As far as he was concerned, she easily outshined every other woman in the world.

He'd thought so ever since the first time he'd met her nearly a decade ago.

Mercedes was breathtaking. Mile-long legs that would wrap around a man perfectly, luscious curves that he could easily fill his palms with, jet-black hair that fell to her waist, exotic steel-gray eyes that saw everything, and alabaster skin that begged for a man's touch.

She was riveting.

And those were just a few things Xander found so fucking desirable about the woman standing there, waiting for him.

In all of his thirty-five years, he had never met a woman who had captured his attention the way she did.

But he knew firsthand that there was more to Mercedes than just a pretty face and a tantalizing body. Truthfully, through the years that they had been friends, he'd been more captivated by her intelligence, her strength, and her wit than anything else.

And she had enamored him. He just had never let her know.

Without a doubt, she was the most tempting woman he'd ever laid his eyes on. And he could guarantee she had absolutely no idea he felt that way.

Because if she did, he knew she wouldn't have agreed to this.

Xander was a pro at keeping his true feelings to himself. After all, he'd spent years doing so. In his business, it didn't benefit him to show his hand too soon. His poker face was without flaw. He prided himself on his ability to hide any and all reaction. And in his defense, he'd been attempting to lure Mercedes to him for longer than he cared to admit. However, as it turned out, subtlety wasn't exactly his specialty. Not where Mercedes was concerned.

He was tired of being subtle. He was also tired of waiting. So, just like everything else, it was time he took control. In the one way that he was intimately familiar with.

Mercedes moved, drawing his attention to her outfit. When he'd picked her up that evening, they'd both been dressed for the formal affair that they were attending. Over dinner, she'd stolen his breath with the sexy black dress that had highlighted her voluptuous figure incredibly well, giving a sexy glimpse at her more-than-impressive cleavage.

However, since they'd entered the playroom, she had changed her clothing. At his request. The black corset with its fiery red ribbons, the short black skirt and knee-high black boots with the four-inch heels was one of the sexiest outfits he'd ever seen her wear, and yes, he'd seen her wear plenty, not to mention less.

After all, this wasn't the first time he'd watched her closely.

Torn between eyeing the woman whose gaze was boring into him and doing what needed to be done, Xander glanced between her and the St. Andrew's cross.

He met her eyes again and nodded slightly.

"Over to the wall." His instruction was gentle yet firm, not offering any room for confusion or argument, which, of course, was the intention.

Time to begin.

MERCEDES CROSSED PATHS WITH XANDER AS SHE moved to the far side of the room as instructed. She met his gaze as she did and noticed the sexy smirk tipping the corner of his lips.

Arrogant bastard.

He seemed to be getting a huge kick out of this. Then again, it wasn't often — *translated to never* — that anyone would get Mercedes to agree to something like this.

Then again — her hesitancy notwithstanding — she had to admit, she was both nervous and excited about what was going on here tonight.

Since the day she'd been introduced to Xander Boone many years ago, they had spent a lot of time together. In the simplest of terms, they were business associates, not to mention friends.

Close, yet very platonic, *friends.*

When they weren't dealing with the ins and outs of the real estate market, they would often spend time together outside of work, as well. A lot of that time was spent at one of Dallas' most exclusive BDSM clubs — appropriately named Kink — where they were both now members.

Their friendship had started almost instantly, and they had grown close through the years. It didn't hurt that they had several things in common that had strengthened their friendship from the start: they both believed that business was business, play was play, and when it came to the latter, they were both looking for something *and nothing* at the same time.

Namely, fun with no strings attached.

Simple.

Uncomplicated.

Just the way Mercedes preferred everything in her life to be.

Only there was one problem... Xander had recently presented her with a proposition that was neither simple nor easy.

Their lives consisted of both work and play, and they went to the extreme on both counts. It was just who they were. Within the category of play, they were both intimately familiar with domination and submission. However, if she didn't know better, she'd have thought Xander had recently received a blow to the head that had clearly warped his good sense.

If Mercedes wasn't mistaken, Xander Boone wanted *her* submission.

And that was where the problem lay. Mercedes couldn't give him that because she *was not a submissive.* Key word being *not.*

She was a Domme, and her reputation was well established and highly respected in their circles, and he knew it. So how the hell he'd talked her into this said a lot about his powers of persuasion.

His request had come one night, about two weeks ago, when they had met for dinner after work. Prefaced with, "Because neither of us has a pet," (as Xander liked to refer to his submissives), "I'd like to call in a favor."

A freaking *favor.*

First of all, for the record, Xander never asked for favors. Hell, he didn't usually ask for anything. So, not only was he low maintenance as far as friends went, it was hard to refuse to help a friend when he looked at her the way Xander had.

That was when things had started to go downhill.

Based on his explanation at the time, and his rebuttal to every one of her suggestions — What about finding a sub or a trainee from Kink? What about that one woman... Yeah, he hadn't even let her finish that sentence — Mercedes was under the distinct impression that Xander was playing a dangerous game with her, trying to get her to submit when there was no way in hell it was going to happen.

Except for tonight.

Somehow he had convinced her to come here, and she had no choice but to deal with it — because a promise was a promise, and Mercedes didn't go back on her word.

Now, as she fought the urge to sneak out when he wasn't looking, Mercedes divided her attention between the power couple and the sexy-as-sin man who was waiting for her to do as he instructed.

It was apparent that Xander's request had something to do with the beautiful couple who had made their way into the room. From what Xander had told her, Logan had been the one to approach him in the beginning. Logan and Samantha weren't vanilla by any means, but according to Logan, they had never experimented with BDSM. Xander had come up with the idea of giving them a little taste of his lifestyle.

Strange request, huh? Actually, it wasn't all that uncommon.

Only, somewhere along the way, Xander had turned the tables on her. Something she would certainly pay him back for at a later date.

It was just a shame that she considered Xander so damned attractive and strangely irresistible — in a platonic sort of way — because she certainly wouldn't have hesitated to tell him to fuck off with his invitation. But in her defense, she wasn't the only one who found Xander physically appealing. Most women did, and just like them, she wasn't immune to his charm. Unfortunately.

At the moment, Mercedes could think of a more apt word to express what she thought about him: incorrigible. Yes, that certainly described him nicely.

Even though she had some reservations about his intentions, or whether or not he had the potential to be reformed, Mercedes had to admit that there was one positive in this entirely screwed up situation: Looking at Xander was a treat for the eyes.

She got the feeling that if you looked up sexy or sophisticated or relentless or alpha male, and let's not forget incorrigible, in the dictionary, there beside the definition would be Xander's picture.

At six foot six inches, two hundred seventy plus pounds, he was an exquisite male specimen. His body was honed to perfection, from his chiseled jaw to his sculpted muscles down to his routinely pedicured feet. His perfectly styled dark hair was an intriguing contrast to his light green eyes, and it was no wonder he'd been repeatedly categorized as one of Dallas's most sought after bachelors.

Not only was Xander intimidating in a physically provocative way, he was also ridiculously successful and insanely wealthy.

Oh, and he was Trouble with a capital T.

Okay, so yes, saying a man was beautiful, especially a man like Xander, would probably be an odd way to describe him, but in Xander's case, it was true. Beauty, at least in his case, wasn't just skin deep, and because of Xander's strength of character, his charm, and his sophistication, he wasn't just the perfect package on the outside. The man was so much more than that.

For the record, no, she did not have a crush on her friend.

Okay, maybe a little one.

Not that she would ever even allude to it.

Fearful that she was ogling him a little too much, Mercedes forced her attention away from Xander and glanced over to Samantha and Logan, noticing they were both watching her intently.

That raised the question, what had Xander told them about her?

As much as she wanted to ask, she was well aware that she wasn't going to get that answer tonight, so she opted to greet them rather than dwell on what he'd said to entice them to join them tonight.

"Nice to see you again," Mercedes called from her spot several feet away. "If you need me, I'll be..." She turned to look at the St. Andrew's cross, for the millionth time wondering what the hell she was doing. Looking back at Samantha and Logan, she followed up with, "Uh ... yeah. I'll just be ... over here."

Not surprisingly, no one said a word in response. Mercedes could tell by the look on Samantha's lovely face that the woman was both confused and nervous. Definitely an interesting combination of emotions.

If she had no idea what to expect, exactly what was she nervous about? That was a question Mercedes routinely asked of new subs who approached her with the same trepidation in their eyes.

On the other hand, Mercedes knew why *she* was nervous and confused. Unlike Samantha, she *did* know what was about to happen. It had everything to do with the damn X that was looming before her.

Both the St. Andrew's cross and *the man*.

"Have a seat," Xander instructed Samantha and Logan from behind her.

Mercedes glanced over her shoulder to look at Samantha once more, offering her a tentative smile, which was returned. And yes, maybe it was just confirmation that she was a little sadistic, because Mercedes was enjoying the hell out of the bewildered expression on the pretty woman's face.

Being a Domme, long past her rookie stage, Mercedes was familiar with what was about to take place. There was just one slight problem: she was on the wrong end of the domination, which wasn't something she was at all comfortable with.

While this particular situation was one she was familiar with, despite the fact that she was on the receiving end, Mercedes was welcoming the twist in her very mundane routine that she called life.

And this was a three-hundred-sixty-degree turn from what she was used to.

CHAPTER TWO

BEING A MEMBER OF ONE OF THE most successful BDSM clubs in the Dallas area, Mercedes was familiar with this scene as well as many others. Demonstrations were a regular thing within the club she attended. No matter how skilled a Dominant thought they were, the mindset in their club was that there was always room for continuing education.

She could easily say that being part of a demonstration wasn't the issue. Nor did she have a problem with an audience. It was a nightly occurrence for her when she opted to play at Kink.

So when Xander had informed her of his master plan to introduce Logan and Samantha to a little bondage and submission, Mercedes hadn't thought anything of it. BDSM wasn't for the faint of heart, but she didn't have to explain that to Xander. When he'd invited her to the opening of Devotion, the new club that happened to be in the exact same warehouse that had provided her original introduction to Xander, she hadn't questioned him, either.

Nor had she thought to tie the two together and come up with her somehow becoming the night's attraction.

Shame on her.

His last and final request had been what had sent her over the edge. Tonight, right here in this very room, Xander Boone wanted to give Samantha a lesson in bondage and submission. The kicker of it all was that he wanted to use Mercedes in his demonstration.

"Why me?" she had asked him that night at dinner, but he'd easily avoided her question, instead continuing to explain his reasons.

According to Xander, Samantha was interested in threesomes, or so he'd been told by Logan. And based on Samantha's explanation as to why she enjoyed them, Xander felt as though she was more turned on by Logan's natural domination of the situation than the actual inclusion of another man.

Made sense. Sort of.

Her understanding of the situation was that Xander had come to the conclusion that Logan got off by watching Samantha pleasured. By another man. Mercedes understood that.

And Samantha had enjoyed being with two men at one time. No questions there, either.

However, Samantha was apparently hesitant because of her past experience and the attachment she'd made with the two men who had been involved in her relationship in the past. That part Mercedes understood, as well.

In order to help them out, Xander had had the brilliant idea to introduce them to BDSM because it could provide the domination that Samantha seemed so fond of, rather than having to introduce a third person for her to get her fix.

Xander had gone on to explain that, since Samantha obviously became attached, it made sense that they might need to shy away from the threesomes and look at another way to get her what she needed.

"Why me?" Mercedes had asked him again after his lengthy explanation, still not understanding why she had to be the one on the chopping block. There were a number of subs who would graciously accept his invitation.

"Because I don't want to use anyone else," he had told her.

Simple. Straightforward. No, it still didn't make sense, yet here she was, agreeing to Xander's plan to act out a scene.

With her as his submissive.

Sometimes she was just too damned nice.

Xander had assured her that she would merely be there as an accessory for the evening, so Mercedes had reluctantly agreed. He was her friend, after all. She could help him this one time. Or so she'd tried to convince herself.

She wasn't in an intimate relationship; therefore, she wasn't stepping out on anyone. Her time was her own. How she decided to spend it was up to her, as well.

Not that this would've been her first choice.

The sharp gasp from Samantha had Mercedes turning to look in her direction again. Her gaze stopped midway across the room, where she noticed Xander absently caressing the flogger in his hands.

Of course he would pick that one.

Mercedes had requested him to use a low-intensity flogger for tonight, and he had laughed at her, then he'd followed his chuckle with, "What's that?"

Okay, fine. He didn't use low-intensity floggers. Then again, neither did she. Most of the time.

But looking at the high-intensity latigo flogger in his hand didn't have her ass singing a happy tune at the moment.

Not that she would let him know that.

Mercedes looked up to meet his intense, light green gaze and found her heart rate kicking up another notch. His mouth was a straight line, but his eyes were laughing at her.

Damn Dom.

"I'm waiting," he informed her as she stared back at him.

He could wait all day as far as she was concerned.

For half a second, she contemplated being a brat, something that she personally had absolutely no tolerance for, but figured that wouldn't bode well for her in the long run. Instead, without argument, Mercedes moved closer to the giant X securely positioned near the wall.

Pushing everything to the back of her mind, she tried to fall into the mindset of a sub. She'd spent enough time with them, knew what they expected of her as their Domme, so she knew what the desired responses were from Xander's perspective.

Easy, right?

Um … no.

The next thing she knew, Xander's enormous body was directly behind her, his front to her back, sandwiching her between him and the wooden cross in front of her.

The man was the human equivalent of a Mack truck.

"Hold this," he instructed close to her ear in that sexy, rich baritone of his, placing the well-worn, braided handle of the flogger in her right hand as he crowded her up against the cross.

Mercedes gripped the nine-inch handle tightly, tempted to slip out from beneath him and show him exactly how it should be used. Instead, she remained motionless, gritting her teeth as she anticipated what was to come.

Xander's giant hands slid from her elbows up to her wrists, sending an unexpected, blinding frisson of heat coursing through her.

Okay, wait.

Back up a minute.

That was *not* supposed to happen.

She wasn't sure whether she was surprised more by how good his touch felt or by how strange it was to have him now cuffing her to the cross. And the cuffing part wasn't what got to her. She'd been there before in other demonstrations. No, it was Xander's touch or, more accurately, her own reaction to it that had caught her off guard.

Once her hands were firmly secured in the padded leather cuffs, Xander slid his palms down her arms, over the sides of her breasts, then down to her waist, but that was where he stopped.

"You ready for this?" She felt his breath against her cheek, his voice low enough so only she could hear.

No. "Yes," she whispered, irritated at how breathless she sounded.

Seriously. She was going to have to give more thought as to why his touch felt so good.

But obviously not right now.

"Then let's get started," he replied just as softly, the hint of a smile in his voice. "First, I want you naked," he stated firmly, his voice louder this time, clearly for Samantha and Logan to hear.

Naked. *Excellent.*

That was the moment Mercedes realized she was about to take a step off of the high dive hovering precariously above the deep end, and she wasn't even sure how far she had to fall before she took the plunge.

"You know your safe word?" he asked, again so that everyone could hear.

She fought the urge to roll her eyes.

"Red," she responded easily, tightening her grip on the flogger handle. She'd never gotten into creative safe words, much preferring the straightforward red, yellow, and green. Red meant stop entirely, yellow meant to slow down, and green meant all systems go.

At the moment, she was stuck somewhere on orange.

"Good girl. If, at any time, you wish to stop, just say red and everything will stop," he said, his tone encouraging.

A shiver danced along her spine.

Xander's hands returned to her shoulders, lightly grazing her skin when he moved her hair out of his way. The warmth of his breath tickled her neck as he leaned in close. When she thought he would say something, he surprised her by placing a kiss to her right shoulder, his tongue briefly trailing along the intricate magnolia tattoo that extended down to her elbow. He didn't linger, but it was enough to send an influx of heat percolating through her bloodstream.

Xander continued to touch her. The heat of his hands on her back made Mercedes bite her bottom lip as she dropped her head slightly, trying to peer down at her feet. *Shit.* This was not good.

Not good at all.

Xander unlaced her corset, slowly and efficiently, his fingers trailing over her naked skin as he revealed it. All she could do was attempt to keep her respiratory system from failing, not wanting to let Xander know just how much he was affecting her at the moment.

The leather corset fell away, and her nipples immediately puckered from the cool air that caressed her overheated skin. *Right. Tell yourself that, and maybe it will be true.*

Within minutes, Xander had her fully naked, save for the thigh-high boots. Mercedes tried her hardest to act as though this were simply clinical, but her damned body was betraying her every thought.

Being naked and being naked with Xander touching her were two entirely different things. Granted, she was sure he'd seen her in various states of undress at the club, but she wasn't sure he'd ever seen quite this much of her at one time.

"We'll leave the boots on," he informed her. "Because they're sexy as fuck."

More chills skated over her skin at his obvious approval.

"Spread your legs for me," he instructed, his hands gliding down her thighs as he knelt behind her. The fact that his face was intimately close to her bottom had her squeezing her internal muscles tightly.

This was nerve-racking to say the least.

When he reached her ankles, she felt the leather straps being secured in place over her boots. Despite the temptation, Mercedes didn't try to see how far she could move. It wouldn't be far; she knew that much. And she wasn't about to let Xander know she'd suddenly developed an overwhelming case of nerves.

Back to his full height, Xander took the flogger from her hand and trailed the long leather strings down her right arm, then across her shoulders. Since he was left-handed and wielding the flogger with his right hand, for now, she knew she had a moment's reprieve.

When he lovingly slid the tails of the flogger over her left arm, she consciously fought the shiver that threatened to rack her body. He was getting into position.

Xander was a big man, with a significant amount of power, and with him standing so close, holding a flogger, she felt a little light-headed and utterly consumed by him.

Refocusing her attention on her part in this scene now that she was an active participant, Mercedes sucked in a deep breath and stared forward, keeping her body loose but on alert. She only wished there weren't a mirror on the wall, because now she had no choice but to watch what Xander was doing to her as well as feel it.

"Have you been a good girl?" Xander asked as he pressed his chest up against her back once more, his eyes meeting hers in the floor-to-ceiling mirror.

Um ... no.

But she didn't say that. She couldn't say anything at first. With his shirt unbuttoned, she felt the heat of his naked chest against her skin, and the only thing she could think about was how warm his body was against hers. And how ... hard.

Oh, shit.

The knowledge that he was physically reacting to this — *to her* — made a zing of pleasure ricochet through her. Never in all the time that she'd known him had Xander shown any interest in her.

Or had he and she'd just missed it?

No. No, definitely not.

Seriously, they were good enough friends that she could walk around her house half-naked when he was there. Not that she did, but if she wanted to, she would've never worried about offending or enticing him.

Considering their dominating personalities were in direct conflict, Mercedes had considered Xander off-limits. After all, one plus one certainly did not equal two Doms. That equation didn't work in her lifestyle, so she'd never worried about it before.

She was certainly worried about it now.

Remembering Xander's question, Mercedes swallowed hard. "Yes, Master X," she answered diligently, referring to him as he preferred to be called in the club — for Samantha's and Logan's benefit only. Master was a sign of respect, and even though she wasn't his sub, Mercedes wouldn't disagree that he'd earned that respect.

When Xander's palm flattened on the inside of her thigh, slowly moving upward, Mercedes bit the inside of her cheek. When the tips of his fingers grazed the curls at the apex of her thighs, she sucked in a sharp breath.

"Are you wet?" he asked, his tone authoritative, his gaze still locked with hers.

He was putting on a show, and she knew it was her turn to flip the switch on her acting skills. Not that she would be entirely acting.

Dammit.

"Yes, Sir," she said, proud of herself for getting the words out.

As though he didn't believe her, his hand continued to roam higher until he was reaching between her legs, cupping her mound. He rested his hand there for a moment before he curled one finger under and slid it through her folds.

"So wet," he growled, the sound incredibly sexy. "So fucking wet."

Mercedes wondered whether he was just as shocked as she was by how turned on she was. Both by him and the situation.

Xander leaned forward, his chest pressing against her. She felt the heat of his breath on her neck, the rise and fall of his chest against her back. "Fucking hell, M. You're gonna kill me here."

She wanted to return the sentiment but clamped her mouth shut instead.

His words were merely a whisper, yet they sounded as tormented as she felt. Mercedes had no idea whether she should be pleased or worried. This was quickly getting out of control. More importantly, this wasn't supposed to be about her. Or Xander, for that matter. This was supposed to be for Samantha's benefit.

Briefly, Mercedes glanced back at the couple through the mirror, noticing that their eyes were focused on her and Xander.

Mercedes had come to terms with giving Samantha a glimpse into the infamous world of BDSM by acting as Xander's sub for a short scene, but her body's reaction was belying her demand that this was only a demonstration.

When he finally took a step back, Mercedes inhaled deeply, but then she suddenly missed the warmth of his body against hers.

Wait. No. No, she didn't. This was a demonstration. Not the real thing.

The flogger tails trailed over her skin lightly again, causing her body to tense with anticipation once more. By the way that the leather consistently brushed over her skin, she knew Xander was focused. It wasn't long before the soothing stroke was replaced by a soft sting that began as he flicked his wrist, the heavy leather strands making contact over and over again. With every additional slap, her body was warming and her pussy throbbing.

She could think of only a couple of occasions when she'd been on the receiving end of those tails, and those instances were purely learning opportunities for her. She'd had to learn how to use one in order to ensure she didn't hurt anyone. But this, this was vastly different.

Never had she actually started to enjoy it. Not like this.

Sure, she had always admired the way Xander used the tools of the trade, and she had to admit, he was incredibly sensual in his movements, but she'd never felt the effect firsthand.

With her eyes closed, the images that floated through her mind lined up with the stinging blows that began across her ass, on her upper thighs, and Mercedes worried that she was going to lose control.

"Is that what you want, pet?" he asked her softly, pulling her back from the brink as his hands traced the heated lines he'd created on her ass.

"Yes, Master X." Shit, that had been an honest answer, and calling him Master hadn't seemed all that strange, either.

She was definitely losing control.

"Good girl," he soothed her. "Do you want me to continue? Do you want me to make you come?"

Fuck no. "Yes, Sir," she replied because she knew that was what he wanted to hear.

Mercedes figured she'd have to fake an orgasm, because honestly, she wasn't into pain like this. She didn't believe it was possible to get her off with any form of flagellation. But he was obviously going to try.

"I'm looking forward to watching you come," he told her, and she had to wonder whether he could read her mind.

Xander slid his hand around to her front, his big finger once again sliding through her slick folds. Only this time, he plunged one finger inside of her, and she cried out, the sensation taking root deep in her core, pleasure detonating on impact.

"Yes, I'm definitely going to enjoy watching you come," he stated again, and Mercedes's internal muscles clenched.

At this pace, she wasn't going to have much of a choice.

But then his finger was gone, and the stinging slap of leather against her oversensitive skin returned.

"Remember, you have a safe word, and you may use it if necessary."

Mercedes didn't say a word. She already knew that, and she feared that if she did speak, she'd give herself away entirely.

Closing her eyes again, she gave herself over to the moment.

The leather kissed her skin over and over, the slaps moving to different places, sometimes staying in the same place for two or three swats. Again, Mercedes didn't make a sound as the minutes ticked by, but her lungs felt restricted as her body flexed and strained against the erotically sensual onslaught.

She tried to focus, tried to determine where he was going to land the next blow, but she found herself drifting. All thoughts disappeared as her breathing increased. The only things intruding on her moment of peace were the sound of the leather as it landed and the bite of pain that sent shards of electrical pulses through her. It was…

Oh, God. She couldn't think anymore.

He was doing it. Xander was sending her toward that mind-numbing place that all subs sought. The place referred to as sub-space. It wasn't unlike Dom-space, as far as she was concerned, but she wasn't supposed to be there.

With less force, Xander trailed over her upper back, then back to her ass, down her thighs, delivering exactly what she apparently needed, because Mercedes found herself floating.

The next time he pressed up against her, the softness of his slacks against her abused skin sent heat coursing through her again. He gripped her right wrist in his big hand high up on the cross while he pressed his lips against her neck and slid his left hand between her thighs, the flogger obviously forgotten.

"Come for me, Mercedes," he exhaled against her ear as he drove two fingers deep inside of her. "Just for me."

That was when it happened.

Mercedes shattered into a million pieces — only it wasn't just her body that was affected. Her mind, or more importantly, everything she thought she knew about herself, unraveled right there in the comfort of Xander's arms.

CHAPTER THREE

LOGAN WOULD CONSIDER HIMSELF AN ASTUTE MAN. Not a lot got past him. So as he sat in the chair with Sam squirming on his lap, the scene before him had definitely caught his attention.

Granted, Logan's cock was rock hard, and it had been even before they'd walked into this private playroom decked out for some serious BDSM activities. The room wasn't overly large, but it was spacious enough to accommodate a St. Andrew's cross near one wall, a spanking bench positioned in the center of the room, and a man the size of Xander Boone.

As he watched what Xander was doing to the beautiful woman restrained to the cross, he was grateful they'd opted for a private scene tonight. All of the other rooms, especially those that were equipped with things such as crosses, chains, and ropes, were monitored by staff for safety and, therefore, open for anyone to watch.

Apparently being an owner of the club had its perks, because the room Xander had procured was off-limits. Thank God.

Sitting in a chair with Samantha on his lap, her attention on the couple about ten feet in front of her, Logan found himself riveted to what was going on. Surprisingly, it didn't have anything to do with the way Xander handled that toy in his hand, either.

No, there was something else going on here. Something between Xander and Mercedes that was more erotic than anything he'd seen in quite some time. The last time he'd witnessed something of this magnitude had been between Luke and Cole that long ago night when the three of them had focused on Sam.

Whatever was happening between Xander and Mercedes, it was … intense. Almost as though the two of them hadn't expected it to happen.

Mercedes had been introduced to Sam and Logan as Xander's friend and business associate, but after watching this scene, he had to wonder whether they were something more than that. From their interactions downstairs, it was clear they were buddy-buddy because they could easily laugh together and practically finish one another's sentences.

However, the intensity between the two of them right now was palpable in the small room, and it didn't matter one bit that Mercedes was strapped to that wooden cross.

So, for the last few minutes, Logan had watched, absorbing the movements, the reactions, and enjoying what was happening to a degree. He'd only been distracted by Sam's sharp gasps that echoed through the room every time that flogger came down on Mercedes's now reddened skin.

For a minute, he thought he would make it through the evening without coming completely undone. After all, they were there to watch, not participate. And that might've been the case, except Sam continued to squirm on his lap, and the way her curvy ass ground against his aching cock was sending him closer and closer to the edge.

But then everything stopped.

Well, almost everything.

While Xander pressed up against Mercedes, obviously soothing her with words after an orgasm that had split the atoms in the room, Logan whispered near Sam's ear, "Do you like watching them?" It was an appropriate, albeit unnecessary, question considering she was still grinding her pussy against his thigh.

"Yes," she replied softly, her body trembling slightly.

He'd be damned. Xander had been right.

After a lot of thought, Logan had decided to approach Xander Boone a few weeks back. Initially, he had intended to proposition Xander about being a third. That idea had dissipated shortly after he'd started talking to Xander, though.

Then, during a long conversation, Xander had suggested that Logan introduce Sam to something that might catch her interest. This certainly had caught her attention, much as it had his.

Logan had openly discussed with Xander some of the things he and Sam had engaged in previously, the conversation surprisingly comfortable. Not at all awkward like he'd initially expected. He had gone on to explain how he enjoyed controlling Sam's pleasure, how beautifully Sam responded during those instances, and how the involvement of a third did something for both of them.

According to Xander, the fact that Sam liked Logan's dominating side could mean that she'd be interested in more interaction of that nature. As opposed to a threesome. Logan had informed Xander about their history and the attachment Sam seemed to have for the men who had briefly entered their relationship.

If he hadn't been convinced during that conversation — which he had been — now more than ever, Logan was absolutely positive that Xander would not be the right man for him and Sam to get involved with. Not as far as a threesome was concerned, anyway.

Xander was a Dom, and although Logan didn't put labels on himself, nor did he participate in the standard BDSM practices, he knew that his own dominating nature would clash with Xander's. Control wasn't something Logan was willing to relinquish, and he got the impression that Xander knew that.

That's when Xander had suggested Logan and Sam learn more about BDSM. Hence, the reason they were there.

Logan watched as Xander let his hands freely roam over Mercedes's lush, curvy body as he took his time, holding her tight and mumbling in her ear. She was gripping the chains attached to the cuffs around her wrist and leaning back against Xander, her eyes closed, her hips continuing to undulate against Xander's hand still wedged between her thighs.

While he took it all in, Logan slid his hand up Sam's bare thigh and beneath the short skirt that she wore. When her hand came down to grip his wrist, urging him forward, he edged underneath the elastic of her panties, sliding one finger through her soft folds.

She was wet. So very wet.

Rather than pull away, he continued to tease her clit with slow, featherlight strokes of his finger.

Because they had played in the hall for a few minutes, Logan knew Sam was probably hovering right on the brink of orgasm considering he'd refused to let her come. For her to sit there and watch while Xander punished Mercedes was rather impressive.

When Logan had brought Sam to this room tonight, he'd had no idea what to expect from Xander and Mercedes. Or even from Sam. Hell, he definitely hadn't expected Xander to whip the dark-haired beauty with the skill and precision of a man who had a lot of practice doing so. Or for Mercedes to take it like a woman who enjoyed it.

Sam leaned back against him now, her back to his chest, her head tilted to the side as she watched Xander continue to tease Mercedes gently. Logan pressed his lips to her neck as he kept his eyes on the pair, realizing then that Mercedes had been freakishly quiet the entire time, though Logan knew that shit had to hurt.

Logan's attention was diverted when Sam tightened her grip on his wrist and pushed his finger inside of her roughly.

"Please," she whispered.

"Please what?" he asked, not keeping his voice quiet. He was well past the point of caring where they were or who was with them. Not that he usually cared, but he always considered Sam first.

"I need you inside me," she whispered, her voice even lower than before, but she didn't stop watching.

She didn't seem to be concerned that Xander and Mercedes were in the same room, either, so he continued, "I didn't hear you." He waited for her to respond, stilling his finger inside of her.

"I need to feel your cock inside me," she said more urgently, her voice just a fraction above a whisper but loud enough that he knew Xander and Mercedes had heard her.

"You want to ride my cock, baby?" he questioned, blocking out everyone else in the room as he pulled his hand free of Sam's grasp.

"God, yes."

"Remove your panties," he instructed forcefully, helping her to stand, which gave him the opportunity to unhook the button on his slacks and release his cock.

Tonight had been a formal affair, which was why he was fully dressed in a tuxedo, but the jacket was unbuttoned, and he managed to ease his slacks down over his hips without leaving the chair.

Sam stood, swiftly sliding her panties down her legs and handing them to him. He slid them into the pocket of his jacket and then pulled her back down on his lap, still facing away from him. Before she got settled, her soft, cool fingers wrapped around his cock as she guided him inside of her.

He bit back a groan, the slick, smooth walls of her pussy sliding down over him.

"Fuck, baby." God, she felt so fucking good.

With him clutching her skirt high on her hips, Sam began rocking on his lap as she faced away from him, watching Xander as he continued to pump his fingers into Mercedes, obviously looking to draw out another orgasm. Logan had no idea how these scenes worked from a logistical standpoint, but he was definitely intrigued by Sam's obvious interest.

As had always been the case, Logan got his pleasure from Sam's. He had no desire to touch or be touched by anyone else, so as far as he was concerned, if this was something she was interested in, he was all for learning a few new ways to please her.

They must've caught Xander's attention, because the man stopped, turning his head slightly to face them as he continued with his quest to drive Mercedes over the edge again.

Xander turned back toward Mercedes, his eyes tracking Sam through the mirror as he spoke to Mercedes. "Open your eyes and watch them."

Logan watched as Mercedes opened her eyes and glanced in the mirror to where they were behind her.

"Do you like watching them?" Xander asked.

"Yes," she moaned.

"Ahh, that's nice," Xander said, his gruff voice lingering in the air. "Watch her, pet. Watch while she lowers herself onto his cock. Just like I want to see you doing to me."

Logan listened to Xander's commentary as it happened, which was oddly arousing. Sam's sweet heat gripped him as his cock slid deep inside of her.

Xander must've realized Mercedes had closed her eyes again, because he offered a more vivid description. "She's riding him, slowly, his cock sinking deep inside of her. But she's watching us, pet," Xander told Mercedes.

Logan gripped Sam's hips tighter as she continued riding his cock, faster this time. She was gripping his thighs, letting herself drop until he was fully inside of her.

"That's it, baby. Ride me, Sam. Show me exactly what you like," Logan urged through gritted teeth, loving how responsive Sam was to Xander watching her.

Across the room, Logan barely noticed as Xander unstrapped Mercedes. Didn't pay much attention when Xander pulled her into his arms, holding her close as he continued to watch Sam.

Logan's own release was barreling down on him, and he found it difficult to focus on anything other than Sam's tight pussy sheathing him as she began to moan in earnest. "Fuck me, Sam. Fuck me hard, baby," he demanded.

"Oh, God!" she moaned loudly.

Xander's eyes came up to meet Sam's as Logan watched, and as though that glimpse were the detonator, Sam's pussy gripped his cock, and Logan couldn't hold back.

Sam moaned again, softer this time, a silent release exploding through her as her pussy clamped on to Logan's cock.

Logan growled in response, coming hard and deep inside of his wife. And when his world had righted itself enough for his eyes to focus, he glanced up to see Mercedes staring back at them.

It was at that moment that he wondered just what possibilities were in store for him and Sam in the future. Although he knew it wouldn't be a threesome with Xander Boone, he did know that he and Sam had a hell of a lot more to explore.

Chapter Four

The following morning…
Wednesday

MERCEDES AWOKE TO THE SUN SHINING THROUGH the open curtains of her bedroom. Unable to get her eyes to adjust to the luminous rays drifting across her bed, she rolled over, burying her head beneath the pillow as memories from the night before assaulted her.

What had she done?

As she inhaled deeply, the scent of fabric softener wafting into her nose, she realized that no matter how hard she wished, last night hadn't been a dream. What she'd done … or rather what Xander had done to her had been real.

Too real.

And if realizing what had happened wasn't bad enough, Mercedes had to accept the fact that she had loved every second of it.

Holy crap, she was in so much trouble.

Never in her wildest imagination would she have dreamed up what had happened last night at Devotion, and sure as the sun was up and blinding with its intensity, Mercedes knew it had happened.

"Are you finally awake?"

Mercedes flew to an upright position, her pillow flying to the floor as she yanked her comforter up over her naked breasts. With what she knew had to look like abject horror on her face, she stared at the man standing in her bedroom. "What the hell are you doing here?"

Xander laughed, crossing to the windows and staring out as he pushed the curtains open even more, allowing the sunlight to all but consume the entire room.

Clutching the blanket tightly, Mercedes gave a second's thought to what she looked like. She was definitely naked, and she knew her hair was a stringy mess all over her head, but there wasn't anything she could do about it at the moment.

"Just checking on you," Xander finally answered, turning to face her.

She could do nothing but stare at him.

Okay, so it wasn't completely absurd to find Xander in her condo. After all, he did own a condo in the same building — the penthouse — directly above hers, so he was nearby.

That explained his presence.

Since they both worked out of their homes, it wasn't even odd that he was home that early in the morning, either.

That explained his timing.

But it did not explain why he was standing in her bedroom, at the end of her bed, mind you, staring at her as though he was anticipating a replay of last night.

Not gonna happen.

"I should've never given you a key," she said with exasperation.

Sliding his big hands into the pockets of his perfectly tailored black slacks that would provide her a mouthwatering view of his nicely sculpted backside should he turn around, Xander didn't appear at all intimidated by her.

Another sexy, seductive laugh escaped him.

"Quit that," she told him, clutching her comforter tight to her chest with one hand and running the other through her unruly hair.

"Quit what?" he asked, grinning that half smirk that had melted the panties off of much weaker women.

"Quit staring at me," she told him. "And get out of my bedroom. I need to…"

Shit, she didn't even know what she needed to do.

"Take a shower," Xander kindly filled in for her. "I've got breakfast ordered. It'll be here shortly."

With that, Xander turned and walked out of the room, leaving Mercedes to stare after him, admiring his finely sculpted…

Good grief, woman. Haven't you learned your lesson already?

How was it possible that the man could make her four-thousand-square-foot condo feel so damn small?

A solid hour later, fully dressed in her heels and one of her most feminine power suits, with its short skirt and formfitting blazer, Mercedes joined Xander in her kitchen. She would've remained in the comfort of her bathroom a little longer, but she had run out of things to do after she dried her hair, and she didn't want Xander to think she was stalling.

Even if she was.

She found him relaxing comfortably at the breakfast table, sipping coffee and reading something on his iPad, a plate of fresh assorted bagels sitting in the center. Without saying a word, she went straight for the coffeepot, hoping like hell a little caffeine would erase the images from last night from her brain. The shower certainly hadn't helped.

"How're you feeling?" Xander asked, not looking up from what he was reading.

"Fine," she grumbled as she rummaged through the refrigerator, searching for the creamer and the cream cheese.

She was far from fine after the events of last night, but the way he was acting so nonchalantly, she got the impression she was the only one of them who was still thinking about it.

"Why are you here?" she asked him as she poured a little too much creamer into her coffee. Seriously? Why were her hands shaking?

"Meeting with Shane," he answered easily.

Shit.

Glancing over at the clock, Mercedes noticed it was fast approaching nine o'clock. She hadn't slept that late in … hell, in as long as she could remember. Her days generally started before dawn on a good day.

"Is he coming here? Or to your place?" she asked, trying to sound casual as she shoved the creamer back into the fridge.

Most of the time, they held their business meetings at Xander's. His condo had double the amount of space that hers did, and he had three offices, his, his assistant's, and an empty one, along with a conference room that he used for God knew what. Unlike her setup, his offices were separate from his living quarters. As for Mercedes, she merely worked out of her condo's secondary master bedroom that she'd had converted into an office.

"I told him to come here," Xander answered as she approached, placing his iPad on the table and sliding the bagels toward her. "You're looking a little pale," he added, tipping his head slightly to the side as he studied her with another of his infamous smirks.

"I wonder why," she blurted, immediately regretting her lack of filter.

She blamed him.

"I hear orgasms will do that to you."

Mercedes glared at him from across the table, letting him know with her eyes that she wasn't going to take his shit this morning. She was not getting into this with him. What had happened last night shouldn't have happened. It was a demonstration that had gotten way out of hand.

So what if he'd given her one of the best orgasms of her entire life. With his fingers.

It wasn't like she was going to tell him as much.

Refusing to dignify his statement with a verbal response, Mercedes reached for a bagel and opted to move the conversation back to neutral ground. "What's Shane coming over to talk about?"

Xander grinned, an all-out, panty-melting smile that had Mercedes fighting to keep from looking away from him. Rather than say something entirely inappropriate, which Xander was known to do from time to time, he morphed into the business professional that she knew him to be, his smile fading away entirely.

"We need to talk about the two properties we're planning to bid on," Xander explained.

"By 'we,' you mean you and Shane are bidding against each other? On both properties?"

Xander kept his eyes on her. "Honestly, I could give a shit less about the land; he can have it if he wants it that bad. I want the Milton building."

Mercedes knew about both properties, the one hundred plus acres off of the toll road up in Frisco and an old office building off of Milton right there in downtown that had just come on the market. Both of them were zoned for either commercial or residential, which was the factor that always put Shane and Xander at odds with one another.

Admittedly, Mercedes had significantly more knowledge regarding the Milton building. After all, Xander had been interested in it since she'd first brought it to his attention, so she had looked into a few specifics and taken him on a tour earlier in the week.

"I think that's smart," she told him. "The Milton building will be your best option of the two. He'll want to turn it into condos, anyway, and there's an overabundance of them in that area. He's better off with the land. Much more opportunity for residential development up that way."

That wasn't going to make Shane a happy camper, but then again, going up against Xander in a bidding war wasn't exactly one of Shane's favorite things to do, either.

Mercedes had known both men for quite some time. She knew how their minds worked because she'd worked with them both on practically a daily basis for the last decade.

She sold commercial real estate, and they dealt in commercial and residential property development, respectively. And many of the property transactions they dealt with were handled by her. Although she had a handful of other high-profile clients, Xander was definitely her bread and butter. He knew it, too.

Before they could go into further detail, her home phone rang. Grabbing the handset that was on the breakfast bar, Mercedes greeted the doorman, letting him know it was fine to send Shane up.

Rising from her chair, Mercedes contemplated getting more coffee before heading to her office. She definitely needed caffeine and a much more structured atmosphere or she would likely do something foolish, such as allow Xander, or worse, Shane, to know exactly what she was thinking. And the absolute last person who needed to find out what had happened last night was Shane Gibson. If he found out, she would never live it down.

"Let's do this in my office," she told Xander when she turned back to look at him, her face flaming when she realized how that sounded.

Shit. She was going to have to get a serious grip.

And soon.

The devilish gleam in his eyes said he'd caught on, as well.

Doing his best to hide his amusement, Xander pushed back from the kitchen table and followed Mercedes through her condo. He didn't, however, try to hide the fact that he was staring at her ass as she moved gracefully through the house.

The woman was fucking gorgeous, and she had an ass that made a man's mouth water. Heart-shaped and the perfect size to fill his hands nicely.

He'd been hoping she would come out of her bedroom after her shower wearing one of those formfitting yoga outfits that she favored when she was home. Casual wear, she called them. Much to his dismay, Mercedes had clearly armed herself for battle wearing a short skirt and a blazer with those damn red heels that gave him an instant hard-on.

Still, it didn't matter what she wore. She was hot as hell. Shit, he was pretty sure she could wear a potato sack, and his dick would still stand up and take notice.

Mercedes cleared her throat, and Xander forced his eyes to move upward. He wanted to laugh because he'd been clearly busted while admiring her perfect ass. Rather than pretend he hadn't been eyeballing her, he tossed her one of the heated looks he'd perfected over the years.

"Sit down," she said with a choked laugh.

He was fairly certain that Mercedes was on to him. How could she not be, though? After last night?

If she seriously thought that what had happened between them at Devotion was just a demonstration, the woman was clearly missing a few marbles. And he knew that wasn't the case, because Mercedes was one of the most perceptive, intelligent women he'd ever met.

He waited for her to take a seat behind her desk before he lowered himself to the chair across from her.

"Mornin'," Shane greeted as he made his way into the oversized room.

Xander glanced back over his shoulder, offering Shane a tilt of his chin in response. The man was decked out in one of those three-thousand-dollar suits he'd recently begun sporting. Although his own watch probably cost more than Shane's entire closet, Xander had to admit, he was impressed with his friend's recent transformation.

Shane Gibson was one of Xander's closest friends. They'd known each other for approximately fifteen years after they'd met during their junior year in college, were both turning thirty-six this year, and although Xander'd started growing his business back in his early twenties, Shane had just recently started getting serious. Now that Shane was starting to rake in the money, he was definitely beginning to look the part, which Xander found amusing considering all the shit Shane had given him through the years.

He wiped the smile off of his face when he looked up to see Shane glaring at him.

Based on the stern expression on Shane's too handsome face, it was clear that this was going to be a tense meeting, and truthfully, Xander would've preferred to spend his time finding a way to get Mercedes naked again.

Twenty minutes later, Xander found himself fisting his hands in his lap as he sat patiently waiting for Shane to calm down.

Tense was an understatement. Shane had lost his cool the moment Xander hadn't given in to his demands. It would've been comical if Xander were in the right frame of mind.

Keeping his composure, he remained as relaxed as he could while Shane paced the floor behind him. Mercedes was sitting at her desk, watching both of them intently, which was the only reason Xander didn't lose his shit.

She'd been the main reason his focus was off all morning, and the last thing he could afford was to let Shane win this round. Clasping his hands together in his lap, Xander crossed one ankle over the opposite knee and glanced at Shane, who was moving up beside him.

"Come on, man. You've got to be fucking kidding me," Shane grumbled, his face contorted with anger and frustration. He turned and stomped back the way he'd come before Xander could say anything.

Uncharacteristically restless, Xander leaned forward, resting his elbows on his knees as he glanced up at Mercedes to see that she was smiling. He wondered if she was entertained by his unease. Probably.

Any other day, he might've taken offense to her obvious amusement at his expense. But today... Today he just couldn't find it in him to get pissed off.

No, today he was apparently going to spend every waking moment thinking about her naked.

The woman had blown his damn mind last night.

Having known her for years, Xander had to give himself a significant amount of credit for keeping his hands to himself all this time. Lord knew he'd been tempted ever since he'd first seen her in that rattrap of an office she had been working out of back when Shane had introduced them.

Rather than try and seduce her, which he knew would've been futile because Mercedes had a firm set of beliefs and his intentions didn't fit them, he'd allowed their relationship to mold into a rather intimate friendship.

Xander didn't have many friends, but those he did have, he kept close. Both Mercedes and Shane were in that category. But unlike any normal friendship, when it came to Mercedes, Xander had suffered some unbearable physical aches through the years, fighting tooth and nail to pretend the woman didn't turn him the fuck on.

Oh, how she did.

But after last night, seeing her in a different light, he wasn't quite sure he could continue on with the charade. Or rather, he wasn't sure he wanted to.

Even if it was obvious that she wasn't happy about the outcome from their scene, no matter how hard he tried, Xander could not stop thinking about the way she'd come apart in his arms. It'd been incredibly difficult to make it through the night knowing she was tucked in her bed while he was just one floor above tossing and turning from an aching hard-on that couldn't be sated.

When Shane approached again, Xander glanced over his shoulder, remembering where he was and what he was supposed to be doing.

"Seriously, X. Tell me you're joking."

"Do I look like I'm joking?" Xander stated firmly, keeping his expression blank as he forced his attention back to the task at hand.

It wasn't a secret that Xander enjoyed the shit out of getting Shane riled up, but this morning he just wasn't feeling it. It was usually the highlight of their interactions, which, these days, seemed to be more and more frequent as Shane's business continued to grow.

Boone Development, LLC, was a light year ahead of Gibson Enterprises, but that divide was shrinking as Shane built a name for himself. And despite the fact that they often found themselves in direct conflict with one another, Xander was genuinely happy for the man.

"I'm making an offer on the Milton building, and you fucking know it," Shane said as he stalked across the room once again. "Why can't you ever make this easy for me?"

"Life's not easy," he told him, knowing his blasé attitude would only piss Shane off more. It didn't change how he felt about the whole deal.

They were currently discussing an undeveloped opportunity zoned for either commercial or residential that had just come up. Shane was interested in buying the property, and Xander didn't blame the guy. Shane was a housing developer, and this particular area was growing by leaps and bounds.

The problem was, there was more residential space than necessary in the area, but he couldn't seem to convince Shane of that. As for Xander, he mainly dealt in commercial property development, and for this particular building, he already knew of a company interested in relocating. Either way, their offers would be quite competitive, but when it came down to it, Xander would walk away with the property. He always did.

"Fuck you, Boone."

That statement and the fierce expression on Shane's face made Xander laugh. He pushed up from his chair — after all, his size was his best intimidating factor — buttoning his jacket as he did. Turning away from Mercedes, Xander thrust his hands into his pockets and addressed Shane directly.

Through the years, Xander and Shane had managed to meet somewhere in the middle on many deals much like this one. By middle, Xander meant more so in his favor. When there was a business opportunity that Xander wanted, he would certainly do what needed to be done to ensure he didn't lose. Pissing off one of his closest friends in the process was usually the end result.

"I'll back off of the land if you want it," Xander informed him. "But I'm not letting go of the Milton building. As far as I'm concerned, this conversation was done before it ever started. So, if you don't mind, I'd prefer to move on to something else."

Business was business, and on that point, he and Shane always butted heads. They probably always would. They frequently found themselves in direct competition, which wasn't necessarily a bad thing.

Despite their business relationship, Xander knew that, by the end of the day, Shane would forgive him. Somewhat. They were also friends.

"Are you handling this for him?" Shane directed his question at Mercedes, clearly annoyed with Xander's lack of cooperation.

"If he asks me to," she said.

"What if *I* ask you to handle it for me?" Shane questioned, thrusting his hands in his pockets and mimicking Xander's stance.

Xander tried not to laugh.

"I can only work for one of you, so you'll have to decide which one that is. You know I won't get in the middle of this. I don't get paid to be a referee."

"I'm not letting this go," Xander told Shane firmly, ignoring Mercedes's comment. "You can bid on the land, and I'll back off, but I'm gonna take this building."

"Fuck," Shane hissed, sliding his hand through his spiky blond hair. "Why do I even bother?" Shane huffed on a frustrated sigh. Although it was phrased like one, Xander knew it wasn't a question.

Glancing over at Mercedes, Xander nodded his head. It was his approval for her to move forward with the offer. She tipped her chin in agreement and leaned forward, her fingers flying over the keys on her keyboard.

"You two don't waste any time, do you?" Shane asked, sounding much calmer than before.

That's the way things worked between them. Shane would get pissed, Xander would tell him how it was going to be, and then Shane would move on with his life. The guy didn't have much stress because of it. Or maybe he didn't have much stress because he worked a lot of it out at the club. After all, the blond-haired, blue-eyed pretty boy was one of the most sought-after Doms at Kink.

"When you're done with that, move forward with my offer on the land."

Mercedes glanced up at Shane and smiled. "Already working on it."

She knew them both so well.

"Y'all going to the club tonight?" Shane's sudden change of subject released the tension in the air.

Looking over at Mercedes, Xander said no at the same time she said yes.

He pinned her with a glare.

Shane then directed his statement to Mercedes, seemingly ignorant to the underlying tension that was lingering between them. "Want me to pick you up on my way there?"

"Yeah, that'll be great."

"You sure you don't want to go?" Shane asked Xander, forcing him to look away from Mercedes.

"I'm sure. I've got another commitment. I'm sure you'll have a good time without me."

"We certainly will, won't we, doll?" Shane said to Mercedes with that damned pretty-boy smile.

She didn't answer, but Xander didn't need her to.

Shane didn't waste any more time, nodding his head at Xander. "I'll catch up with you later."

"Later," Xander called after him as Shane darted out of the office.

Xander listened to his friend's footsteps down the hall, then across the Travertine entryway, and then finally when Shane opened and closed the front door behind him.

As soon as he knew they were alone, he turned his attention back on Mercedes. "There is no way in hell you're going to the club tonight."

CHAPTER FIVE

MERCEDES DIDN'T KNOW HOW SHE MANAGED TO keep from cracking her keyboard right in half when Xander spoke.

She inhaled slowly through her nose and then out through her mouth as she tried to control the anger that snaked its way into her bloodstream and threatened to burn her to a crisp.

The man had balls; she'd give him that.

She could handle a lot of things, such as Xander being an asshole when it came to his business dealings, but she damn sure didn't do well with anyone telling her what she could or couldn't do.

"Last I checked, you don't make my decisions for me," she told him, grateful she'd managed to hold on to some semblance of calm.

"The hell I don't," he bit out.

Mercedes clamped her jaw shut, afraid if she didn't, it just might hit the floor. Never, in all the time she'd known Xander, had he talked to her like that.

The man was clearly delusional.

Taking a deep breath to calm herself, Mercedes got to her feet and moved around to the front of the desk, where Xander stood. She crossed her arms over her chest, keeping her back straight, her chin up as she approached him.

"Excuse me?" She couldn't go nose to nose with him because he was several inches taller than she was. But she did meet his eyes. "Is there something we need to talk about?" she asked him curtly.

"No," he bit out. "As far as I'm concerned, there isn't anything to discuss," he argued, sounding not at all like the calm, confident man she knew so well.

"Well, I think there is." Mercedes took one measured step back, not wanting to crane her neck as she argued with this insufferable man. "What the hell is wrong with you?"

"*Me?* What the hell is wrong with *you*? Do you not remember anything that happened last night?"

"Yeah, actually, I do," she answered abruptly. "I remember going to Devotion with you to help you with a demonstration. That's what that was, right? A demonstration? Nothing more, nothing less? As a favor to you, I was your assistant, if I recall correctly."

Xander exhaled sharply, but he didn't look away, the smooth skin on his freshly shaven jaw taut, that telltale vein at his temple giving away his true frustration. "It was more than that, and you fucking know it."

"I don't know anything of the sort," she lied.

Yes, Mercedes could classify what had happened between them as un-fucking-believable. But it was a fluke. A stroke of luck. Inconvenient timing. Strange alignment of the planets. Call it what you would.

She knew it had never happened to her before, but what Xander didn't seem to understand was that it would never happen again.

Nev. Er. A. Gain.

"You're lying," Xander said, his eyes locked on her. "You know how I know? Because you can't look me in the eye when you say it, Mercedes."

Keeping her eyes locked with his, just to prove him wrong, Mercedes argued, "I think you forgot one little detail about last night. It was your idea. You're the one who needed my help on a demonstration. A *demonstration*, Xander. Nothing more."

Xander didn't say a word in response, so Mercedes continued. "Oh, and get this," she added sarcastically, recalling the email she'd received just a short while ago. The one that had made her damn near choke on her tongue. "Logan McCoy emailed me a few minutes ago. He wanted to let me know that Sam definitely has an interest in D/s lifestyles." Mercedes frowned. "Thanks to you and your brilliant plan, he thinks I'll be a good person for her to chat with. The man thinks I'm a submissive."

Despite her outrage, Xander's expression didn't change. He just stared down at her, his hands in his pockets, looking as relaxed and comfortable as always, even though the tightening of the muscle in his jaw gave him away entirely. She had to admit, he wasn't usually so easy to read.

"And that's a bad thing how?"

Mercedes fought the irritation that was eating away at her. "You know good and damn well that I'm not a submissive," she bit out. "But after your little scene last night, they seem to think I am."

"Fine. Do you want me to set them straight? I'll do that. That doesn't mean you can't give her information on the subject."

Mercedes didn't respond as she continued to glare at him.

Even though they hadn't talked in depth about what had happened, Mercedes knew there was no way Xander would believe she'd willingly go from being a Domme to his submissive just because he'd given her an orgasm.

Hell, it didn't work that way. She didn't want to be a sub. Not his or anyone else's. There might've been a time in her life when being passive had seemed natural to her. Too bad life had changed her, and she'd soon learned that taking the reins and being in control was the easiest way to get to the top. She'd made it her mission, and somewhere along the way, she'd built a reputation as an extremely successful entrepreneur, not to mention, as one of the most formidable Mistresses in her circle of friends.

She wasn't looking for a personality overhaul, thank you very much.

Throughout their friendship, she had reminded Xander that she was the dominating half of her relationships, and she had no interest in switching sides. Not for anyone.

Especially not for him.

Nothing had changed.

She was suddenly compelled to move away from him and to change the subject. Without haste, she went back behind her desk and, as gracefully as she could manage, slid down into her chair, keeping her eyes on him. She waited for him to sit, which, surprisingly, he did.

"I need to know what your initial bid for the Milton building is going to be so I can get a contract drawn up," she told him, morphing into her role as his real estate agent.

Business was probably the only safe subject they could discuss at the moment.

"Get me comps and some information on the company selling, and I'll let you know."

"I'll get right on that." Grabbing her pencil and a note pad, she focused on the task at hand.

Mercedes jotted down the notes, taking more time than necessary, hoping he'd get the hint and head out the same way Shane had.

When she looked back up, she found Xander staring at her, his expression unreadable. "What?" Mercedes asked, her voice soft but insistent. "Why are you looking at me like that?"

"No reason," he grumbled, pushing to his feet.

Mercedes continued to watch him, holding her breath as she waited to see if he'd say something more or just leave her be.

When he turned, making his way toward the door, she couldn't decide whether she was grateful or disappointed that he'd opted to go.

"Get the comps and come talk to me. I'll be in my office."

Mercedes nodded, and Xander turned and left.

WALKING AWAY FROM MERCEDES WHEN HE WANTED nothing more than to address what had happened last night was harder than he'd thought. But somehow he managed to make his way out of her condo, into the elevator, and up to the penthouse without turning around.

Barely.

Once inside, he went straight to his office. It was the only way he'd be able to keep his mind off of the woman who'd single-handedly driven him to distraction.

"Hey."

The moment he dropped into his chair, Xander looked up to see his assistant, Leah, standing in his doorway.

"I didn't hear you come in," she told him.

"Just walked in."

"Everything okay?"

As much as he liked Leah, he definitely wasn't interested in sharing his personal business with her. She was a sweet girl. Too sweet, actually. Why she stuck with him, he had no idea.

Leah Ingram had been his assistant for the last two years. She was young and cute and so damned innocent it made Xander's teeth hurt to talk to her sometimes. He was constantly trying to watch what he said to her, afraid he'd offend her sensitive ears.

But the woman was the best damned assistant he'd ever had. She juggled college and work and, from what she'd told him, very little else. She was never late, never asked to leave early, and never, ever called in sick.

With strawberry-blonde hair, pale brown eyes, a china-doll face that looked far younger than her twenty-five years, Leah was the picture of a sweet virgin.

Xander thought she was absolutely adorable, and he genuinely liked her. But she made him nervous because of how fucking innocent she was.

Oh, and the woman had caught Shane's attention, and Xander knew his best friend stayed as far away from Xander's offices as he possibly could. Xander suspected he was scared to talk to her because he didn't want to risk slinging a curse word and causing her to crumble.

"I'm good. What time's my next meeting?"

"Eleven thirty," she answered instantly. "You're scheduled to call Malcolm Hirsh." Even her sweet, lilting drawl was cute.

Fan-fucking-tastic. Just what he wanted to do today.

Hirsh was a persistent bastard who'd been driving him batshit crazy for the last three months. Xander owned a piece of property that he'd been sitting on for the last five years or so. He had no intention of doing anything with it just yet, but Hirsh, the owner of the adjacent property, was looking to expand his operations. He wanted Xander's land. But he didn't want to pay anywhere close to what Xander wanted for it.

"Thanks." Glancing over at the clock on the wall, Xander noticed it was only ten. He looked back at Leah, who was still standing in his doorway. "Why don't you take the rest of the day off?"

Her eyebrows darted up into her hairline before she was able to mask her expression. "Are you sure?"

"Very." At the moment, he had other ideas of how to pass the time, and he didn't need an audience.

"Okay, then. I'll... Let me just finish what I was doing and then I'll go. But I'll see you tomorrow morning, right?"

"Of course," he answered, trying to soften his expression. He was thinking too much, and he knew that Leah was sensitive whenever he got into one of his moods. He wasn't sure why that was, but she shied away from him most of the time.

"Thank you."

He had no idea what she was thanking him for, but he watched as she disappeared around the corner. He wiggled his mouse to get his screen saver to disappear, and he pulled up his calendar.

"Hey, Leah," he called out.

"Yes, sir?" she asked, rushing back to his door.

"Clear my calendar for the rest of the day before you go. I'll take Hirsh's call, but that's it."

"Yes, sir."

Xander tried to work for the next few minutes, waiting for Leah to leave, but he had a difficult time focusing. Thankfully, his assistant didn't take long before she was saying good-bye and heading to the door.

Before the front door probably even shut behind her, Xander had picked up his phone and dialed.

"Yes?" Mercedes asked, making the word into two syllables when she answered.

"Meet me in my conference room in ten minutes. Bring the comps with you." Xander didn't wait for a response; he hung up the phone and then took a deep breath.

It was now or never.

CHAPTER SIX

MERCEDES KNEW SHE SHOULDN'T HAVE BEEN ALL that surprised by Xander's abrupt phone call, but she was. It wasn't his fault, either. She felt as though she were walking around in some sort of alternate universe, confused about where she was and where she was going. Imagine walking around on the ceiling and trying to figure out if you were the one upside down or the furniture was.

That's how she felt.

Printing out the comps she had pulled up as soon as Xander had left, she grabbed a pencil, her cell phone, and the paper now sticking out of the printer. She didn't know if it had been ten minutes or not, but she was ready to get this over with.

It was a regular occurrence for Xander to summon her to his office to discuss business, and usually she'd be prepared for anything he could throw at her. But this time she felt strange as she rode the elevator to his floor.

When she stepped up to his front door, she was tempted to knock, but she knew that would've also been weird, so she turned the knob and walked in. Closing the door quietly behind her, she took stock of the living area. Empty, just as she'd expected.

A few seconds later, she was walking into the conference room — which, by the way, Xander had never requested that they meet in.

"What are you looking at?" she asked as she moved closer, watching him stare out of the floor-to-ceiling windows, his hands thrust in his pockets in typical Xander fashion.

"Just admiring the view." He turned slowly to face her, and a smile crept across his lips. "However, this view *is* considerably better."

Mercedes rolled her eyes. Now this was getting ridiculous. She had thought for sure he'd be over this by now.

Maybe the guy just needed to get laid; she didn't know.

Watch her, pet. Watch while she lowers herself onto his cock. Just like I want to see you doing to me.

Shit. A chill raced down her spine at the memory of his words from the night before. She could still hear the rough gravel of his voice, evidence that he'd been just as affected by what had happened as she had.

But it didn't matter. She couldn't help him.

Maybe it would do him some good to go to the club tonight instead of her. She'd be more than happy to back off if he needed to head out and release some of the tension that was clearly building up.

She wanted to tell him as much, except the idea of Xander with another sub, or any woman, for that matter, made her stomach churn.

A sudden snap had her glancing down to her hands. She'd broken her pencil right in half.

Fucking great.

At least it wasn't her cell phone she had snapped right in two.

Looking back at Xander, she noticed he was on the move, and she went the opposite direction, keeping the small conference table between them at all times. She didn't wait for him to ask her to sit; she just dropped into the chair closest to the windows. Expecting him to take a seat on the opposite side, she immediately regretted having sat down when he remained standing.

Crap.

"Nervous?" he asked, his eyes darting down to the broken pencil in her hand, his hands still casually inserted into his pockets.

"Not hardly," she lied.

"You don't like that I'll admit to admiring you, do you?"

Frustrated that he wouldn't let it go, Mercedes met Xander's gaze head on and said harshly, "Whatever, Boone. There's no one to impress anymore; you don't need to try and flatter me."

Xander was beside her in a flash. His abrupt movement startled her, causing her to drop both halves of her pencil, the papers, and her cell phone onto the table. As he loomed over her, she looked up at him, her body stone still, her eyes wide, and her mouth slightly open as she tried to figure out what the hell he was going to do.

Before she could come to a conclusion, he was taking her hand, pulling her to her feet, and then backing her up a few inches until she was flush against the window he'd been gazing out of just a few minutes before.

How the hell had that just happened?

"What are you doing?" she asked, her voice low, her anger apparent. "Let me go."

"No. Not until we hash this out."

"Hash *what* out?" she asked as she tried to push him away unsuccessfully. Albeit, she hadn't been using as much force as she should have, not to mention Xander Boone wasn't going to budge unless he absolutely wanted to.

Xander gripped her hips gently, holding her in place with relative ease. He wasn't going to hurt her; she knew that. And she wasn't at all scared of him. She just wasn't sure she could hold out being this close to him. Not after everything she'd been feeling since last night.

The man, despite all of the warnings that she'd always given herself where he was concerned, drew her in, made her want things she shouldn't want, and he'd proven that effortlessly at Devotion. But she still had time to turn things around, to ignore everything that had happened between them and move on with life as normal.

When she stopped pushing against him, he loosened his grip, and she surprised herself when she stopped putting up a fight.

"So talk," she said after a long, deafening silence.

Xander moved, and Mercedes glanced down as he reached for her hands, linking his fingers with hers before lifting her arms up over her head and pinning them against the glass.

Okay, this was not good.

When she looked back up into his eyes, Mercedes knew he would see more than she wanted him to. She couldn't deny the fact that her body was humming. Being this close to him, his hands holding her so easily in place, was doing funny things to her insides. Sort of the way things had gone last night.

Again, there was the problem. She had to remind herself of the most important thing.

She. Was. Not. A. Submissive.

Not at all.

And that's what Xander wanted.

Her entire life revolved around her hard-earned control — in and out of the bedroom. There was no room in her life for a man who wanted to order her around, to insist that she do what would please him. As the pathetic tale went: been there, done that.

"Young lady, you will not be leaving this house." "I don't recall approving you to wear that." "Get off the goddamn phone." "You won't get a penny from me. If you want it, work for it." "Dammit, Priscilla, I didn't give you permission to buy her that."

Her father's words rang inside of her head, the constant orders and restrictions, his infallible ability to ensure she never got what she requested. He'd ridden her hard from the time she was little, never giving her an ounce of freedom because he had preferred to keep her and her mother under his thumb.

She damn sure wouldn't let any man control her like that again. It was the very reason she'd left home as soon as she'd graduated from high school even though her father had moved out the day she'd turned eighteen.

"Please don't," she whispered to Xander now, the words more a plea than a command. She did not want to fight with him, and she found that her resistance to him wasn't nearly as fortified as she'd once believed.

"Don't what?" he asked, sounding way too curious.

"I don't want to do this," she told him.

She *didn't* want to do this, no matter what her traitorous body was projecting.

Shit, who was she kidding? She did want this. She wanted him up against her, wanted to feel the warmth of his body the way she had last night. Even while she had slept alone in her bed, she'd ached for this man although she knew there was no chance in hell that she would ever cross over to the dark side.

"I'm not asking you to do anything."

"No?" Mercedes glared at him.

Infuriating Dom.

He was asking for everything, and he very well knew it. They'd been friends for too long. She knew how he operated. And what that said about her, because she'd allowed him to manipulate her to this point, she didn't want to think about.

"Fine. Then how about this? I *can't* do this," she told him. "You know I can't, X. It's not who I am."

Xander unlinked their fingers, but he kept her pinned with her arms still above her head, one giant hand circling around her wrists while the other moved down to cup her cheek. To her horror, she leaned into his touch.

"But you want to, don't you?" he asked, his tone gentle.

"No! I don't. I already told you that!" she yelled.

When Xander merely stared back at her, Mercedes fought the urge to scream at the top of her lungs. It was either that or break down in tears because this man — this Dom — was wearing down her resistance. Clearly she wasn't as convincing as she was trying to be.

He didn't say anything for a long time, and Mercedes realized what he was doing. Damn it. He was pulling that psychological, manipulative bullshit on her. Xander was letting her think it through, giving her time to come to a decision on her own. It was the way he operated, how he handled all of his subs. He would never force anything on anyone, which meant if a woman wanted something from him, she'd have to agree up front.

Damn it.

"Let me go," she ground out through gritted teeth. She was not going to give in to him. No way in hell.

Xander didn't budge. He just continued to pin her with his hand on her wrists and his beautiful eyes peering down at her, probably reading her mind, if she had to guess.

That wasn't good, either. Especially considering the questions running loose through her brain.

If she were so adamant that she didn't want this, why was her body burning for him? Why was she feeling things she hadn't felt in ... well, in years? Why was she suddenly wanting to relive what she'd felt last night when he was touching her?

God, this was too confusing.

Staring back at him, she suddenly hated herself for allowing him to wear her down, but she knew that she couldn't lie to him. She wasn't built that way. The truth was the only way she knew, because without the truth, what was left?

"Tell me, Mercedes. Tell me that last night wasn't just a demonstration. You felt more, didn't you?"

"Maybe. I don't know," she finally said, rationalizing her thoughts. She didn't know anything anymore. In the span of one night, he'd flipped her world upside down, and she didn't know which way she was going anymore. The emotions that churned inside of her were unexpected and left her hovering on the brink of insanity.

"Tell me this," he prompted. "Last night, what did you feel?"

What had she felt? An easier question would be what *hadn't* she felt. He'd made her feel more in twenty minutes than she'd felt in years, and that scared the shit out of her. She wasn't looking for anything. She was content with her life, and what he represented was nothing more than danger to everything she'd created for herself. And she knew that one wrong decision could very well damage their friendship beyond repair.

Was she willing to risk it?

Mercedes looked away, breaking eye contact with him. He didn't allow her to disengage, though. He just curled his finger beneath her chin, turning her head back so that she was facing him, and she let him.

"Tell me," he ordered as he dropped his hand to his side.

"I'm used to being in control. You know that." He didn't say anything, so she continued. "I'm in control of every aspect of my life — business and personal. And that includes my sex life. I control my destiny. I decide what and when. That's who I am, Xander. What we did last night goes against who I am."

"But you enjoyed it."

It wasn't a question.

This time Mercedes didn't look away. "Yes. I did. Are you happy now?" she bit out. "That doesn't change anything. I still crave the control."

Sort of.

"Do you?"

She hated when he did that. She didn't want to talk about this.

"Yes, dammit," she snapped. "What happened last night…" Mercedes closed her eyes briefly and then reopened them, a renewed sense of purpose filling her. It was her turn to get answers. "Remember that night at Kink when you volunteered to let Mistress Desiree demonstrate on you because no one else had the balls to do it? How did that make *you* feel?"

"Like I was in someone else's body," he told her, his answer surprisingly honest.

"Then you know exactly how I felt, X," Mercedes stated firmly.

"When are you going to stop lying to yourself, Mercedes? To us both?" he argued, his voice low, his tone even. "I was with you, remember? You came apart at the seams when we were together."

Yes, she had. Against her will.

Okay, no, not really. But still.

"And you think that's all I need? An orgasm?" Mercedes tried to pull away again, but Xander held her wrists more firmly.

Xander opened his mouth. Closed it.

She wanted to know what he had to say. But then actions replaced words, and Mercedes found herself giving in to something she'd dreamed about since the moment Xander had put his hands on her last night.

As he looked into her eyes, he tightened his grip on her wrists just a little and moved his free hand up, his knuckles lightly grazing her nipple as he did. Then he was sliding his fingers into her hair, cupping the back of her head, as he leaned down, pressing his lips to hers.

He was kissing her.

For the very first time.

And sweet mother of mercy, the man could freaking kiss.

Mercedes was pretty sure her knees were going to give out.

In contrast to the heated argument they were having, Xander's lips were soft, his hand gentle as he held her.

She hesitated only briefly before she gave in, kissing him back with delicious intent. Her legs weakened, her body ignited with sensation as the kiss penetrated her bloodstream, moving through her entire body in a rush.

It didn't take long before the passion of the moment overwhelmed them both.

Holding her head firmly, Xander controlled the kiss, and she let him. It would serve no purpose to try to top him. He wasn't going to allow it. And, truth be told, she wanted to remember what it felt like to be dominated, to let go of the control, to concede to someone else for even a brief moment.

Just this once.

She pressed up against him involuntarily, unable to stop herself. What this was between them wasn't normal. It wasn't run of the mill. And dammit all to hell, it wasn't only about sex although it would appear that way from the outside looking in.

But what most people didn't realize about her was that she used her Domme status to keep her distance from people. The habit had been ingrained in her since she was a teenager, growing up in an abusive household with an overbearing father, then reinforced time and time again through a series of bad relationships when she was older.

Being in control meant she didn't have to give up anything, didn't have to answer to anyone, and being a Domme in the lifestyle she coveted meant she could be satisfied physically without ever having to give too much of herself. As far as emotional ties, there weren't any. Because she didn't allow them.

But this was Xander. Her friend. A man she admired, a man she suddenly craved, which meant she would want more. Nothing about Xander was easy, and if she gave in to him at all, even one tiny bit, she feared she'd lose a part of herself that she'd been holding on tightly to for as long as she could remember.

The kiss lingered, the passion between them fanning the flames as she was engulfed by the same overwhelming sensations that Xander had instilled in her last night when he'd used nothing more than his hands and a flogger to send her careening into the abyss.

Seemingly unwilling to let go, he consumed her, tasting, teasing, seeking all that she was willing to give him.

And she let him.

Long minutes later, when he pulled back, Xander remained steadfast, holding her wrists, palming her head gently as he stared down at her. Why that made her feel good, she didn't know.

But she did. She felt … safe in his arms.

It had been an incredibly long time since a man had looked at her the way Xander was looking at her now. Maybe it was her fault because she'd refrained from taking on a full-time sub for a couple of years now, disinclined to commit to something she didn't think she was ready for again.

The only thing she knew was that she shouldn't feel good. She wasn't supposed to *want* this.

And that was the main reason she had to push him away.

There was a long pause before Mercedes reluctantly said, "If you're looking for a submissive, I suggest you consider taking Sam on. I think she'll satisfy that urge and you'll both get what you want. Hell, you'll even get a threesome out of the deal, and we all know how you feel about that."

Did that make her sound jealous? God, she hoped not, but she couldn't help herself. The idea of Xander dominating Sam, the thought of Sam crushed between Logan and Xander made her crazy, but she knew if she didn't push him away, she ran the risk of pulling him close, and it wasn't in her best interest to do so.

"You, not Sam," Xander said brusquely, his words coarse as though he were just as affected by this as she was. He brushed his thumb over her cheek, but he didn't finish his sentence.

"Me what?" Mercedes finally asked when it was clear he wouldn't go on. Sucking her bottom lip between her teeth, she waited.

"I want *you*," he finally said. The gravelly tone of his voice had pleasure igniting beneath her skin.

Mercedes's heart did a somersault, but she stopped it mid-flip, refusing to give in to the promises she could hear in his tone.

"That's bullshit, and you know it," she argued, trying to keep her voice even. "I'm a challenge for you, X. That's all I am. I've seen the women you play with. They're meek and … they don't pose much of a challenge. Hell, most of them aren't even true submissives; they just want a shot at your money."

"If you think I'm looking for a woman who doesn't challenge me, then you don't know me as well as I thought you did," he replied softly.

Mercedes forced her eyes away from his. He saw too much.

"Look at me," Xander demanded. This time he used only his words, not his hands.

Her eyes darted up quickly, too quickly. She knew he saw that she was still hovering on the fence that separated *undecided* and *hell no, this is emotional suicide.*

"Let me show you," he pleaded gruffly. "Five days. Starting right now. That's all I'm asking for."

"Five *days*?" That was *all*? Shit, that was only the beginning. "You think you can turn me from a Domme to a submissive in…? Wait, why five?" she asked curiously, all other thoughts coming to an abrupt halt.

Xander smirked, a glint of humor in his radiant smile. "Five's my lucky number. You know that."

She *did* know that. Just like seven was her lucky number. And twenty-three was Shane's. They'd had a long conversation one night over a bottle of vodka. *That* had been interesting.

But it wasn't the point.

"Xander—" She stopped herself, trying to realign her thoughts once more. Calming down, she followed up with, "I like being in control."

"Do you?" he asked, sounding unconvinced and rightfully so since he still held her up against the window, and somewhere along the way, she'd forgotten that she had pressed her body up against his, her breasts against the hard planes of his chest.

But it didn't matter that she was physically attracted to this man. This *Dom*. She did like being in control. And she was good at it. She was successful. She was independent. And she'd kept the attention of more subs than she cared to count through the years. They kept coming back. It didn't seem to matter that she never promised them anything. That said something about her; she knew it did. But it didn't explain these mixed-up emotions churning in her belly.

She wasn't giving up yet, though.

"Are you saying you want to top *me*? That in five days I'll just hand over the reins to you?" she asked. "That's a little optimistic, X. Even for you."

"That's exactly what I'm saying." He answered easily that time, his restraint palpable.

Having him dominate her was something she'd never even considered until last night at Devotion. Since then ... well, since then she'd thought about little else.

Confusion overwhelmed her. No matter what she wanted, regardless of whether she gave in to it or not, it still didn't explain what Xander's ulterior motive was.

"Why me, X?" Knowing she was moving into dangerous territory, Mercedes stared into crystal green eyes, searching for the truth. He didn't answer her question, so she continued. "And once you break me? Once I'm nothing but a puddle at your feet? Then what? Are you telling me you wouldn't get bored with me like you do all the others?"

Mercedes knew him. Xander hadn't had a serious relationship since the day she'd met him. He played at the clubs, took some of them home, but they never lasted more than a week at the most. He claimed that it was due to work. He didn't have time for anything else.

Right.

Mercedes wasn't willing to give up the friendship they'd developed for a few days of sex.

No matter how good she suspected it would be.

CHAPTER SEVEN

ALTHOUGH XANDER HEARD EVERY SINGLE WORD MERCEDES said, he didn't believe her for a second. Oh, she gave a convincing argument with her direct questions, trying to turn this around on him.

And maybe she had a point. Xander hadn't had a real relationship in as long as he could remember. He'd been content with work and play, keeping the two completely separate, yet knowing that work would ultimately take priority over anything else.

That was before last night. Before his entire thought process had changed at the hands of this one woman. Or rather, when he'd finally gotten his hands on this woman.

After years of subtly trying to get her to see him the way he saw her, Xander had finally been handed an opportunity too good to pass up. Thanks to Logan's request, Xander was given the chance to get her in a position where he could convince her that he was the man she needed. Because she was who he *needed*. Who he *wanted*. The woman he longed to have beside him. And not just as his friend.

In all of the years he'd played at the clubs, all of the pets he'd commanded, never once had any one woman touched a place so deep inside of him the way Mercedes had.

Not that he could share that with her just yet, because it would likely come back to bite him in the ass, and right now, he just wanted a commitment from her. Five days. That's all he needed to show her exactly how good the two of them could be together.

Hell, he could still feel the way her body had relented to his last night. The way she'd come apart in his arms. It had taken right at ten minutes to bring her down from the sexual high, which he believed was what really pissed her off.

Not him. He'd loved every fucking minute of it and yearned to do it again. So much so that Xander couldn't even contemplate the idea of being with another woman ever again. He wasn't even sure he could simply play with a sub, because the only person he would be thinking about was Mercedes. And he couldn't stand the thought of her with someone else, either. He knew himself, knew that he'd lose his shit if he saw her with another man.

Nor was he willing to just let her go. If required, Xander was more than ready to fight to convince her.

He understood her reaction. Hell, he'd be thoroughly confused if, somewhere along the way, he showed any sort of submissive tendency, as well. But Xander knew her, knew that she'd never submit to another man.

Only him.

And that fucking made his dick hard.

To know that she would never kneel at another man's feet, would never give up the control she held close to the vest... It made him want to dominate her in every way.

Starting right fucking now.

"It can't happen, X," Mercedes told him, drawing him back to the present.

Staring down at her, watching the storm clouds brew in her eyes made him want her all the more. She could argue with him until the end of time, but he wasn't willing to be thrown off course. Not now. Not after last night. After they'd made it this far.

Xander opted to take a more direct approach. Shifting so that he could slide one knee between her thighs, he released her hands and gripped her hips, forcing her skirt up high and grinding the steely length of his cock against her belly. All while he crushed his mouth to hers.

She was so soft in his arms. The abundant swell of her breasts against his chest, the heavenly feel of her generous hips against his palms. She was perfect for him.

He was hanging by a thread, holding her close, reveling in the heat that generated between her legs. When she began grinding her pussy against his thigh, he knew she was done. No matter what she said or what she told herself, this combustible energy that generated between them was hard to resist.

No, not hard. Damn near impossible.

"Xander," Mercedes moaned when he gripped her hair, tilting her head back so he could deepen the kiss. Thrusting his tongue into the sweetness of her mouth, Xander almost came when she grabbed his ass and jerked him closer.

It was a stalemate. He held tightly to her hair; she held on to him with her relentless grip. Breaking the kiss and staring into her eyes, Xander opted to go with the cold, hard truth.

"I'm going to dominate you, Mercedes. I'm going to have you begging me, pleading for me to make you come. I'm going to show you exactly what it feels like to lose absolute control. And I'm going to do it over and over again until you don't want to think about anyone but me."

Her eyes went from soft gray to a thunderhead, blackened with resistance. Or was that need?

Mercedes slid her hand down between their bodies and began stroking his rigid erection through his slacks. Xander fought the urge to thrust into her hand. What he wouldn't give for her to jerk him off right then and there. Or better yet, for her to drop to her knees so he could watch his cock slide in and out of her pretty pink lips.

He wished he were naked. If he thought she would be game, he would strip them both right then and there. Toss her across the table and fuck her senseless. Xander wanted her more than his next breath, but he knew he could only push Mercedes so far, and right now there was a delicate balance that he couldn't afford to throw off.

"I don't have any desire to submit to you," Mercedes explained as she stroked his cock roughly. "If you think I can be forced into enjoying it, you're wrong. And on top of that, we both know we'll tire of each other before long."

Xander didn't hear anything after the word "force." He'd never had to force a woman to enjoy anything.

"Force you to enjoy it?" Xander asked incredulously as he slid his hand up her thigh slowly, easing his finger beneath the lace of her panties. He grazed her clit with his fingertip and then eased lower until he found her soaking-wet entrance. "I don't think force is necessary, baby."

Xander fought to keep his eyes open even though she continued to stroke him more firmly, and he wanted nothing more than to get lost in the sensation of her intimate touch along his aching cock.

Mercedes suddenly stopped, gripping his cock painfully, forcing him to inhale sharply as she tried to control the situation.

Determined to fight fire with fire, Xander pushed his finger inside of her slowly.

"One of these days, you're going to learn that not everyone wants what you want. *This* is what I want," she said, tightening her grip on his dick and making him damn near choke on his tongue. "I want a man with my collar around his neck. I want a man who is on his knees and naked when I come home. Begging me, pleading for me to let him come. I want a man shackled to my bed, one I can have my way with whenever I choose. I want a man who knows that I can offer him the greatest pleasure ever to be had."

"Baby, I can assure you that you'll never get a collar around my neck, nor will I ever be on my knees unless I'm lapping your sweet pussy, and you damn sure won't have a chance to tie me to your bed. But I assure you, I already know how intense the pleasure is." He paused, sliding his index finger deeper and twisting, searching for... There it was.

Mercedes released the stranglehold she had on his dick as she cried out with pleasure, bucking against him, trying to get closer as he rubbed her G-spot with his finger, forcing her closer and closer to the edge. Still gripping her hair, he pulled her head forward until his mouth brushed her ear. "And I promise you, I'll make you come as many times as I possibly can." He nipped her ear. "Starting now."

Mercedes's body went stone still, her breaths slamming in and out of her lungs as her climax gripped her. She thought she was hiding it, but Xander felt the way her pussy clamped on to his finger, the way she trembled in his arms.

He didn't care if she came quietly or if she screamed so that the fucking neighbors came running to help her. Either way, he was going to make her come again. Very, very soon.

When she finally relaxed, Xander pulled her to him, ignoring the hard-on that was now pounding incessantly between his legs. She might not want to be close to him at the moment, but he couldn't seem to let her go.

MERCEDES WASN'T SURE HOW MUCH MORE OF this she could handle. Xander had somehow found a direct link to her pleasure receptors, and he could set her off faster than anything, including her favorite vibrator.

Now that she was boneless from another intense climax at this man's hands, she wasn't sure how she was going to be able to continue to deny him.

Eventually, he was going to realize she was on the verge of giving in.

Oh, hell, he already knew that much. She was the only one who believed otherwise.

When she finally caught her breath, Mercedes pulled out of Xander's arms and looked up at him. She reached down to readjust her skirt but realized he'd already done that.

"I've got to take a call in a few minutes," Xander said, still hovering above her. "It'll be over at noon." He paused long enough to tip her head back so that she was looking at him. "I want you to seriously think about what I've requested. If you choose to give me the five days, I expect to see you in my office at that time."

"A little quick, don't you think?" she retorted, suddenly unsure of herself.

"No, I don't. If I had my way, I'd be inside you right here. Right now."

A tremor of need shook her from the inside out. The raspy tone of his voice said he was on the edge, too.

"Five days, Mercedes. I want you for five solid days."

"I don't think I'll last five hours," she told him honestly. She wasn't a submissive. It wasn't like she could flip a switch and become something she wasn't. That's what happened in romance novels, not in real life. And this damn sure wasn't…

"Give me five days to prove you wrong."

…a romance.

Could he read her mind? She hoped not.

Regardless, Mercedes wasn't going to give him an answer right then. She had until noon, which was… Shit. It was only a little more than thirty minutes away. Not nearly enough time to make a life-altering decision like that one.

Xander leaned down, pressing his lips to hers gently, and then he pulled back. As soon as he stepped away, she feared she might just slide down to the floor. Had it not been for the windows at her back, she would've done just that.

She watched as his impressive form walked out of the conference room without looking back.

Dropping into the chair closest to her, Mercedes spun around and stared out the window. How was she supposed to make a decision like this?

Five freaking days. Was the man serious?

And when the hell had she even decided she might possibly be able to do this?

What was she supposed to do now? Did she write out a list of pros and cons? Probably wouldn't help, because she knew good and damn well the pros list would be significantly longer than the cons.

After all, this was Xander Boone she was talking about.

The man was infuriating, he was sexy, he was intimidating in a crazy provocative way, and he was downright relentless when he wanted something. She'd seen it on a recurring basis with the properties he wanted. He didn't take no for an answer, and he didn't even have to resort to threats to get what he wanted.

He just got it.

People rolled over for the man. He had such a persuasive personality; he could get someone to agree, and they would somehow think that the idea had been theirs in the first place.

And now he'd put her in his sights.

Mercedes knew what her answer was going to be. It wasn't an easy decision, but she didn't have a choice. As much as she wanted to tell him no, she knew she wouldn't. Giving him five days to prove himself wrong seemed the lesser of two evils. She wasn't going to be able to give up control. Not even to him.

Now she just had to come up with a plan to come out a winner at the end of all this. Because being a loser, which meant she'd give her heart and soul to this man, wasn't even an option.

CHAPTER EIGHT

LOGAN HELD SAM'S HAND AS HE LED her around to the passenger side of his truck. They'd worked from home for most of the morning and were just now heading into XTX for an impromptu, not to mention highly inconvenient, Wednesday afternoon meeting with Xavier Thomas, President and CEO of XTX Industries. Not by choice, mind you. If he had his way, Logan would push the meeting to tomorrow and crawl back in bed with his beautiful wife.

Preferably with Sam naked and riding him. Reverse cowgirl style.

Logan shifted as his cock stirred at the mental image.

Holy shit, if he didn't get his mind out of the gutter, he was going to go caveman and haul her back in the house without thinking twice.

If it weren't for that damn meeting...

"You okay?" he asked her as they neared his truck, hoping she didn't hear the need in his voice. For whatever reason, he wasn't all that interested in tackling any major obstacles today, unless, of course, one of them was Sam naked.

Shit.

"Fine, why?" Based on her startled response, she was clearly off somewhere else in her head. At least he wasn't the only one.

"You seem distracted."

Sam turned and smiled up at him, and Logan stopped before reaching for the door handle. He waited for her to talk, because obviously she had something on her mind.

"Can we go to Devotion tonight?"

How had he known she was going to ask that?

Logan fought the urge to smile. It was true; Sam had come into her own. Sexually speaking, of course.

The woman was a force to be reckoned with when it came to business, but it wasn't until a few months into their relationship that she'd really opened up to her sexual desires. And yes, with Devotion now open, he suspected she would want to experiment at his twin brother's new club, especially after last night.

"Tonight?" he asked, pretending he wasn't all that interested. He wasn't particular about where they went tonight just as long as he could relax a little.

"Yes," she said, clearly catching on to the game he was playing. "You know you want to," she whispered, leaning into him and up on her toes, her mouth brushing his.

"What's in it for me?" he asked, knowing full well what was in it for him.

"Anything you want."

"That right?"

"Mmm hmm," she murmured, her lips pressing to his when he leaned down closer for her kiss.

"Anything?"

Sam's eyes opened wide as she stared up at him. "What'd you have in mind?"

He could see the anticipation in her gaze, knew she'd be begging him to take her back to Devotion so she could relive last night. Purposely not answering her question, Logan redirected, wanting to understand what she was hoping to get out of tonight. "What if Xander isn't there tonight?"

"What if he is?" she countered, feigning innocence.

Leaning over, he swatted her on the butt and then gently urged her toward the truck. They could easily resume this conversation on the way to work. After all, if she continued teasing him like this, he had no qualms about throwing her over his shoulder and carrying her right back into the house. Xavier would just have to get over it.

After she had settled inside, Logan made his way around to the driver's side, his mind now going in an entirely different direction. What if Xander *were* at the club? He hadn't had the chance to talk to him after the scene last night. There hadn't been time that morning, though he had sent Mercedes an email after scrounging up her contact info, but she had yet to answer him.

Once he pulled out of the driveway, Logan glanced over at his wife, then turned his eyes back on the road. "Are you interested in what you saw last night, baby?"

He had asked the same question on their way home from the club, but as far as he was concerned, Sam hadn't answered him as honestly as he would've liked. He figured she was holding back for whatever reason, and he wanted to understand before they moved in that direction. He had firsthand experience in what the aftermath did to her when these extracurricular activities didn't go the way she hoped.

"Are you referring to the watching? Or are you asking if I'd like to try something like that?" she asked.

"Participating," he clarified. He already knew his wife was a voyeur. He happened to like that particular trait of hers.

"I think it would be interesting to try."

"Interesting?" Her use of the word confused him.

Sam was quiet for a while, and Logan didn't press her to talk. He knew her. When she was ready, she would answer him.

They were halfway to the office before she finally spoke.

"Is this BDSM stuff something you're interested in?"

Logan glanced sideways at her. "Depends. I could be persuaded into trying." Hell, tying her to the bed was one of his favorite pastimes. He damn sure didn't have any desire to be tied up himself, but she'd already managed that once. He had never let her do it again.

He felt her eyes on him when she turned to face him. He could sense her mind working. She was going to overthink this again. Not that he didn't want her to. There were times when Sam needed to think things through, and this was one of them.

Logan wasn't much into the BDSM scene, never had been interested, but he knew from her reaction last night that Sam had enjoyed herself immensely. She'd told him so — in explicit, cock-hardening detail after they'd fallen into bed last night.

But no matter which way you looked at it, BDSM was a far cry from a threesome, at least based on what he'd seen last night.

"I don't know what I want anymore."

"Talk to me, Sam." This was the first time he'd ever heard her frustrated when she talked about their sex life. He knew things had been a little vanilla for the last year and a half because, after Tag, they'd been hesitant to find someone who might be able to fulfill a role that they both were trying to define individually.

She didn't want casual. Logan feared permanent.

They were at an impasse.

"I don't even know how to explain it."

"Baby, you're gonna have to try. This is your show. If you want to try something new, I need to know what it is."

"You're not interested in asking Xander to be...?"

"No," he told her now, keeping his eyes on the road. "I don't think Xander is the right person." Logan glanced over at her when he said, "But I won't deny that I had thought about it."

"I had, too," she told him, sounding surprised by her own admission.

Logan knew that she had. He knew his wife better than anyone in the world. He knew what she liked, what she didn't like, and what she feared. When it came to their sex life, they were on the same page.

"Do you think Xander would be willing to help us with this BDSM stuff?"

He knew she was redirecting the conversation much as he had earlier. She was good at that. Instead of trying to turn the conversation back to the bigger question — was a threesome what she really wanted? — he went ahead and told her what he thought. "I think Xander's open to giving us a few pointers. As to how far *I'll* be willing to go, I don't know."

That was nothing but the truth. Logan enjoyed trying new things. As far as what he wasn't willing to do, he had a very short list. He would be the first to openly admit that he enjoyed watching Sam with another man. And he knew she enjoyed it, too.

Apparently his wife needed that *something more,* too, because ever since Luke had been involved in their sexual encounters back in the very beginning, Sam had craved having another man. But then Tag had been a part of their lives for such a short time, and she'd never been the same after that.

Logan understood Xander's belief that Sam was drawn to Logan's domination. He got that. But that didn't mean she wanted to venture down the road that neither of them was familiar with.

Logan knew there were people who didn't understand various sexual kinks — and yes, he had many — but he also knew it wasn't necessary for him to explain them. People were entitled to their desires, and he and Sam embraced theirs. Openly. Honestly. Together. And as far as Logan was concerned, that was all that mattered.

But BDSM? That was an area that Logan knew nothing about aside from the glorified aspects that could be found on practically any website.

Sure, the scene from last night had been hot as hell. He'd enjoyed watching, but that didn't mean he would enjoy taking a flogger to Sam. Shit, he was more worried that he would hurt her, and that was the last thing he wanted to do.

The pain, yeah, well, it wasn't really his thing.

And just because Xander believed Sam was more interested in Logan's dominating side than an actual threesome didn't mean it was the truth.

"You can't tell me that you didn't like what you saw last night."

Logan glanced at Sam and chuckled. "Baby, I buried my cock in your pussy. I don't think there was any disguising the fact that I liked it. I won't deny that. That doesn't mean you'd enjoy it if you were in Mercedes's shoes."

"Are they together?" Sam asked, damn near giving him whiplash with her abrupt change of the subject. Again.

"I don't know." If she would've asked him that question before last night, he would've said no, but after seeing Xander and Mercedes together ... now he had to wonder.

"If they aren't, do you think you would reconsider Xander for a threesome?" Although she asked the question directly, Sam sounded incredibly nervous.

"No," he stated firmly. He hadn't yet explained exactly what he and Xander had talked about, but he figured now was as good a time as any. "Sam, Xander's not the right man for what you're thinking. He's a Dom. He's not going to willingly walk into a situation where he isn't in control." Logan knew that from what Xander had told him. "And you know I'm not willing to give up control."

Logan heard her shuddered breath, saw her force a smile.

"I need you to do something for me, Sam," Logan said, waiting for her to acknowledge him before he continued. "You need to think long and hard about what you want. If you want to pursue this BDSM stuff, I'm game. If you'd prefer to find a third for the future, I'm open to that, too. I just need to know which you want more.

"Unfortunately, I think you're going to have to make a choice here. I don't see you getting both. And definitely not with Xander."

Logan knew his wife, knew she was going to do some serious thinking. And he'd wait. Patiently. Because when Sam finally decided what it was she wanted, he knew she'd do what she felt would make them both happy. That's just the way she worked. And that's one of the main reasons he continued to fall in love with her a little more each day.

CHAPTER NINE

XANDER HUNG UP THE PHONE AND LOOKED up from his desk. He had heard his front door open for the second time about three minutes ago, and there were only a handful of people who had a key to his house. The housekeeper, the cook, his assistant, Leah, Shane, and yes, Mercedes.

Needless to say, he'd been only half paying attention to Hirsh's incessant rambling on the other end of the phone because he'd been more interested in who was there, praying that Mercedes had come back.

His heart had pounded frantically in his chest when he'd heard her leave. If he hadn't been on the phone, he would've gone after her, but he wanted to get Hirsh off his back once and for all. Not that that's what had happened.

A quick glance at the clock on his computer and he noticed it was right at noon. It had to be Mercedes.

Fighting the urge to go in search of her, Xander remained where he was. The whole point was to make her come to him. If she didn't, then that was his answer. It wasn't the one he wanted, and he wasn't certain he would stop pursuing her, but at least it would give him some idea of what he was up against.

Opening his email, he skimmed through the items in his inbox. There wasn't anything pressing, and he knew his calendar was clear for the rest of the day, but he had to do something to keep from jumping out of his seat and going to search for her.

If he had to guess, Mercedes was pacing the floor in his living room, trying to convince herself to turn around and go back home.

Looking up from his computer screen, Xander watched as Mercedes stepped into his office.

For a moment, he thought his heart would pound right out of his chest.

Leaning back in his chair, he studied her. She didn't look much different than she had earlier, although somewhere along the way, she'd lost the blazer, which he considered a good thing.

Her silky onyx hair was flowing loosely down her back and over her shoulder, her crisp white shirt had two buttons opened, revealing just a hint of her gorgeous cleavage, and her black skirt was back to how it'd been before he had gruffly thrust his hands beneath it.

She looked prim and proper and so fucking sexy it made his teeth hurt.

"I'm here," she told him.

"I see that." He made a point not to look pleased, but he definitely was. So much so that his cock was now straining against his slacks, begging for attention. On the flip side, though, Xander was leaving what happened next up to her, so his dick was likely going to have to be patient.

He'd asked her to come to him, and she had, which meant she was accepting his proposal. If she weren't, Mercedes would've emailed him with the bad news. She wasn't big on conflict, and she tended to avoid it whenever possible. So it was good news that she was standing there. Except he knew Mercedes, which meant she would have a few stipulations to go along with her acquiescence. Now he just had to wait to see what those were.

She moved closer, her arms loose at her sides. Not only was she still mostly buttoned up like the business professional he knew her to be, she had also put on even taller heels. He happened to prefer the ones she'd had on earlier, but these were nice, too. They'd come right out of her Domme wardrobe; he recognized that immediately.

If Xander had to guess, the shoes were a power play. Being that she was roughly a foot shorter before the five inches added to her height, she probably felt less intimidated by his size now. Without her shoes on, he could easily rest his chin on the top of her head. With her shoes, her forehead would be level with his chin, but the woman would come eye to eye with most men she encountered.

"So, how does this work?" she asked, looking around at anything but him.

"How does what work?" he questioned, playing her game right along with her.

Mercedes met his gaze head on, and he saw the frustration in her eyes. She was doing this, but she wasn't exactly happy with her own decision.

It was a start. That's all he needed.

He waited to see if she would clarify.

She didn't, which left him in charge.

Pushing up from his chair, Xander didn't waste time as he made his way over to her. Taking her hand, he pulled gently, encouraging her to come with him.

If she wanted to know how this was going to work, he'd show her. In his opinion, talking was overrated when it came to certain things.

Mercedes wasn't new to this scene; she wasn't naïve enough to think he'd be gentle with her just because they were venturing into the unknown together. Five days was barely enough time to convince her that this was the right thing to do, so he couldn't afford to take his time seducing her slowly.

Just as he'd expected, Mercedes hesitated briefly, pulling against his hold on her hand, but then she gave in, following behind him.

Taking his time, he led her through his office, then through the main floor of his condo before approaching the stairs. He didn't look back at her, unwilling to give her an out just yet. Once they reached his bedroom, he'd give her another chance to change her mind, but the most important thing was to get her there first.

A minute later, they were walking into his bedroom. Once inside, he shut the door with a gentle click and then turned to face her.

Her face registered nothing of what she was feeling. Then again, Mercedes was good at masking emotions. Almost as good as he was.

Xander figured he could credit her bastard of a father for the way she kept her emotions on lock-down. According to the conversations they'd shared, Phillip Bryant was a fuckup of the worst order. Xander only prayed he never ran into the guy, because he wasn't sure he'd let the man walk away with his body intact. Hell, he wasn't sure he'd let the man walk away period.

Shaking off the thought, Xander focused on Mercedes. "Take off your shoes," he commanded, ensuring she didn't take the statement as a request.

Her eyes widened only slightly, but then she did exactly what he asked, stepping out of her shoes and leaving them on the floor beside her.

"Now your blou—" Before he could get his instructions out, she stopped him by holding her hand up.

"Me first," she said.

Xander took a small step back, raising his eyebrow in interest and pushing his hands into his pockets. He was aiming for casual, although he was having a damned hard time keeping his hunger for this woman under control. "Go ahead."

"We're going to do this," she began, glancing around his bedroom briefly before meeting his eyes once more. "I'll agree to five days, no holds barred."

No holds barred? Oh, hell. He was definitely intrigued.

Xander didn't smile, but he wanted to. Victory was a sweet, sweet thing. He didn't think Mercedes would appreciate his celebrating, so he forced a bored expression.

"But you have to agree to something first," she informed him.

To his surprise, she reached up and began to unhook one of the buttons on her blouse, this one just beneath her magnificent breasts.

"You've got my attention," he told her, trying to keep his eyes on her face. It wasn't as easy as he hoped it looked.

The single button came free from its mooring, the crisp white fabric separating slightly to reveal the generous swells of her breasts cupped in white lace beneath.

"I'll agree to play this game with you. You can do your best to make me submit," she told him as she freed another button. "I'm not at all convinced that it'll work, but I'll give you a shot."

His first instinct was to tell her that this damn sure wasn't a game he was playing, but he kept it to himself. "And?" he implored her, waiting to hear her stipulations.

"You have to let me top you."

Xander laughed out loud. There was no fucking way.

"I'm serious," she told him, her hand working to reconnect the button on her blouse.

Had he been any other man, he might've succumbed to her threat, but Xander didn't take kindly to teasing. If she wanted to work out a deal, he was game, but he didn't play that way.

"Unbutton it," he barked, standing up straight as his hands fell to his sides.

Mercedes's eyes flared with what he assumed was surprise, maybe mixed with an ounce of heat. The woman might believe she was dominant, but he could see the underlying submissive inside of her.

What made him crazy was the fact that she truly believed she was more in control by being a Domme, as opposed to a submissive. He knew she was well aware of Xander's and Shane's views on Doms and subs, but she'd never embraced their way of thinking. Which was another reason he felt as though her reasons for becoming a Domme weren't the same as most.

She wanted control.

Of herself.

That's where she'd failed along the way. That's where so many people went astray.

The Dom didn't wield the power ... the submissive did.

Now, he was going to work on teaching her that very lesson.

MERCEDES'S FINGERS STILLED ON THE BUTTON SHE'D just managed to hook back. The look in Xander's eyes was fierce, and it sent a trickle of heat fluttering beneath her skin. She loved that look. Loved to watch him when he turned all of that masculine dominance on one of his subs. He was a sight to see.

Had she been watching him do that to someone else, she would've applauded him for taking the reins. Being that he was taking what little control she had away, Mercedes wasn't quite sure how she felt about it.

As though they had a mind of their own, her fingers worked the button loose once again before sliding to the next.

"Now continue to remove your blouse while you tell me your requirements."

Mercedes complied, unable to stop herself. She wasn't exactly sure how she was going to continue to think, much less talk, because she was distracted by the look in his eyes, the impassioned way he continued to watch her.

"Tell me," he ordered.

"You have to agree to let me top you. Twice," she said, her breaths betraying her as she began to gasp for air as she released the last button on her shirt.

Moving on to release the buttons on the cuffs at her wrists, she continued. "I'll agree to submit to you, however you see fit, for the next five days. But at least once during that time, I want to dominate you. In public. And then, after all the silliness is over, I get to dominate you again. In public. At a venue of my choosing."

She barely noticed the slight quirk of his eyebrow, but it was there.

Honestly, Mercedes was stunned that he hadn't laughed in her face or told her to get dressed because there was no way in hell he'd agree to her terms.

"Drop the shirt," he said, his words no longer holding a hint of the gentleness she'd sensed in him earlier. He'd gone into full Dom mode. Not that she believed he had another setting.

Mercedes allowed her shirt to slide down her arms and fall to the floor behind her. Now practically naked from the waist up, Mercedes felt the overwhelming heat that had been simmering in her veins since the moment he had left her standing in his conference room.

Twenty-four hours ago, if someone had asked her if she would ever be in this position, she would've laughed her ass off.

Now? Well, she certainly wasn't laughing.

"Now the skirt."

Mercedes knew she needed to stand her ground. He was clearly stalling, probably hoping she'd give in and retract her stipulations once she was naked. No chance.

"Do we have a deal?" she asked him as she reached to her side and unhooked the clasp on her skirt before lowering the zipper.

"In public, huh?" he asked, this time sounding amused.

"Yes. Public. Once at Devotion," she explained as she gripped her skirt, keeping it from falling to the floor. "And the other at a place and time of my choosing."

She knew exactly when she was going to call him to the carpet, but she couldn't very well tell him that she'd reserve her date for the grand opening of Alluring Indulgence Resort, which they'd just recently heard would be happening sometime at the beginning of next year. It was a good thing she was a patient woman, because it was going to be a long wait. But definitely worth it.

"What's required of me?" he asked, his eyes continuing to glance up and down her partially clad body.

"Whatever I want," she told him.

He nodded, his eyes still scanning her from head to toe.

"Hard limits?" he asked.

Okay, so he had her there. If he had hard limits, she'd have to comply. It was the only way she worked. "Yes, you can tell me your hard limits," she agreed.

He chuckled. "I wasn't talking about me. I was talking about you. What are *your* hard limits?" he asked, turning the question back on her.

God, she'd given some thought to what her hard limits were while she'd been pacing her living room, trying to talk herself out of this. She knew she should have at least one, maybe two, but she hadn't come up with any. Her rationale had been that if she was going to do this, then she wanted to go all in with this man. She wanted to give herself over to him completely, to let him take control. It was the only way to prove to them both that this was not what she wanted.

She'd been unable to come up with anything she refused to do, because, ultimately, she trusted him; there was no doubt about that. They'd been friends for so long she knew everything there was to know about him. He would never hurt her. Never.

"I don't have any," she finally said, her breath coming out in a rush.

"None at all?" he asked skeptically.

"None," she confirmed.

"So you're good with sex in public? Being naked at the club? Me using toys on you? Floggers, canes, whips?"

Those were just a handful of things she knew he was really thinking about. "I have no hard limits," she reiterated.

"Drop the skirt," he commanded, his tone gruffer than before.

Releasing the material from her fist, she allowed her skirt to slide down her legs. Once it pooled at her feet, she stepped out of it, moving closer to Xander.

"Have I told you how fucking beautiful you are?" he asked.

Mercedes wasn't sure whether he'd meant to say the words out loud, but she answered him anyway. "No."

"Fuck," he muttered. "You steal my breath, Mercedes."

Holy shit. The honesty in his tone nearly had her knees going weak beneath her. She'd never heard him talk like that. Not to anyone. Ever.

Fearing that he was trying to distract her, Mercedes reminded herself that she was still waiting for an answer.

"Do we have a deal?" she repeated as she waited for his next instruction.

"Take off the bra," he told her, his eyes locked with hers.

Without hesitation, Mercedes reached up and unhooked the front clasp of her bra, promptly dropping it to the floor. Xander hadn't answered her yet, not verbally, anyway, but she could see his response in his eyes.

They were going to do this. They were going to submit to one another.

It was only a matter of time.

CHAPTER TEN

XANDER WAS DOING HIS BEST TO FOCUS on the conversation and less on the dazzling, nearly naked woman in front of him. It wasn't easy. Even if he prided himself on his ability to keep his composure, there were still some temptations that weren't easy to ignore. Mercedes was just such a temptation.

While he contemplated his answer to her question, he was busy grazing her incredible curves with his eyes, wanting to put his hands on her, to feel once again how soft her skin was. To cup her breasts in his hands. He wanted to put his mouth on her, to suck her nipples until she was writhing beneath him, begging for more.

He would've assumed that just the idea of submitting to anyone, let alone in public, would've sent his dick into hiding, but truthfully that wasn't the case. Or maybe it was the fact that Mercedes had told him she didn't have any hard limits. That, in itself, was enough to make him damn near lose his mind.

To know that she trusted him enough to know he'd only push her as far as he felt she could go, well, it was humbling.

"Just to confirm," he said as he took one step closer. "You'll give yourself over to me for five full days. Starting now. No hard limits. And in return, I have to agree to submit to you on two occasions. Once at Devotion, the other at a time and place of your choosing?"

He knew what she had up her sleeve. She was going to play her card in a public place that would put him fully on display. Somewhere that might intimidate him. If she believed he wasn't on to her plan, she was sadly mistaken. He'd just recently asked her to join him at the opening of Alluring Indulgence Resort, and though it wasn't planned for roughly six more months, it was clear she was thinking that would be her venue of choice.

Not that he really gave a shit. He knew the Walkers would likely find it amusing, but that was the least of his worries.

"That's correct," she said on a breath, her eyes still locked with his.

"Remove your panties," he instructed, not looking away.

Without reservation, Mercedes reached down and slid the silky white panties down her legs, stepping out of them as well, which put her a mere foot or so away from him.

His eyes locked on the patch of dark hair between her legs, then he trailed them up over her generous hips, admiring the small tattoo he'd only been privy to when he had seen her playing at the club. He continued upward, over her gently rounded belly, past her bountiful breasts. He was distracted briefly by the ornate tattoo that encircled her entire arm from her shoulder down to her elbow. He'd always loved that tattoo. She'd gotten it before he met her, and according to her, it was a reminder of all that she'd been through. The flower represented her, and the intricate detail around it was the chaos she'd lived in since she was younger. As with a lot of her personal details, whenever he would ask, she would shrug him off, telling him it wasn't important. Little did she know, but everything about her was important to him. And she should know that by now because he'd never let her retreat from him before because he was her friend. He was in her corner, no matter what.

He looked up, meeting her gaze head on.

He wanted to tell her that they had a deal. He wanted to tell her that he'd pretty much do anything for this chance. For him, it was so much more than getting her to submit to him. He'd wanted Mercedes for so long, had ignored that hunger and pretended he could handle merely friendship. But this woman was all he'd ever wanted in one magnificent, enticing package.

He had to have her.

And if it meant he'd have to submit in front of a crowd of people just to prove himself to her, then so be it.

"Please tell me we have a deal," she whispered, her arms still hanging down at her sides.

"We do," he finally conceded, unable to keep his hands off of her a moment longer.

Taking one step forward, he cupped both of her shoulders, skimming his hands down her arms and then back up. She was warm and soft. His self-restraint was being tested, because as far as Xander was concerned, he hadn't waited just a few minutes for her to get undressed, to stand before him completely and utterly vulnerable.

No, this certainly wasn't something he'd come up with on the fly. He'd been waiting for this for years.

"Turn around."

Mercedes turned away from him, giving Xander a perfect view of her back and her ass. He took a moment to skim over her soft skin, ensuring that there weren't any marks left from their scene the night before. Although he'd double- and triple-checked prior to them leaving Devotion last night, he couldn't help himself now.

She was flawless. Perfect in every way.

For a man his size, he was always conscientious about the women he was with. He didn't pursue tiny women. He had no interest in being gentle, which meant he needed a woman who could handle him. Mercedes was that woman.

Moving up against her, Xander reached for her hands, linking their fingers and lifting her arms. "Put your hands around my neck," he advised, leaning forward, which was the only way she'd be able to reach around him.

Her fingers were cool against the overheated skin of his neck. He closed his eyes briefly, enjoying the feel of her touch.

Pressing his lips to the curve of her neck and shoulder, Xander slid his hands over her hips, her waist, higher, until he cupped her breasts in his hands.

"You have such beautiful breasts," he mumbled as he lifted them. "Perfect pink nipples that will look so pretty clamped."

Her body tensed briefly, but Xander didn't allow it to throw him off course. Pinching her nipples, he kissed her neck again. "But not yet. First, I want you to look up into that mirror."

Xander glanced up to meet her gaze in the oversized cheval mirror that his designer had picked out, saying something about suiting his personality. For him, it had always been just a mirror. But right now, it was a portal to ecstasy.

"For the next five days, I'm going to own you. Every part of you. Do you agree?"

Mercedes only nodded, but her eyes never left his.

"Answer me," he insisted, keeping his tone low. "That's one thing I won't compromise on. You will tell me what you're feeling. Especially when I ask."

"Yes," she whispered. "For five days, you'll own me."

Xander wasn't a praying man, but right then and there, he sent up a silent plea that five days would turn into much, much longer.

MERCEDES WATCHED THE IMAGES IN THE MIRROR closely. Xander's body pressed up against her back, his face serious as he observed her in the reflective glass. What she saw wasn't at all what she'd expected to see.

There, reflecting back at her, was a naked woman — her — but she saw more than just an abundantly curvy body that she knew was a far cry from perfect. Not that she'd ever cared about perfection. She liked who she was, how she looked, her inner strength. But right now, with Xander's big hands grazing over her skin, the fire she saw in his gaze, well, it made her feel incredibly feminine and ... powerful.

How could that possibly be the case when, for the last ten minutes, she'd undressed in front of him at his command? Could it be the way he was looking at her? Or possibly the way his hands drifted over her skin reverently, like he was cherishing every touch.

Whatever it was, it was heady. Enough to make her breath lodge in her throat.

He didn't appear to be in a hurry, didn't seem to need more than what they were sharing at that moment, and she felt an exhilarating rush of lust burst in her bloodstream.

She'd had a hard time admitting that he would own her for the next five days. In fact, she'd said the words while, at the same time, she was thinking that she'd never last that long. But the longer she stood there, the more Xander touched her, all while their eyes met briefly in the mirror, she knew he had won before the game ever even began.

She might never truly submit, but that didn't mean she wasn't going to fall for him.

"I want to touch you," Xander mumbled against her ear.

He was touching her, wasn't he? She didn't speak the words out loud, though.

"Come here."

As he stood up straight again, her hands fell from around his neck. She let her arms hang down at her sides while she glimpsed the woman in the mirror one last time. She couldn't help but wonder whether she would recognize the woman by the end of the weekend. She was sure if Xander had anything to say about it, she would.

Mercedes took Xander's hand when he held it out to her. Following behind him, she allowed him to lead her to his bed. Seriously? Was he going to get down to business so quickly? That wasn't like him at all.

"Sit," he said, motioning toward an oversized cedar chest that sat at the foot of the bed.

Not meeting his gaze, Mercedes sat as instructed, her knees tightly clamped together in front of her while she kept her arms in close to her body, suddenly feeling incredibly modest.

She watched as Xander moved across the room. When he grabbed a chair and returned to set it in front of her, she wondered what he was going to do. Surely if he wanted to have a conversation, he could afford her a measure of dignity and allow her to get dressed.

"Spread your legs," he insisted.

Okay, so apparently her dignity just took a dive out the window. It was a twenty-story drop. There was no way it would be intact when she finally got around to needing it again.

Mercedes's nerves were suddenly at war inside of her.

Swallowing hard, she stared back at Xander. She could do this. She knew she could. She would just need to pretend that this was a lesson, a demonstration of sorts, one that she could use when she was the one in control again. It wasn't like she didn't have an idea what he was going to do. She'd done the same to her subs multiple times.

Squaring her shoulders and straightening her spine, she spread her legs, keeping her attention focused on Xander's handsome face.

"Very pretty," he remarked, his eyes sliding down her body and then stalling between her now spread thighs.

She fought the urge to snap her knees closed.

You can do this, she reminded herself.

Xander inched the chair closer to her, closing the gap between them.

"Put your feet on my knees."

Okay, so that was going to be an awkward position. Not wanting him to see the mortification that was probably clearly written on her face, she avoided his eyes by looking directly at his chest as she did as she was told.

With her feet resting on his spread knees, she had to lean back on her hands to hold her upper body up, while her pussy was on full display for him, and he was taking every opportunity to glance between her legs.

She was not going to survive this.

"I'm going to shave you later," he informed her, one finger gently grazing the dark curls at the apex of her thighs.

Her first instinct was to argue. It wasn't that she was against the idea, because she was usually bare down there, but recently, she'd decided to do something different. Translated to: she'd gotten lazy, and rushing out to the spa to get waxed hadn't been high on her priority list. She preferred to be bare, so in some sense, she was still in control. Not that she would tell him as much.

Remembering that he'd be making her decisions for the next five days per their agreement, she didn't say a word.

"I want us to lay out the rules, Mercedes," Xander said, surprising her with the topic.

Here she was, splayed wide for him, and he really wanted to have a civil conversation? She was going to lose it; she knew it.

Sucking in a deep breath, she tilted her chin up, ignoring the fact that he'd put her in an incredibly vulnerable position. "What are the rules?"

If she wasn't mistaken, Xander's lips tilted slightly into one of those sexy smirks of his.

He was pressing his luck.

"For four nights, you will sleep in my bed."

"But—"

"No buts," he argued. "Once I'm finished, you can tell me your thoughts and we'll discuss."

God, he sounded like such a fucking Dom.

"Fine," she retorted sarcastically.

Xander's hand lifted, and before she could react, he smacked her splayed pussy, sending a zing of heated pleasure racing through her. She moaned.

Oh, God. She actually moaned.

Heat suffused her face, but this time it was embarrassment that laid claim to her body. The body that betrayed her with such an enthusiastic reaction to his intimate touch.

"Keep up with the smartass comments, and I'll bend you over my knee."

Mercedes clamped her lips shut, not trusting herself not to argue. It was in her nature. She was the one who was generally in control. This was the exact reason she didn't submit. It went against everything in her because she didn't want someone to order her around.

"Five full days. Four nights. My bed," he restated. "You'll live under my roof during that time. You'll be permitted to go to your condo to handle your business dealings. When you aren't working, you'll be here with me."

"Tell me I'm going to cook and clean for you and we're done," Mercedes argued, venom injected in her tone. He was pushing her to her limit.

Xander glared at her, his eyes hard. She was so transfixed in his gaze that she didn't see him move. When his hand slapped her pussy once again, she screamed. An intense, pain-filled pleasure jolted her system. Before she could think or breathe, Mercedes found herself lying across Xander's huge thighs, her breasts crushed against his leg.

"Five," he told her. "Count them out."

There wasn't a pause before his hand came down on her bare ass, and she knew instantly that he wasn't going to go easy on her.

Oh, God. The humiliation was unbearable, but somehow she dug deep, grasping every ounce of her pride as she lay motionless across his lap.

"One," she groaned through clenched teeth, her breath rushing out of her.

Another slap followed immediately on the same ass cheek, and this time she swallowed her scream. "Two."

"Three more," he said, the heat of his hand caressing the sting on her ass.

The warmth disappeared, and she braced herself for the impact, but it didn't come immediately. It was exactly what she would've done, leaving her sub anticipating the next move.

Oh, fuck! Mercedes screamed when his hand landed on the crease where her ass met her thigh, the pain excruciating yet strangely erotic at the same time. "Three."

There was no way she was going to last through two more. Her ass was burning, and the heat had engulfed her entire body. She felt like she would implode at any second.

He spanked her again, this time on the opposite cheek. "Four."

Tears slipped from her eyes, and she blinked, wanting to take them back. There was no way she'd break right now. She refused. Sucking in a deep breath, she held it as she waited for him to finish.

The last one came in the same spot as the one before, and she choked on a gasp that ripped from her chest, the pain lancing through her nerve endings.

"Five."

"I'm proud of you," he said, his voice steady and calm.

Mercedes knew that Xander didn't overreact. He never punished a sub out of anger. That's not what it was about. Too bad, in her current position, she wasn't feeling all that calm, or seeing any rationale behind the punishment.

Biting her tongue to keep from yelling at him, Mercedes waited for him to move, wanting desperately to get off of him, but at the same time, she wanted to feel the safety and security of his body against hers.

Not to mention, she was pretty sure she wouldn't be sitting for at least a good half hour. Her ass was on fire.

CHAPTER ELEVEN

XANDER HAD TO TAKE A MOMENT TO breathe, to try to rein himself in. To ignore the overwhelming urge to sink his cock into this amazing woman, to make her beg and plead while he plowed her over and over until they were both barely able to breathe from the desperate need for release.

Watching as Mercedes's beautiful bare ass blushed a pretty red beneath his hand had nearly been his undoing. And the way she'd reacted had been more than he could've asked for. She'd taken every swat, counting them out as he'd instructed, without squirming or trying to pull away.

And when he'd said he was proud of her … that was an understatement.

She slayed him with her trust. If she ever thought he was in total control just because she was the one submitting, she was definitely wrong. He might own her body for the next few days, but this woman was rapidly taking ownership of his soul. It was inevitable, he knew. And it was a risk he was willing to take because, God willing, by the time their five days came to an end, she'd belong to him in every way that mattered.

Xander shifted, helping Mercedes to her feet. Once she was standing, he leaned forward and pressed his mouth to her reddened ass, the skin warm beneath his lips.

Taking her hand, he eased her back toward the cedar chest, motioning with his head for her to sit. He knew it was going to be uncomfortable now that her ass was reddened by his hand, but it was part of the punishment.

"Feet up," he instructed again, wanting her back in the same position she'd been in earlier. He liked her splayed out for him. He knew that insisting she was naked and on display took away her sense of control.

To his surprise, she didn't argue. She didn't even wipe away the tears that had left tracks down her cheeks. Leaning forward, he thumbed away the wet streaks while keeping his eyes locked with hers. There was defiance in the magnificent gray color, which made her eyes darker than he'd ever seen them.

"Now where were we?" he asked, leaning back and letting his hand trail slowly over her breast, her belly, and once again grazing the perfect triangle of dark hair on her mound.

Yes, he'd certainly be shaving her later. He wanted her bare. The idea of her bare folds glistening made him hotter than hell.

"You told me that I'd spend every minute that I'm not working here with you."

"Right. And you won't be going to Kink tonight, either," he said, knowing he was going to hit a sore spot with her.

To his surprise, she bit her bottom lip, but she didn't argue.

"I'll call Shane and let him know," Xander told her.

"About us?" she asked suddenly, her eyes widening as though the idea of Shane knowing about their deal was horrifying.

He decided to test her. "Yes."

"What are you going to say?" she questioned.

"Whatever I want." He didn't elaborate. He would tell Shane exactly what was going on because he chose to. End of story.

"Now, do you have any questions?" he asked her.

"Will we be going to Devotion?"

"Yes. I want somewhere we can play. We'll be more anonymous there." He was doing that for her, wanting her to realize he was thinking about her. At Kink, she'd be mortified to submit to him. He got that.

Mercedes nodded, as though his answer was acceptable. Xander waited for her to ask more questions. She didn't.

"Are you on the pill?" he asked.

"Birth control shot, yes."

"You've seen my recent medical records, but if you want, I'll get you a copy." Routine testing for sexually transmitted disease was a requirement to be members of Kink, and at Devotion, too, so they were both familiar with providing them. Just last week, Xander had sent his with her to Kink. And prior to the soft opening of Devotion, he'd seen hers when he'd submitted her application for membership.

"Why?" she asked.

"Because," Xander told her, sliding his finger along her wet slit, "when I'm inside of you, I don't want any barriers between us." He paused, dipping the tip of his finger inside of her. "Does that bother you?"

If it did, Xander wouldn't hesitate to use a condom. He'd never had sex without one, never been in a relationship that had made it to the point where he would trust a woman enough. Most of the time, he was too weary that a woman would try and trap him by getting pregnant. A morbid thought, maybe, but one he had to consider with everyone he decided to spend time with.

With Mercedes, trust wasn't an issue. The issue was that he wanted her with his body and his soul, and, at least for now, he doubted the feelings were reciprocated.

"I've never..." she began, swallowed. "I don't..."

She clearly couldn't form an answer, so Xander helped her out. "You've never had sex without a condom?"

"No."

"Are you scared to?"

There was hesitation in her eyes, but he waited her out this time, wanting the truth.

"A little. But not because of what you're thinking. I just… It seems too intimate."

Xander agreed. "That's the point, Mercedes," he told her, his voice low. "I don't want anything between us. Nothing. I want to feel you in every way possible."

She seemed to think it over for several seconds, and then she nodded her head. "Okay. No condoms. Unless we're at the club," she answered, the breathless tone of her voice belying the unaffected expression she tried to force into place.

Xander nodded. It was a requirement at Devotion that condoms be used in any public scene. It was also suggested that condoms be used at all times.

"Good," he told her as he pulled his finger back. "Do you have any other questions for right now?"

She looked like there was something she wanted to ask, but she kept her mouth closed.

"The only thing I ask of you, M, is that you're honest with me. Open and honest about everything. Answer me verbally when I question you. Talk to me when you have concerns. You know how this works; I don't need to explain it to you."

"I know how it works," she said snippily.

"Good, then I think we're on the same page."

"Yes, we're on the same page." Mercedes paused briefly. "Just remember we made a deal. I get to dominate you, as well. And there are no hard limits."

"Trust me baby, I doubt that's something I'll ever forget." The idea of Mercedes dominating him was ludicrous, but he wasn't about to tell her that. He'd made a deal, and he wouldn't go back on his word. And just like her, he'd give her his complete and total trust. She would do with it what she wanted.

And in the end, they'd both be stronger for it.

MERCEDES WAS HANGING BY A THREAD, AND she wondered whether Xander knew it.

Here they were, having a somewhat casual, although extremely important, conversation, yet he continued to tease her with the very tip of his finger against her clit. It was driving her absolutely mad, but she'd held back, refusing to let him see her weakness.

"Now what?" she asked, trying to keep her composure but falling apart little by little as each second passed.

"Now I'm going to make you come," Xander said, surprising her. "With my mouth."

"Oh."

Xander grinned that devious, seductive smirk that made her legs weak. Thankfully she was sitting down, so she didn't have to worry about falling over.

"Up on the bed," Xander instructed, tilting his head in the direction of the bed behind her. "Just scoot back until your ass is on the edge, then pull your knees in against your chest."

Wait, what?

Mercedes tried to envision what that position would look like. It didn't take much of an imagination to figure it out.

Slowly, hesitantly, she moved back, using her hands to walk herself up onto the mattress. It was firm yet soft, and the duvet that covered it was plush and cool against her tingling skin. When her ass was on the very edge, she stopped.

Trying her damnedest not to think about the fact that she was here with Xander — her friend — or about how uncomfortable this situation was, she did as he asked, driven solely by selfish need. Lying back, she pulled her legs against her chest, which put her even more on display than before.

Hoping he didn't see the heated blush that overcame her, Mercedes stared up at the ceiling.

"Pull your knees wide," he instructed.

With her knees still drawn in against her body, she used her arms to pull them apart. Cool air being pushed down from the ceiling fan caressed her overheated pussy.

The chill was immediately replaced by warmth, and her insides clenched painfully. Xander had pushed the cedar chest out of the way and was kneeling at the foot of the bed, his mouth now delightfully close to where she needed it.

"I've wanted to taste you for so long," he said affectionately, making Mercedes suck in a breath. She continued to be shocked by his words, but more by their delivery. It was as though this wasn't a spur-of-the-moment decision but rather something he'd considered for a long time.

Could that be true? Could he really…

"Oh, God!" she moaned when his tongue lashed against her swollen folds, teasing her as he went.

Keeping her hands on her knees, she tried to hold herself still, not wanting him to stop as the pleasure consumed her. It was intense, to say the least. Chill bumps broke out over every single inch of her skin as the incredible sensation of his mouth on her sensitive skin overwhelmed her.

"Feel good?"

"Yes," she moaned again as he lapped at her pussy once more.

"Then I'll continue," he told her. "Oh, and Mercedes?"

"Yes?" she asked breathlessly, wishing she could tell him to shut up and make her come.

"You can come when you're ready."

"Thank you," she said, honestly meaning it. If he'd asked her to hold off, she wasn't sure she'd be able to, and strangely, she didn't want to disappoint him.

The firm press of his tongue as it caressed her, delicately sliding over her clit on each torturous upstroke, had her body trembling. The man certainly knew what he was doing. There was no hesitation in his movements, no questioning whether he was doing it right, and that in itself was so fucking hot Mercedes was sure she'd explode soon.

Holding out wasn't an option. It'd been far too long since she'd had a man between her thighs like this. It was intimate and required that she get emotionally closer than she cared to. Something she'd refused to do for the last year or so.

Pressing her head into the mattress, she tried to lift her hips, wanting to bring Xander's mouth closer, to apply more friction, maybe tempt him to add a finger.

"Oh, God," she moaned when he sucked her clit into his mouth, using his tongue to lash over the sensitive bundle of nerves until she was shaking from the orgasm that was threatening to break free.

"Come for me, pet. Whenever you're ready," Xander said, his tone firm, unyielding. And so fucking sexy.

When he pressed two fingers into her, his mouth once again latching on to her clit, she knew she was doomed. She wasn't going to be able to last. Not that she needed to, but it felt so fucking good she didn't want it to end.

"Please," she pleaded, unsure exactly what she was asking for.

Xander intensified his oral ministrations as he began fucking her with his fingers. Slow, deep strokes penetrated her, forcing her closer and closer to the edge.

She had to focus on holding her legs up and open as he drove her completely insane.

And then, when she thought she'd rein herself back in, she shattered into a million pieces. Brilliant, colorful fractures of light broke off behind her closed eyelids as her orgasm consumed her.

"Fucking beautiful," Xander said quietly, pulling her attention to him.

Mercedes opened her eyes, fully expecting him to still be kneeling on the floor between her legs, but he wasn't. He was leaning over the bed, his hands on either side of her head as he held himself above her.

Letting go of her legs, she relaxed into the mattress, her gaze locked with his. Right there, in the beautiful green glow of his eyes, Mercedes was positive she saw something. Something that was very much like a promise.

He leaned in, pressing his soft, warm lips to hers, and she fought the urge to hold him to her. Instead, she allowed him entrance into her mouth, tasting herself on his lips and tongue. This wasn't new to her, but with Xander, there was something discreetly unique to their mating.

And that was probably what she feared most.

When he pulled back, not moving, just staring down at her, Mercedes reached up and touched his face with the tips of her fingers. "Thank you."

"No, baby, thank you."

CHAPTER TWELVE

XANDER SAT AT HIS DESK, STARING OUT the office window overlooking downtown Dallas, his mind still reeling from what had happened a few short hours ago. With the phone pressed to his ear, he listened to the monotonous ringing while he sat patiently waiting for his friend to answer, doing his best to focus on something other than the memory of the way Mercedes tasted against his lips.

"What's up?" Shane asked when he finally answered his phone.

Not in the mood to beat around the bush, Xander opted for getting right to the point. "Wanted to let you know that Mercedes won't be going to Kink tonight," Xander told Shane bluntly.

Mercedes had informed him that she had a call that she had to take and had disappeared back to her condo shortly after he had helped her to get dressed. Not wanting to let her go, Xander had resigned himself to doing just that. As much as he wanted to keep her at his side every single second for the next five days, he knew he couldn't.

"Why not?" Shane asked curiously.

"I'm taking her to Devotion."

"*You're* taking her?"

"That's what I said."

"Mind if I meet you there?" Shane asked, a modicum of uncertainty in his tone.

Xander turned his chair to stare at his blank computer screen. "Not at all."

"Cool. See you, what? At nine?"

"I'm taking her to dinner first, so yes, around then."

Knowing he should hang up and let the call end on that note, Xander paused, fully expecting what came next.

"What's going on, X?" Shane asked, his tone turning serious all of a sudden.

Xander sighed. He knew he needed to explain to Shane the deal that he'd made with Mercedes and the recent development that had already changed their friendship, at least as far as Xander was concerned. Shane deserved that much because he cared about Mercedes, almost as much as Xander did. And on any given day, Xander would usually invite Shane to dinner with them.

Not tonight.

He'd already informed Mercedes that he was going to enlighten Shane as to what was happening between them, but he wasn't quite sure how to spit it out. If he offered up too much information, Shane would quickly realize this was something more than just a few days of playtime. He had absolutely no intention of anyone figuring out that what Xander wanted was a hell of a lot more than playtime. Not before he could convince Mercedes, at least.

"Fuck," Shane exhaled, clearly making his own assumptions based on Xander's lack of answer. "Man, do you know what you're doing?"

Okay, so clearly he didn't need to explain, but Xander scrounged up a considerable amount of *let's just play along* and answered with a question of his own. "What are you talking about?"

"I always suspected you had your sights set on her, but seriously, X, she's…"

"She's what?" Xander asked, his frustration escaping.

"She's not a submissive."

That's what you think, Xander thought to himself. Out loud, he said, "I never said she was."

"No, but if you're getting cozy with her, then you're thinking you can change her. Man, that's not gonna happen. You're gonna ruin your friendship with her. Not to mention your business relationship."

Xander had given that some serious consideration, as well. However, he spent his life taking risks, and this was one he couldn't find it in himself to regret. At least not at this point. The alternative — sitting back and hoping Mercedes might pursue him — would probably have him waiting a lifetime.

Unacceptable.

"Let me worry about that," Xander told Shane. He wanted to say he had it all under control, but he wasn't sure that was the case, so he bit his tongue.

Shane sighed, clearly dropping the subject. "I'll see you both tonight then."

With that, they disconnected the call.

Shane was right; he'd be seeing them both. The remaining question was one only Mercedes could answer: how much of herself was she going to let people see?

WHEN MERCEDES STEPPED OUT OF HER CONDO a little before seven, she took a deep breath, trying to settle her unruly nerves. She was an absolute mess and had been ever since Xander had made her come ... with his mouth.

Lord, did the man have an amazing tongue. The memory sent a rush of heat shuddering through her.

Willing to do just about anything to put some much-needed distance between them after that mind-blowing event, Mercedes hadn't lied when she'd told him she had a call she couldn't miss. It had been a well-timed saving grace. As to how well she'd handled that call, she didn't know. Her mind had continued to wander back to Xander's bedroom.

God, what a difference a day could make.

As she stood in the hall just outside of her front door, she wondered whether she should just go back into her condo and pretend none of this had ever happened. The only reason she was out there was because she wasn't sure she could resist jumping Xander if he took two steps inside.

However, it didn't seem to matter whether she was out in the hall or safely tucked away in her condo; her thoughts still drifted to Xander and the deal they'd made. Part of her wanted to back out; the other part of her wanted to move full steam ahead.

If she pushed hard enough, she knew Xander would back off. He might not be happy about it, but he wasn't the type of man to ever cross the line. Too bad she couldn't even convince herself that she wanted him to, because if she didn't even buy it, he definitely wouldn't believe her if she tried to tell him.

The elevator dinged, drawing her attention down the hall.

Her breath halted in her chest as she watched Xander approach, looking devilishly handsome and positively intimidating with his hands thrust into the pockets of his expensive slacks, his dark, forest-green tie a nice contrast against his crisp white shirt, and his hand-tailored jacket accentuating his immense upper body.

In her opinion, there was nothing sexier than a self-confident, well-dressed man. And that was a more-than-befitting description of Xander Boone.

Watching him as he moved toward her, Mercedes recalled the first time she'd met him. Upon first glance, he'd overwhelmed her with his sheer size. It hadn't taken long before he'd overwhelmed her with his personality, as well. And to this day, Xander was probably the one man she admired more than anyone else. And not just because of how incredibly striking he was.

"You look beautiful," he said by way of greeting, invading her personal space and pulling her to him, his lips brushing against hers briefly.

"Thank you," she managed to reply, suddenly feeling a little unsteady on her feet.

Definitely a good thing she'd decided to meet him in the hall. "Are you ready?"

Mercedes wasn't sure she'd ever be ready for this man, but she responded with a firm yes.

"Perfect. Did you pack your things?"

Xander had called her to let her know he was taking her to dinner and that they would be making an appearance at Devotion later for an invitation-only BDSM theme night. During that conversation, he'd asked her to pack enough to last her through the weekend.

"I did," she confirmed.

"Good. Gerard will have your things delivered to my condo, and Janelle has agreed to come by and put them away," he informed her as he held out his arm, a signal for her to hold on to him.

Gerard was their beloved doorman who handled so much more than just a door in their building. And Janelle was Xander's housekeeper. Well, if she'd had any inclination that Xander would be discreet in regard to their deal, she was wrong. It was obvious that her secret was going to be out soon.

Nestling her hand into the crook of his arm, she allowed him to lead her back to the elevator.

Lord. The man smelled incredible. Clearly he'd pulled out all the stops.

"You mean I'll have room in your closet?" she asked, hoping to disguise the nerves that hadn't settled at all since he'd stepped foot out of the elevator.

"And your own drawer in my dresser," he told her with a wide grin.

Butterflies went on the attack immediately, making her belly flutter. She was not immune to this man, no matter how much she wished she were.

They rode the elevator to the ground floor and were met by Gerard, the doorman, who greeted them both by name. Once they stepped out into the humid night air, Mercedes noticed Xander's limo waiting for them.

Xander took her hand from his arm and held on to it while he helped her into the back of the limo, the driver standing to the side holding the door open.

"We'll be at our destination in under fifteen minutes, Mr. Boone," Carson, Xander's limo driver, informed them as Xander climbed in behind her.

"Where are we going?" she asked when the door was closed and they were alone.

Xander moved to sit beside her, not leaving an inch of space between them, his big, warm hand resting on her thigh.

"Dakota's," Xander replied, referring to one of his favorite restaurants, a five-star steakhouse, no less.

As the limo pulled away from the curb, Mercedes made a last-ditch effort to calm her nerves. It wasn't like she hadn't shared more than her fair share of dinners with Xander. They often would go together, especially when he wanted to go to Dakota's because he knew she liked the place.

She knew she should feel comfortable with him because they were such close friends, but this felt decidedly different. Mostly because Xander was touching her. Constantly. Oddly, she found that she didn't mind his touch. It was intimate yet casual, but not at all innocent, which left her a little rattled. She could practically feel the tension radiating beneath his skin, and that made her own skin tingle.

Thankfully, the drive was a short one, and it wasn't long before Xander was leading her into the restaurant. After being greeted by name, Mercedes followed the host to a table in the back while Xander remained right behind her, his hand making her skin sizzle where he kept it at the small of her back.

Xander, ever the gentleman, pulled out her chair after waving off the host's attempt and waited until she was seated comfortably before taking the chair across from her. She would've been surprised by the fact that he didn't take the seat next to her, but if you'd ever been out to dinner with Xander, you'd realize that the broad expanse of his upper body left him little room to share at a small table such as the one they were now sitting at.

So, their seating arrangement wasn't unusual.

What was different from normal was the fact Xander took her hand from across the table and caressed the backs of her fingers with his thumbs while the host detailed the wine list for them.

As usual, Xander nodded politely but didn't order, rather waiting patiently for their waiter to arrive.

"Good evening, Ms. Bryant, Mr. Boone," the familiar waiter said with a face-splitting grin when he approached them less than a minute later.

"Good evening, Tony," Mercedes greeted back, smiling up at the handsome young man. It didn't seem to matter what time of day or night they chose to go to the renowned steakhouse, Tony was always there to serve them. She had her suspicions that Tony was called in even on his days off if Mr. Boone chose to make a reservation.

"Tonight I'd like as little interruption as possible," Xander informed him in that deep, booming tone that he used when speaking business. Strangely enough, Xander kept his eyes on her, not bothering to address Tony directly.

"Of course, sir," Tony answered, not looking at all taken aback by the request. "I'll bring the wine momentarily."

"Thank you," Mercedes said as Tony turned and disappeared across the restaurant. They would not be placing an order because, for the last few years, whenever she accompanied Xander, they always had the same thing. Tony would no doubt ensure they had a perfect dining experience, without interruption.

Not bothering to pull her hand out from underneath Xander's, she stared down at their hands, wondering if he felt the way she trembled. It was an involuntary reaction, one she wasn't at all proud of.

"Shane called," Xander informed her, drawing her attention back to him.

She raised her eyebrow, a silent acknowledgement that she was listening.

"He's going to meet us at Devotion later."

Mercedes swallowed hard, but her gaze didn't waver from Xander's. She'd already given herself a pep talk earlier. This was a commitment she'd made, and now she had to deal with the fallout. A deal was a deal, and worst case, if she couldn't survive this first test, she'd easily let Xander know at the end of the night.

For now, she was committed to the next few hours, no matter what was on the agenda. She had no idea how Shane was going to react to whatever Xander had planned for her at Devotion, but she couldn't very well argue after she'd entered into this agreement with her eyes wide open.

"You don't care to know what he said?" Xander asked, a nearly indiscernible tilt to his full lips the only sign that he was amused by her reaction.

"Of course I care," she said with a matching smile, trying to hide her reaction to his teasing.

When Xander didn't offer more details, Mercedes laughed. "Quit playing with me, X. Just tell me what he said."

"He said he's looking forward to seeing us tonight."

"He didn't ask any questions about why I wasn't going to Kink? Or about why you and I were going to Devotion together?" Although the notion of their going out to various places together wasn't completely absurd, Mercedes knew Shane was rather perceptive. Not to mention suspicious.

"Of course he asked why," Xander admitted, sitting back when Tony arrived to pour the wine.

Mercedes tasted the rich red that Tony offered and then signaled her approval before turning her attention back to Xander.

"And?"

"I told him that I was taking you to dinner and then taking you to Devotion. I didn't feel the need to explain my reasoning to him."

Mercedes knew his explanation hadn't been accepted without more questions. Rather than push Xander, she sat back, waiting patiently.

He laughed. A brilliant, rich sound that made her insides jump to attention. She loved when he laughed. It was such an amazing sound, probably because it was so rare. At least like that, anyway.

"I told him he'd be seeing a lot more of you tonight."

"You did not!" Mercedes gasped.

Xander laughed again, which settled her somewhat. The man was incorrigible.

"No, I didn't. But you and I both know that it's going to happen."

Mercedes wasn't all that worried about Shane seeing more of her, as Xander put it. It wasn't like he hadn't seen plenty of her before. When they played at Kink, the individual playrooms were all open to the public. The private rooms could be viewed if the participants chose, so there were plenty of times Shane could've witnessed a scene between her and one of her subs.

What she was worried about was what Xander had planned.

"Are you going to use one of the main playrooms?" she asked, referring to the large glass rooms that were centered on the main floor.

"I haven't thought that far ahead yet," he told her, another devious smirk teasing his lips.

It was official; she was not going to survive the night.

CHAPTER THIRTEEN

"HOW'S YOUR MOM AND DAD?" MERCEDES ASKED after Tony delivered their meals a short while later.

They'd already made it through the salad course, shared another glass of wine, and managed to talk about very little. Mercedes was nervous, there was no doubt about that. In a sadistic sort of way, Xander liked the idea of her being nervous. It meant she viewed this dinner as something more than two friends or two business associates enjoying a meal together.

And this was definitely more than that.

"They're good. Right now they're enjoying the sights in Columbus, Ohio." At least that's where they'd been when he'd talked to his mother early that morning.

"Are they planning to head back here anytime soon?"

Xander took a sip of his wine as he watched Mercedes. "Not if they have anything to say about it."

His parents, married for going on forty years, were retired and, after plenty of discussions, had decided they wanted to set out to see the world. Or more specifically, to tour any state within the US that they could physically drive to. Xander had bought them a recreational vehicle with all of the bells and whistles, and he was pretty sure they hadn't looked back since.

That'd been three years ago.

He talked to his mother every day to catch up on what they were doing or for her to grill him about what he was doing. Didn't matter if the call lasted three minutes or thirty, he still made a point to talk to one or both of them every day.

"Where are they off to next?"

"As of this morning, they hadn't decided. Either Michigan or Pennsylvania. I think they're going to stay right where they are, though, for at least a week."

Mercedes looked up at him, concern in her eyes. "Is everything all right?"

"Yes," he told her, cutting his steak. "At least that's what my mother is claiming. My dad took a fall, but she assures me it isn't anything to worry about. I told her I'd fly up to check on them, but she insisted that I not." That conversation hadn't gone over well, but when Xander had finally calmed down, he'd agreed. For now.

Of course, at that point, Stella had changed the subject, wanting to know what Mercedes and Shane were up to since she'd apparently heard enough to suit her fancy about Xander's day-to-day.

Xander's parents loved Mercedes. They had asked him more than once whether he was ever going to settle down with her and, if he wasn't, whether or not Shane was going to show better sense than he apparently had. He'd laughed, knowing what he did. Settling down wasn't the issue. Neither was the notion of settling down with Mercedes.

Xander knew that there were plenty of men and women who had relationship phobias or a constant need to push people away for whatever reason. Xander had none of those. He didn't cringe at the prospect of getting married, settling down, having kids. It might happen one day. He was even fairly optimistic at thirty-five. He'd had a good childhood, he was close to his parents, and he didn't feel the need to come up with some sort of reason he couldn't get attached.

What he did have a problem with was finding the right woman. They all seemed to take a keen interest in his bank account long before they showed much interest in him on something more than a sexual level. That's usually about the time he would part ways.

"Maybe you should surprise them," Mercedes said, pulling him back to the conversation.

"You mean fly up there?"

"Sure, why not? I know you. You're probably itching to go check on them."

There was no doubt that Mercedes knew him better than most people. Ever since his mother had informed him that his father had fallen, he'd been anxious to find out for himself just how his father was doing. However, since it wasn't something he intended to do tonight, he decided to change the subject.

Because he'd much rather talk about Mercedes, he said the first thing that came to his mind. "How's your mother?"

Mercedes looked up at him, gracefully laying her fork on her plate, then dabbing at her mouth with a linen napkin before reaching for her wineglass. He saw the moment she attempted to shut down, and he immediately regretted the question. But rather than backtrack, he simply waited for her to answer.

"She's fine. Still in rehab."

It was the fourth drug rehab her mother had been in during the last two years. The woman was strung out, and she didn't have any problems reaching out to Mercedes when she'd blown her last dollar on drugs. Mercedes, being the soft-hearted woman she was, usually assisted financially, but he and Shane had finally managed to convince her it was time to stop enabling her mother.

That hadn't been a particularly exciting conversation, but they'd gotten through it after a heated screaming match. But in the end, Mercedes had agreed with them and then somehow convinced her mother to go into rehab. Unfortunately, her mother was using Mercedes's money to pay for it, but as far as Xander was concerned, it was better than Priscilla blowing it on coke.

"Do you think this one is working?" he asked, encouraging her to open up a little more.

"About as good as the last one," she answered sharply.

He had no doubt that Priscilla was only in rehab to ensure that Mercedes didn't give up on her completely. He'd heard all the stories. She didn't share with many people, he knew, but she had opened up to him. And Shane.

Priscilla Bryant had had a hard life. Married to a son of a bitch, she had taken the coward's way out, staying with him so she wouldn't have to get a job to support herself or her daughter. That was about the only good thing Mercedes's father had done for either of them, she'd told them.

For the last few years, Priscilla had jumped from job to job, mostly cleaning services that paid little more than minimum wage. But once she got tired of going to work, she just didn't. And then she'd call Mercedes, ask for money, and Mercedes would grudgingly give it to her, knowing there was no way her mother would ever pay her back.

Xander knew Mercedes was not fond of talking about her family. If at all possible, she preferred not to talk about her mother. She absolutely hated to talk about her deadbeat father, who'd disappeared from her life just a few months before Mercedes graduated from high school. According to her, she was happy he'd left. To hear Mercedes tell the story, the abusive bastard had stuck around long enough so that he wouldn't have to pay child support to Mercedes's mother and not a moment longer.

"How about we move on to a lighter subject?" Mercedes requested, picking up her knife and fork and pinning Xander with a look that told him she was not at all interested in the subject.

Fine. He knew when to back off, just like he knew when to push back. For now, he'd let her have her way.

Two hours later, Xander led Mercedes out of the restaurant and to the waiting limo. They'd taken their time through dinner, and once the conversation had detoured to business, it'd seemed as though Mercedes's tension level had receded a few notches.

Holding her hand while she climbed inside, he glanced over at Carson. "We're going to Devotion. No interruptions. And I don't care how long it takes us to get there. If we arrive before I give you the go-ahead, continue to drive until I tell you."

"Yes, sir," Carson responded, his face showing absolutely no emotion.

The man had worked as Xander's personal driver for not quite eight years. He knew exactly what to expect. He was paid well for his discretion and had never once interfered or questioned Xander's instruction. It was the main reason he was still on the payroll.

Xander climbed into the limo and allowed Carson to shut the door behind him. Reining himself in, Xander waited until the limo had approached highway speeds before he turned his full attention to Mercedes.

"Take off your shoes and come here."

Mercedes glanced over at him, clearly startled by his request. To her credit, she didn't question him, rather turned to face him slightly.

"On my lap," he instructed when it was clear he hadn't been detailed enough.

Mercedes's perfectly groomed eyebrow cocked skeptically, but she didn't argue. He watched as she slipped her shoes off, leaving them on the floor of the car before moving in front of him.

He glided his hands up the outsides of her thighs, relishing the warmth of her bare skin as he slid his hands beneath the short, billowy skirt, pulling her toward him so that she could straddle his legs. She clearly understood what he wanted, because she slowly eased atop him, her knees on each side of his thighs.

"Much better," he told her, caressing her cheek as he stared back at her. "I like you close."

"I like being close," she admitted, startling them both with her unguarded response.

He studied her momentarily, taking his time as he continued to caress her smooth cheek with one hand while sliding his other hand higher and higher on her thigh, but never giving in to the temptation to take it further. Not just yet.

"You're committed to this?" he asked finally, despite the fact that it wasn't so much a question as it was an acknowledgement.

"I am," she told him without reservation. "For tonight."

"And what about tomorrow?" he questioned, not exactly thrilled with her response. They had five days, and he did not like the idea of her backing out after one night.

"Let's take it one day at a time."

"I'm not going to go easy on you because you're threatening me," he informed her. "In fact, you might find yourself punished."

"It's not a threat," she assured him softly, her hand coming up to rest on his cheek, mirroring the way he was touching her.

God, he loved her touch. Loved the feel of her delicate fingers on his skin. He wanted her to touch him. Everywhere.

Rather than force the issue, he let it drop.

"Do you have any idea how much I've wanted you? Or for how long I've wanted you?" he asked, not expecting a response.

"No," she whispered, her head tilting slightly as she leaned her cheek into his palm. "Tell me."

"How about I show you."

Letting his finger slide down her cheek, he trailed his hands along each side of her neck, over her collarbone, until he reached the swells of her breasts. The turquoise minidress she wore was beautiful, he had to admit. It accentuated her curves, but more importantly, he loved that it was strapless. And short. Did he mention he liked that it was short because it showed off her magnificent legs?

The woman had killer legs.

If he'd had the chance to request her to wear something, it would've been exactly this.

Reaching around behind her, he deftly unhooked the tiny hook and lowered the thin zipper down her spine until the dress fell free to reveal her breasts.

She'd gone without a bra tonight, and that realization made his dick harder than he'd thought possible.

Glancing up, he noticed she was watching him, so he continued on his quest to get personally acquainted with every inch of her. Dropping his head, he focused his attention on her left breast, making a wide circle with his tongue around her areola. He took his time, tasting her, teasing her, inhaling her sweet, sexy scent. Intermittently, he would glance up, wanting to see the expression on her face.

He moved on to tease her other breast, offering the same attention before leaning back and looking up at her.

"Don't stop," she whispered, her fingers sliding into the hair at his nape. "Please don't stop."

"Didn't plan to," he assured her as he leaned in again, this time focusing his attention on her nipples, using his tongue and teeth to tease them into tight buds.

Sliding his hand into the inside pocket of his suit jacket, he pulled out a small box, and once he was satisfied with how her nipples stood erect, he pulled back and looked at her again. Holding up the box, he waited for her to open it.

She offered him a small smile as she reached up and flipped open the lid to reveal a set of crystal nipple clamps he'd ordered just for her. It was amazing how fast things could be delivered when money was no object.

Mercedes lifted the chain made of stunning rose gold from the box, holding the clamps in each of her hands. They were going to be so fucking pretty on her.

Unable to resist, Xander leaned forward again, sucking her right nipple into his mouth, this time more aggressively, firmly teasing with his tongue until Mercedes was writhing on his lap. When her head fell back, he released her, making quick work of the clamp and settling it into place as she gasped.

He tightened the tension on the clamp, going slowly until she was wiggling against him, her other hand threatening to drop the other clamp.

"Don't let it go," he warned her as he continued to admire the jewelry now in place.

Gripping her waist, Xander once again tormented her other nipple, lingering longer than he intended when she began to moan in earnest. Once he was satisfied, he pulled back and just as diligently attached the other clamp, tightening that one, as well. A small crystal dangled from each clamp while the chain looped down between her breasts.

"Beautiful," he said as he admired her puckered nipples. "Do they hurt?"

"A little," she admitted, her breaths ragged and choppy.

"Have you ever had your nipples clamped?"

"Not by a man, no," she told him.

Xander cocked his eyebrow, waiting for her to explain.

"I own a pair because I wanted to know what they felt like. I happen to like them." She grinned.

"I happen to like them, as well." Quite a bit.

With his hands on her hips, he pulled her closer, nestling the hard length of his erection between her thighs, wishing like hell he could bury himself inside of her right then.

He would've, too, if it hadn't been for the fact that the first time he took her, it damn sure wouldn't be in the backseat of a limo. No, he was reserving his first feel of her pussy sheathing him for later that night. It was a damn good thing he had an endless supply of patience, because Mercedes had the potential to push him to the breaking point.

Unable to keep from enjoying how pretty her nipples looked with the rose-colored gold dangling from them, he admired her a while longer, reaching into his pocket once again and retrieving a much smaller box.

"More?" she asked, her chest rising and falling as though she was anticipating his next step.

This one was going to take a little finesse on his part, he knew. The nipple clamps were one thing, because they were for her pleasure as well as his. The next thing he wanted to give her was more than that. It was a symbol.

One he fully expected her to balk at.

THE WEIGHT OF THE NIPPLE CLAMPS WAS making her crazy. The sensation was both tantalizing and a little painful at the same time, but the pain was a good one. An erotic one that heightened her awareness and left her hungry for more.

In truth, she hadn't expected it. At least not tonight.

Why, she didn't know.

This was Xander. A man who liked to keep people on their toes. And he didn't work on anyone else's timetable. Ever. This was his show, and she had fully accepted she was just along for the ride.

Mercedes fought the urge to cup her breasts, to squeeze them to release some of the pressure. It was a good thing she had a tremendous amount of control. Not that she was showing much of it tonight.

As she watched, Xander held out the other box, not moving to open it or have her do the honors. In fact, he looked worried. Studying his reaction caused her to forget all about the consistent throb in her nipples. For the time being.

"What's that?" she asked, suddenly incredibly nervous.

"Don't panic on me yet, pet," Xander said reassuringly, his eyes never leaving her face.

She watched, anticipation and dread doing a number on her already frayed nerves. In truth, she hadn't been all that surprised by the nipple clamps. They were an expected adornment with Xander. Maybe not tonight, but she'd definitely anticipated them. Xander was quite fond of them, she knew. But now that they were in place, she couldn't imagine what other torture devices he might be hiding.

Xander flipped the box open to reveal an exquisite diamond rose on what looked to be a white gold chain.

Her heart stuttered in her chest when he lifted it from the box, and she realized exactly what it was. Her first instinct was to move away from him, to get as far away as possible. He must've known, because his hand snaked around to her back, holding her firmly in place.

"If you absolutely refuse to wear it tonight, I will understand," he told her.

Mercedes met his eyes for the first time since he'd retrieved the chain, and what she saw staring back at her certainly wasn't what she'd expected. He had said the words, but she knew without a doubt that if she refused, he'd be more hurt than angry. And that bothered her more than anything.

"Just for tonight?" she asked, her hands trembling.

"Tonight, and any night we're at Devotion."

"Xander…" She couldn't even finish her sentence.

There was absolutely no way she was ready for this. Although the jewelry was delicate and beautiful, what it symbolized was something she wasn't ready for. Shit, it had only been a few hours since she'd agreed to this deal, and now he wanted to…

God, she couldn't even think it.

"Why?" she asked, bewildered by what he was offering.

Xander reached up and cupped her chin, forcing her to look at him when she couldn't tear her gaze away from the chain dangling from his fingers.

"It's not permanent, and it doesn't mean anything unless you want it to. It's more so that there are no questions from anyone else, M. I don't want any questions as to who you belong to."

"It's a collar," she said, as though that could possibly be news to him. More accurately, it was what she'd refer to as a day collar, one designed to show ownership, but not used in play.

"It is," he confirmed. "One I had designed for you today. Like I said, it's not permanent, but I do want to ensure that there are no questions. For the next few days, you belong to me. Completely to me."

Shit. She knew what it symbolized, and she understood his reasoning. It still bothered her.

Mercedes had taken plenty of subs over the years. Only once had she ever collared one. And that had come back to bite her in the ass hard.

A little over two years ago, Mercedes had let herself get just a little too attached to a man. A sub. Or at least she'd thought he was submissive. In the club, he'd played the part to perfection. And for the months leading up to her collaring him, she had thought she loved him.

But in the light of day, Mitchell hadn't been anything that he proclaimed to be. Oh, sure, for the six months they dated exclusively, he'd pretended rather well. It hadn't been until she had officially collared him that he'd shown his true colors. He had even gone so far as to propose to her. When she'd told him she wasn't quite ready to go that far yet, he'd shown her who he really was.

That one devastating night, she'd learned his true nature. He was a submissive when people were watching. He was an asshole when they weren't. The first time he'd laid a hand on her, she'd kicked his ass out. Well, technically Xander had kicked his ass out because Mitchell had refused to leave her condo while he tried to convince her that he was sorry.

How she'd been so blind, she truly had no clue, but it had been a rough few months for her.

Regardless, she didn't take the notion of collaring a submissive lightly, and she knew by the way Xander stared back at her, not moving as he waited for her response, that he didn't, either. Now that she thought about it, in all the years that she'd known Xander, never had he collared one of his pets, even a few he'd coveted for longer than just a couple of days.

"Oh, God," she breathed. "I don't…"

"It's all right, pet," he said soothingly, lowering his hand.

No holds barred.

The thought fluttered through her mind, reminding her of why she was here and what she'd agreed to.

Before he could return the necklace to the box, she reached out and grabbed his wrist. She'd signed on for this, and she wouldn't go back on her word. If this would please him, Mercedes was willing to give it a shot. No matter how uncomfortable it made her.

"I'll wear it," she whispered, shocked by her agreement.

Obviously Xander was shocked, as well, because he just stared back at her as though she'd lost her mind.

She had. She truly had.

"Lift up your hair," he instructed long seconds later, his voice not as steady as it had been previously.

He was just as affected by her concurrence, and that sent a torrent of courage flooding through her. That and a sense of empowerment that she hadn't expected.

Raising her arms, Mercedes caught her breath when the nipple clamps pulled, the weight of the chain pulling tighter. She moaned but managed to lift her hair up.

Xander reached behind her, his large fingers moving deftly, and then a moment later, he was finished. How he could hook something so small with such precision was beyond her, but clearly he knew what he was doing.

Dropping her hair, she looked directly at him and noticed he was staring at her neck. She reached up, her fingertips brushing across the small rose that settled comfortably against her throat. When she swallowed, she could feel it, which meant she would constantly be reminded that it was there.

Probably exactly how he wanted it.

"Fuck," Xander growled. "M."

The next thing she knew, Mercedes was crushed against him, Xander's powerful arms flexing as he held her close, his mouth fused to hers as he devoured her whole.

She didn't hesitate, fully engulfed by the flames that ignited when his mouth met hers. The deep rumble in his chest didn't subside as he thrust his tongue against hers. She was going to disintegrate into ash if he kept this up. The passion that smoldered between them was more powerful than a wildfire fanned by high winds.

"I'm not sure how much longer I can wait," he said when they came up for air.

"For what?" she asked, confused and more than a little breathless from that mind-blowing kiss.

"To be inside you. I want to feel the heat of your pussy surrounding me," he breathed, his lips brushing against the skin of her neck while his hips jerked beneath her.

She wanted it, too. She wanted nothing more than to remove the barriers between them and sate the ever-intensifying ache that was continuing to grow more painful with every passing second.

"What are you waiting for?" she asked him, cupping the back of his head and holding him close to her.

Xander must've taken hold of the chain that connected the nipple clamps, because suddenly there was an influx of pleasure-pain that bolted through her nipples, making her cry out from the sheer ecstasy of it.

"For that reason," he said on a rush. "Because I want to make you come a million different ways before I bury myself inside of you."

She wanted to tell him that the only thing he needed to do was to continue talking like that, and she'd come from his voice and his words alone.

And she feared it would be the honest-to-God truth.

CHAPTER FOURTEEN

AFTER XANDER HAD SIGNALED FOR CARSON TO make it to their final destination, he helped Mercedes right her dress, effectively hiding the nipple clamps. He hadn't particularly wanted to, but he'd been under the impression she needed a minute.

As soon as the limo came to a stop in front of Devotion, Xander eased out into the stifling evening air and then helped Mercedes out behind him once she'd slipped her shoes back on. Carson came around to handle the door, handing him a small bag as he did.

"Thank you," he told the man. "I'll text you when we're ready."

"Yes, sir. I'll be waiting."

Taking Mercedes's hand, he led her to the main doors of Devotion and then held one open for her.

With a quick nod of his head, he greeted the woman who was manning the desk and the security guard who was standing off to the side. The woman didn't have much work to do tonight because the club still hadn't officially opened to new members and tonight's festivities were by invitation only. And he could only hope security wasn't necessary, but one could never be too careful.

With his fingers still linked with Mercedes's, he made his way through the next set of double doors that led to the actual club.

At that point, Xander released her hand and placed his at the small of her back, directing her toward the first bar. He noticed she was suspiciously eyeing the small bag that he was carrying, but he refused to share the details with her just yet.

Xander had a plan, and every time he eyed the collar around her neck, he became more and more anxious to get the night started. Only he wasn't looking to rush her, and being that Mercedes was the one who was going to be in the uncomfortable spot tonight, he knew he needed to give her a little time to get acclimated to their surroundings. Figuring out of sight, out of mind was the best option, Xander stowed the bag underneath the first bar that they came to. He then grabbed the attention of the bartender and ordered them drinks.

While they waited, he took the opportunity to observe the goings-on of the club.

It was still fairly early, but the place was jumping, more people than he was expecting considering this was a test run of what they hoped would become a regular theme night.

Tonight's theme … BDSM.

He was surprised to see that the attendees had embraced the concept. At least they had if their state of dress was any indication. Last night's attire had been formal; tonight was all about play. He noticed that, without explicit direction, some people came up with some rather interesting ideas.

Most of the early arrivals donned leather, some not so appealing, some rather intriguing, all having one thing in common: an apparent effort to reflect the glorified, often stereotyped lifestyle many were just now exploring.

Overall, Xander liked the feel of the place. Everyone was into it, from novices to experts and varying degrees in between.

As was usual, the shutters over the windows were closed, the lights were dimmed, which left the club backlit by the red lights that surrounded the bars. The music was loud, a sexy bass beat thumping through the cavernous space. There were lines of people around the bars, others sitting at the scattered tables, some on couches, and even some against the wall.

Because of the theme, they'd added some scenery, which included a St. Andrew's cross, a very interesting Sybian saddle machine that Trent Ramsey, the somewhat obnoxious actor turned club owner and one of Xander's longtime acquaintances, had found necessary to include. Off to the far side, Xander noticed someone had brought out a swing, as well.

Of course, those pieces of equipment were already reserved in advance for the night, as were the glass-enclosed playrooms. Mistress Serena was in one, but only one of the other three was occupied at the moment.

Xander had originally intended to use one of them tonight, but after careful consideration, he was leaning toward utilizing one of the more private areas. Then again, that all depended on the way Mercedes responded to him.

Tonight he intended to test her again.

He was the Dom — *her* Dom — and she was his submissive, and he fully expected her full cooperation and attention throughout the night. If she could manage to rein in some of her defiance, he'd gracefully reward her by keeping her out of the public eye.

However, if she chose to defy him, which up to this point he wasn't sure she would do, he would easily lay claim to one of the glass rooms as punishment. Because of the latter, he had first dibs on the third room just in case.

Either way, he fully intended to make tonight interesting.

After all, he didn't have a minute to waste. Five days wasn't nearly enough time for all the things he had planned for her. But for now, he'd proceed with that time frame in mind.

Retrieving the drinks that the bartender handed over, Xander turned to Mercedes, offering hers to her first.

"Thank you," she said with a smile when he handed her a glass filled with a clear liquid.

"You're welcome," he replied, studying her as she sipped from the glass. Figuring it was as good a time as any to lay out the ground rules, Xander continued. "Tonight, I want you to refer to me as Master or Sir," he told her boldly, wanting to set the boundaries immediately.

Up to this point, they'd merely been on a casual date, something Xander found himself hoping for more of in the near future. Well, the only difference might've been him placing the nipple clamps on her and collaring her in the limo.

"Can you do that?" he asked when she didn't answer immediately, needing her verbal confirmation that she was on board.

"Yes, Sir," she mumbled.

He noted the sarcasm in her tone. She was adept at the rules of this game, so he didn't feel it necessary to call out her transgressions as they were made. If she wanted to play that way, he'd gladly dole out his punishment accordingly. On the other hand, she knew what would please him because she knew him so well, so she had the option of playing by the rules.

The choice was completely up to her.

"One-drink limit tonight," he informed her as he sipped his Glenlivet. That was a hard and fast rule that they were both used to. Anytime he planned for a scene, he knew that alcohol didn't mix well. The safety of his sub was, above all else, his utmost priority.

And tonight, he fully intended to focus all of his attention on the beautiful pet he planned to stake his claim on in every way possible.

LUKE MCCOY WAS DOING HIS BEST TO keep his eye on everything that was going on around him as he stood near the bar. It wasn't that hard to do considering he knew he had a second set of eyes doing the same not far away. Cole was less than ten feet away talking to Sierra, but Luke knew he was well aware of everything that was going on.

As he waited for the bartender to hand over the three drinks he'd ordered, Luke scanned the room, noticing that Xander and Mercedes had just arrived. Good thing, too, since tonight had been his new business partner's suggestion in the first place. If he were completely honest, the whole BDSM thing didn't do much for him. Well, that wasn't completely true. He did find it rather tempting to tie Cole or Sierra to the bed whenever the opportunity arose. But that didn't mean he was into all the shit that was going on around him tonight.

In fact, he was tempted to rush Cole and Sierra out the door and haul them home as fast as possible. From there, he'd be more than happy to show them his version of BDSM, which would involve a pair of handcuffs, some scarves, and him being buried to the hilt in one or the other of them as soon as fucking possible.

"You all right?"

Luke glanced over to see Trent Ramsey standing next to him, giving him one of his infamous smirks.

"Never better. You?" he answered easily, turning his attention back to the groups congregating around the wide-open space.

"Just fucking dandy," Trent said with a grin. "Looks like those Walker boys are gonna have to work extra hard to compete with this place, don't you think?"

Luke fought the urge to roll his eyes. "Last I checked, it wasn't a competition." Then again, he'd been telling Trent that for months. The guy didn't get it. He was hell-bent on ensuring that Devotion was above and beyond anything the Walkers could come up with. Had Luke not been a silent partner in the up-and-coming resort that the Walker brothers were building, he might've cared more than he did.

"Try telling them that," Trent said, nodding his head toward the far side of the room.

Luke followed his gaze and noticed Travis Walker had made an appearance. Son of a bitch. Wasn't that interesting? He was going to have to head over and talk to him. At least that would give him an excuse if he found he needed one.

"Has Xander been introduced to Travis?" Trent asked when Luke didn't say anything more.

"Yeah," Luke answered. He wasn't going to let Trent know that Xander's name had also been added to the long list of financial backers for the Alluring Indulgence Resort. It would likely make his head explode, and for the time being, Luke was content with not having to deal with Trent being in a panic. At least tonight he seemed to be in a good mood.

Then again, with plenty of half-naked women sending looks his way, the man really shouldn't have a care in the world.

"Everything okay over here?"

Saved by a beautiful woman.

Luke smiled down at his wife, putting his arm around her and pulling her closer to him while he glanced over to see where Cole was. His husband moved up against his other side and immediately picked up the conversation with Trent. God, he loved that man. Cole always knew when Luke needed rescuing, and he would always need to be saved from Trent. The man had the ability to drive him absolutely fucking crazy. But thanks to Cole, it looked like he'd be able to hang on to his sanity for a little while longer.

"Couldn't be better," he told Sierra, turning his full attention to her. "I thought you'd be talking to Sam."

"I was. For a couple of minutes. I plan to meet up with her again once they get settled."

"Problems?" Luke asked, glancing around to see if he could locate his twin. He hadn't had a chance to talk to him.

"Not that I know of," she said, pulling his attention back down to her. "So, what's on the agenda tonight?"

Luke retrieved a drink from the bartender and handed it over to her before pulling her close once more. "That's completely up to you," he told her as he smiled.

"Really? I get to choose?" she asked sweetly.

Oh, hell. The woman had that devious grin that had the hair on the back of his neck rising. In a good way. "Did you have something in mind?"

"I've always got something in mind," she assured him.

After last night and the impromptu ceremony that Sierra had sprung on him and Cole, Luke wasn't sure he'd be able to keep his hands off of her even if she'd asked. By the expression on her pretty face, she definitely wasn't thinking about retreating to a quiet room all by her lonesome.

And for that, he loved her all the more.

"Baby, just say the word," Luke told her.

Looking around the room once more, Luke found himself smiling. It wasn't just the club, or the success of the previous night, or even tonight. It was all of it combined. His wife, his husband, and their daughter. Life was looking up for them, he knew that much.

And if anyone who knew him from before were to see him now, they'd probably wonder just what had happened to him. That was easy. Love. That's what had happened to him.

And now it was time to celebrate.

CHAPTER FIFTEEN

MERCEDES STOOD BESIDE XANDER, TRYING TO APPEAR casual and unconcerned. Truth was, her nerves had taken to breakdancing, and she wasn't sure how much longer she could tolerate the tension that was building to a crescendo.

The look in his eyes, the one that said things were about to get real, wasn't helping. The only positive, they were at Devotion and not Kink. She'd be mortified if they'd gone to their regular haunt because she was known there. Here, she was just another nameless face, and if Logan McCoy had mentioned anything, people were already believing she was a submissive.

Ha! The joke was on them.

Shit.

Mercedes's gaze landed on Shane standing on the far side of the room. He looked up just in time to see her watching him. Without hesitation, he excused himself from the group he had been conversing with and was hastily heading their way.

She could do this.

That statement went on a constant loop in her head, and she held tightly to the imaginary repeat button to ensure she didn't forget it. She only hoped that if she thought it enough times, she'd soon believe it, because at the moment, she was worried that backing out of the whole thing was high on her priority list.

"You look incredible," Shane said when he approached, leaning in and kissing her firmly on the lips.

She smiled up at him, hoping he didn't realize just how terrified she was now that he was there.

The sound that came from behind her stopped her heart for a millisecond. She looked up to see Xander glaring at Shane, and that's when Shane must have realized his faux pas.

"Shit," he mumbled, staring back at Xander. "I'm... Shit."

Shane was tongue-tied, and Mercedes knew why. If she had to guess, Xander was currently burning a hole in Shane's face with just a look. Shane had kissed her right on the lips, something that they did all the time. It meant nothing. They were friends.

But until tonight, she'd never been wearing a Dom's collar.

"Sorry, man."

Mercedes had known Shane longer than she'd known Xander, but not by much. They were good friends, possibly even closer than she and Xander. She spent a lot of time with Shane during her downtime. It wasn't strange for him to stop by her condo just to chat. Where Xander was the quiet, observant one, Shane was chatty and loud, the life of the party much of the time.

Shane's gaze dropped to her neck again, and then his eyes darted to Xander, who was now standing directly behind her. Just when she thought he wasn't going to say anything more, he broke the silence.

"That was fast."

Crap.

Xander's body moved even closer to hers, his hand sliding to her hips as he pressed his front against her back. He was like a living, breathing security blanket, and for a moment, she felt a measure of relief. With him standing there, she could almost envision herself absorbing some of his strength.

She would need it if she wanted to survive the night.

"You're good with this?" Shane asked, his question directed to her.

There was another unmistakable growl that came from Xander, and she smiled. Territorial much?

"Of course," she lied. She was committed because she'd made a deal. Didn't necessarily mean she was good with it; however, she needed Shane to know that she was on board.

The expression on Shane's face softened and then he laughed.

"M, I'm not sure how he managed to talk you into this, but darlin', I fully intend to watch this one play out."

Mercedes didn't smile even when the Texas twang he worked so hard to disguise slipped out. In fact, another emotion took root. Mortification. She wasn't sure how she would endure Shane watching a scene. Especially one where she was a submissive. It went against everything she'd worked so hard to build for herself, and here, tonight, she got the impression Xander intended to strip her of all her control.

Because he could.

"Back off, Shane," Xander growled from behind her.

"Yeah, what he said," Mercedes said, trying to lighten the mood. "It's fine. And if you want to watch, be my guest."

Xander's grip tightened on her hip, and that was when she realized she had overstepped. Tonight he was in the lead. He was in control, and she didn't have a say in the matter. She knew that based on the way Xander played at the club.

Shane's eyes darted back and forth between the two of them, and then he laughed again. "Yeah, good luck with all of this. I'm still not sure how he talked you into it, but yeah…" Shane stopped talking, but his sparkling blue eyes were lit with amusement.

"Did you come here to play?" Xander questioned, his hand loosening somewhat.

"I did, actually."

"Did you bring Clarissa?" Xander asked.

Mercedes's gaze darted behind her. Clarissa? She turned her attention back to Shane while she waited for him to answer.

"Not tonight. She had something to take care of. I promised I'd bring her to the next one."

"Clarissa? *My* Clarissa?" Mercedes asked, confused.

"Technically, she doesn't belong to you, doll," Shane said with a chuckle. "But, yes, we're talking about your friend Clarissa."

Holy shit. Clarissa and Shane. That was an interesting combination. Then again, Clarissa was an unattached submissive, and she had known that her friend thought rather highly of Shane.

"Are the two of you…?" Mercedes couldn't get the words out.

"We're just playing," Shane assured her. "Nothing serious."

Maybe not for him, Mercedes thought to herself. She made a mental note to call her friend first thing tomorrow. As much as she loved Shane, she wasn't at all sure he was the best man for Clarissa to be playing with.

"So who's your victim tonight?" Xander asked, his tone gruff.

When Shane looked over his shoulder, Mercedes glanced in that direction. There, on the other side of the room, was a pretty blonde and an equally pretty brunette staring back at them.

Yep, that's the way Shane played. It wasn't surprising to see he'd set his sights on two women for the night. It took a lot to hold Shane's interest, and although he was a fun-loving, laid-back charmer most of the time, when he went into full Dom mode, his entire demeanor changed.

He liked a challenge, and subs loved him for it. He didn't play around, didn't entertain the notion of relationships any more than Xander did. In fact, he made that point clear up front, and surprisingly, women still flocked to him. No doubt hoping they would be that someone special who could change his take-no-prisoners approach.

God, she prayed Clarissa wasn't thinking she might be the one to change him.

Mercedes would've warned them if she could. But it wasn't her place. And honestly, she enjoyed watching Shane and his inane ability to bring even the most defiant of subs to heel.

Then again, she had more than enough to think about. Like her own submission, and how, if at all, she was going to pull that off.

She glanced around the room as she waited for Xander's next command or for Shane to make another snide comment.

It seemed most of the people she'd been introduced to the night before were also there tonight.

Off in one corner, she caught a glimpse of the incredibly handsome Luke McCoy and his husband, Cole Ackerley, talking to Trent Ramsey, and Sierra, Luke and Cole's wife, cozied up to Luke's side. That wasn't surprising, especially after the impromptu ceremony they'd had the night before.

While Xander and Shane's conversation echoed around her, the memory of that ceremony came to the forefront, still having the ability to bring tears to her eyes. She hated that underneath it all she had a soft heart, but witnessing the three of them pledge their love for one another like that had been beyond anything she'd ever seen.

Before she had a chance to linger too long on the memory, Mercedes spotted Samantha and Logan McCoy making their way through the club. She glanced up over her shoulder to see Xander was watching them, as well. Turning back, she noticed that they'd stopped to talk to a couple she didn't recognize, but she purposely looked away, hoping they wouldn't feel her eyes on them.

It wasn't that she didn't want to interact with them, but if she was going to have to endure what she'd been through last night — although likely on a much grander scale — she wasn't sure she wanted such an intimate audience this time. Because no matter what she tried to tell herself, this time wouldn't be a demonstration.

Unable to help herself, her attention was drawn back their way, watching Samantha as she interacted with her husband and the other couple. Yes, Mercedes could definitely see the woman's allure. Not to mention her very blatant submissive tendencies. That thought reminded her that she'd told Xander he should take on Sam as a submissive because she was clearly more his style.

She swallowed the rest of her drink in one gulp and then turned to set the empty glass on the bar behind them. She needed to get her head on straight, and thinking about Xander with another woman, sub or otherwise, was so not helping.

"Are you ready?" Mercedes asked Xander abruptly, interrupting his conversation with Shane.

Shit.

His eyes landed on her, hard yet slightly amused, and she immediately realized her mistake.

This was not her show, and she'd promptly fallen into her usual routine of directing the evening to the way she expected it to go.

Without a word, Xander downed what was left of his drink and then placed the empty glass on the bar before turning to face her fully.

Damn. Damn. Damn.

She'd well and truly fucked up that time. She'd known earlier that she'd pushed her boundaries with her sarcasm, but now she could see the retaliation in Xander's glimmering gaze.

And the chill that raced down her spine didn't have anything to do with the temperature in the room.

Chapter Sixteen

Xander was adept at controlling his reaction but even more so at expressing his thoughts with just a look. He hoped like hell Mercedes wasn't having a problem reading his thoughts. The way her pretty gray eyes widened told him she was not far off on assuming what he was thinking.

Rather than address her transgression right there in the middle of the club, he opted to give her direction, a little foundation they could build on. They'd be moving this party somewhere else in the very near future, but until then, he wanted to make sure they were on the same page.

Based on her attitude thus far, they weren't even reading from the same book.

Xander fully intended to change that.

Right fucking now.

"I want you at my side at all times. Not in front of me, not behind me," he ordered, making sure his voice remained hard. "From this point on, I'll make the decisions, understand?"

He shouldn't have had to explain himself that much. Had she been one of his regular subs, he'd have bent her over his knee and spanked her ass, drawing any and all attention to her.

Apparently he was losing his fucking touch. This woman was getting to him more than he should be allowing, that was for damn sure.

Her reaction was exactly what he'd expected. She was likely trying to figure out what she could do to pull him back from the edge. What she didn't seem to realize was that it was a little too late for that.

Undermining his authority as her Dom while in public was one violation he would not tolerate. It was a blatant sign of disrespect, and he deserved more than that.

Xander knew this wasn't going to be easy, and it damn sure wasn't going to fall into that neat little box that he usually reserved for his subs. But it certainly was going to be worth it even if he had to remind himself that Mercedes wasn't a sub. Well, technically, she was tonight.

But he couldn't be too lenient on her, because the woman knew damn well what she was doing. She probably knew exactly what his response would be, too. He'd seen her in action more times than he could count. She didn't take this sort of attitude from the subs she played with. Ever.

No, Mercedes Bryant was hard-core, demanding respect from anyone, especially from her subs.

Keeping his eyes trained on her, he waited for her to respond. She didn't, and it pissed him off a little because he knew she was doing it on purpose. She was testing him.

Topping from the bottom.

Fuck. How had he not seen that?

"Do you understand me?" he asked, his voice echoing his frustration.

For a brief moment, he wondered whether Mercedes was going to lose every ounce of her gumption. He knew the way her mind worked, and if he had to guess, she was quickly rethinking this.

Mercedes had made it crystal clear by her actions that she absolutely detested feeling vulnerable and weak, and at the moment, with the way Xander purposely glared at her, he was sure she was feeling exactly that.

Rather than use words like he'd instructed her to, she nodded, and his frustration flashed hot and bright.

Without hesitating, Xander smoothly reached around and fisted her hair firmly but gently, pulling her flush against him. He wasn't hurting her, not even a little bit, but he knew the aggressive action had certainly caught her attention.

She looked like she was ready to tell him to go to hell.

To his surprise, she didn't move, and she didn't say a word.

But he never said anything, either, just continued to pin her with his eyes.

It must've dawned on her that he was waiting for a response. A verbal one, because she finally answered.

"Yes, Sir," she responded breathlessly.

"That's more like it," he said, his tone fierce. He leaned down until his mouth brushed her ear before he continued. "Tonight, you belong to me, pet. All mine. I advise you to get into the right frame of mind, or you really won't like what I have in store for you."

Or maybe she would. Maybe that's what this was. She was pushing him. The idea made him laugh, except it made perfect sense.

Fuck.

Was she seriously anticipating punishment? Submitting to him by acting out and forcing him to take a harder stance?

"I'll leave the two of you alone," Shane told them, and Mercedes did try to pull away from him then.

Xander didn't allow her to move; he kept one arm banded around her waist, his other hand still fisted in her hair. "We'll catch you later," Xander told Shane firmly, never breaking eye contact with Mercedes.

Once Shane had retreated, he released his hold on her, holding on long enough to ensure she was steady on her feet before letting go completely.

"Don't move," he told her as he slipped back to the bar and retrieved the small bag that he'd stashed earlier. While he was there, he whispered instructions to the bartender. Once he received a nod of agreement, he went back to Mercedes.

"Since you're clearly having problems understanding who is in control, we're going to do this the hard way."

Holding the bag out to her, he waited until she reached for it. When she looked back up at him, he gave her a wicked smile.

"Go change. I expect you back here in ten minutes. Not a minute longer. Understand?"

"Yes. Sir," she said, tacking on the "Sir" at the last minute.

"Hurry up, your time starts now."

Xander watched Mercedes, the bordering on indecent yet fucking sexy as hell way her hips swayed, as she headed toward the changing rooms closer to the main doors. Part of him expected her to sneak out through the main entrance and never return. That's probably why he kept an eye on her until she disappeared into the first room.

"Please tell me you know what the fuck you're doing."

Xander turned to see Shane glaring at him.

"I thought you were going to do your own thing," Xander retorted, suddenly wishing he had another drink.

This was going to be a long night, and as much as he anticipated it, he was already getting worked up.

"Do you really think she's up for this?"

Xander stared back at his friend, irritated by the fact he was being questioned, but understanding Shane's reason all the same. They'd both always looked out for Mercedes. Even if she was capable of taking care of herself, she'd come to mean so much to them that they made sure she was never hurt.

"I won't hurt her," Xander told Shane now, fury igniting just beneath the skin at the implication.

"Whoa, hold up. I know that. I never thought you would, but seriously, X. She doesn't look comfortable with this."

Xander laughed, his anger slipping out on his exhale. "Are you fucking serious right now? When has it ever been about comfort? The whole point is to push them out of their comfort zone."

"By 'them,' I assume you're referring to subs," Shane stated angrily. "She's not a sub."

Xander inhaled deeply.

It was true, he respected Shane. Hell, he even respected the man's opinion, but he was seconds away from losing his shit.

"If I thought she couldn't handle this, I wouldn't have made a deal with her," Xander finally said, holding on to his control with a tight grip.

"A deal?" Shane asked.

Xander noted the incredulous tone to his friend's voice.

"Yes. Five days. She's giving me five days."

"For what? For you to *dominate* her? Are you serious?"

"Yes," Xander answered bluntly.

"Is that all you want from her? To play a fucking game of who can top who first?" Shane asked, his back going ramrod straight.

Xander lowered his voice and looked Shane directly in the eyes. "No, it's not a goddamn game. Not for me at least. I want every fucking part of her, goddammit. You should fucking know me better than to think otherwise."

"Son of a bitch." Shane exhaled, his defensive posture softening. "You lov—"

"Don't even fucking say it," Xander bit out. The time for talking was over. He wasn't one to explain his reasons, but he understood Shane's need to protect Mercedes, so he was making an exception, but he could only be pushed so far. "This conversation is over. You let me handle this."

Shane thrust his hand through his blond hair, making it even more unkempt than it already was, and still the man looked like it'd been done on purpose. "Fine. Just..." Shane stopped abruptly and glanced behind Xander, his eyes widening.

Xander steeled himself and turned around. "Son of a bitch," he breathed out heavily.

"My sentiments exactly," Shane said, a low whistle escaping him.

If Xander had thought for one minute that Mercedes looked hot in that dress she'd had on, well, he clearly hadn't known the definition of hot.

The woman had just managed to steal his breath.

And that was something not many people had the ability to do.

Mercedes felt naked. Well and truly naked.

Granted, she didn't have much covering her, so it only made sense.

As she made her way across the club, it felt like she had to walk a mile to reach the spot where Xander still stood, and all the while it seemed as though everyone's attention was on her. Although she knew that wasn't the case.

Or at least she hoped that wasn't the case. She didn't have enough nerve to look around to find out for sure.

With the way Xander's intense gaze raked over her as she closed the distance between them, she felt like she was standing there without a stitch on. Then again, the outfit he'd asked her to change into had fit into a tiny bag, so it went without saying that she was rather underdressed.

"You look fucking amazing," Xander breathed out roughly, reaching out and taking her hand as he pulled her close.

She was tempted to curl up in his arms so that he could shield her from the eyes that were boring holes into her much-too-exposed skin.

The skimpy purple baby-doll nightie was quite impressive. The expensive silk was softer than anything she'd ever felt. Had she been in the comfort of her own home, she probably would've admired herself in the mirror, but here, standing in the middle of Devotion, she felt her anger building.

If Xander hadn't been so involved in his conversation with Shane, he would've realized she'd taken more than the ten minutes he'd allotted her to change. In fact, she'd redressed once before finally succumbing to her punishment.

And here she was, dressed in her heels, a barely there thong, and a wisp of a top that showcased every one of her assets.

Including the clamps that pulled at her now beaded nipples.

"Excuse us," Xander said to Shane, never taking his eyes off of her.

Xander studied her blatantly for another moment before linking their fingers together and leading her away from the bar.

Crap.

She followed Xander, knowing full well he intended to take her somewhere so that he could dole out his punishment for her defiance earlier. Part of her was anxious to get on with it because she needed something to take her mind off of the fact that she was practically naked.

They didn't make it far before they had company.

Logan and Samantha.

Mercedes stopped, doing her best to remain at Xander's side as he had instructed earlier. From this point on, she was going to make a point to do as he asked. Since she'd already defied him enough to earn a severe punishment, she was hoping to earn back a few brownie points. Even if it killed her.

Had she been her own sub acting out like this, she knew for a fact that she wouldn't have fared nearly as well. Xander was being way too tolerant. It made her feel good, but that's only because she felt as though she still had the upper hand. It made her want to push him at the same time.

She'd committed herself to this — no holds barred. And he'd done the same. So why did he seem to be holding back as much as she was?

"I hear this was your suggestion," Logan said as he approached them, nodding toward the open space, apparently referring to the themed play going on around them.

"It was," Xander agreed, his fingers tightening around hers, adding a level of comfort she hadn't realized was missing. "I'm rather impressed with the turnout. Glad you could make it."

"We are, too," Logan added, pulling Samantha to his side gently. "I think my brother's even more impressed. Sounds to me like Sierra has taken a particular interest in some of the equipment."

Xander grinned as he glanced across the room. Mercedes followed his gaze, noticing he was looking at the Sybian saddle machine. She fought the urge to smile.

Yeah, if Sierra got a taste of that, she could imagine her husbands might just run out and buy her one. The machine was interesting, but she could imagine the look on Luke's and Cole's faces as they watched her on it.

"What about you?" Xander asked, directing his question to Samantha. "Are you here to play tonight?"

She looked embarrassed by the question, but she squared her shoulders and smiled up at Xander, then over to Mercedes.

"If I can talk him into it, yes."

Mercedes decided that she really liked Sam. The woman embraced her desires, and that was truly refreshing. She knew so many women and men who merely fantasized, never taking the plunge to explore those fantasies. And here, at the club her brother-in-law owned, Mercedes imagined Sam felt safe.

As she should.

"Well, I think you'll find plenty to keep your attention tonight," Xander said, glancing down at Sam and then back to Logan.

Mercedes noticed a small amount of disappointment in Sam's eyes, but she was pretty sure she saw relief mixed with it. Had she been hoping for another scene with them?

For some reason, the idea wasn't as off-putting as she would've thought. Although, tonight, Mercedes wasn't really looking to have an intimate audience. Especially not now that she'd riled Xander up with her disobedience.

Mercedes held her breath, hoping Xander wouldn't invite the couple to join them. Not tonight. Please, not tonight.

"I'll be acting out a scene with Mercedes tonight. If you're interested in watching, we'll be one of the main attractions."

Mercedes noticed Xander's discreet head tilt in the direction of the glass-enclosed rooms that acted as the main stage for the club as a whole. Okay, so she wasn't going to get a reprieve tonight.

She could handle being on display. That wasn't a problem. She didn't mind being one of the main attractions, either. What she feared most was what Xander had planned for her.

"In fact, I think they just got the room ready," Xander said, drawing Mercedes's attention.

Oh, God.

She looked back at the third room to see a spanking bench had been delivered at some point. If her heart hadn't just taken to galloping in her chest, she might've admired it for a moment. Instead, she had the urge to throw up.

"We look forward to checking it out later," Logan told them, glancing between the two of them as he held out his hand to Xander. "I'll catch up with you both later in the week."

Mercedes forced a smile, swallowing hard. She looked over at Sam, their eyes meeting briefly, and she saw what looked like admiration peering back at her.

Why in the world would the woman want to be in her shoes at the moment?

"Definitely. We'll have lunch so we can talk. Good to see you, Sam," Xander said as a good-bye, smiling tentatively at the pretty blonde while Mercedes clung to his hand like a lifeline.

Yeah, she was seriously going to have to conjure up some level of calm or she was not going to make it through the next few minutes, much less the evening.

CHAPTER SEVENTEEN

XANDER LED MERCEDES AWAY FROM SAM AND Logan and over to the glass room that he'd reserved prior to arrival. After opening the door with a code, he stepped back and allowed her to go in before him.

Once inside, he closed the door behind them, ensuring that it locked so that they wouldn't have any uninvited guests. It was one thing for voyeurs to linger as they watched through the twenty-foot-tall glass walls, but Xander had no interest in any additional participants.

Tonight it was just him and Mercedes in the room.

"What do you think?"

"It's … interesting," she said as she glanced around the room. "It's a little … bright."

She didn't sound quite as cool as she was trying to appear. It made his dick hard to know her anticipation level was rising. That was what he expected.

If she pretended this was just another demonstration, she wouldn't get out of it what he wanted her to. To know that she'd passed the point of being able to distance herself from the situation pleased him.

Xander smiled at her. "I'll take care of the lighting in a minute. Right now, I want you to climb onto the bench."

Mercedes looked up at him for the first time since they'd stepped into the room. Her eyes were wide, her throat working as she swallowed hard. There was a question in her penetrating gaze, but just as he had expected, she didn't ask it.

Taking her hand, he held it as he led her closer to the bench. She paused momentarily, but he didn't rush her, merely watching as she mentally worked it out. As much as he wanted to encourage her, to slide his hands over her thighs and coax her into place, he wasn't willing to do it. This was up to Mercedes.

"Remember, you have a safe word, pet. I expect you to use it if, at any time, you feel the need to stop."

Mercedes glared up at him, and he fought the urge to laugh. She clearly didn't like the idea of safe wording out, but she of all people should understand that it wasn't an admission of defeat.

"Yes, Sir," she said through clenched teeth.

Xander released her hand when she knelt on the lower padded bench. Sliding his hand over her ass, he only offered his touch briefly before taking a step back.

What Mercedes might not have realized was that there were separate controls for the room that would allow as much or as little outside interaction as he wanted. There was no way to seal off the room entirely, but he had the option of limiting visibility by pushing a single button. There was also the option of muting the speakers that allowed anyone to hear them.

The glass walls were made of a switchable privacy glass. They could go from clear to frosted, limiting those who were outside of the room to see only shadows, rather than a full view. For right now, he was going to leave the walls clear. And the speakers on.

Despite Mercedes's hesitancy, Xander knew for a fact that she had no issues with being watched. He had no preference. He allowed his subs to dictate how much privacy they had, and it often depended upon their actions, whether they were obeying him or acting out. Being a member of a sex club, though, usually meant that one was intimately acquainted with public exhibitionism. Otherwise, if you weren't interested in the audience, all of this could be done in the privacy of your own home.

Once Mercedes was in place on the bench, her abdomen resting comfortably over the narrow, horizontal padded bench, he moved closer. Her breasts were unbidden, her rib cage resting on the bench while her chest hung slightly over. He couldn't wait to free her breasts from the silk that was currently clinging to them. On this particular bench, there was an armrest where her elbows rested. And to reduce the strain on her neck, she would be able to lay her forehead on a narrow padded bar that connected between the ends of the armrest.

Thanks to the design, he had the option of strapping her down, her thighs and her forearms. Just the thought of restraining her had his cock lengthening.

He would get to that. In a minute.

"You look incredible in that position," he told her, his tone low and soothing.

She didn't move.

He paused, not moving closer.

"Thank you, Sir," she said.

Clearly an afterthought.

They'd be working on that shortly.

"You're welcome, pet."

Stepping up behind her, he placed his hands on her lower back, slowly pushing the silk top upward, exposing her creamy skin. "I'm going to remove this now. We've gathered quite a bit of an audience, and I'd very much like them to see as much of you as possible."

"Yes, Sir," she whispered, her voice a little rougher than before.

She was getting turned on. Exactly what he had hoped for.

Keeping his pace slow, he pushed the nightgown higher until he could easily slip it over her head, her long, silky hair falling over her left shoulder as he did. She didn't move when the silk pooled in the crook of her arms, and he again praised her for it.

Leaning over her from behind, because he couldn't resist, he placed his forearms on the remaining space on the bench that was exposed at her sides. He tucked his arms against her, sandwiching her between his chest and the bench but making sure not to put his weight on her. Reaching beneath her arms, Xander fingered the chain that was hanging down, the one connected to the clamps on her nipples.

Mercedes moaned when he tugged, causing the clamps to pull.

"You look so fucking pretty right now. Bent over, your ass and pussy at my mercy. You make my dick hard, pet. So damn hard."

Mercedes's breath hitched, and the harder he tugged on the chain, the more she moaned. But she didn't respond, otherwise, which was what bothered him.

He couldn't help but wonder whether she was testing him again.

"You're going to look even prettier when your ass is red, won't you?"

"Yes, Mas— Sir."

Xander caught Mercedes's slip, and an emotion he wasn't familiar with ripped through him. She'd purposely refused to call him Master. He had no idea why that hurt him so much, but it was like a knife through his chest.

Rather than dwell on it, he shoved it away, refusing to let it get to him. It wasn't a requirement, and what he needed to focus his attention on was getting her off.

That's the punishment she would receive from him tonight. He fully intended to make her soar, bring her to orgasm as many times as he possibly could until she was pleading for him to stop.

MERCEDES REMAINED AS STILL AS POSSIBLE, HER breath slamming in and out of her lungs in perfect rhythm with the pulsing beat of the music playing overhead. She was trying not to break down before things even got started, but her nerves were getting the better of her.

She continued to remind herself that this was Xander, a man she trusted with her life. There was no fear of him hurting her physically; she knew that. It wasn't what she was worried about.

The problem she had was letting go. Handing him the reins, letting him control her pleasure.

Last night had been different. It hadn't been intentional.

The scene they'd done together had been mutual. She had been playing a part. That was a far cry from what she was doing now because *playing* the part of his submissive and *being* his submissive were on opposite ends of the spectrum.

She didn't want to disappoint him. Yet she already had.

Mercedes didn't flinch, did her best not to react at all as Xander's hand trailed over her skin once again. He worked his way over her butt, caressing her thigh with his warm hands. She knew what he was doing, but she tried not to think about it.

While he worked the buckles that would hook around her thighs, expertly restraining her to the bench, she remembered the way he'd tensed a moment ago. She had nearly called him Master, but for some reason, at the last minute, she'd opted to go with the more impersonal Sir.

It had been a cheap shot; she knew that much. One that she would've noticed as a Domme, as well. For his sub to refer to him as Master X, or simply Master, was one of the highest honors he could receive as a Dom. At least according to Xander.

It meant acceptance.

She'd purposely changed her tactic although she had wanted to call him Master, for reasons she couldn't even fathom at this point. And he had obviously noticed, just as she'd expected.

Xander worked the buckles on her forearms, and she kept her head down, her eyes on the concrete floor beneath her. She wouldn't be able to look at him. Not at this point.

Shit, she was doing well just to breathe.

An overwhelming mix of emotions was stirring inside of her. Defiance, panic, anger, submission. The least of which was the latter, but she was trying.

The hardest part was the fact that she wanted Xander to touch her. She wanted to touch him. Up to that point, she hadn't had the pleasure of putting her hands on him, unless stroking him through his slacks earlier that morning counted. Since she hadn't had the pleasure of touching him skin to skin, she didn't consider it. And just the thought of exploring him inch by inch was driving her crazy.

Once he had her properly restrained, Xander's hands caressed her bottom again, and she fought the urge to groan. God, his touch was exquisite. The way his big hands formed to her body perfectly, it was as though he was built specifically to touch her.

"Lovely." Xander's word caressed her skin as smoothly as his hands, causing Mercedes to suck in a breath.

The more she thought about it, the more she realized she could handle whatever pain he dished out, whatever punishment he felt she deserved. But it was his reverent tone, the way he seemingly admired her that was breaking down her resistance.

The worst part about it: Mercedes didn't associate approval with submission.

Which was a new lesson for her as a Domme. She gave her approval when it was earned, lavished her subs with kind words when they did what she expected them to do, but never once had she put herself in their shoes. To hear it, the tone of Xander's voice ringing with the honesty of his words, caused her chest to swell with an emotion she wasn't sure she was ready to feel.

She'd always associated submission with the inability to be in control. Her subs wanted her to take all control from them. Some let her do it easily; others were resistant. But all in all, they needed that from her.

For her, losing that control wasn't an option. It meant someone else could overpower her, rob her of her strength, shatter her self-confidence.

Even though she could look at submission from a clinical perspective, through the eyes of a Domme, she still resisted the idea of letting someone have so much power over her.

Mercedes stopped thinking when Xander slid her panties down over her hips, leaving them to rest around her thighs. She'd already been exposed; the G-string he'd provided for her to wear had done little to cover her. But this was about making her feel vulnerable and being on display for him. Her panties provided a constant reminder of that fact. She was sure that was his intention.

"Are you wet, pet?" he asked, his fingers slipping down the crack of her ass.

She didn't answer him. She couldn't.

"Shit!" Mercedes screamed when Xander's hand landed firmly on her ass, the heat from the contact blooming instantly.

"Answer me," Xander boomed, his voice echoing in the small, enclosed space, jerking her to attention.

He sounded … angry.

She saw him move into her field of vision, felt his hands as they fisted into her hair as he lifted her head. The next thing she knew, she was looking at him. There was no anger in his beautiful green eyes, only dominance.

"Answer me when I speak to you. Do you understand me?"

"Yes, Sir," she whispered, keeping her eyes locked with his.

"If you want this to end, you know what you have to say. I'll let you go, and we'll move on with our lives. But in the meantime, you will not top from the bottom, do you understand?"

Top from the bottom?

Oh, God. Was that what she was doing?

Crap.

Now that she thought about it, yes, that's exactly what she was doing. She was holding out on them both in her attempt to keep control. Not only was she denying herself pleasure, she was also denying him his. And that was unacceptable. Even to her.

"Yes, Sir. I understand, Sir," she said in a rush.

"Good." He leaned in and pressed his lips to hers in a kiss so gentle, so sweet, she felt it to her toes.

That's exactly when she knew…

If she wanted to please him, which she did, she was going to have to do what was necessary.

Mercedes was going to have to submit.

CHAPTER EIGHTEEN

XANDER PEERED INTO MERCEDES'S EYES AFTER HE kissed her, willing her to feel what he was feeling. To know what he wanted from her.

That's when he saw it.

But before he could swallow the lump that had formed in his throat from her nonverbal acceptance, she had him dangerously close to going to his knees with what she said next.

"I'm ready, Sir. I'm at your complete mercy, Master."

Xander's heart thumped painfully hard against his ribs as he continued to stare into her eyes, wanting nothing more than to believe what she was telling him.

She'd called him Master.

"Thank you, pet," he whispered back, releasing her hair. He was surprised his voice worked at all.

Mercedes continued to hold her head up briefly before she breathed in deep, her back rising and falling from the effort. And then she rested her forehead again, and he knew it was time to begin.

No holds barred.

Admittedly, he'd been holding back.

Now wasn't the time to hold back on her. She deserved his full attention.

Xander removed his suit jacket, laying it over the chair in the corner. He then went to work on his shirt, removing the diamond cuff links and tucking them into his pocket before rolling up his sleeves.

After dimming the lights, he reached for the toy bag that he'd had Carson bring in a while ago and retrieved the items he'd brought especially for tonight. Especially for Mercedes.

Ensuring he was just out of her visual range, Xander opened the packages, not attempting to be quiet about it, either. He wanted her to be curious, but he wasn't willing to divulge his secrets just yet.

It wasn't just about the spanking he was going to deliver tonight. In fact, he'd be using his hand for that, just because he enjoyed the feel of her ass beneath his palm. The other toys ... well, those were solely for her pleasure.

Once he had the plastic removed from the first toy, he snatched up the lube, and then he crossed the room, taking his place once again behind her. Unable to resist the temptation to touch her, he leaned down and pressed his lips to the center of her back, trailing his tongue along her spine, stopping at the crease of her ass.

Her soft inhale reassured him. She was with him, just like she'd said she was.

Setting the pump-action bottle of lube on the floor beside him, Xander made sure she'd be able to see it. But he kept the other item discreetly hidden in his hand.

He placed open-mouthed kisses over her ass, along her right cheek, then the left, teasing the cleft between them with the tip of his finger as he went along until he was separating her cheeks completely, sliding his tongue slowly downward, over her asshole, and ending at the slick entrance to her pussy. Delving deep into her cunt, he teased her relentlessly until she was bucking against his mouth.

"Fuck," he growled from behind her. "You taste so good."

That elicited a moan from her, and Xander felt his body morphing rapidly into his role. She'd shaken him up both with her refusal to call him Master and then when she'd seemingly submitted — all in. And now, he wanted nothing more than to hear her scream his name.

Squatting down on his haunches, he retrieved the lube and pumped a generous amount over her asshole, then rubbing the small end of the toy through the slickness until it was thoroughly coated. She was squirming beautifully.

Fuck.

He had to wonder just what the fuck he'd been thinking. If she thought she was being disciplined, then she had absolutely no idea the physical pain he was in. His cock was like a steel rod. He could hardly think for wanting to slam into her, to sink into her depths while her pussy clamped around him.

Focus.

"Do you know what I'm going to do to you, pet?" he asked as he continued to tease her puckered hole with the blunt end of the toy.

"No, Master."

"Do you want to know?" he questioned.

"If that is what you want, Master."

Perfect answer.

"You've got such a pretty ass, pet," he told her as he squeezed her right cheek with his hand, using his left to continue teasing her. "I look forward to taking you here later," he added, pressing the toy more firmly against her asshole.

Mercedes groaned, her hips pushing back slightly against his hands. She liked that idea. And didn't that just make his dick all the more excited.

"You'd like that, wouldn't you? To feel my cock slide in your ass? To feel me deep?"

"Yes," she breathed out roughly, "Sir."

"Has anyone taken you here before?" he asked, almost as an afterthought, his hand stilling. It was something in the way she'd said "yes, Sir" that had tripped him up.

"No, Sir."

Fucking hell.

Xander stared down at the toy in his hand. She'd never... Shit. That was the last answer he would've expected from her, and yet he had no clue as to why. Just because she enjoyed playing at the club didn't necessarily mean... Shit. He couldn't even gather his thoughts.

"Please, Master," Mercedes whispered, and he knew she was encouraging him. She would've picked up on his pause.

"Thank you, pet," he told her, letting her know how much this meant to him.

Xander retrieved a latex glove and slipped it on his hand. Once he was ready, he slid one finger into her, the tight ring of muscle gripping him. "Relax, pet. I'm going to fuck you with my fingers first. Then I'm going to put in a plug. There's no way you can handle me like this."

"Yes, Sir," she moaned, her hips thrusting back hard as she tried to force his finger deeper. She was limited by the restraints and tempting him more than he had anticipated.

Pushing back to his feet, Xander thrust one finger into her ass, working her slowly before inserting two. He took his time, building her up, driving her crazy before he began scissoring his finger and finally pulling out. Without giving her time to think about it, he began slowly pushing the small blue plug into her ass, letting her acclimate to the size until it was fully seated inside of her.

"I love the way that looks," he told her as he ripped the plastic glove off of his hand and tossed it into a nearby waste receptacle before gliding his hands over her smooth, warm skin. "Are you ready for me to continue?"

"Yes, Master," she moaned, her head still down, her hands fisted. He could see her thighs straining as she knelt on the bench.

When she began to relax, he retrieved the other toy he'd purchased for this particular occasion and took his position behind her once more.

Glancing up, he noticed they had developed a rather large audience. Several people he recognized were watching, including Luke and Sierra, Logan and Samantha. And even Trent Ramsey had stopped by for the show. They had an unobstructed view of the plug in her ass as well as the slick juices coating her pussy.

"You've drawn quite a crowd, pet. I think they're enjoying seeing your ass and pussy displayed for them. But I bet they're waiting for me to make your pretty ass blush. What do you think?"

"Yes, Sir," she groaned. This time there was more tension than pleasure in her tone.

"Good. Then it's time to get down to business."

MERCEDES TRIED TO RELAX. SHE TRIED TO focus on her breathing now that the discomfort in her ass had subsided. She knew Xander had a thing for anal sex, she'd seen him in action at the club, but for some reason, she hadn't expected him to move in that direction quite so fast.

She'd been wrong.

The plug felt as though it were massive, but she imagined it was one of the small ones, possibly medium. Not that it really mattered, because it was still not the most pleasant feeling. Considering she wasn't used to anything more than a narrow vibrator that she would use on herself from time to time, this felt like someone had driven their fist inside of her ass.

She heard the sound of plastic again, and her mind went into overdrive, trying to figure out just what he was going to do now. She already had a plug in her ass and clamps on her nipples. Surely he wasn't going to use anything else.

Leaving her in suspense, Xander once again placed his hands on her ass, kneading the muscles gently. He was standing between her spread knees, and she could feel the soft material of his slacks against the insides of her calves. She tried to focus on how warm his hands were, how silky that material felt against her legs, but the tension was already beginning to build while she waited for him to do something.

Anything.

Shit.

She really didn't care.

She was right at the breaking point, having to bite her tongue to keep from crying out for him to put her out of her misery, when his hand came down on her ass. She did cry out, but there were no words as the pain ricocheted through her.

"Do you like being spanked?" Xander asked her, his tone deeper than she'd expected. It took everything in her power to answer him.

"No, Sir," she said truthfully.

"Then why do you insist on disobeying?"

God, could she really answer that? "I don't know."

His hand came down on her other cheek, and as she jerked in response, she thought she felt the bench move beneath her.

"Not good enough," he told her. "Now answer my question. Honestly."

"Because I want to, Sir," she told him, bracing for the impact.

Instead, his hand caressed what she could imagine was a bright red imprint on her sore butt.

There was only silence, which was off-putting in itself until she heard a small noise. It sounded like a vibration. And that's when she felt it, her insides beginning to tingle from...

The plug in her ass was vibrating, and her clit began to pulse strangely from the sensation. She wanted to clamp her legs together to add a little pressure, hoping to intensify the stimulation that wasn't enough to send her over the edge, but her restraints kept her from doing so.

"Very nice," he said with such approval Mercedes closed her eyes. "Now tell me how many swats you think you've earned tonight, pet."

How many?

Crap.

She was going to have to think about that one for a minute. That was a question she was used to asking of her own subs. A too-low number would have Xander tacking on more; a too-high number would have her asking for something she didn't necessarily want.

"You think on that for a minute," he told her as she heard him shuffle behind her. "Let me know when you have a number."

Mercedes wondered what the hell he was going to do and why he insisted on making her crazy. That's when warm, moist air blew across her clit, and she knew what he was about to do.

His tongue slid against her, and she cried out. "Oh, God, yes."

It felt too good. Between the vibrations in her ass that had subsided to a more tolerable level, the only thing she could focus on was his tongue on her clit. More than anything, she wanted him to fuck her. She'd been riding a fine edge all day, ever since earlier in the afternoon when he'd made her come with his mouth.

Holy shit. Had that really been today?

She felt as though he'd been tormenting her for days, not just mere hours. Heaven help her if he did decide to hold out, because she wasn't sure she'd be able to survive not feeling him inside of her soon.

He doubled his efforts with his tongue, and then the vibration in her ass intensified, making her shriek from the pleasure that coursed through her.

"Did you come up with a number?" he asked, his voice moving with him.

He must've stood back up because his tongue was no longer teasing her, but he had replaced it with… Oh, shit. She could tell it wasn't his finger. It was too big. Way too big.

Remembering he'd just asked a question, Mercedes managed to respond. "Yes, Sir. I've come up with a number." Never mind the fact that that was a lie. But it would buy her a few seconds, at least.

The vibrations in her ass increased, making her legs tremble as he pushed something deep inside of her pussy. Now she was full. So freaking full, and it was... Oh, God. It was amazing. If only he would add some friction, pull out and thrust the toy inside of her again because she was suddenly on the verge of begging to come.

"How many, pet?"

"Seven," she said, not really thinking about the number, just shouting out the first thing that came to mind.

His gruff chuckle had the fine hairs on her arms standing up. Oh, God. Not enough, obviously.

"Did you pick seven because it's your lucky number? Or because you really believe you only deserve seven?"

Leave it to Xander to want to clarify everything.

Damn Dom.

He knew her all too well. "It's my lucky number, Sir."

The vibrator seemed to settle deeper inside of her, but he didn't pull it out, much to her dismay.

"Do you need to be fucked?" he asked her, surprising her with the change of subject.

"Yes, Sir." That was an easy question to answer.

"How badly?"

"Very badly, Sir."

God, she sounded like such a ... submissive. But right at that moment, it seemed right. She wasn't questioning her reaction to him. The fact that she was letting him tease her beyond mercy or knowing that there were probably a group of people getting off on her public humiliation made it hotter.

The humiliation she was actually enjoying tremendously.

The fact that Xander seemed only focused on her was enough to allow her to give in to him.

For a brief second, the vibrations in her ass stopped completely, but she still felt the fullness from what she assumed was another vibrator in her pussy.

Doing her best to focus on her breathing, she wanted to try and gain some semblance of control before he...

"Oh, God!" she groaned as the vibrations started up again, this time in her ass, her pussy, and against her clit.

"Come for me, pet."

Coming on command had never been something she could even fathom doing, but the stimulation was such that she had no hope of staving off the orgasm that grew stronger and stronger until…

"Fuck yes!" she screamed as she came, thankful she was tied down, because she was pretty sure she'd have been a puddle on the floor otherwise.

CHAPTER NINETEEN

XANDER WASN'T SURE HE'D EVER BEEN MORE impatient in his entire life. And he'd been wearing thin for longer than just the drive home from Devotion.

After delivering the fourteen licks that he'd determined — because, seriously, seven wasn't even remotely close to enough — to Mercedes's beautiful backside, he'd made her come at least three more times in the process, but it wasn't until the final orgasm that he'd known he might not be able to make it all the way home before he had her.

It'd taken several minutes to rouse Mercedes after her last powerful orgasm, but once he did, he had quickly bundled her into his coat and then led her right out of the building, without saying a single good-bye.

At that moment, nothing had mattered except getting her home and spending the rest of the night buried deep inside of her. While he had helped Mercedes into the limo, Carson had gone back inside to retrieve her discarded clothing and returned promptly.

Although Xander would've been content to look at her wearing his coat and little else, she'd insisted on getting dressed in the car. Back into the stunning turquoise dress.

Sitting by and watching her had been a bonus. The woman was so graceful, even when she was maneuvering into her clothing in a moving car with limited space.

As the car came to a final halt, Xander let out a long exhale.

About damn time.

Carson pulled the limo up in front of their complex, and Xander didn't waste any time before climbing out. Once again wearing the sexy dress, Mercedes insisted on walking, although he would've preferred to carry her. Instead of arguing, because it wasn't going to do him much good, he just took her hand and remained silent until they reached the front door of his condo.

Once inside, though, Xander purposely ignored the fact that she had wanted to walk on her own, and he lifted her into his arms, paying absolutely no attention to her immediate rebuttal.

"Hush," he ordered. "Keep in mind, you've probably earned a few more licks tonight. Enough to keep me busy for a while."

Mercedes instantly quieted.

"Does it seem like this day will never end?" she asked as she wrapped her arms around his neck, resting her head against his shoulder.

Xander made his way up the stairs and to his bedroom without saying a word. If she thought the day had been interminably long, she had no idea how he felt right at that moment. Rather than deposit her on the bed like he would've preferred, he took her into the master bathroom.

"If you tell me we're going to shower, I'm going to tell you how much I really like you," she mumbled drowsily.

"Well, get prepared to like me," he advised her as he set her on her feet in front of the long vanity.

After turning on the water, he waited for it to warm while he easily undressed Mercedes. Once she was naked, he took his time removing the clamps from her breasts.

"Oh, fuck," she groaned when he released the first clamp, using his hands to stimulate the soft, warm globe while the blood rushed back to her nipple. When he reached for the other clamp, Mercedes gripped his wrist.

"I've got to take it off," he informed her.

"I know. Just … give me a minute," she said, her breath rushing in and out.

When she finally relaxed, nodding her head at him, Xander reached up and removed the other clamp. Placing his hand over her breast, he squeezed as he leaned down and pressed his mouth to hers. Kissing her was like heaven and hell mixed together. She was so sweet, so damn responsive, but the way she kissed him back made his dick ache all the more. He needed her. But they still needed to get the shower out of the way.

Once the steam began to fill the bathroom, Xander urgently removed his clothes, wrapped Mercedes in his arms, and led her into the glass enclosure.

"Oh, God, the water feels good," she said as the warmth cascaded over them.

"You feel even better," he told her, placing a kiss on the top of her head. "But don't think I'm through with you yet, pet."

In fact, he was just getting started.

"Haven't you had enough?"

Had enough? Was she kidding? He hadn't had anything yet, except for hours and hours of self-imposed torture. At this rate, his balls should've been glowing a nice neon blue. He was scared to look down for fear they would be.

Instead, he chuckled, amused by her obvious exhaustion. He'd fucked her with a dildo, and she'd clearly forgotten that he had yet to come once since they'd agreed to this just that morning.

He was looking to change that in the very near future.

Xander pulled away from her, looking down into her eyes as he cupped her face in his hands. "Not nearly enough."

There was the hint of a smile on her lips that made everything seem to right itself. Like all of the events of the last few hours wouldn't have to be categorized as one big failure, because if her smile was anything to go by, he'd at least done something right.

What, he didn't know.

"As much as I'd love to linger in here," Mercedes said drowsily, "I'd much prefer a nice soft bed."

Xander wouldn't argue because he felt the same way. "As soon as I shave you, we'll make our way to the bed."

The drowsy smile on Mercedes's face flashed to something akin to surprise. Ahh, so she'd thought he was joking about that, had she?

"Turn around," he instructed, reaching for the bottle of shampoo that hadn't been in his shower that morning. It must've belonged to Mercedes and had been delivered as expected by his housekeeper, Janelle, while they'd been out.

Reaching for the detachable shower head, Xander wet the long, silky strands of Mercedes's hair before applying a generous amount of shampoo. The scent that filled his shower was unmistakably hers. He didn't pretend to know much about flowers, but he could distinctly discern the scent of lavender that drifted on the humid air around them.

After washing her hair, he used the conditioner, as well, and then proceeded to soap her body, taking the time to observe the creamy, smooth skin of her ass, ensuring there weren't any marks. Once he was satisfied, he turned his attention between her legs. When she began to moan softly while he soaped her up, he smiled. She was right back to where he wanted her. Aroused.

When he was satisfied with how clean she was, Xander took a step back before snatching his own body wash from the shelf. He lathered himself, going as slowly as he could manage while Mercedes watched him — or more accurately, watched his hands as he thoroughly soaped his rigid erection. He lingered on his cock longer than necessary, but the way her eyes glazed over was almost enough to send him into orbit. He was that fucking close.

He had to stop her when she reached for him.

"Not yet, pet. You'll get your turn in a minute." If he let her touch him now, he'd come in her hand, and when he came, he fully intended to be inside of her. Fuck, he hoped he lasted even that long.

"Lean back against the wall and put your right foot on the ledge," he told her as he reached for the pink can of shaving cream sitting near the shampoo.

"Have you ever done this before?" she asked him, sounding worried.

"Do you really want me to answer that?" he asked sternly. He wasn't interested in going into detail about his past experiences, but yes, he'd certainly been in this position more than once.

"No, I don't," she finally said with a small smile.

"Trust me, pet."

Xander filled his hand with shaving cream and lathered her mound before dropping to his knees in front of her. The hard tile of the floor would've bothered him if he hadn't been distracted by the pretty picture she made standing above him, her cunt open for his perusal.

Not wanting to draw out the process for longer than necessary, Xander didn't tease her much as he focused on the razor in his hand. Instead, he worked diligently, reapplying shaving cream when necessary, rinsing thoroughly, until she was completely bare.

That was when he knew he'd reached his tipping point.

MERCEDES WOULD ADMIT TO HER FEAR. WELL, not out loud, but she'd definitely admit her nerves were at war inside of her. And it had nothing to do with Xander wielding a razor between her legs.

In fact, that had been quite an experience. The man was precise about everything he did, and shaving was something he was especially good at.

What he was also good at was driving her crazy.

For the last half hour, she'd stood in the shower with him, only briefly able to touch his stellar body. Now, as he led her across the bedroom, going directly for the bed, she prayed they would not pass go or collect anything on their way.

She was tired of waiting.

Touching him was something she ached to do, and after all of the amazing things he'd done to her body since noon that day, she wasn't sure she could wait much longer.

"Please tell me it's my turn," she whispered, trying to keep her request as unintimidating as possible. She truly wasn't trying to top him. At the moment, domination and submission weren't even on her radar.

She just wanted to freaking touch him.

Xander turned to face her, the backs of his knees against the mattress. When he pulled her against him, his big, warm body lining up with hers, she sucked in a breath.

The man was perfection. All sleek, formidable muscle, long and corded beautifully.

And his cock.

Sweet mercy. He was big. Huge.

Not that he looked impressively large against his way-bigger-than-average frame, but Mercedes could feel the heavy weight of his cock against her belly, and she knew he was well above average.

Right now, she wanted to measure him. With her mouth.

"Do you think you've earned a turn?" he asked, that wicked gleam in his brilliant green eyes.

"No," she said truthfully. As far as a submissive went, she'd failed miserably for most of the day. And up until their scene at Devotion, she truly hadn't put forth much effort. Not until she'd realized exactly what she was holding out on.

Knowing how much pleasure she could offer Xander by giving him her submission, she'd finally relented. And holy freaking Toledo, had it been worth it.

"Good answer," he said as he cupped her chin. "Thank you for being honest."

"Always," she told him, meaning it.

Mercedes saw an unfamiliar emotion pass in his eyes, and she tried to pinpoint what it might be, but before she could get that far, Xander was pulling her down onto him.

"I want to feel your hands on me," he whispered gruffly. "I've waited a long time for this, Mercedes."

He'd said her name. Not pet. Not M, his nickname for her. He'd said her name.

"I have, too," she told him truthfully. She had. Definitely all day and probably even longer than that if she had to guess. Even if she hadn't realized it, Mercedes had been secretly wanting this. Perhaps for a really long time; she wasn't sure. But right now, she didn't want to think about any of that.

Now that she was lying on top of him, she had a little control on her side. But she held back, letting him take the reins. When he pulled her head down so that their mouths met, she held back longer than she'd thought possible.

And that's when everything went out the window.

It was no longer Dom versus sub. This was all about two people, a man and a woman who wanted one another with a desperation that threatened to suck the oxygen out of the room.

The kiss lingered for long minutes, but the hunger intensified. They were a jumble of hands and lips and tongues as they reached and searched and stroked. Mercedes felt his smooth, warm skin beneath her fingertips, the crisp hairs of his legs against her shins, the heavy stalk of flesh against the apex of her thighs as Xander ground his hips against hers.

Oh, how she wanted this man. She could get lost in him for hours, and she fully intended to.

Pulling her mouth from his, she fought for air as she ran her lips down his neck, over his collarbone. She didn't try to pull away when he repositioned himself so that he was fully on the bed, ending with her straddling his legs as she caressed the hard angles of his chest.

She made her way to his nipples, using her tongue and teeth to twist and pull the titanium bars that ran through his nipples. God, that was so fucking sexy. She'd never been with a man who had his nipples pierced, but fuck, it was hot. And she learned that the more she tugged, the more he moaned his pleasure.

"Does that hurt?" she asked curiously, not stopping in her pursuit to torment him the way he'd done to her all day long.

"Just a little," he said on a groan. "In a very good way."

So, it was true, Xander enjoyed that small bite of pain — just like she'd learned that she did.

"God, yes," he groaned, palming the back of her head and holding her to him as she teased his nipple relentlessly.

He only released her enough so that she could move to the other side, savoring the feel of his smooth skin against her lips, the cool metal against her tongue as she continued to nip and pull — harder this time — until he was bucking up against her.

Fearing he was going to rush this before she was ready, although she wouldn't have complained if he'd driven his cock inside of her right then, Mercedes made a wet path with her mouth down the center of his abs, lingering long enough to outline each gentle ripple of muscle with her tongue. Moving lower, she trailed the sexy muscles that formed a V, moving back up slowly, first one side, back down. Then the other.

She briefly stopped on the tattoo on his left side. There, perfectly aligned just beneath the line of his V, was the word *Trust* in plain black bold letters. Seeing it made her heart pound wildly.

Mercedes knew all about the tattoo. She knew the meaning because she'd heard people talk about it at Kink. It was Xander's motto: Without trust, what was there? According to him, when he finally trusted someone implicitly, and they trusted him in return, he would know that was the woman he'd spend the rest of his life with.

At least that's what she'd heard.

Looking up at him, Mercedes saw that he was watching her intently. Her breath lodged in her throat as she realized just what they were doing here. Was this the trust he was looking for?

She tried not to read too much into it, choosing to pretend she wasn't thinking about the fact that they were about to take this to the next level.

With his head propped on a pillow, he had his hands now casually behind his head as though he'd be able to resist what she was about to do to him.

She smiled.

He smiled back.

Without asking, she leaned down and sucked him into her mouth. It took some work, but she managed to take him almost all the way to the root, the thick shaft filling her mouth completely until her gag reflex kicked in. Only then did she pull back, laving the silky smooth length of him with her tongue.

"Fucking shit," Xander groaned, his hips thrusting up, the impact of his large body jarring her, but she didn't release him. "Mercedes, baby, I... Oh, fuck yes."

Not wanting him to stop her, she began sucking him, taking him deep while she wrapped her hand around the base of his cock, squeezing firmly, unwilling to let him come. Not that she expected him to. This was Xander. He had more self-control than anyone she knew.

"Mmm," he groaned as his hand once again resumed its position in her hair. He didn't use force, just a gentle pressure as she sucked and stroked, doing her best to go slow, but loving the intensifying sounds of his pleasure.

"Come here," he groaned loudly, and the next thing she knew, Mercedes was turned around, straddling his head.

Without questioning him, she continued to focus on sucking him, fearful that he would distract her to the point she wouldn't be able to pleasure him the way she wanted.

It didn't take but a second for that to happen, and Mercedes found herself grinding against his mouth, desperately riding his face as he tormented her clit with his wickedly talented tongue.

"Oh," she said, wrapping her lips around his cock to keep from crying out. She did her absolute best to focus on him, to ignore the absurdly amazing feeling of his lips on her, his tongue thrusting into her.

As much as she wanted to maintain control of the situation, it was only a matter of seconds before she lost.

A violent, amazing, wonderful orgasm ripped through her, shattering her into a million tiny fragments as her body locked up, and she totally forgot what she'd been doing.

CHAPTER TWENTY

HE WOULD ADMIT IT HAD BEEN A power play. One designed to keep him from coming deep in her throat, because the way Mercedes was mastering his cock with her mouth had been unlike anything he'd ever felt before.

Rather than give in too soon, he'd redirected his attention to eating her pussy until she came.

And now she was resting against him, allowing him a moment to catch his breath and pull himself together. But he didn't wait long.

Carefully, he rolled her off of him and then repositioned them both until he was kneeling between her thighs, his elbows resting beside her head, his cock tucked against the warm, wet heat of her pussy. He fought the urge to sink into her.

Barely.

"Hi," she whispered long seconds later.

"Hey," he said with an answering smile, but the smile gently faded, and another emotion bubbled up inside of him. "I need to be inside of you," he told her.

It was more of a warning. Or rather, a request of sorts. He didn't intend to use a condom, and although they'd had the conversation earlier that day, he wanted to make sure she was still on board with the idea.

He'd had an emotional moment when he'd noticed Mercedes studying the tattoo on his side. He'd had the word *Trust* etched into his skin years ago, a daily reminder of what he was searching for. When he'd witnessed her looking at it, then up at him, he'd known that she understood.

She was *the* woman. She was the one he trusted. The woman he wanted to spend the rest of his life with. He had known it for years and years, even if she hadn't realized it. But he hadn't said anything to her minutes ago because he feared he would freak her out. That and he had hardly been able to swallow past the lump that had formed in his throat.

Mercedes reached her hand between them, gripping his cock, and he groaned. "I need you, too," she whispered back, the raspy inflection of her voice making his blood boil.

"Just like this," he said, making sure she understood.

She didn't hesitate, just shifted so that he was aligned with her slick entrance.

"Yes," she said, leaning up and pressing her lips to his, "Just like this."

Oh, damn.

Xander's muscles tensed as soon as the head of his cock breached the scalding entrance to her pussy. He had a long way to go, and for the first time in a very, very long time, he had to pray he wasn't about to do what every man feared — come prematurely.

But she felt so … fucking perfect. That was the only way to explain it. Mercedes was perfect. Every inch of her skin was molded to him, her leg was now wrapped around his hip, her ankle pressing into his ass as she encouraged him to go deeper.

"I'm taking my time," he warned her.

"Don't bother," she urged with a grin. "I'll be right there with you. And then, after we've slept for a few hours, I'll wake you while I ride you."

Lord have mercy.

Xander's hips took on a life of their own, and he thrust forward, his cock tunneling deeper as Mercedes cried out beneath him.

He immediately stilled.

"Don't stop," she pleaded. "Please don't stop."

Her ankle pressed harder against his ass, and Xander couldn't resist sliding even deeper. Wanting to find the position that would send her over as fast as he feared he would be going, he pushed himself up onto his knees and gripped her ankles, holding her legs straight up. With her hips elevated off of the bed slightly, the backs of her knees against his ribs, and her ankles near his head, he began shallowly thrusting into her, never retreating fully until he was rocking faster, the sweet grip of her cunt on his cock making his head spin.

"Harder," Mercedes pleaded, her hands clasping onto his thighs as she tried to pull herself toward him. "Deeper."

Unable to speak because he was overwhelmed by more than just physical sensation, Xander kept his eyes locked with hers as he began to increase his pace. It wasn't until he had her practically bent in half, her legs now over her shoulders, and was pounding hard and deep into her that she began chanting his name over and over. Just the sound of her voice and his name on her lips had him nearing closer to the release he was beginning to crave like a drug.

"Fuck, baby," he growled. "Your pussy's so damn tight. So fucking perfect." He continued to ramble, not quite sure what he was saying, but as that telltale tingle started in the base of his spine, he couldn't stop himself.

"Xander! Oh, yes! Xander, I'm coming!"

And that's all it took for him to lose it. He came hard and fast, and the only thing that kept him upright was the fear of crushing her. He wasn't sure how many minutes passed before he had control over his body once again, but by then, he knew it was too late.

What had just happened between them, what could be easily classified as an earth-moving experience, had likely just sealed his fate.

Pulling out of Mercedes, he immediately missed the silky warmth of her body surrounding him. But he managed to force himself to his feet and over to the bathroom. He took care of business and then returned with a warm washcloth. Attempting not to wake her, Xander cleaned between her legs before making the trek once more to toss the cloth into the hamper.

He crawled back into bed, pulling her as close as he could and practically wrapping himself around her. It was then, as his mind began to drift into sleep, that he knew without a doubt that he'd never be able to willingly let her go.

MERCEDES DIDN'T KNOW WHAT TIME IT WAS when she came awake suddenly. It didn't take her long to acclimate to where she was. She heard Xander's heavy breathing, the heat of his body surrounding her, the safety of his arms immediately bringing her out of her dream.

As she lay there, she tried to ignore the dream, tried to ignore everything except for the man spooning behind her.

For the first time in a very long time, Mercedes didn't want to flee the bed when a lover was there. Not that she'd taken a lover in a really long time, but even though her memories of all the others were blurry, she knew without a doubt that this was different.

How, she wasn't sure.

Aside from the fact that she still feared she couldn't be what Xander needed — a submissive — there was a shameless hope that maybe, just maybe, they stood a chance together.

Not that she was thinking about forever.

Definitely not.

Okay, maybe a little.

Wait.

Forcing her eyes open, Mercedes glanced out at the Dallas skyline brilliantly lit against the inky night sky. The view, even from his bed, was incredible. She didn't have exactly the same view as he did, and as she lay there, trying to be quiet and listening to him breathe, she tried not to think about how much she never wanted to leave this place.

She wasn't talking about his condo or even his bed. No, Mercedes was talking about his arms.

Never in her life had she felt for someone what she was beginning to feel for Xander. Okay, so maybe it was because they were friends. Great friends. Longtime friends. She had never been in a relationship that had such a strong foundation as this one.

Not that this was a relationship.

Hating where her mind was drifting to, but not willing to let go of the security of Xander's arms around her, Mercedes decided to listen to her body rather than her heart.

Rolling onto her back and then over to her side so that she was facing Xander, she discreetly — or what she hoped was discreetly — wrapped her leg over his hip, gently urging him to roll over, too.

He did.

He didn't say anything, either, but his breathing had quieted, so she figured he must be awake.

Fine, she'd do this his way.

Rather than jump on him immediately, which she had to admit was a damn fine plan, Mercedes began stroking him slowly until his cock was thick and hard, pulsing against her palm. Then and only then did she climb over him, slowly lowering herself onto him until she was completely impaled by his impressive erection.

Before she could move, Xander's hands slid up to her hips. He didn't rush her, and he didn't open his eyes, either. Instead, he just pulled her down onto him, her breasts crushed against his chest while he filled her completely.

Their mouths met; their tongues began a lazy slide back and forth, back and forth as he began to pump his hips, driving himself deep inside of her.

And in her mind, that moment would go down as the first time she had truly made love.

Never once did Xander rush; never once did he break the kiss, either. The friction intensified, but his pace never did. Slow and steady, until Mercedes could take no more. Her body began to tingle, that gentle pulse that started between her legs and radiated outward, through her core, her arms, her legs, her fingers and toes.

She was fully engulfed by the man, and the orgasm that rippled through her wasn't earth-shattering like before, but it was, without a doubt, the most amazing orgasm she'd ever had. It consumed her entire body. And Xander, being the Dom that he was, had controlled every movement, every single satisfying movement.

And only when she settled did he increase the pace, pumping his hips faster until another orgasm was building, faster, hotter, this one like a tsunami rather than the gentle rolling waves of the first. It was then, as he claimed her body, sent her soaring one more time, that he came hard and fast inside of her.

It wasn't long before Mercedes gave herself over to sleep, knowing that this man had forever changed her.

But in ways he probably hadn't expected.

CHAPTER TWENTY-ONE

Day one, officially...
Thursday

THE FOLLOWING MORNING, XANDER FOUND HIMSELF IN his office, a cup of coffee in hand as he stared at his computer screen just as the sun was beginning to filter light through the thin layer of clouds overhead. He'd been up for at least two hours, having left Mercedes to sleep in a little longer.

He knew she was usually an early riser, but he hoped she'd stay in bed. And unless she had snuck out of his condo without him knowing — which was damn near impossible — he figured she was still asleep. Considering it was only six, he hoped that was the case.

Right on time, his phone rang, and he snatched it up, even though he knew Mercedes couldn't hear it.

"Morning," he greeted.

"Why is it you're always up so early?" his mother asked.

"Me? What about you?"

"It's not early for me."

His mother was definitely a morning person. Maybe that's where he'd gotten it from, he didn't know. But this was the same way they began pretty much every conversation they'd had for the last few months.

"How's Dad?" he asked, getting right to the point.

"He's doing better," Stella told him.

"Okay, spill it, Mom," he ordered when she hesitated.

There was a long sigh, and then his mother's voice once again filled his ear. "He's fine, really. We went to the emergency room, and they x-rayed him thoroughly. No broken bones, but he'll be sore for a few days."

"What happened?" Xander asked as he leaned back in his chair, unable to disguise the worry in his voice.

"It was silly, really. I don't think he'd want me to tell you."

Xander's mind immediately went in the wrong direction, and he sat up straight. "Okay, you know what? Never mind. Forget I asked."

Stella laughed, her soft, elegant tone drifting back. "Not that. Oh, dear."

Xander could imagine her blushing to the roots of her short, dark hair.

How had she known what he was thinking?

"But regardless," she said with another laugh. "He's fine. Just being a man, soaking up the attention for a little while."

Xander knew his father, and he understood what his mother was saying. So, maybe it was true that they both generally allowed Stella to dote on them more than necessary. Xander knew it made her feel better, which was why both he and his father had never told her that she was a little overbearing, especially when someone was hurt.

"Do I need to come up there?" he asked seriously.

"No, I don't think it's necessary. But if it'll make you feel better, we'll never tell you not to."

Xander grinned. That was his mother. That was her way of saying she wouldn't mind him visiting. It had been at least three months since he'd seen his folks. They were always travelling, and in order to make sure they didn't have to change their plans, he would make time to fly to wherever they were, allowing his mother the opportunity to give him a guided tour of whatever city they were invading at the moment.

"I think I should come visit," he told her firmly, knowing ultimately that she wouldn't put up a fight.

"Fine. If you insist."

Xander laughed out loud. "I insist, Mother."

"Good. Then that's settled. I'll let you know when we move on and where we're going. But for the next few days, I'm going to make him stay right where we are. At least until I know for sure he's not going to hurt himself again."

"Is he around?"

"Of course."

"Can I talk to him?"

There was some shuffling on the phone, and then his father's gruff tone sounded in his ear.

"What did she tell you?"

"That the two of you were hanging from the rafters and had just moved on to swinging from the ceiling fan. Something about hot monkey sex, Dad. It wasn't a good visual, and I have absolutely no interest in talking about it," Xander said deadpan.

"Oh, dear Lord," Stan Boone groaned. "Why in the world would she tell you something like that?"

Xander laughed again. "Please, Dad. Do *not* go into detail. I really don't want to know."

"Good, then I won't. When are you coming to see us?"

That was his father. Always right to the point and never ashamed to let him know that he preferred him to come visit. That sealed Xander's plans, so he answered with, "Give me a couple of days. I'll let you know when I can head out."

"What are you working on? Buying up the other half of downtown?"

"I'm trying," he chuckled as he shook his mouse to make the monitor come online.

"Seriously. Did you hear anything more on the Milton building?"

"Not yet. Mercedes is putting in an offer for me. I'm hoping we'll know something more by the end of the week."

"That's a smart move, son." Stan wasn't into real estate by trade; however, he was interested in everything that Xander did, so through the years, he'd made a point to know the ins and outs of the real estate market.

"I thought so," he answered easily.

"Are you going to X-hale tonight?"

Shit. Was it the third Thursday of the month already? Xander pulled up the calendar on his computer. Yep. It was. "Yeah, I'm going over there."

"Tell Shane hello for us," Stan told him. "One of these days, maybe we'll be back down there. You can take me again."

Xander was pretty sure he heard something in his dad's voice, something very much like longing. But he didn't question him, rather saying, "I'd like that, Dad."

Going to X-hale — the cigar bar Xander had purchased and renamed roughly four years ago — was a monthly thing, something both he and Shane looked forward to. For the year before his mother and father had headed out on the road, Xander would invite his father, as well. Not that he'd gone often, but the few times he had, Xander knew the man had enjoyed himself.

"Look, Dad. I've got a conference call in a few. Tell Mom I love her and that I'll see you both in a couple of days."

"Will do," Stan answered. "And try not to think about your mother and me on those rafters, will you?"

Xander laughed, just as his father had probably intended, as the call disconnected. Leave it to his father to try and torment him. The man was always trying to come up with something.

MERCEDES WAS DRESSED AND DOWNSTAIRS JUST IN time to see Xander walking into his kitchen. She was carrying her shoes and heading for the coffeepot, hoping she didn't look as harried as she felt.

Snatching a cup from the cabinet, she dropped her shoes on the floor and grabbed the coffeepot. God, even one cup would go a long way to improving her morning. As it was, she wasn't sure she could function without at least a little caffeine.

"I can't believe you didn't wake me up," she chastised him when he came up behind her.

"You looked so peaceful. If I had my way, you'd still be in my bed," he mumbled close to her ear, pulling her hair back from her neck and placing a kiss to the sensitive spot that made her shiver.

"I have a meeting," she told him, pulling away to glance at her cell phone. "Shit. I'm late."

"Where's your meeting?" Xander took her coffee cup from her hand and placed it on the counter before turning to the refrigerator to retrieve the creamer.

"Not far from here," she informed him. "I'm meeting a client." Fidgeting with her shoes, Mercedes finally managed to get the damn things on, and when she turned back to Xander, he was holding out her coffee mug.

Mug.

Not cup.

He'd transferred her coffee from a cup to a mug, and he was sending her on her way.

"Be careful. Call me later."

Mercedes stopped. She stared up at Xander. "You're sending me on my way, just like that?"

"Just like what?" he laughed. "You've got a job to do, M. I wouldn't dream of getting in the way of that."

Yes, she did have a job to do. But for some reason, she'd expected him to be … demanding or something. Insisting that she stay and do something. Hell, she didn't know.

He stepped close, placing his hands on her hips as he pulled her against him. "Trust me, if I could keep you tied to my bed, you'd be there right now. And I'd be buried so deep inside of you, you'd never be able to let me go."

Mercedes sucked in air. When he talked to her like that... It did strange things to her.

"Well," she said on a breath. "I better go."

"Yes, you better." Xander pressed his lips to hers. He didn't linger, didn't tease. Just quick and sweet. "By the way, it's Thursday," he told her as though she didn't already know what day it was.

"And?"

"And I'm going to X-hale tonight."

He looked disappointed, but Mercedes knew he enjoyed going to the cigar bar. It was one of the highlights of his month and had been for years. So much so that he'd acquired, redesigned, and renamed one of his own a few years back — what had previously been known as Smoke had become a much more refined establishment appropriately named X-hale. According to Shane, the name had been Xander's ego hard at work.

"Okay." At the moment, Mercedes didn't have any plans for the night, but she wasn't going to tell him that. If she did, she feared he might just change his plans for her. And that was the last thing she wanted. "I'll call you later to find out what time you'll be home."

Xander nodded, but he didn't say anything.

It was Mercedes's turn to assure him, even though every second that passed made her that much later. "I'll be here tonight. Just like I promised."

Xander's eyes softened, and she realized that was exactly what he'd been worried about.

Breaking the eye contact, she held up her coffee mug in salute. "Thanks for this. I've gotta go, but I promise, I'll call you later."

"I'm holding you to that."

Of course he was.

Several minutes later, Mercedes was walking through the parking garage. On the way down from Xander's condo, she had called her client, informing her that she was a few minutes behind. She didn't make a habit of running late for anything, and she still wasn't sure how she'd managed to be so careless that morning.

Because you slept like the dead after Xander rocked your world.

Okay, so there was that.

Once inside her Lexus SUV, Mercedes placed her coffee in the cup holder, staring down at it for a moment. Xander had prepared that for her. Just like…

No way. Do not go there.

It was a simple task, one anyone would've done. She was not going to read any more into it. Just because they'd had phenomenal, top-of-the-head-exploding sex last night did not mean they were a couple.

This was still a deal. One that would only last a few more days.

Mercedes's phone rang. Thank God.

Hitting the button on the steering wheel to activate the Bluetooth, she greeted the caller. The number that came up on the navigation screen was unfamiliar.

"Mercedes?"

"This is she," she told the female caller.

"This is Samantha McCoy."

"Hello, Samantha," she answered, trying to hide the confusion in her voice.

Oh, God.

If Sam was calling to discuss her desire to· learn about submissives, she just might run her car into a wall.

"Please call me Sam. I just wanted to call to see if you had plans tonight."

Tonight? Right. The boys — including Logan — would all be at the cigar bar. "I, uh—"

Sam interrupted. "Some of us are going to go out to a … you know … a toy shop." Sam paused, and Mercedes smiled. The woman was nervous.

She didn't encourage Sam to continue because she had no idea what the woman was requesting.

"We wanted to see if you wanted to go with us."

Wow. That was a surprise.

"An invitation to a sex shop?" Mercedes said with a laugh. "I have to admit, I don't get those types of invitations much. At least not from a woman."

Sam laughed, some of her anxiety seeming to fade away. "Yeah, well, me, either. But we figured since the boys get their night out, we'd do something that would ... benefit them, too."

Mercedes liked the idea of a girls' night out without men. She hadn't been able to spend a lot of time with Clarissa, her closest friend, because Clarissa's schedule was even more bogged down than Mercedes's. But tonight, she certainly didn't have anything to do because Xander would be gone, and she feared if she sat at home, she'd only find ways to pick apart everything that had happened over the course of the last two days.

"Sure, I'd love to go," she told Sam.

"Perfect," Sam said enthusiastically, just short of a squeal.

Mercedes listened while Sam gave her the details: time, place, what they'd be doing before in case she wanted to join them for drinks. When Sam finished with the instructions, they said their good-byes just as Mercedes was pulling into the parking lot of her destination.

A group of girls at a sex shop.

Why the hell not? It could be fun.

And it would be her chance to set the other women straight. After all, they were probably still under the impression that she was a sub.

CHAPTER TWENTY-TWO

"THAT IS NOT WHAT HAPPENED, AND YOU know it," Shane argued with a choked laugh. "She was… Shit. I don't even know what she was after. I could see it in her eyes, she wanted me laid out like a platter, and I got the feeling she wanted to feast on my blood."

Xander laughed. The stories Shane told about the subs he encountered never ceased to entertain him and the others. He was pretty sure that Trent hung on to every single word Shane spoke, like he was some sort of Dom god or something.

"Did she? Lay you out like a meal?" Tag Murphy asked from where he relaxed in one of the leather chairs, a glass of Hennessy in his hand.

"Not a chance," Shane bolstered. "I didn't run," he said, glaring at Xander before turning back to Tag, "no matter what anyone might tell you. However, I did walk fast. That woman scared the shit out of me."

A round of laughter echoed in the small area.

They'd gathered at X-hale as was their ritual on the third Thursday of every month. Xander owned the upscale cigar bar, but he didn't run it. He left that to John Rhinehart. And he didn't regret it, either.

He'd much rather enjoy his time there, not worry about whether it was being run the way it should. In turn, he paid John well to manage the place.

John was adamant that their clientele was high class, which meant their membership fees were astronomical to ensure they kept it that way. And in turn, they stayed relatively busy with the upper-crust males who sought a few hours of time to themselves. Usually during the week.

This specific night was closed to the public because Xander had reserved the place. The bar didn't hold many people, catering to a maximum of thirty at any given time. And that was if the poker room in the back was at capacity.

Tonight, they weren't playing poker. Instead, the entire group, including a new face Xander hadn't seen before, had gathered just to chat. Luke and Logan McCoy had arrived, along with Cole Ackerley, Alex McDermott, Tag Murphy, Trent Ramsey, Shane Gibson, and the newcomer, Elijah Penn.

Pretty much the same core group that gathered every month to enjoy cigars and a little top-shelf liquor. Because Xander had wanted to discuss some business, he'd informed Trent to limit his monthly guests. The man knew more people than the rest of them put together, and he was bringing someone else into the fold.

Tonight, Trent had introduced Elijah Penn, Senior Vice President of Global Sales of a company that boasted to be the industry leader in storage and server virtualization. Logan McCoy's ears had perked up at the title; that was for damn sure. Xander didn't doubt that Elijah was some bigwig at a Fortune 500 company. The people Trent knew were usually at the top of their industry, whatever that might be.

After the initial introductions were made, Xander had noticed that Logan and Elijah had sparked up a conversation. Apparently they knew of one another because of their close business ties. They'd never officially met, or so Xander had overheard. Up until Shane started telling his latest tale, the two men had been engrossed in a rather animated conversation, clearly having hit it off.

At the moment, everyone had migrated to the lounge area, filling the chairs that formed a wide circle. Luke and Cole were the only two standing, and they were propped near the wall closest to the group. There were a couple of side conversations, but for the most part, the discussion had eased back as a whole.

"So, are you a member of Devotion?" Alex McDermott asked, his question seemingly directed at Elijah. It had to be, since Alex would know that the rest of them were members, if not financial backers.

"I am," Elijah confirmed. "As of a week ago, they accepted my application, and I was able to attend opening night. I was not, however, able to make it last night," he went on to explain with the slightest hint of a British accent.

According to Trent's earlier introduction, Elijah had been in the United States for roughly two decades. At forty-two years old, Elijah Penn spent the majority of his time working, which involved a significant amount of travelling all over the world. He had enlightened them with a little of his history, also informing them that he routinely went back to visit his aging parents. He had, however, assured them that he considered Dallas his home. That had been his excuse for many of his "American-isms" anyway.

"Are you planning to attend later this week?" It was Logan's turn to ask a question, and Xander glanced over at him, then peered at Elijah for a response.

Xander wasn't privy to the applications that were submitted, but he knew if he wanted to, he could get his hands on them. Based on Logan's sudden interest in Elijah's attendance, he figured Logan was interested in getting his hands on Elijah's, as well.

"I'll be out of the country until early Sunday," Elijah informed them. "However, I hope to make it there on Monday."

Logan nodded. "I'd like to introduce you to my wife."

"I'd like that very much."

Elijah and *Samantha*? It was obvious which direction Logan was heading, but Xander tossed around the idea in his head for a moment. "Are you into threesomes?" Xander asked Elijah bluntly.

Elijah didn't seem at all put off by the question. "As a matter of fact, I am," he answered easily. "Why? Are you offering to include me?"

Xander laughed stiffly. "Not a chance." Xander had no intention of sharing Mercedes, but he knew for a fact that Logan was interested in pursuing something that might have some lasting benefits. He'd known from the beginning that suggesting Logan and Sam might find some interest in BDSM was a gamble. But it had provided him an opportunity to get cozy with Mercedes, and he'd taken it. Yes, he was a manipulative bastard when he needed to be. "But definitely good information to have."

"Are you married?" Shane asked casually.

"Thirteen years this month," Elijah confirmed.

Everyone's attention turned to him. That would've had Elijah married sometime in his late twenties if Xander's math was correct. But what Xander couldn't wrap his head around was that he was married, but he was interested in a threesome with other couples? There was no way Logan had understood Elijah's situation correctly if he wanted to introduce this guy to Sam.

"I met Beth through a business conference when I was fresh out of college. She stole my breath the moment I saw her. I pursued her for three years before I finally wore her down and convinced her to marry me," Elijah explained with a huge grin. "Of course, she wasn't the type of woman to ever jump into anything, so she insisted on a long engagement. Two years later we were married."

Everyone's attention was focused on Elijah. Xander watched him carefully. The man wasn't disguising just how much he loved his wife.

"My Beth passed away four years ago," Elijah told them when no one said a word, anguish dripping from every word. "As far as I'm concerned, we're still married. We always will be."

You could've heard a pin drop.

"I'm sorry for your loss," Cole said, taking a step closer to Luke as he did.

"Thank you. We were together for a very long time. As you can imagine, you don't get over the love of your life. And I have no intention of replacing her."

Shane nodded as though he understood. Xander didn't. Nod, that is. He had a good idea of what Elijah was saying. He wasn't sure he'd ever get over Mercedes if something were to happen to her. God willing, he would never have to.

He didn't care if they were together for five days or fifty years. The woman was seared into his soul at this point, even if she didn't know it.

But after last night...

"How's Dylan?" Luke asked, gently changing the subject and directing his question at Alex, who was standing nearby.

While the others picked up the conversation, Xander watched Elijah for a moment longer. No matter how hard he tried, he couldn't fathom what the man must've gone through or the pain he must've suffered from losing the one person who would forever hold his heart.

Xander shook off the thought and then turned his attention to the explanation Alex was giving. Dylan Thomas was doing better. Not great, but better, Alex said.

The depression he'd been living under since his wife passed away from cancer nine years ago had taken a drastic turn after his son graduated from high school last year.

From what Xander understood, Dylan felt as though he wasn't needed anymore now that his children were practically grown, despite the fact that everyone, including his children, tried to convince him otherwise.

Xander knew that people handled grief in many different ways. Such as Elijah continuing to celebrate his anniversary every year and still wearing what appeared to be his wedding band on his left hand. Or Dylan, who had never managed to find himself after spending so many years taking care of others.

"She died from cancer," Alex was saying.

"My Beth did, as well. Brain cancer. She battled for two very long years before the good Lord decided it was time."

"Dylan hasn't been able to move forward. We all understand that he'll never let her go. We don't expect him to," Alex told Elijah. "But we want him to accept that he has to keep on living. His sister, Ashleigh, my fiancé, tries to get him to talk, but he doesn't open up much."

"It's difficult to move forward. I understand where he's coming from. But, in the same regard, we each have to find something that will keep us content in the meantime," Elijah agreed.

Xander felt all eyes on him. Apparently the conversation had taken a turn they weren't all comfortable with, so they were probably looking to him to save them all.

"So, Logan," Xander began, realizing it was time to liven things up, "do you know anyone seeking a CEO position?"

And just like that, the conversation moved to business.

"OH. MY. GOD. DO PEOPLE REALLY BUY this stuff?" Ashleigh exclaimed as they perused the aisle of the sex shop that Mercedes considered the "less than desirables." The particular item Ashleigh was referring to was known as an anal toss ring. And it was exactly what you would expect it to be. An anal plug with a stem that would... Yeah. Needless to say, if you wanted to stand across the room and toss rings, you now had a target to hit.

"That's funny," McKenna said with a laugh.

Mercedes had had the pleasure of talking to McKenna in depth at the bar they'd met at an hour before. They had only been talking for five minutes when they'd hit it off.

"But I happen to like this one," McKenna told them, picking up a large box. "It's an Area 51 blow-up doll."

"A what?" Ashleigh asked incredulously.

"It's an alien blow-up doll," Samantha informed Ashleigh.

Mercedes laughed at the outrageous expression on the pregnant woman's face. She kind of found it difficult to believe that the woman wrote erotic romance and had absolutely no idea about stuff like this.

These were tame compared to some of the things Mercedes had seen, but she didn't say as much. For the time being, she was just enjoying their enthusiasm.

When she had arrived at the bar, Mercedes hadn't been sure what to expect. She'd met Sam, and she'd had a brief introduction to Sierra at the opening of Devotion, but tonight was the first time she had been introduced to McKenna and Ashleigh. Her stomach had been in a knot when she first arrived, but it hadn't taken long before they loosened her up with the banter between them. It was clear that these women were close to one another.

They'd practically absorbed Mercedes right into the fold without question.

"It has three boobs," Ashleigh told them.

"And don't forget the three love holes," McKenna added with a snicker.

"Look at this," Samantha called from a few feet away. "It's called a happy hopper."

"Oh, God. That's hilarious," Sierra said as she broke out into giggles and moved past them.

"What do you do with it?" Ashleigh asked.

"You sit on it. And … hop."

McKenna laughed outrageously as Ashleigh stared in disbelief at the giant blow-up ball that was equipped with three different-sized dildos attached to the top.

"Hey, you've got to see this stuff," Sierra called from the next aisle over.

Mercedes followed the rest of them as they maneuvered through the store, picking up and giggling at several more of the items on the shelf before making their way over to Sierra.

Ahh, yes. The BDSM aisle.

Sam glanced over at Mercedes, their eyes connecting briefly before Sam looked away, trying to hide a smile.

"This is some serious stuff," Sierra said as she picked up a box. "It's called The Humiliator."

"Do people really use this stuff?" Ashleigh asked again.

"They do," Mercedes assured them. Granted, she didn't know anyone who used a ball gag with a toilet brush attached to the end, but to each his own. "As for that, I'm sure someone has had endless hours of pleasure."

They all laughed, just as she'd expected they would.

"Have you used any of these things?" Sam asked, her tone more serious than before.

"All the time. I'm frequently encouraging my subs to think outside of the box."

"Your subs?" Sam asked, her eyes wide. "But I thought—"

"That's what Xander wanted you to think," Mercedes said before Sam finished.

"So you're not a submissive?"

"No, not by a long shot."

Sam didn't seem convinced, but the woman was kind enough to keep her comment to herself. It was clear by the expression on her face that she didn't believe her.

Along the wall, there were different forms of kinky toys, including blindfolds, muzzles, spreader bars, as well as wrist and ankle restraints. In another section to their left, there were hoods and dungeon irons, not to mention a myriad of suspension equipment and even a section for pony and puppy play.

Mercedes noticed Ashleigh had turned white as a sheet as she continued to take stock of the various toys people used to entertain themselves.

"Do you have a favorite?" McKenna asked her now.

"I like cock and ball shackles," Mercedes told them honestly. "Cock rings and ball weights are always a good time, as well."

"You're a Domme?" Sierra asked, apparently trying to sound unsurprised.

"I am," she assured them.

"Well, I'll be damned. That's fucking cool." Leave it to McKenna to be impressed. "We definitely have to have lunch sometime soon. I'd be honored if you'd let me pick your brain. I've considered doing a BDSM series for my online magazine, and you'd be perfect."

Mercedes smiled, but she wasn't about to make a commitment.

"So how do two Doms hook up?" Sierra questioned her.

"They don't usually."

"So you and Xander are … what? Experimenting?" Sam asked, her expression unreadable.

"You could say that."

The girls must've been happy with her response, because they moved on, continuing to pick up and discuss the assorted selection of toys and sexual apparatus that they came across.

Mercedes was enjoying their reactions, hanging back a little bit when Sam came up to her side. "Whatever it is between you and Xander, I don't think it matters what the norm is."

Mercedes turned to face Sam more directly. "Is that advice?"

"No, just observance. I'm the last person who could give advice. I can't even figure out what I want these days, much less help someone else. But I've seen the way the two of you look at each other."

Mercedes was quiet, still waiting for Sam to finish her thought.

"Let's just say, you don't see that every day."

And with that, Sam went to join the others, leaving Mercedes to dwell on her comment.

And yes, Samantha was partially right. You didn't see it every day.

But that didn't mean it was meant to be.

CHAPTER TWENTY-THREE

XANDER WAS SITTING IN THE DARKENED LIVING room when Mercedes arrived. When he had walked in the door half an hour ago, he hadn't bothered turning on lights or lamps before he dropped onto the sofa. Hell, he hadn't even turned on the television to try and pass the time.

His only thought had been waiting for Mercedes to show up. He hadn't been able to convince himself to go upstairs to shower and wait for her, either. Truth was, he wanted to see her the moment she stepped through his door. Simply put, he had missed her.

And their brief conversation by phone that afternoon hadn't satisfied him in the least. It was the first time since he'd opened the cigar bar that he would've preferred to be anywhere else but there. As long as he was with Mercedes.

But in order to prove to himself that his life could still be normal even when he didn't feel normal, he'd continued with his routine. Only now, the woman who'd sent his normal day-to-day into a dizzying spiral was opening his front door and stepping inside.

"Hi," she said when she noticed him sitting in the shadows.

"Come here," he said in response. He hadn't meant it to come out so forceful, but he'd slipped.

She must've heard something in his tone, because she smiled. "Over there? Where you are?"

"That's right." He smiled back at her, his entire body filling with light just from the radiance of her face. "Right here. On my lap."

"Mind if I take my shoes off?"

"Not at all. In fact, I'd be more than happy if you'd get completely naked."

"Is that an order?" she asked warily.

"Not yet."

Mercedes kicked off her shoes and padded across the hardwood floor. When she hiked up her skirt a little, standing directly in front of him, he held out his hands to her. With their fingers linked, he eased her onto his lap so that she straddled him.

"You smell like smoke," she told him with a grin. "I kind of like it. Did you have fun tonight?" she asked.

"It was a good night, yes." He wouldn't go so far as to say it was fun. Between talking business and missing Mercedes, he would've enjoyed himself more if he'd just spent the night in with her. "What about you?"

"We had a good time. I like them."

Mercedes had informed him that Sam had invited her for a girls' night out. When she hadn't elaborated about where they were going, he had inquired. And that's when she'd informed him they would be going to a sex toy shop.

"Did you find anything you liked while you were there?"

"There was this one chastity cage that I had my eye on."

Xander laughed, but there wasn't an ounce of humor in the sound. Because he knew Mercedes could be quite vindictive when she wanted to be, he opted to change the subject before she got any ideas about putting one of those things on him. After all, he had agreed to let her top him. If she went hard-core on him, he might just have to wave the white flag. Especially if she got anywhere near his dick with any sort of cage.

"Have you seen my dungeon lately?" he asked, knowing she hadn't. That got her attention instantly. "Don't worry, pet," he whispered as he slid his hand behind her neck, pulling her closer to him. "Tonight, I don't intend to tie you down or punish you."

He pressed his lips to hers gently.

"No? Change of heart?" she asked softly.

"Not at all. But tonight, I'm interested in pursuing what we started last night."

No matter how hard he'd tried, throughout the day, Xander had thought of little other than what had happened between them last night when they'd finally fallen into bed. They'd burned up the sheets, and he had been ready for a replay since the second he'd woken up. Now that she was there with him, he didn't want to stop touching her long enough for her to get naked. Although he would since it would be for a worthy cause.

Pulling her closer so that he could feel the heat between her legs against his throbbing hard-on, he slid his hands down her back and cupped her ass in both hands.

"I want to be inside of you," he stated gently. "I've waited all damn day, and I've finally run out of patience."

Mercedes's eyes softened as she stared back at him. "Me, too."

God, he was still shocked when he heard her say things like that. He expected her to try and play it off as a joke. Or even to argue. But her easy acceptance and admission had hope flaring in his chest.

Sliding his hands down her hips, he made his way to her thighs and then pushed her skirt up even higher so that he could feel her bare skin against his palms.

"Stroke me," he encouraged her as he leaned forward, urging her to kiss him.

When her mouth met his, he was sure they would spontaneously combust. The air crackled and sizzled around them. She was fire in his arms, ablaze with a desperation that mirrored his own. He wasn't about to let her go, clothes be damned.

Somehow, bless her, she managed to free his cock without ever pulling her lips from his. He sucked on her tongue while he reached for her panties. There was no way he was letting her up so he could work them down her legs. He'd just have to replace them later.

A soft ripping sound had Mercedes pulling back from him, and he fought the urge to laugh.

"Did you just rip my panties off of me?" she asked suspiciously.

"I did."

She stared back at him for a minute, not saying anything. Then the corners of her mouth turned up in a mind-blowing grin.

"That's fucking hot."

And then her mouth was back on his, and Xander thought of nothing except having her slide down onto him.

When she rocked forward, lifting her ass from his thighs, he gripped his cock, and she did exactly that.

"Fuck," he growled. The sheer pleasure of her sheathing him damn near had him seeing stars. Just like the night before, the lack of a latex barrier had his blood pressure spiking dangerously. She was hot and wet. Fuck. "Mercedes..."

He meant to say her name as a warning, but it came out as something else entirely.

She didn't seem to need clarification, because she began to rock gently, her hips shifting as she rode him right there on his living room sofa.

"I'm not gonna last long," he warned her when she increased the pace.

"Good."

"Good?" he asked breathlessly as he tried to focus on not exploding too prematurely.

"Yes," she mumbled against his lips, her hands sliding into his hair. "I want you to come inside me."

Fuuuuck.

Xander couldn't resist. He gripped her hips, guided her, and then pulled her back down until he was slamming into her, both of them holding the other tightly. He had no intention of letting go until she did, but if she kept this up, his head was definitely going to explode.

"Xander," she moaned, pulling her mouth from his. "It's too good. Oh…"

"Come for me," he said. It wasn't a command, just gentle encouragement. He watched her, loving the way she looked as she hovered above him, wantonly riding his cock.

Sliding one hand around between her legs, he used his thumb to rub her clit, urging her closer and closer. He wanted her to come with him, but he was racing toward the edge, dangerously close to losing it.

"X!" Mercedes shocked him with her scream as her head fell back, her pussy clamping down on to his cock as her orgasm gripped her. He wasn't sure if it was the heat of her body, her urgent cry, or the way her fingernails dug into his shoulders, but he followed her over, his cock jerking and pulsing inside of her.

Long minutes later, when their breathing finally returned to normal, Mercedes lifted her head from his shoulder and looked down at him.

"How was that for round one?" he asked when she met his gaze.

"Round one?"

"Most definitely."

"What did you have in mind for round two?"

Sliding his hands around to her ass once more, he gripped her firmly.

And then stood, holding her to him, his cock still firmly lodged inside of her.

"What are you doing? Oh, my God, Xander. Put me down."

"Not a chance," he told her as he made his way to the stairs.

"I am way too heavy for you to carry."

Xander didn't respond because the comment was absurd. Clearly she wasn't too heavy, because he was already climbing the stairs, tempted to take them two at a time just so he could get to his destination faster. He would've, too if he had any inclination of pulling out of her.

But he didn't.

Because the jarring impact of her body against his had him primed and ready for round two.

CHAPTER TWENTY-FOUR

Day two…
Friday

BY THE TIME MERCEDES MADE HER WAY downstairs the next morning, she had managed to shower, dry her hair, apply her makeup, and still hadn't run into Xander.

She was only a little disappointed.

Waking up in his bed for the second morning in a row had been an experience, to say the least. She'd awoken feeling relaxed, despite the dream that had once again taken the liberty of disrupting her sleep.

Although she hadn't been overwhelmed by the urge to run and hide from the man she'd just spent the night with, she had been a little perturbed that he'd left her alone. Again.

Knowing Xander, he was probably on the phone, never mind the fact that it was still early. The man did little other than work.

Too much.

As she made her way downstairs, she listened for him, trying to pinpoint his location. With coffee the only thing on her mind, Mercedes headed to the kitchen, hoping to find him there.

Nope. No Xander.

But there was coffee, which was all that mattered. After pouring a cup, she padded through the house, making her way to his office. That's when she heard his voice. He sounded angry, but she couldn't make out what he was saying.

Since he'd instructed her to be with him every moment that she wasn't working, Mercedes figured she had a right to violate his workspace even when he was on the phone.

When she walked in, the frustration that was written all over his face immediately morphed into something else entirely as soon as their eyes met.

"Look, I don't give a shit. I didn't authorize it, so you figure it out. I'm not willing to sell just yet. Let him know that I'll consider if the price is right, and what he's proposed is ludicrous. I've got to run. Talk to you later. Hey."

Mercedes smiled as soon as the receiver made its way into the cradle. "Good morning. Looks like you're having a good day already."

"I am now. Come here."

Without thinking, she moved toward him, sipping her coffee as she did. When she was within touching distance, Xander reached for her. Rather than worrying that they'd get a surprise scalding, Mercedes set the cup on the desk and moved into Xander's arms.

"I was hoping you'd sleep longer," he told her as she perched on his lap and he pulled her close.

As she got comfortable, she realized that she spent quite a bit of time sitting on his lap. For some reason, the idea didn't bother her at all. "I would have, but I woke up alone."

"Sorry about that. I tend to get up early, and I didn't want to wake you."

"What time did you get up?"

"Four."

"Hmm, I think there might be a nap in your future," she said with a smile.

"I like that idea."

For the first time since she'd walked in, Mercedes realized he was dressed. Completely. Like, with a tie and everything.

"Going somewhere?"

"I've got a meeting this morning."

"Oh."

"I figured you had things to do today," he began.

Mercedes tried to push off of his lap, immediately ashamed of her assumption. His arms tightened slightly, her escape attempt failing.

What was she thinking? That Xander would've just changed his entire day because she'd spent another night in his bed? Or possibly because *she* felt there was a connection between them that wasn't just related to casual sex? Or that just because her calendar wasn't crammed full that morning that his wasn't? Granted, it was Friday, and she knew the man probably had plenty of things to do.

As did she.

"I do. I need to follow up on the Milton building. I'm hoping to hear something back today." No, actually she wasn't, but it sounded good. Xander leaned over and kissed her, but Mercedes turned quickly, offering him her cheek. "In fact, I need to go make a call."

To her surprise, Xander leaned back, releasing his hold on her as she abruptly stood. He simply cocked an eyebrow, pinning her with a look that promised punishment later.

"I'll talk to you later, then."

Okay, so he probably knew she was upset. So what? If it meant she could put a little distance between them, then it was worth it. Clearly she'd gone and lost her mind, thinking that a couple of nights in his bed had changed things.

Obviously not.

"Mercedes," Xander said sternly when she turned to walk away.

Knowing she was going to earn some form of punishment and not really giving a shit, she waved him off without turning back. "I'll catch you when you get back."

As she made her way down the narrow hall, she heard him say, "You're damn right you will, pet."

At four thirty in the afternoon, Mercedes made her way down the narrow hallway that led to Xander's office. It was the first time she'd been back since her less-than-graceful retreat that morning.

Somehow she'd managed to avoid Xander's phone calls throughout the day, and luckily he hadn't pressed the issue. Then again, she had conveniently disappeared for the majority of the day, which meant he was likely going to be questioning her relentlessly.

She'd just spent the last two hours with a client, showing him two recently listed condos not far from her own building. Needless to say, she wasn't in the best of moods, because not only had she shown him both condos twice, but he'd insisted on nitpicking every last detail until finally he'd decided he wasn't interested.

She would never get those two hours back.

But on the positive side of things, she'd been able to get her mind back in working order. No longer was she reliving the time she'd recently spent in Xander's arms. And more importantly, she wasn't thinking any of those crazy thoughts about him.

Things were back to normal.

As normal as they could get anyway.

Only now she had to face Xander once again. Probably because she'd ignored his calls throughout the day, he had left a lengthy voice mail not long ago, reminding her of the deal that they'd made, among other things.

"Hey, it's me. Call me perceptive, but I've figured out that you're avoiding my calls. It hasn't stopped me from calling you yet, and it won't stop me in the future, so if you don't mind, just answer the damn phone. It would be a hell of a lot easier than me having to have a one-sided conversation with your voice mail." Pause. *"I can only assume that you're on your way home, and yes, I'm here waiting for you. So, whether you show up in five minutes or five hours, I'll still be here.*

"We have a deal, Mercedes. And I've never gone back on my word, and I know you haven't, either, and now isn't the time for either of us to start." Another pause. "Damn it, woman. Either give me a call or I expect to see you within the hour. And if you're lucky…" Exasperated breath. "No, wait. You've long surpassed luck. Like I said, I'll be here waiting."

Incorrigible.

Damn him.

Xander had the ability to make anyone feel guilty, and he'd successfully piled a shitload of guilt on her plate although he probably hadn't meant to.

Or maybe he had.

Mercedes stopped short just outside of Xander's office door.

After all of the time they'd recently spent together and the way she'd lost control at each and every turn, getting way too emotionally involved, Mercedes should've wanted to stay as far away from him as she possibly could.

But that wasn't the case.

Surprisingly, at some point during the day, she had started to miss him despite the fact that she was doing her best not to think about him at all.

Shaking her head to clear her brain of the random thoughts, she took a deep breath. She'd gone and lost her mind, that's all there was to it.

She raised her hand to knock but was stopped by the sound of Xander's voice before she had the chance.

"Come in."

"Hey," she greeted when she moved into the vast open space. Along with praying that she sounded normal, she hoped like hell she didn't look like a woman who'd been working herself into a frenzy all day.

Or, more importantly, she hoped he had forgotten all about what had happened just that morning in this very office when she'd panicked like a scared child, running away as fast as her legs would carry her.

"You look exhausted."

Okay, that was a good sign. Maybe.

"I am," she told him, dropping to the leather sofa across from his desk. "I just spent two hours showing Charles Markom two condos that, of course, he thinks are beneath him."

Xander leaned back in his chair and steepled his fingers together over his flat belly as he studied her. She could see the amusement in his eyes, but she didn't rise to the bait.

"He's still giving you the runaround?" Xander asked.

"I think that's all he wants from me," she told him. "I'm seriously considering not answering the phone next time he calls."

The amusement in Xander's eyes disappeared.

Crap. She'd gone and done it now, putting her foot right in her mouth by mentioning not taking calls.

"You enjoy doing that?" he asked, his tone lacking any jest. He was serious.

Knowing that anything she said at that point would be used against her, she kept talking, pretending not to realize he was upset with her. "I don't want to even think about him. Right now, I just want to sit here. Right here. The only thing that could make it better would be pizza and beer," she said, and he laughed, just as she'd hoped he would.

"Pizza and beer?"

Okay, so it was true, she wasn't much of a pizza eater, nor was she a beer drinker, but her comment had effectively redirected the conversation.

"How about I get Italian delivered, and we share a bottle of wine?" Xander offered, sitting up in his chair.

"Even better," she replied, dropping her head back on the cushions and closing her eyes. Maybe if she feigned sleep, she'd be able to avoid any further discussions.

While she dozed slightly, she listened as Xander placed an order to one of their favorite Italian places just down the street. She was tempted to tell him to cancel dinner, and she'd just slide deeper into the cushions and call it a night.

Before she could get too deep into slumber, Xander's voice brought her back.

"It's not time for bed yet."

"And why not?" she asked drowsily, her eyes still closed.

"Because I said so."

Oh, crap. She knew that tone all too well. Opening one eye, she peered over at him. He was still at his desk, his forearms casually resting on the top. Sitting there with his tie loosened, his jacket gone and sleeves rolled up, his hair not as perfectly styled as it had been that morning, he looked like sex personified. Although the man could rock a suit like no one else, Mercedes liked the disheveled look even more.

Her body instantly came alive, sleep all but forgotten.

"Stand," he instructed as he got to his feet. Not moving, she watched as he made his way over to the door and closed it. The click as the lock engaged had her body going on full alert.

Slow, measured footsteps carried him across the oversized office until he was standing within a foot of her. She briefly glimpsed the Dallas skyline from the floor-to-ceiling windows that ran the length of two walls, but then his big body was in front of her, blocking her view of anything but him.

"Are you asking to be punished even more?" he asked, his voice assuredly calm.

Okay, so he hadn't forgotten about that morning. And he probably hadn't forgotten the fact that she'd ignored his phone calls all day, either.

To her absolute horror, her body began to hum with anticipation. Not only had she believed that she was too tired to get turned on, she was also shocked that she was reacting to his dominance so easily.

"Can I take my shoes off first?" she asked, sitting up straight.

"If you want to add another five swats, sure."

Mercedes was wide-awake then. He wasn't playing. Pushing to her feet, she didn't look away, anticipation now making her body sing.

Xander backed up a few steps and perched on the edge of his desk as he stared back at her. "Remove your clothes," he insisted. "Keep the shoes on."

Damn Dom.

Her shoes were killing her feet, but he probably knew that. Had she not ignored him or run away, she knew he would've gladly given her permission to remove her shoes, but he was in full Dom mode, the intensity in his gaze penetrating her through and through.

Mercedes didn't think to argue further, which either said a lot about how tired she was or it said a lot about the complete three-sixty that her life had taken in the last forty-eight hours.

It was still hard to believe it had only been a little more than two days since they had made their deal.

Trying not to rush, and doing her best not to think, Mercedes removed her clothes, piece by piece, leaving her favorite pair of Guccis on as Xander had instructed her to.

As she stood before Xander completely naked, the one thing she knew for sure … she was too damned tired to think about anything right now.

ADMIRING MERCEDES'S COMPLETELY NAKED FORM, XANDER LET his eyes graze every dip and curve of her graceful body. In her heels, her legs were a work of art, and he found he would be content just to stare at her for as long as she would let him.

Although he knew they had to be damned uncomfortable at this point.

Considering the disappearing act she'd pulled on him that morning, he wasn't compelled to give in to her requests, though. She needed to think about what she'd done. It was only fair, since he'd spent the majority of the day wondering whether she'd back out of their deal. With the way she was looking at him now, he figured it was still a possibility.

Just that morning, she'd run out of his office like the place was on fire. As if that weren't bad enough, she'd ignored all of his phone calls throughout the day until finally his irritation level had reached an all-time high. He'd left a lengthy voice mail expressing as much.

So, as far as he was concerned, his need to dominate her was warranted. She deserved punishment for her actions, and he fully intended to make sure she thought about what she'd done before she allowed it to happen again.

After making her wait a solid two minutes while he admired her, Xander rose to his feet. "Lie across the desk," he told her as he walked around his desk and opened one of the drawers.

He'd retrieved one of his paddles earlier in the day and slipped it into his desk drawer, anticipating this moment.

Mercedes glared at him, and he fought the urge to smile. Oh, yes, she was definitely defiant; he had no doubt about that. But he damn sure wasn't going to let her get away with the little stunt she had pulled. Running away from her feelings, which he truly believed was what had compelled her to hide out throughout the day, was unacceptable.

Mercedes closed the distance between herself and the desk. Her eyes tore free of his when she leaned over, her chest resting on the wooden top.

"Very nice," he said approvingly as he tapped his hand with the small wooden paddle. "How many licks do you think you've earned today, pet?"

Xander walked back around the desk, coming right up behind her and pressing his straining erection against her ass, letting her know just how much the sight of her bent over his desk did to him.

She didn't answer his question, so he took a step to the side, and without hesitation, he slapped her ass with the paddle, making her jump.

"Tell me, pet," he said firmly. "I don't appreciate being ignored."

"I don't know," she breathed out.

"You want me to pick a number?"

"No," she said hurriedly.

Xander smacked her ass one more time. "What was that?"

"No, Sir. I don't want you to choose a number."

"Then you better come up with one fast." Xander set the wooden paddle on her back and squeezed her ass with both hands, kneading the muscle and marveling at the way her ass brightened from the paddle.

"Ten, Sir."

"Ten?"

"Yes, Sir. Five for leaving this morning and five for not taking your phone calls."

Well, at least they were on the same page. She knew just what had gotten him so worked up.

"And you think ten is enough for what you did?"

"No, Sir. But I'm not sure I can handle more than that. Not with the paddle."

He liked her honesty. And because she'd been prepared with a detailed answer, he decided to give her a reprieve.

"Ten it is," he said as he retrieved the paddle from where it rested on her back. "Count them off."

Xander didn't linger, didn't tease her. He landed ten swats on her ass and the backs of her thighs in rapid succession while she counted them out. And once he landed the last one, he dropped the paddle to the carpeted floor and leaned over her, his cock intimately nestled against her ass.

"Don't do that to me again," he whispered, knowing she would hear the torment in his tone. He'd spent the entire day wondering what she would do. Fearful that she would try and back out of their deal because she was feeling too much too fast. He knew Mercedes. She avoided emotion at all costs — at least where intimacy was concerned. She gave all of herself to her friends but little to nothing to her lovers.

Xander wanted all of her.

"Yes, Sir," she whimpered.

Xander eased off of her, letting his hands slide down her naked back. Gripping her hips, he pulled her so that she would stand. When she was fully upright, he said, "Turn around and look at me."

When she turned to face him, her eyes were downturned, something he found he did not like one bit. "Look at me." He wanted to see the emotion in her eyes, to read what she was thinking. The woman would not hide from him anymore.

Their eyes met, and he slid his hand down between her legs, gently teasing her bare pussy lips.

"Kiss me," he demanded, doing his best to keep his hands to himself. He wanted her to make the first move. If she wanted him as much as he wanted her, she would do as he instructed.

Mercedes didn't rush forward, and Xander figured she was trying to test him. What he wanted to do was to pull her flush against him and crush his mouth to hers, but ever since that morning, he had realized she was extremely skittish. She just hadn't told him why.

Yet.

Then again, what had happened the last two nights had been monumental, and it'd left him in a state of confusion for the better part of the day. It wasn't hard to understand that what was going on between them was more than a well-planned strategy to dominate this woman in every way possible. No, this was significantly more.

This perfect woman, this amazing Domme, had, without thinking, handed all control over to him under her own steam. It had been a moment he would remember for the rest of his life.

He knew her. He knew that Mercedes was probably questioning herself, wondering if she was losing her touch. Rather than ask her to embrace this side of herself, he was trying to let her feel her way through it on her own. She'd get there; he knew that much. And it was a damn good thing he was a patient man.

Then again, he fully intended to regain his control of the situation right here, right now.

He sensed what she needed, and right now, it wasn't the aggressive, no holds barred — as she'd put it — sex that they were so good at. As much as he ached to dominate her, he needed Mercedes to give in to this as much as he already had.

Cupping her cheek, Xander locked his gaze with hers as he leaned in close, taking things slower than he might've liked. But this was about her. Not him.

When his mouth settled on hers, Mercedes wrapped her arms around his neck, bringing them even closer. As his mouth settled over hers, she surprised him by sliding her fingers into his hair.

He fucking loved when she touched him. When she seemed to need the contact as much as he did.

She teased him with her tongue slowly, and he was cognizant of the way he responded, refraining from pushing her too fast. It was a tremendous effort because, for a large part of the day, he'd replayed the way she had looked leaning over him, riding him for all she was worth right there in the middle of his living room. Then he'd get lost in the memories of the two of them making love in his bed.

She'd certainly thrown him for a loop, and Xander was pretty sure he'd gone into this with his eyes wide open.

He knew she could feel the slight vibration of his body as he held himself back, but he didn't try to press her.

Pulling his lips from hers, he said, "I need to be inside you, pet. Right here. Tell me you need it, too."

"I need to feel you inside me," she answered, her eyes searching his as though she were trying to look for something deeper.

It was the exact same way she'd been looking at him that morning before she had freaked out and disappeared.

Mercedes's hands slid around, and she removed his already loose tie, watching his face as she did. Xander made sure she saw everything he was thinking.

Once she was finished, he slowly unbuttoned his shirt, keeping his eyes on Mercedes while he did. Once he had the damn thing undone, he shrugged out of it and allowed it to fall to the floor near his feet. Unable to wait long enough for her to undress him because he wasn't sure he'd survive her sensual touch without going entirely mad, he didn't waste any time removing the rest of his clothes.

When he was naked, he pulled her against him again, and without breaking eye contact, Xander slid his hands down to her ass and then hefted her up until she was forced to wrap her legs around his waist. He carried her over to the door and pressed her back against the solid wood surface.

He wanted to praise her for not saying anything about being too heavy for him to carry, but he didn't. Instead, he said, "Tell me exactly what you want from me." Xander loved when she told him what she wanted. Because he didn't hear it very often, just the soothing request from her lips made it all the more exquisite.

"I want to feel your tongue. On my mouth, my breasts, my pussy."

Xander couldn't deny the electrical current that charged through him at her words. Mercedes was very vocal about what she wanted, and he assumed that was her dominant side that spoke up so easily. But her submissive side was much more prominent, if only she'd give in to it more.

Unable to resist, Xander crushed her into the solid wood as he thrust his tongue into her mouth, devouring her. She tasted like sweet sin, a temptation unlike anything he'd ever known before. He took his time, plundering her mouth until they both had no choice but to come up for air.

Sucking in as much oxygen as he needed, Xander shifted her higher and then sucked her nipple between his lips, teasing the tip with his tongue before sucking her more fully into his mouth. With her arms wrapped around him, she was gripping his head, while her legs squeezed him tightly. Laving both breasts repeatedly, Xander didn't stop until she was begging for more.

He had no choice but to let her down so that he could complete her request. As soon as her feet were on the floor, he lowered himself to his knees. "Put your leg over my shoulder."

Mercedes complied, placing her left leg over his right shoulder, the sharp heel of her shoe digging into his skin, and Xander tried to remain in control.

Using his fingers, he separated her slick folds, exposing her so he could admire her beautiful pussy. After teasing her with his thumb briefly, he dove between her legs with his tongue, delving into her pussy without giving her a second to think about it. Her soft moans filled the air as she trembled in his arms, grinding against his mouth as he fucked her with his tongue.

"Xander."

His name was a plea on her lips, and his chest swelled. She wasn't holding back, just as he'd hoped, and a tremendous amount of pride swelled in his chest.

Releasing her clit from between his lips, he only stopped long enough to tell her to come whenever she was ready. Then he was delving back into her sweetness with his lips, teeth, and tongue, gripping her hips to hold her in place, making sure she knew he had her.

When she began moaning his name in earnest, he thrust two fingers inside of her, and she detonated on impact, flooding his mouth as he lapped at her sweet pussy.

And to think, he was just getting started.

CHAPTER TWENTY-FIVE

MERCEDES BARELY MANAGED TO CATCH HER BREATH before Xander was standing again, lifting her into his arms. Just when she thought he'd thrust inside of her, filling her the way she so desperately needed, he moved, carrying her over to the sofa and depositing her onto her back. He slipped her shoes off of her feet, and then he was there. Crawling over her and warming her with his naked body.

He kissed her, allowing her to taste herself on his lips as he once again tormented her mouth with his mind-blowing kisses. He was driving her out of her mind, pulling her back to the brink once more.

More importantly, he was making it difficult to think. Which was probably his intention. There was no denying the fact that the man knew exactly how to play her body with exquisite accuracy.

Just as soon as he had arrived, plying her with bone-jarring kisses, he was gone, his mouth leaving a blazing trail over her skin, returning to her breasts, working her into another heated frenzy instantly. She thrust her hips, trying to tell him what she really wanted, but he was a man on a mission, and she knew there was no stopping him.

As much as she enjoyed the ethereal torment he was applying to her sensitive nipples, Mercedes wished he would slam into her, filling her with his cock.

She wanted nothing more than to hold on to him as she flew apart in his arms.

He made her groan in disappointment when he turned his attention to the bright artwork that decorated her shoulder. He used his tongue to trace the tattoo, but to her surprise, he didn't linger long before he slid down between her thighs once more.

Okay, so maybe she wasn't exactly disappointed, but her groans were certainly tinged with impatience.

His rough chuckle made her smile. Yes, the man was relentless, and he had a one-track mind. Since she'd been the one to ask for it, she couldn't be all that upset.

"Oh, fuck!" she moaned when Xander lifted her leg, bracing his palm beneath her thigh and opening her wide as he delved into her with his tongue over and over.

Mercedes knew she wouldn't last. She couldn't resist him, and when he turned the heat up, she didn't stand a chance against him. "Yes," she moaned. "Just like that, X. Suck my clit."

Her entire body shuddered when he wrapped his lips around her clit, his tongue lashing as he pressed two fingers inside of her again. When he groaned against her, the vibration of his mouth sent her over the edge, her body fracturing from the inside out as her orgasm took her.

Xander didn't allow much time to pass before he was hovering over her, staring down at her as he gave her a moment to catch her breath again. She welcomed the reprieve, but she prayed he wasn't finished yet.

Sliding her hands around his neck, she pulled him against her. He was stronger than she was, which meant he didn't fall on top of her, although she wouldn't have minded.

She wanted to feel him against her. Everywhere. What was coursing through her had long surpassed mere desire and somewhere along the way morphed into a desperate, aching need.

"Beg me," he said, his breaths ragged. She heard the urgency in his tone that time, and she welcomed it. He might be the almighty Dom, but to know she got to him... It was empowering. "Beg me to make love to you."

"Please," she answered easily, her voice rough with her own desire. "I want to feel you."

"No. Beg me to make love to you," he said firmly.

Mercedes stilled. She stared back at him as her heart began a rebellious thump in her chest.

Make love.

She wasn't sure she could handle hearing those words. She'd been thinking that's what they'd done the night before and the night before that, but they'd both seen where that had gotten them. She'd run out of his office that morning like a scared child. Running from what she was already beginning to feel for this man.

As she looked into his eyes, she noticed that he wasn't backing down. He didn't seem in the least bit intimidated by her reaction.

Oh, Lord. This man knew her better than she knew herself. The moment she'd walked through his office door, she'd felt more like herself than she had in years, even if she'd still been on the defensive. She'd spent too much time trying to hide her own needs in order to ensure she kept herself distanced. If she didn't, she knew she would get hurt again.

But this man, her best friend, had read her easily, and his gentle yet insistent tone stole her breath.

He was breaking down her resistance, and she was too weak to deny him anymore. She wanted him, wanted every part of him.

"Tell me that's what you want, Mercedes."

"Yes," she breathed out roughly. She was too tired to deal with the conflicting emotions. "I want you to make love to me. I need it. I need you."

Xander growled, a rough, animalistic sound that sent shock waves of pleasure through her as he settled between her thighs. Digging her fingernails into his shoulders, Mercedes pressed her back into the sofa, pushing her hips forward as Xander held himself above her, rocking into her gently at first.

"Oh, God, that feels so good."

"You feel good," he said. "You feel so fucking good, baby. When I'm inside of you, I don't ever want to leave. I could spend the rest of my life right here."

She wasn't sure whether it was the heat of the moment that made him say the things he was saying, so she tried not to take them to heart, but it was so hard to do. He sounded so sincere. His eyes were a soft green as he stared back at her, and for a moment, she felt as though he could see clear to her soul.

His warm body surrounded her, consumed her. The way he thrust into her gently, his hips jerking at the last moment to send him deeper before he retreated, had her body singing. The man knew how to please her. He knew just how to use his body to achieve maximum pleasure.

Sliding her hand into his hair, Mercedes held him to her, bringing his mouth down to hers briefly. But more than she wanted his kiss, she wanted to watch him, to see the ecstasy brewing in his beautiful eyes, to know that he was feeling the exact same thing she was feeling.

"Fuck," he growled, thrusting deeper, every muscle in his big body taut.

She moaned, reveling in the glorious friction that ignited every pleasure receptor in her core.

He slid his forearm beneath her head, lifting it so that she was closer to him as he hoisted her leg up, changing the angle as he penetrated her impossibly deeper.

"Xander."

"Tell me, baby. Tell me how it feels."

"It's… Oh, God!" Mercedes didn't think it could get any better, but then he ground his pelvis against hers, lodged to the hilt, filling her to bursting, before he pulled out and slid home once more. "It's perfect."

Mercedes bit her bottom lip as she watched him, waiting for that moment when she knew he'd reached the pinnacle and was ready to plummet into euphoric bliss right along with her.

Their bodies were slick with sweat as they moved together, the frantic pounding of her heart the only sound she heard.

"Come for me, Mercedes. Come with me."

Mercedes latched on to his hair tighter, holding him to her as he buried his face in her neck. His pace intensified, his thrusts bottoming out inside of her, the delicious friction causing that ever-growing tingle to start in her womb, making her insides glow.

"Harder," she begged although she wasn't sure she could handle much more. Apparently she could, because her orgasm built to a crescendo as Xander mercilessly drove deep inside of her, penetrating her thoroughly.

"That's it, baby," Xander growled, his body going stone still as his cock pulsed inside of her. "Fuck."

A sharp bolt of pain lanced her shoulder when Xander nipped her skin, but it didn't hurt. Not in that way. No, this was a sensation that she felt clear to her soul.

Because Xander hadn't just bitten her. He'd claimed her.

And there was no way in hell she could deny it. She was completely his. In every way.

Time stood still until they managed to catch their breaths, but Xander didn't move from his position. She didn't want him to.

Mercedes let her internal muscles milk him, enjoying the hungry growls that continued to rumble in his chest. For the first time in as long as she could remember, Mercedes felt herself falling for a man.

This man.

CHAPTER TWENTY-SIX

Day three...
Saturday

ON SATURDAY EVENING, XANDER WAS TIDYING UP the kitchen after tossing the remnants of their dinner into the trash. After a surprisingly leisurely day, one they'd spent together at his condo doing literally nothing for most of the day, Xander had finally given in and cooked dinner for Mercedes.

He wasn't much of a cook, he would be the first to admit, but he was capable of working a stove. The sausage and vegetable risotto, a dish his mother had made quite often when he was a kid, wasn't fancy, but it had been decent. Not as good as his mother's, but edible. That's all that mattered.

So, after he'd slaved over the stove for all of thirty minutes, they'd shared a meal while they talked about the upcoming week.

Mercedes had gone on to tell him about the official offer she'd put in on the Milton building yesterday, and how she was now waiting for the counter offer, fully expecting it to come on Monday. There was no doubt about it; the seller would certainly counter. Not that Xander blamed them.

Now, as they made their way to the living room, he was falling into his normal evening routine, which, for the next hour, would consist of watching the news.

"I think I'm going to head to my place and take a bath," Mercedes told him hesitantly.

"No," he responded easily, keeping his voice soft. "You can take a bath here." He wasn't about to let her disappear on him again. After all, they had agreed that she would stay with him unless she was working, and he'd been impressed that she'd spent the entire day at his place, never once using an excuse to go home.

Progress, especially after the rocky day they'd had yesterday.

"But—"

Xander glared at her, effectively silencing her.

"My bath works just as well as yours does."

To his surprise, Mercedes didn't argue. Instead, she pinned him with a glare of her own before turning her attention on the stairs that led up to the master suite.

Neither of them said anything more, and the next thing Xander knew, Mercedes was making her way upstairs. When she was halfway there, he called out to her. He waited until she turned to look down at him.

"I'll be up in a little while to help you out. Don't get out until I come get you."

He could tell that his instructions weren't exactly what she wanted to hear, but he'd give her props for not complaining. Xander didn't budge until she'd made it to the top of the stairs.

Once she was there, he reached for the remote and flipped on the television, dropping onto the sofa. As he sank into the cool leather, he immediately remembered the way Mercedes had looked perched atop him, riding him. And then yesterday in his office, when he had thrust inside of her on a similar sofa... Shit. He wasn't sure he'd ever look at black leather the same again.

God, she'd come completely undone right there in his office. The memory was enough to heat his blood and send it pooling south. He wanted her.

Then again, he was certain he was nearing sainthood since he'd refrained from taking her a million different ways throughout the day.

As he stared at the television screen, not seeing anything other than the bright glow of the images, he thought back to the first time he'd asked Mercedes to dinner all those years ago. The setting hadn't been exactly what he'd hoped for, but all in all, it'd been interesting, to say the least.

From the moment he'd met Mercedes, he'd been intrigued by her. Even if he had come to accept there wasn't a snowball's chance in hell that there would ever be anything between them. Mainly for the fact that she was a Domme, and he was in no way submissive.

He wouldn't lie, he had never really come to terms with it. It had just taken him a little while — nearly a decade — to find a way to show her just how he felt about the whole thing.

If his memories served him correctly, it had been during their first dinner out — unfortunately that had been business, not pleasure — that he'd found himself seeking a way to get under her skin the same way she had him.

They hadn't been alone that night, either. They'd been joined by the Realtor of one of the clients Xander had been working with and the man's assistant. He hadn't been happy to find out they had chaperones, but at the time, he'd figured Mercedes had invited them on purpose. To protect herself from him.

He was right, because that night she'd made her feelings on the subject crystal clear.

"You don't know what a submissive is?" Mercedes asked skeptically. She was speaking directly to Tim Johnson, a high-profile Realtor who was working for the seller of a property Xander was in the process of acquiring.

As they sat in the upscale restaurant, the waiter having just brought out baskets of bread for the foursome congregating at the table, Mercedes had apparently latched on to one little comment that Tim had said jokingly.

"Nothing more than the glorified stuff I've seen on television," Tim admitted, his full attention on Mercedes.

Xander watched Mercedes, waiting to see what she'd say. How they'd gotten on the topic originally, he wasn't sure, but it was interesting to see that Mercedes was completely open to the discussion.

Mercedes seemed to study Tim for a moment before she continued. "Do you like to be in control, Mr. Johnson?"

Xander grinned, hiding it behind his wineglass. He noticed the way Tim shivered outwardly, an obvious reaction to Mercedes's sexy voice. Xander could only imagine the fantasies the man was having where she was concerned. Hell, he'd had a few of his own in recent weeks.

Tim glanced over at Xander, who was sitting beside Mercedes, but his gaze didn't linger elsewhere for long. The man was probably trying to determine what he wanted to say.

Xander leaned back in his chair and watched things play out between the two of them.

"Depends," Tim finally admitted, his voice lower than before. "If we're talking business, I do. When it comes to other things, I could be persuaded to give up control."

"Persuaded?" Mercedes asked seriously, sipping her wine as she stared back at him. "Or is it something you prefer?"

Xander had a feeling that the question was loaded. He got the impression there was only one correct answer where Mercedes was concerned.

"It's something I prefer," Tim's assistant stated firmly.

Xander's gaze darted to the pretty young woman sitting to Tim's left. She wasn't looking at her boss, which was probably a good thing because her open admission seemed to have shocked Tim somewhat.

Based on Mercedes's reaction, she hadn't expected it, either.

"Do you play at a club?" Mercedes asked casually.

"I have, yes," Clarissa Tinsley admitted, her cheeks turning pink.

"Well, Xander here" — Mercedes glanced over at him — "is a Dom." He wasn't sure why, but somehow she had successfully pulled him directly into the conversation. He fought the urge to laugh at that.

"Is that right?" Clarissa asked sweetly, her eyes glazing over slightly.

"Mercedes is being too kind. She's a Domme herself, but she doesn't like to brag," he said with a smile. "I'm a member of Kink," he admitted, sipping his wine and making sure they all noticed his casual disinterest in the conversation.

What he wanted to do was to talk to Mercedes directly. Preferably about something other than business, but until today, she'd managed to keep their brief relationship on a steadfast professional level.

He had hoped to change that tonight.

She had successfully cock blocked him by inviting these two.

"Is your husband a Dom?" Mercedes asked Clarissa, and Xander heard the subtle irritation in her tone. It seemed as though she hadn't been looking to spread the word of her Domme status.

Fair was fair, in his opinion.

"I'm not married," Clarissa admitted, her eyes immediately going down to the table.

"Well, Mr. Boone might just be interested in showing you the ropes."

Lord, was she serious?

Keeping his reaction to Mercedes's blatant assumption hidden was difficult, but he prided himself on his ability to maintain his composure at all costs. He also thought she might've been testing him, so he decided to play into her hands.

"If you're interested in seeing the club, I'd be more than happy to have you as a guest," he told Clarissa, watching Mercedes out of the corner of his eye.

"What is it that you like about being a submissive?" Tim asked this time, surprising them all with his interest.

When Clarissa seemed to be thinking things through, Xander added, "Don't overthink it. Tell him the first thing that came to your mind. Why is it something you prefer?"

"I don't want to be in control all the time," Clarissa offered easily.

"I could never do that," Tim said, laughing. He appeared as though he was suddenly uncomfortable.

"No?" Mercedes asked. "Is that because you want to be in control of your business?"

"I would never give up control of my business."

"Who said you had to?" Mercedes asked.

Xander wondered why she seemed to be pushing the issue.

"I just assumed," Tim said, glancing around to look at the three of them.

"But aside from that, you'd give up all control?" Mercedes asked Tim, resting her elegant forearms on the table, her beautiful hands wrapped around the stem of her now empty wineglass.

The waiter must've noticed her body language, because he was immediately at her side, refilling her glass.

"Thank you," she told him with a brief glance.

"I think it's a possibility."

Xander's attention jerked back to Tim. Had he been answering Mercedes's question? Was this guy a submissive? Or was he just playing with Mercedes?

There was only one way to tell.

"So, you'd be interested in being dominated by a woman?" he asked, signaling for the waiter to refill his glass, as well.

"I think it would be fun," Tim said.

Xander could see that Tim was making every effort to keep from looking at his assistant.

Yep, the conversation was definitely uncomfortable for the man, but at the same time, at least it wasn't business.

Xander focused on the television screen, noticing the words scrolling across the bottom for the first time. He didn't pay them much attention even now, but as he watched the jumble of words, the memory of that first dinner date began to fade. He did his best not to think about the events that had happened shortly after that dinner, either.

As it had turned out, Tim was very interested in being dominated, and Mercedes had been all too kind by agreeing to show him the ropes. It was their introductory scene at Kink. Xander would never forget it, either. If he was correct, Tim wouldn't, either. The man had been smitten, just like several of the unattached male subs that night. Needless to say, Mercedes had garnered a reputation at the club.

If they could only see her now, he thought to himself.

Pushing up off of the sofa, Xander untucked his polo shirt from his jeans. On his way up the stairs, he unbuttoned one of the buttons near his neck. Once he was inside his bedroom, he reached behind his head, grabbed a handful of cotton, and pulled his shirt over his head, discarding it on a chair nearby.

He made his way to the master bathroom and propped himself against the open door, staring at the beautiful woman soaking in the oversized Jacuzzi tub.

Xander was pretty damn sure that each and every time he saw her again, she was even more beautiful than the last time.

Black hair piled haphazardly on top of her head, her naked body covered with mounds of white bubbles. She was sensational. Her eyes were closed, her arms resting along the sides of the tub.

For once, Mercedes looked entirely at peace.

"You decided to join me?" she asked sweetly, not opening her eyes.

"Not tonight," he informed her, pushing away from the wall. Rather than join her in the tub, he decided for a quick shower. And then they'd play a little before bed.

Hoping to give her a few more minutes to relax, he took his time in the shower, glancing over at her through the glass walls. Xander liked the fact that she was watching him. In fact, she never seemed to look away, unabashedly watching as he soaped up.

"Are you making me get out?" she asked, smiling.

"It's time. I was hoping to show you something before bed."

That seemed to catch her interest.

"What are you going to show me?"

"Wouldn't you like to know," he teased.

God, he loved the way she seemed so comfortable in his bathroom, relaxing in his tub, sharing the space with him. It just felt … natural.

Reaching down, he waited for her to take his hand. Once she'd hit the button to release the water from the tub, she took his proffered hand, and he assisted her to her feet. Taking the handheld shower sprayer that was attached to the tub, he turned on the warm water and rinsed her thoroughly.

The water sluiced over her generous curves, and he watched as every glorious inch of her was uncovered. As usual, he found himself intrigued by the intricate magnolia flower tattoo on her shoulder that wrapped around her upper arm all the way to her elbow. It was feminine and so damn sensual. As was the other one on her hip that contained a pair of cuffs, a collar, and a flogger hidden in the brilliantly colored flowers.

Once he was sure he'd washed all of the soap from her creamy skin, Xander turned off the water, took her hand, and helped her out of the bath onto the plush rug sitting in front of the tub. From there, he retrieved a towel and proceeded to dry her completely. When he was satisfied, he took his terry cloth robe from the back of the door and wrapped it around her.

Mercedes smiled up at him, and Xander's heart skipped a beat. He was beginning to crave those smiles.

Taking her hand in his, Xander led her down the hall to another room on the second floor. There were two additional bedrooms, but this one he'd had converted.

Into his own personal dungeon.

Keeping his eye on Mercedes, he watched for her reaction.

She already knew about the dungeon, but he'd never actually shown it to her. Mainly because she had never asked, and he'd never had a reason to.

Until tonight.

CHAPTER TWENTY-SEVEN

MERCEDES HAD BEEN ESSENTIALLY BONELESS AFTER HER bath. But as she allowed Xander to lead her to his dungeon, she knew her stress was about to come back tenfold.

It wasn't that she'd thought she wouldn't visit his dungeon at least once during the five days she'd be there, but honestly, she'd been hoping for longer — preferably a month — to acclimate to her new *temporary* life before he ventured this direction. Although that wasn't part of the deal.

Apparently Xander had other ideas.

Xander flipped on the lights in a rather impressive room and allowed her to step inside before he put his hands on her shoulders and eased the robe down and off of her, leaving her very, very naked. As naked as he was.

An involuntary shiver racked her body, and it had nothing to do with being cold. In fact, the air was comfortable, and her body was warming nicely just from the idea of what was to come, yet there was a little bit of hesitancy that was lingering in the forefront of her mind.

Her fight-or-flight instinct was kicking in, as well, warning her that she might soon regret what she'd signed on for.

Then again, he'd openly punished her in front of a large group of people at Devotion, and she'd found out just how much she could enjoy that type of submission.

Even if she was still confused by it.

All of that aside, if she really thought about it, this place had some positive things going for it. One, it was nice. Not seedy or dirty, just immaculately clean and well designed. And two, they did not have an audience, which meant she'd be able to maintain a little of her dignity while he did whatever he had planned for her.

Mercedes would openly admit that she was impressed with Xander's setup. He'd gone all out by incorporating the necessary equipment for all of his kinks, including a rather intricate suspension rig that would rival any she'd seen in any club — it was equipped with a narrow padded platform that appeared to act as a bed with a number of straps to secure his submissives. He also had a medical setup in one corner — for those extremely kinky play scenes. Another corner had a St. Andrew's cross. And the final section had a rather plain-looking bench — probably used for regular whipping, if there was such a thing.

All in all, Mercedes liked it. The floors and walls were an inky black, the lights were blue, which offered a seductive, eerie glow to the room.

"I'm going to go easy on you tonight," he told her.

She would've believed him, too, if it weren't for the wicked glint in his eyes and the smirk on his sexy lips.

"Let's play, shall we?" he said, taking her hand and leading her toward the suspension rig.

Another shiver raced down her spine.

"Are you cold?" he asked, pulling her against him.

Mercedes pressed up against his equally naked body, relishing the heat of him as he wrapped his arms around her.

"No," she said honestly. She wasn't cold, but she would definitely take whatever warmth he was willing to share with her.

"Good."

After pressing a kiss to her forehead, Xander led her to the suspended bed. Stopping in front of it, he let her go and then worked the rigs until the bed lowered just a little, making it easier for her to sit on the edge. She did so without argument, knowing it wasn't going to do her any good tonight.

The next thing Mercedes knew, she was expertly secured. Her wrists were attached to cuffs above her head. Her feet rested on brackets that protruded from the end of the bed, and her ankles were cuffed in padded leather. The position of her feet left her legs spread wide.

Completely exposed.

Once again.

"You're so fucking beautiful," Xander said gruffly, the desire in his tone apparent.

Mercedes watched him closely. Not because she was scared but because she just wanted to watch him. The way he moved, the way he appeared so comfortable in his own skin.

He moved over to a setup on the wall, grabbing items left and right, opening packages, before finally returning to the foot of the makeshift bed and standing between her thighs.

"Does your housekeeper clean this room, too?" she asked, her anxiety getting the best of her.

Xander grinned, his eyes lighting with his amusement. "Yes, she does."

She heard a cap being opened, and she knew what he was going to do. The position he had her in left her ass slightly hanging over the edge.

"Has she ever asked you about it?" Her voice wavered with the question, her nervousness ringing loudly in the room.

Xander chuckled low and deep. "No, we haven't sat down to discuss it."

Just like the last time he'd played with her ass, Xander pulled on a latex glove before coating his fingers with lube, making her body clench accordingly. She knew what he was preparing her for, and there was absolutely no fear.

In fact, Mercedes was anxious for him to do what he'd promised the other night at the club. She'd known then that he was going to prepare her, and she was grateful for that. Anal sex wasn't on her list of things she usually engaged in — okay, so it was on her list of things she never did, at least not with another person.

But that didn't mean she wasn't anticipating it.

Her body burned hot, almost immediately when he pressed his finger against her anus, teasing her slowly.

"You've never taken another man here?" he asked, obviously wanting her to clarify for him again what she'd said at Devotion.

"No, Sir." Her words vibrated with… Oh, good grief. She wasn't sure if it was nerves or anticipation that filled her more.

The look he shot her was fully of passion and … possessiveness, maybe?

"Do you know how much I want to slide my cock right here?"

Mercedes shook her head as he teased her with the tips of his fingers.

"I've dreamed about it, pet."

She watched as he reached for the butt plug he'd opened a moment before. As though he was tormenting her, which he kind of was, he coated the end generously with lube before he returned his fingers to her anus. This time he slid one finger inside of her slowly.

Mercedes closed her eyes as the initial bite of pain came and went. It wasn't long before he began fucking her with slow, deliberate thrusts of his finger in her ass. Her pussy was wet, her entire body in tune with the strange intrusion.

"So tight. I can't wait to slide my cock in your ass and fuck you hard. Do you want that, M?"

"Yes, Sir," she answered immediately, too turned on to be appalled by her behavior.

This man knew her too well, knew just how to play her body to make her crazy with lust. It was as though he'd paid attention to her through the years.

And maybe he had.

Either way, Mercedes wanted this.

This she could handle. Playtime. In a dungeon. It wasn't about romance and emotion; this was about pure, unadulterated fucking. Something that would keep her from getting too attached to this man.

At least more so than she already was.

Refusing to think about that, Mercedes focused on his fingers — plural because he'd added a second — as he penetrated her, thrusting a little deeper, a little harder.

"Oh, God," she moaned when her insides tightened.

"Feel good?"

"Yes," she moaned.

And it did. It felt so good.

His fingers retreated, and she felt the blunt head of the anal plug as he pressed it against her.

"Breathe, pet. Bear down for me."

Mercedes did as she was told, and it wasn't long before the plug was lodged in her ass.

"So fucking pretty," he exhaled roughly.

She was breathing, just like he'd told her to. In fact, she was panting, willing the pain to ease. And it did, within a few brief minutes. By the time he stepped away to remove the glove, she just felt full.

"I'm going to lift you up some more," he told her as he used the levers on the side of the machine.

And he did; he lifted her several inches. It was slow going, but she was suspended even higher off of the floor.

"You've got such a pretty pussy, pet," he told her as he stepped between her legs once again. "So pretty."

She watched as he leaned forward, his head lowering between her thighs before the warmth of his mouth caressed her sensitive flesh. God, yes! She wanted to beg and plead, but she knew if she did, he wouldn't continue, and she wanted nothing more than for him to continue.

And he did.

Oh, God, how he did.

Xander used his fingers to separate her pussy lips, holding her open as he sucked her labia first, then slid his tongue over her, lightly grazing her clit, sliding down to her vaginal opening, and then back up. He repeated the movements several times, making her squirm.

"Is this what you want? For me to eat your pussy?"

"Yes," she whispered.

"Yes, what?"

"Yes, Sir."

"Beg me, pet. Beg me to eat your sweet pussy."

"Please eat my pussy, Sir," she said without an ounce of shame. It felt too good.

At this point, she was way past caring what he made her do. As long as he didn't stop doing that.

XANDER TOOK HIS TIME. HE WANTED TO tease Mercedes until she was begging him to fuck her. Ever since he'd walked into the dungeon with her, noticing the way she seemed to easily accept what they were about to do, he'd been hard as stone.

Even when he'd retrieved the anal plug, the haze of lust he could see burning in her eyes hadn't dissipated. She might've burned hotter at that point.

Just the knowledge that he was the first and only to take her ass was nearly his undoing. She awed him with her trust.

And now, as he drove his tongue inside of her, he knew it wouldn't be much longer before he'd be sliding into her body.

He wasn't going to promise to go easy on her tonight.

Seeing her strapped down, naked, and writhing was hotter than hell. It was a dream come true, one he'd had for more years than he could count. And now that he had her there, at his mercy, he wanted to do nothing more than to take her in every way possible.

"Xander. Oh, God, I'm going to come."

Rather than say anything, he increased his efforts, wanting to drive her wild, to make her scream his name.

"Yes! Oh, God, it feels so good. Don't stop. Please don't stop."

While Mercedes rambled, her body tensing, he directed his efforts to her clit, flicking his tongue over the engorged bundle of nerves over and over. Knowing that she'd fly apart as soon as he thrust his fingers into her tight cunt, he held off for as long as he could. But finally, the need to be inside of her, to fuck her until he couldn't see straight took over, and he couldn't wait.

Driving two fingers into her pussy, Xander doubled his efforts, focusing on her clit.

"Oh, fuck! Yes!"

Mercedes screamed beautifully as she came, her pussy clamping down on his fingers as her body convulsed with her orgasm.

He only stepped away briefly, retrieving a condom and the clit-stimulating vibrator he'd opened earlier from the counter. Once at her side again, he covered himself and then grabbed the lube, coating his cock hurriedly.

Working the plug out of her, he tossed it into the sink nearby.

"I need to be inside you," he told her, his eyes focused on her. "I'm going to fuck your ass, Mercedes. I'm going to take you right here. Right now." He wanted to say, *the only one who will ever take you like this*, but he didn't add that part. "And when you come again, I expect you to scream my name. Do you understand me?"

"Yes, Sir" she moaned, but she didn't look at him.

He moved around near her head, fiddling with the suspension chains, lifting the front of the bed so that she could see exactly what he was doing. When he was satisfied, he returned to the foot of the padded platform.

"Eyes on what I'm doing. I want you to watch while I take you."

Mercedes glanced up at his face and then back down between her legs. "Hurry," she pleaded.

Smiling, Xander gripped his cock firmly and then prodded her ass slowly, pushing into her. He continued to watch her, doing his best to ensure he didn't hurt her.

"So tight," he growled as sweat trickled down his temple.

His cock was slowly sliding deeper, but he still had a ways to go before he was fully inside of her. When he'd taken her pussy before, it always took some finesse to fill her completely because he wasn't a little man, nor was he average. But like this, shit, he wasn't sure she'd be able to take him all the way.

"Please, fuck me, Master," she begged, her raspy voice sending a chill down his spine.

Master.

Aww, fuck.

When she called him that, there was no way he could resist. He went as slowly as he could until finally his balls were pressed against her bottom and sweat was coating his neck.

"I'm going to fuck you hard. Can you handle it?" he asked, praying like hell she didn't say no.

"Yes, Master. Fuck me," she begged.

Xander slid out of her slowly, but this time, he didn't ease his way into her ass. He thrust forward, swallowing a groan as the pleasure accosted him. She was so tight. And in this position, with her propped up, she was even tighter. But he couldn't stop.

He pulled out, thrust forward. Repeating over and over as their breathing increased, soft growls and moans filling the air as they both headed toward release. With the tiny vibrator on his finger, Xander pressed against her clit and Mercedes's eyes widened.

While he increased his pace, thrusting harder, faster, over and over, he moved his finger in small circles over her clit.

"Yes! Xander! Please!"

"Come for me, pet. Come for me. Scream my name when you do. I want to hear my name on your lips."

Focusing solely on the amazing pleasure coursing through him, Xander pounded into her, harder, faster, deeper. His thighs were screaming from the position, but he didn't care. His balls were drawing up close to his body, sweat popping out on his arms, his legs, his chest. He was completely and totally consumed by this woman.

"Ahh, fuck," he growled, unable to stop himself as he fucked her hard. "So good, baby. So fucking good."

Sliding his thumb into her pussy, Xander fucked her ass and her pussy while he pressed the vibrator to her clit.

"Oh, shit! Oh, shit! I'm going to come, Xander. Yes! Don't stop! Oh, God! Xander!"

Xander gritted his teeth when her body clamped down around his cock. A rough sound escaped his chest as he pounded harder, once, twice, three more times until he couldn't hold back any longer.

"Fuck yes, Mercedes! I'm going to come deep in your ass. Fuck, baby." And with that, Xander let go completely.

CHAPTER TWENTY-EIGHT

Day four...
Sunday

SUNDAY MORNING CAME WAY TOO EARLY. BY the time Mercedes forced her tired body out of Xander's bed at seven, she was once again alone. This time she was grateful for a little time to herself, though. She'd had that same dream, the one that had been haunting her for days now, and she needed a moment to pull herself together.

Making a detour to the bathroom, she opted for a shower. Her body was still sore from the night before, and she hoped a little warm water would help to ease some of the discomfort.

A full hour had passed by the time she made her way downstairs. Rather than searching for Xander, she headed to the kitchen, hoping he had made coffee again. When she reached the brightly lit room, she found Xander sitting at the kitchen table, his iPad in front of him.

"Good morning," he greeted as soon as she stepped through the arched doorway.

"Good morning." She didn't slow as she headed for the coffeepot.

"We're taking a little trip today," he informed her after she'd poured her coffee and doctored it to her liking.

"Where?" she asked as she lowered herself into the chair across from him.

"Ohio."

If she was right, the only thing in Ohio was his parents. Well, not the only thing, but definitely the only thing Xander would need to go there for. "Is everything all right?"

"As far as I can tell," he assured her as he glanced down at his iPad and then back up to her. She didn't want to think about what it meant when he pushed the tablet away and focused on her. She didn't dare to hope. "Come here."

Okay, she dared.

Making her way to him, she held her coffee close to her chest but then released it when he reached for it first.

With the cup on the table, Xander pulled her closer, but he didn't try to get her to his lap. Instead, the man shocked the hell out of her when he wrapped his arms around her waist and rested his head against her belly.

Mercedes did the only thing she knew to do. She held him back. Sliding her arms around his head, she teased the hair at his nape gently. She didn't even know what to say.

For the first time in all of her life, the man seemed … vulnerable.

Thankfully, she didn't have to come up with something to say because, a minute later, he pulled back and looked up at her. "The jet will be ready in an hour. I didn't know if you had anything you needed to do this morning."

"I've got a call to take, but I can do that from anywhere," she told him, reaching for her coffee cup again as she took a step back. "Do I need to pack anything?"

"No. We'll be coming back tonight. I've got a meeting tomorrow morning that I can't miss."

Well, then. "Okay."

An hour later, almost exactly, Carson was dropping them at a private airport where Xander's personal jet awaited them. She'd only been aboard this plane once previously, and that had been when Xander had taken an interest in a property in New York of all places. He'd taken her along so they could check it out. Although her real estate license wasn't instated there, he'd insisted that she go with him.

But this wasn't a business trip. It was personal. Extremely personal because his parents were involved. Which meant that Mercedes would be spending time with his mother and father, probably in close quarters.

Until a few days ago, that prospect wouldn't have bothered her. Now, it did. Mainly because she had no idea what she was going to say to them. Would they realize she had fallen in love with their son? Would they pick up on the tension that radiated from Xander? She certainly had, and she knew it hadn't been there the night before, so she was all the more confused.

Rather than bother him, she pretended to work, and for whatever reason, he left her alone.

For the entire flight.

By the time they stepped foot out of the plane onto Ohio soil, she was more or less to the breaking point. Xander had been on the phone for much of the trip. And when he hadn't been, he'd appeared contemplative as he spent his time staring out of the small window. He hadn't asked how she was doing, and she hadn't interrupted him once.

Now, as they climbed into the limo that was waiting for them, Mercedes knew she had to say something. Anything.

But she couldn't find her voice.

"We're going on a field trip today," Xander informed her shortly after the door to the limo closed behind them.

"Field trip?"

"Yeah, my dad wants us to check out the Pro Football Hall of Fame."

Hmm. That sounded … interactive.

And maybe that was a good thing. That meant less time for Mercedes to stumble over her words. Maybe.

"And then we'll have lunch."

Lunch. Okay. Lunch was good.

She didn't respond, just thumbed through her phone, glancing at her email although she didn't see any of the words on her screen.

What had happened between last night and today? Why was Xander acting so strangely? Or was he?

Maybe it was her. Maybe she was the one acting strangely, and he was just adjusting to her mood.

Crap.

Once the limo was in motion, Mercedes took a moment to glance out the window. That was when Xander reached for her hand, sliding his fingers through hers. She had to fight the urge to look at him, but the relief she felt in her chest was palpable.

When he didn't speak, she knew she had to, and the words finally tumbled out of her mouth. "Are you all right?"

"I will be," he answered, glancing down at their linked fingers.

"Is your dad okay?" Mercedes knew he'd been worried about his father ever since he had learned of the fall.

"My mother is insisting that's the case," he told her as he looked sideways at her. "She's hiding something from me."

Oh. Well, that definitely explained his mood. "Did you talk to her today?"

"Yes. I called her this morning to let her know we were flying in to see them. You would've thought I was threatening to take them back home to Texas or something with the way she clammed up all of a sudden."

Mercedes knew how close Xander was with his parents. He was always sharing stories about his parents, his childhood. She knew he did it because he loved them, but also because he had always hoped to get her to open up about her family.

Yeah, well, Xander had soon learned that she hadn't lived the Brady Bunch life and had no desire to share the horror stories of growing up with her father.

"You nervous?"

Mercedes glanced down at his mouth, then up to meet his eyes once more. "Why would I be nervous?"

"You're meeting my parents," he told her with a smirk.

"I've already *met* your parents," she retorted with a smile. "Many, many times."

"But this is different."

"How so?"

"This time you're meeting them as my sub."

That statement got the tension ratcheting up another notch, her chest suddenly feeling tight once more. "Since they don't know you're a Dom, I seriously doubt you'll tell them I'm your temporary sub." She hoped he wouldn't.

There was a light that seemed to turn off in his eyes, but Xander tried to pretend he wasn't affected by whatever she'd said. "Maybe I'll tell them all about it."

Crap. Temporary. That's what she'd said that had bothered him. And she suddenly wished she could take it back, because she wanted to put a smile on his face. Instead, she gave him a weak grin and said, "Maybe you won't."

What had started as a who-could-top-who double dare just a few days ago had quickly morphed into something entirely unexpected, and Mercedes had to wonder whether he felt what was transpiring between them the same way she did.

It was more than just sex. A lot more.

At least for her it was.

Before Mercedes could question him, which she wasn't even sure she wanted to do, the limo came to a stop, and Xander reached for the door. Once outside, he held out his hand to her, and she reached for it, taking comfort in the strength of his hand against hers. Even when she was out of the car, he didn't let go of her hand, and that simple gesture had more relief flooding her.

Yeah, it was plain as day … she'd fallen for this man.

Head first.

XANDER FIGURED IT WOULD TAKE SOMETHING EPIC to shake him up. Today, it had been a combination of things.

Ever since he'd woken up at three o'clock that morning with a warm, soft woman curled up to his side, he'd known. His life had been altered. Irrevocably.

Never had he imagined one beautiful woman would be the reason he felt off-center. Nor had he ever expected that one single woman could keep him together at a time he thought he might just fall apart.

Okay, so maybe he had anticipated that Mercedes Bryant held the power to make him feel things he wasn't used to. Thinking that and knowing that were two very different things, though. And the way she made him feel … well, it scared the shit out of him.

No, he wasn't thinking about running and hiding in a closet and hoping she'd hightail it out the same way she'd come in.

Actually, he was feeling the exact opposite.

Xander was ready to lie at her feet and reveal every single emotion she made him feel. Starting with love.

Yes, that was correct. Love. The big L word that terrified most people.

It didn't terrify him, but he knew Mercedes would likely run for the hills if he did confess as much to her. He had an overwhelming urge to tie this amazing, beautiful woman to his bed and never let her go.

Only he knew he had to keep his distance. They were only a few days into this, and he knew without a doubt that Mercedes wasn't as comfortable with her feelings as he was with his. And wasn't that a fucking shame, because Xander had never in his life felt what she made him feel when she was near.

"Have you ever been here before?" Mercedes asked as they made their way up the steps toward the building whose sign boasted the name and the glass windows gave them a glimpse inside.

"Once," he told her. "With my father."

"And he wants to go again?" she asked with a grin.

"My father would probably go every single day if we lived here." It was true. Stan Boone was a football fan. He was also Xander's biggest fan. And it wasn't just because he'd played football in high school and then in college. His father loved football, but Xander knew he loved him more.

"Has your mother been here before?"

"Not that I know of. You'll both be Hall of Fame virgins."

Mercedes laughed, and Xander realized what he'd said. He couldn't help it, he laughed as well and tightened his grip on Mercedes's fingers. He loved having her there with him. Especially like this.

Once they stepped through the main doors, Xander's eyes attempted to focus on the lighting change, but before he could make out more than mere shadows of the people standing inside, he heard her voice.

"Xander!"

It was his mother.

Xander released Mercedes's hand as Stella approached, her smile making her entire face light up. Unable to do anything more, he stood there with his arms open wide. Stella walked right into them, and he hugged his mother, kissing her on the cheek before taking a step back.

His father did the same, and they shared a quick hug and a pounding slap on the back — it was a guy thing.

"It is so good to see you," Stella said to Mercedes as she hugged her tightly before taking her hand and leading her toward the exhibit on the other side of the room.

"You look great," Mercedes told his mother as she glanced back at Xander and his father, who had fallen into step behind the women. "As do you, Mr. Boone."

"I definitely don't mind when a beautiful young lady calls me Mr. Boone, but I prefer Stan, Ms. Bryant." Xander's father teased Mercedes, making her blush.

"Stan," she tacked on, followed by, "How are you feeling?"

The four of them came to a stop.

"Much better," he told her as Xander glanced over at his father. "Let's get this show on the road, shall we?" Stan redirected.

Mercedes met Xander's gaze, and she knew as well as he did that Stan had purposely avoided saying more. Fine. He would give his father a brief reprieve for a few minutes, but he fully intended to ask him for the details. The real details this time.

Xander spent the next half hour following his mother and father and Mercedes through the many exhibits that highlighted football's greats and the numerous details about the history of the game. It was true, he had been there once before, but even now, he felt a bit nostalgic.

No, he didn't miss his football days. Not in the least. He had moved on to bigger and better things, and he didn't have to worry about a potential life-altering injury changing the course of his career. He'd made that decision long before that could happen.

"How about some lunch?" Stella asked, turning around.

"I could handle lunch," Xander told her. He wasn't starving, but he would get the chance to talk directly to his father. And he knew his father was doing his best to avoid Xander's questions, which was why he'd been hearing all about football for the last thirty minutes.

The café they entered was nothing more than a snack bar with chairs and tables, but Xander wasn't picky. It didn't hurt that they were the only people in the place aside from the ragged-looking guy behind the counter. Okay, so maybe he wasn't ragged, maybe he was just trying to stay awake, because it was clear today was not a day he was hustling to keep up.

The four of them ordered and then took their seats at one of the few tables. Once they were seated, their baskets of food and bottles of water in front of them, Xander decided now was as good a time as any to talk to his old man.

"How're you feeling?" he asked. It was the same question Stan had managed to avoid earlier, but as far as Xander was concerned, he hadn't gotten a good enough answer.

Stan sighed. "I guess it's safe to say I'm getting a little old to be swinging from the rafters."

Xander looked up then, looking over at Mercedes. She was staring at his father with wide eyes. When she looked over at him, he smiled at her and just shook his head.

"Hush," Stella said, laughing. "We were certainly not swinging from the rafters. No matter what Xander told you."

"We?" Mercedes asked, obviously realizing they were joking.

"How was the trip?" Stella asked. Leave it to his mother to try and change the subject.

"Quick."

"Well, I guess that's a luxury that's worth the price, huh?" Stan asked.

Xander laughed.

Although his parents hadn't ever hurt for money, they weren't by any means wealthy. They were comfortable, having always managed their money efficiently. And Xander hadn't grown up with a silver spoon in his mouth, either. But once he'd made his first million at twenty-five, he'd vowed to ensure that they didn't have to worry about money. He didn't spend extravagantly, but he did prefer to travel and dine in style.

Glancing over at the snack bar behind his father's head, he grinned. Okay, so maybe not always in style.

"It's worth the price, Dad."

"Where's Shane?" Stella asked as she picked at her hamburger. Or what looked like a hamburger.

"Working, I'm sure."

"He should've come with you."

No, he shouldn't have. But Xander didn't respond. That's the way his mother was. It was her little way of pressing the issue. The Mercedes issue.

Knowing they would rather talk about anything but his father's health, Xander decided it was now or never. "How are you really feeling?"

"Better than I was. Nothing's broken, thank the good Lord, but there for a couple of days, I wasn't so sure they hadn't been looking at someone else's x-rays."

"How'd you *really* fall?"

Stan glanced over at Stella before meeting Xander's gaze once more.

"I was heading out of the RV, planning to sit outside and watch the sun set. While I was walking, I had a sharp pain in my chest that stole my breath there for a moment. I guess I lost my balance, and that's when I took a tumble down the stairs."

Xander swallowed hard, glancing between his mother and his father. Stella had purposely left off the fact that his father had had chest pains. He wasn't sure whether he should be grateful or pissed. He'd have been on a plane in a heartbeat if he'd known that. And maybe that's what she'd been trying to keep from happening.

And Xander realized then that his father had been the other reason for his melancholy mood that morning. He had known something had happened. Something more than his father just falling. Knowing didn't do anything to settle his fears, though.

"Did they do any tests?" Xander asked, not caring which of them answered him at this point.

"Yes, they did tests," Stella assured him. "Everything is fine. He didn't have a heart attack."

Xander wasn't sure he was breathing. He was looking at his father, a picture of good health, and wondering just what the hell he would do if something ever happened to him.

Throughout his life, Stan Boone had been a stalwart supporter. He'd been right there beside him, rooting him on through all of the sports he'd played throughout his childhood, right up until college, when he'd accepted a full scholarship. To play football. Stan had even been there when Xander had decided football wasn't what he wanted to pursue anymore.

Sure, he was close to his mother, talking to her every single day, but Xander would be the first to admit that Stan Boone was the role model he'd mirrored himself after.

The idea of not having his father in his life had the potential to bring Xander to his knees.

CHAPTER TWENTY-NINE

MERCEDES WANTED TO REACH OVER TO XANDER and hold his hand. It was a strange feeling, but she couldn't seem to shake it.

As she listened to the conversation between him and his parents, she caught a glimpse of a much younger Xander, the one who looked up to his father as though the man had hung the moon. When Stan had mentioned he'd had chest pains, Xander's entire demeanor had changed, and right before her very eyes, he'd let down that guard he kept in place at all times.

She'd wanted to wrap her arms around him so that she could latch on to him until the moment passed.

But she hadn't.

And then, as though nothing had happened, Xander's walls fell back in place, and he transformed into the professional she knew him to be. Even if this was as far from a business setting as they could get.

"It's nothing to worry about," Stan assured Xander. "I've gone in for a few more tests, and they haven't found anything."

"I don't want you to hide that from me again," Xander stated bluntly, the full brunt of his fear aimed at his father.

Mercedes couldn't imagine what he was feeling.

"You've got more important things to worry about than me," his father told him.

"Bullshit," Xander ground out through clenched teeth, his eyes narrowing. "Nothing is more important."

Mercedes knew that Xander loved his parents. He was close to them in ways Mercedes had never known personally. She'd been introduced to Stella and Stan years ago, spent plenty of time with them when they were in town because Xander was always inviting her.

As she watched them, she had a craving to feel that emotion he rarely showed turned on her. Would he look at her as though the entire world revolved around her?

Did she want him to?

The last question wasn't easy to answer mainly because she was confused. About everything.

"How're things with you?" Stan asked, and Mercedes realized he was talking to her.

"Good. Really busy at the moment."

"The housing market's making a comeback, huh?"

Mercedes knew Stan wasn't all that interested in talking about real estate, but she sensed he was doing his best to change the subject, so she responded, "Looks that way."

"Tell us about Ohio," Xander interrupted, saving Mercedes at the last moment. When she looked up into his eyes, she saw something she'd never seen before.

And this time, she was the one whose chest was tightening.

But this had nothing to do with pain.

An hour and a half later, Xander was walking Mercedes back to the limo. They'd walked his parents to their car, and after Xander had said a few brief words to his mother, they were on their way.

When they reached the car, the driver opened it for her, and then Xander spoke to the man as she climbed inside. The only words she could make out were *detour* and *scenic route*. Although she pretended not to hear anything, Mercedes's heart rate sped up.

Rightfully so as it turned out, because the moment Xander climbed into the limo behind her, she noticed the intense expression on his face.

"Come here," he ordered, his tone laced with nothing but pure dominance.

She complied easily, without question. Or reservation.

There wasn't a lot of room to maneuver in the backseat of the limousine, but there was enough. For what she sensed he wanted, anyway.

Xander spread his legs and guided her onto her knees on the floor between them. She kept her eyes locked with his, waiting for his next command.

"Unfasten my pants," he told her.

Mercedes did.

"Put your hands on my cock."

She did that, too.

All the while, she continued to stare into his eyes. Xander might've been fighting the emotion that was tearing him up inside, but she could feel it radiating from him. He might've been commanding her, but there was a plea in his eyes. He needed this.

He needed her.

Mercedes continued to stroke him slowly, watching him as she did. Xander shifted, forcing his slacks down farther, freeing his cock completely.

"I want to feel your mouth on me," he said huskily.

Mercedes didn't say a word, doing as he wanted. And she didn't do it because he ordered her to. She did it because she wanted to. She wanted to relieve him of his pain. Whatever was eating away at him, she wanted to soothe him. And if this was what he needed from her, she'd gladly offer it.

It was a true testament to everything she'd been feeling for him lately.

Being a submissive — his submissive — wasn't at all what she'd thought it would be. Giving up control to someone was not that easy, but when it came to Xander, Mercedes found that she was willing to do damn near anything to please him. Even if she still held back at times. Even if she still had a burning urge to dominate him, to prove to them both that she wasn't the type of woman to be walked on.

Although Xander had proven in recent days that submissive didn't mean she was being reduced to less of a person. The opposite, actually. She felt empowered when she was with Xander, especially when he was looking at her the way he was now.

Lowering her head, she swiped at the head of his cock gently, just a breath of air and the very tip of her tongue. Xander's thighs tightened, and Mercedes continued.

To her surprise, Xander didn't put his hands in her hair. He didn't try to guide her mouth to his cock, nor did he try to thrust up into her mouth. No, he let her lead, allowed her to take control although they both knew he was still dominating every single second they were together.

Xander's hands fisted at his sides, proving that he was holding back. It only made her want to push him harder. Using every skill she possessed, Mercedes did her best to drive him crazy. Adding her hands to the mix, she tugged at his slacks, forcing them down to his knees, cupping his balls, kneading them gently while she continued to lick and suck, never moving too quickly. She wanted him to let go, to finally let go.

But he didn't.

Just when she thought he was going to lose it, Xander moved, pulling her up from the floor until she was straddling his legs. He crushed his mouth to hers, sliding his fingers into her hair and holding her close. His other hand moved around to her back, gliding beneath her shirt and caressing her skin gently.

"Let me feel you," she told him when their mouths separated. "Let me feel you inside me."

Since she had on a skirt, it wasn't difficult to adjust herself so that she could take him. The only thing in their way was her panties, but to her surprise, Xander made quick work of that by ripping them off of her.

That made two pair. And yes, it was just as hot the second time to have him desperate enough to rip her clothes off.

Pleasure ignited in her core. A burning lust that had only been smoldering for the last few hours, never completely burning itself out. And now, it flared into a blaze of heat so powerful she wasn't sure she'd survive it.

When Xander guided himself inside of her, Mercedes let him. She let him control everything from that point, because the only thing she could focus on was how good he felt as he thrust inside her over and over.

He pulled her mouth back to his, kissing her until she could hardly breathe, hardly think for wanting him.

"Mercedes," he growled as he pulled his lips from hers. But he didn't move away; he just held her to him as she continued to lift and lower herself onto him while he met her thrust for thrust.

XANDER WAS LOSING CONTROL. HE WAS A wreck, and he had a feeling that Mercedes knew it. At the moment, the only thing that was keeping him together was her arms around him. He was so lost in her he feared he was going to say something that would send her running from him, but he couldn't seem to focus.

The way her body clasped him, pulling him deeper, holding him tighter, Xander didn't ever want it to end.

Never.

He wanted to feel her surrounding him just like this for the rest of his goddamn life.

Never had he lost control like this. He hadn't even known he was capable of it.

It was the emotional overload, he knew that much. Between what he was feeling for her and what he'd learned at lunch, he wasn't doing a good job of keeping the emotion on lockdown.

"Look at me."

Mercedes's voice called to him, and he lifted his head, meeting her gaze. God, he loved this woman. He'd cared about her for a long time; he'd even loved her. But not like this. Not with all that he was and all that he ever would be.

It didn't have a damn thing to do with the sex, although he wasn't sure two people had ever been more perfect for one another. In all of his life, after all of the women he'd been with, never had he felt this. This blazing inferno that scorched him to his very soul. Mercedes was all that he wanted, all that he needed, and the world could probably come crashing down around them, and he just wouldn't care.

"Aww, fuck," he groaned when she tightened her muscles around him.

Gripping her hips to still her, Xander sucked in a breath, trying his damnedest not to lose complete control.

"Let go, X. Let go for me," Mercedes encouraged.

Looking into the brilliant gray depths of her eyes, Xander realized she wasn't trying to top him. She just wanted him to let go. To give in to her.

Shifting, he lifted her slightly and angled himself so that he could thrust up into her, driving his cock deeper, harder. He was in control, but so was she even if she didn't realize it.

"M," he growled.

"Come for me," she said, her hands coming to rest on his face, holding him so that he had no choice but to look at her. "Come with me."

"Fuck!" he growled, his release pulled from him by her and the sweet words that shredded him from the inside out.

He continued to drive up inside of her until she was groaning, her hands tightening on his face, but she kept her eyes on him.

"Come for me, baby," he said softly. "Let me feel all of you."

With that, Mercedes came, her eyes never closing, and what he saw reflecting back at him gave him hope.

CHAPTER THIRTY

Day five...
Monday

TOSSING AND TURNING AS THE DREAM PULLED her deeper, no matter how hard she tried, Mercedes couldn't force herself awake, so she let it consume her.

The clock on the wall read just after five when Mercedes stepped into her condo. Having just finished with a rather intense meeting with a pain-in-the-ass client, she was ready for a little downtime.

More than ready.

Glancing around, she noticed that everything seemed the same as when she'd left early that morning. Her housekeeper had come by, but that was the only evidence that anyone else had been there.

But there was someone else who was supposed to be waiting for her. Because she'd instructed him to before she'd left that morning.

Xander would be there. She knew it.

Because that's what he would do. He would follow the rules to the letter, do exactly as she instructed. Without question. Without argument.

It wasn't real. He wasn't a sub. But she was sure he'd play the part because that was what they'd agreed to.

Of all the subs she'd taken in the years she'd been a Domme, Xander would be by far the most obedient, even if he'd only been acting as her sub for just a few short hours.

For whatever reason, his unerring ability to please her was starting to drive her a little crazy. First it had been a phone call, his easy ability to call her Mistress. And the emails from him, letting her know what he was doing and where he was going.

He was the perfect pet. Compliant, obedient, always agreeing. She knew she should be counting her blessings but found even that difficult because this wasn't Xander. The man whose body had become that of a subservient submissive lacked something.

Emotion.

Then again, she was pretty sure Xander did that on purpose, although she would never accuse him of topping from the bottom. He knew what she wanted, what she expected. And vice versa. They'd been friends long enough that they understood each other that well.

During their brief few days together, Xander had allowed her to explore a part of herself that she hadn't known still existed. He had driven her to want things she'd sworn she didn't want. But it was him. Only him who made her want these things.

But today was supposed to be the day that everything would change.

For both of them.

Quickly ridding herself of the killer heels she'd been wearing for the last few hours, Mercedes snatched them up in her hands before carrying them into her bedroom. When she stepped into the master bedroom, her beautiful sub was kneeling on the floor facing the door, his glorious body on display for her. She shut the door with a gentle click to alert him of her presence and then let her eyes roam over him.

His hands rested on his thighs, his cock semi-erect between them. His collar, the one she'd surprised him with just that morning, was around his neck, a thick, black leather collar that fit him perfectly. She'd left it on the dresser before she'd left for work. Another point in his favor — he'd found it and read the instructions.

The only other things on Xander's incredible body were the nipple piercings and the magnificent tattoos that decorated his otherwise perfect skin.

As she moved slowly across the room, she could see the word Trust *tattooed on his side, following the rigid line of muscle that arrowed down toward his groin.*

"Have you been there long?" she asked as she moved toward the bathroom.

"No, Mistress."

She didn't say anything more even though the fact that he'd referred to her as Mistress should have thrilled her immensely. Just like every other time he'd said it throughout the day, it sounded hollow, and that bothered her.

Instead, she left him kneeling while she went through the oversized bathroom to her closet. Once inside, she put her shoes back in their place and then proceeded to change clothes. Her office attire wouldn't do for tonight. She had an image to uphold, after all.

Twenty minutes later, she ventured back into the bedroom, completely dressed. On the other side of the room, lying on the top of her dresser were the clothes she'd personally picked out for him to wear to the club tonight. After retrieving the pair of leather pants, a black T-shirt, which would be removed as soon as they were inside, and his black lace-up boots, she returned to where he was still kneeling on the floor.

Before she asked him to rise, she admired him some more. Hell, seeing him on his knees, doing exactly as she'd instructed was heady enough, but the idea that he might be doing it solely to please her made her burn for him.

Sub or not, Xander truly was the most immaculate male specimen she'd ever seen. Without an ounce of fat on his body, the man weighed somewhere near two seventy-five, give or take a few pounds. At six foot six inches, he was massive, and Mercedes, not being one of those slight, skinny women, appreciated every single inch of him. In comparison, she felt incredibly feminine and sometimes even fragile when his arms were around her.

"Stand," *she instructed as she set his clothes on the bed next to where he was kneeling.*

When he was upright, Mercedes moved in close, letting her body brush slightly against his nakedness. Even at five foot eight inches, with her five-inch heels adding even more to her height, Mercedes had to look up into Xander's eyes.

The heat she hoped to see reflected there would've made her body warm another degree, but that's not what she saw. No, what she witnessed in Xander's beautiful green eyes was a void, as though he couldn't think or feel for himself unless she told him exactly what to do.

She wasn't fond of that look.

Their previous conversation rang loud in her head.

"Remember that night at Kink when you volunteered to let Mistress Desiree demonstrate on you because no one else had the balls to do it? How did that make *you* feel?"

"Like I was in someone else's body."

That's exactly what it was. He was somewhere else, but his body was there for her taking. He was doing as she wished, but his heart wasn't in it.

Had she expected it would be?

Pushing the question out of her mind, she slid her hands, palms down, over his taut stomach, up over the thick planes of his chest, and then around his neck, pulling his head down easily until her mouth met his.

"I missed you," *she whispered before pressing her lips to his. The kiss rapidly escalated, and Mercedes had to force herself to pull away from him.* "Get ready, and we'll leave in a few minutes," *she told him as she planted another short kiss on his lips.*

"Yes, Mistress."

*That's what she heard when he called her Mistress...
Absolutely nothing. The word was right, but it was hollow.*

*Needing a moment to herself, Mercedes left the bedroom and
headed to her guest bedroom, where she kept her toys. She'd also
stashed a few things she'd retrieved just that morning from
Xander's personal dungeon.*

*She wanted to add a couple of things to her bag tonight, toys
she knew he had in his vast arsenal, the ones she'd eyed when they
had previously visited his dungeon. Not that she needed any other
toys for Xander, because she'd already stocked up from her own
collection, choosing exactly what she thought would make him
lose his mind.*

*And that's what she was going to do. She'd only been
anticipating it since the day they'd made their deal. To prove to
him that she wasn't what he wanted her to be. She was a Domme.*

*Not wanting to waste any more time, she grabbed the items
and made a beeline for the front door. It was time to do this.*

Mercedes woke with a start, glancing around the room to find
herself alone.

Holy crap.

Covering her eyes with her hands, she tried to calm her
breaths. She was slowly going crazy, and that dream wasn't
helping.

It'd only been four days that she'd been practically glued to
Xander's side, pretty much handing herself over to him on a silver
platter, yet that dream continued to torment her and had since the
first night she'd slept in his arms.

She could close her eyes and still see how incredibly handsome Xander looked with her collar around his neck. But it was his responses in the dream that always tripped her up night after night. Every time, she expected to see something different, but it was never there. It was like he was just a shell of himself. Like his body was there, but someone else had entered the right response, the right actions, hell, the right way to breathe into his brain, and that was all he knew how to do.

Sighing, she rolled over to her side.

Was this a sign? Was her subconscious telling her that she couldn't do this anymore? Being a sub was... Shit. It was confusing was what it was.

The dream seemed surreal, sort of like a premonition. She couldn't help but compare her own responses to Xander's domination against the dream version of Xander and his responses to her. There were no similarities. She seemed suited for submission, while he ... did not.

There was no way to deny that her body was eagerly anticipating Xander and his commands. She burned hotter and brighter than ever before when she gave herself over to him completely.

But she had a difficult time accepting her desire to submit. Especially considering what she'd been through as a child. The hell that her father had put her through every single day of her life. She didn't want to get herself in that position ever again. Never could she allow someone else to have that sort of control over her.

It didn't feel that way with Xander, but the fear was still close, coming to the surface with every passing minute.

"Let her go out with her friends, Phillip," Priscilla argued while Mercedes stood just around the corner, watching her parents in their kitchen.

"I told her no," Phillip yelled. "I don't want her out of the house."

"She's sixteen. She needs to spend time with her friends."

"She's too stupid to have friends," Phillip screamed, and Mercedes flinched as though she'd been slapped.

Too stupid? Had her father really called her that?

Sure, he'd called her many names before — pest, tramp, pain in the ass, not to mention some much, much worse. But stupid?

She made straight As; she didn't miss school, didn't even ask to stay home when her temperature had been over one hundred and she had been throwing up all night.

She knew better. Her father would've stayed home, keeping her right under his thumb, telling her to quit faking it, to grow up. And if that didn't work, if he didn't get the reaction he wanted, he would hit her.

Never did he spank her like she'd heard some parents did to their children when they were bad. No, he backhanded her. Once he had even punched her in the stomach.

Just like he did to her mother.

And that's what made this situation all the more surprising. Her mother was standing up for her. She was sixteen years old, and for as long as she could remember, Priscilla had never stood up for her against her father. Not once.

But here Priscilla was, standing up to her father, a gleam in her once pretty gray eyes.

"Let her go out," Priscilla said through gritted teeth, shocking Mercedes with her boldness.

"Fuck you," Phillip argued. "She's staying right here. Until she turns eighteen. Then she can do whatever the fuck she wants. She can go out and fuck the defensive line for her school's pitiful excuse for a football team for all I care."

What? Mercedes couldn't believe her father was saying such disgusting things. She was a freaking virgin.

"You're too hard on her," Priscilla said, that eerie glow still in her eyes.

"And you're a pitiful excuse for a human being," he barked. "But I fucked you once and you fucked me for the rest of my life. So this is what you get. But don't worry, the day she turns eighteen, neither of you will see me again."

"I hate you!" Priscilla yelled.

"Not nearly as much as I hate you," Phillip growled.

Mercedes didn't stick around to listen to more. She turned on her heel just in time to hear the loud smack that she'd been waiting for. He'd hit her mother. Again.

As she closed her bedroom door, Mercedes took a deep breath. It wouldn't last long; she knew that much. Even abusing them took too much effort for Phillip. Instead, he would leave her mother lying on the floor wherever she fell. And once Priscilla pulled herself up off the ground, she would head to the medicine cabinet to find something to alleviate the pain.

That's how it always happened.

Mercedes blinked, and the room came into focus.

God, she hated thinking about her parents. She wanted to scream at them for all they'd put her through. It was their fault she was the way that she was.

It was why she insisted on dominating people. It was why she'd become so successful. She'd turned her hatred for them into success because she hadn't had a choice.

And that's why she didn't want to give up control. She'd spent every single day of her life up until she was eighteen years old living with a man who wanted to punish her because he felt as though his life sucked. She was a mistake, one he wished he could take back. But since she'd been born despite his desire for her mother to have an abortion, Phillip Bryant had made it his mission to ruin their lives, as well.

"Good morning."

The sexy, rough grumble of Xander's voice startled her, but she tried to play it off, turning her head slowly to see him moving toward her.

"Morning," she said, her voice still raspy from sleep. Yeah, that definitely wasn't emotion lodged deep in her throat.

"Sleep well?"

She didn't answer, but she forced a nod. That was the best she could do, because honestly, she didn't know if she had or not. It all seemed to depend on how she interpreted that dream.

"Do you know what today is?" he asked.

Mercedes frowned, doing her best to think. "Monday?"

"It's Monday," he confirmed, a sexy smirk on his lips. "It's also BDSM night at Devotion."

Oh, crap. That meant...

"That means today is *my* day," she said, trying to sound excited by the idea. Maybe that's what the dream was about. Or at least why she'd had it last night. Because today was the day she would own Xander Boone, even if for just a little while.

"*Tonight* is your night," he corrected as he crawled over her, his muscles tensing as he held himself above her.

He was on the wrong side of naked, in her opinion, wearing only a pair of black boxer briefs and a mischievous smile, the titanium bars in his nipples drawing her attention to his chest. She gazed at him momentarily, her eyes trailing down until they stopped on the word *Trust* scrolled along his side.

Trust.

That's what it all boiled down to, wasn't it?

"And that means?" she asked, lifting her gaze back up, hoping for clarification as she reached up and fingered his nipples.

She needed a distraction. And he was perfect for the role.

"I agreed to let you top me. You wanted the first time to be at Devotion. That means while we're there tonight, I'll be at your mercy. Until then," he mumbled, nuzzling his mouth against her neck, "you're mine."

Why that didn't bother her, she had no idea. Four days ago, she probably would've argued and told him that wasn't the deal. But technically — and yes, Xander was all about technicalities — it was. She had only requested that she be allowed to dominate him in public — once at Devotion and another at a place of her choosing. When she wanted. Didn't mean it would be during their five-day time frame, either. No, she was reserving that date for a time and place that would offer the most optimum payback.

Pretty optimistic of her, she knew.

If she were completely honest with herself, she'd never thought this night would happen when she'd originally requested it, so, for now, she'd let him have his way.

But tonight…

Yeah, tonight he was all hers.

CHAPTER THIRTY-ONE

As part owner of Devotion, Xander had several reservations about what was about to happen. For one, submitting to Mercedes, even if it was a one-time — or rather two-time — deal, wasn't at the top of his list of things he wanted to accomplish in his lifetime.

Actually, it wasn't even on the list.

However, he had seen that familiar spark in her eyes earlier when they'd left his condo, right after she'd given him strict instruction as to how the night would go. He had complied half-heartedly, hating himself for agreeing to this in the first place.

If the woman thought it went against *her* nature to submit, she had no fucking clue what it was like for him. Even if it meant he was fulfilling a fantasy of hers — her words exactly — he felt the animal beneath his skin itching to get free.

When they'd arrived at the club, he had allowed the valet to take his Escalade while he walked Mercedes inside, still being the perfect gentleman he was raised to be. But it was the moment they'd stepped into the club proper that his world had tipped on its axis. And not in a good way, either.

She'd warned him of her expectations, so he'd gone along with it. After all, tomorrow morning — when their time was officially over — would depend on his participation tonight, even he knew that much.

Thankfully, she had allowed him to wear his comfortable attire, which consisted of leather pants, his shitkickers, and a plain black T-shirt. She'd handpicked everything from his closet earlier, and he'd been impressed.

But that's where his comfort level took a quick nosedive.

It wasn't that he had a problem being partially naked in public. That didn't bother him in the least. But removing his shirt so that everyone could see the thick black collar that now wrapped like a noose around his neck wasn't thrilling him at all.

Shit, at this point, he wasn't sure he'd even be able to convince his dick that this would be worth his while.

As he reached for the drinks he'd ordered at the bar, he felt the weight of the huge leather cuffs that wrapped around his arms, and he fought the urge to groan. Another of Mercedes's "surprises" for him tonight.

The woman was pushing her luck. Up to this point, he thought he'd been somewhat of a good sport about this. Thank God he'd be the one in control as soon as they made it back to his condo, because he was going to tan her ass for putting him through this shit.

He made his way back to where Mercedes was standing, handing her the drink she'd requested. As he stood beside her, he kept his attention focused solely on her. It was that or possibly rip the fucking collar off of his neck and use it to bind her hands behind her back so he could take her nine ways to Sunday right there at the fucking bar.

The look she shot him would've had a weaker man cowering. She was going to push his limits tonight; it was written clearly in her beautiful gray eyes.

His attention was drawn to a sound across the room, and Xander looked up to see Shane laughing at something Luke McCoy said.

Just fucking great.

It looked like Mercedes was going to have her work cut out for her tonight because he wasn't feeling especially submissive. Exactly the opposite. And maybe that's what she needed. Topping from the bottom was something he despised, but it was also something he could master in the situation he was currently in. Based on the way Mercedes had submitted to him so sweetly over the last few days, he knew it wouldn't be tough to accomplish, either.

He glanced around the room as he waited for her to command him to do something, wishing like hell they'd just get on with it. As it was, it seemed everyone who was anyone was there tonight.

Of course, he noticed Sam and Logan were sitting on one of the couches closer to the glass-enclosed rooms talking to Sierra and Cole, who looked way too cozy at the moment.

He wondered how long before Mercedes noticed they'd shown up tonight. Or how long it would take for her to interact with them. If it had been him in control, after all that had happened since their first trip to Devotion, he could easily figure out a way to work Sam and Logan into tonight's festivities.

Shit.

Glancing down, he noticed she was watching them intently, probably trying to mentally will them to see her. Or him. Or both of them.

Fucking hell.

If she had any intention of inviting them to watch, or worse, participate, he was going to lose his shit.

Then again, Mercedes was acting different tonight. Quite frankly, she'd been acting strange since he'd found her lying in his bed that morning. She'd been lost in thought when he'd approached, and it hadn't been until he'd spoken that she'd even realized he was in the room.

They'd been apart during the day because work had gotten in the way, but as soon as she'd walked into his condo that evening, she'd taken the reins and was holding them tightly, fully morphing into the Mistress she was known to be.

His only hope would be to get her naked so he could slake his lust inside of her. If that were to happen, he didn't give a shit who stood by to watch. So, maybe, if he were lucky, he might just get something out of this.

Then again, if she wanted to keep it one-on-one between the two of them, no one around to see how hot she made him burn, he was all for that, as well. He could think of a million ways to make her scream his name, didn't matter if she believed she was the top or the bottom. He didn't give a fuck either way.

"Are you ready?" Mercedes asked him several minutes later as she set her empty glass on the bar.

He downed what was left of his Glenlivet before turning to face her. Just for the hell of it, he didn't answer, just nodded his head. The way she cocked her eyebrows almost made him smile, but he managed to hold it back. Just the little act of not verbally responding was enough for her to think about all of the ways she could punish him, and quite frankly, Xander was looking forward to seeing her do her worst.

"I want you one step behind me at all times," she ordered, and he immediately remembered the first theme night they'd attended just a few short days ago. He'd said something very close to that to her.

When she turned away, just because he could, he took a moment to admire her beautiful body. The woman made his blood burn hot, and it didn't matter if she was wearing the demure silk that he preferred to see her in or in the sexy Domme-wear she sported now. Hell, she could've been naked, because when she got that air of confidence about her, he lusted after her all the more.

Again, it was all about stirring things up a bit.

He followed Mercedes, knowing full well she intended to head over to Shane, because that was going to be her way of punishing him for what he'd put her through the last few days. And since he'd already defied her once since their arrival, he knew she'd be keeping track of his transgressions from here on out.

Considering he knew Samantha and Logan were watching, Xander decided tonight might just be the night to introduce them to what it meant to be a defiant sub. After all, he could be a teacher no matter which role he was in.

"Shane, good to see you," Mercedes greeted as the pair hugged and kissed one another briefly.

Xander didn't allow the chaste kiss to upset him, although he had the urge to punch Shane in his too pretty face. Rather than give the man something to remember, Xander stood one step behind her as instructed and glared down at Shane with a smirk on his face.

"Looks like your sub's a little cocky tonight," Shane said, unable to disguise his amusement with the situation.

You're a dead man, Xander mouthed, making sure Shane read his lips perfectly.

Shane laughed, causing Mercedes to turn and look back at him, taking a moment to study him as she did, and Xander made sure the smirk was gone.

"It would seem so," she said absently. "I think I have a good idea of how to take care of that, though."

Xander cocked an eyebrow as he met her gaze, unwilling to look away. He wanted to know what she had in mind. He'd half hoped she would've laid out her plan for the night prior to their arrival, but she'd kept the majority of the details to herself. It appeared she was going to surprise him. That was okay, too. He liked surprises. Monotony wasn't all it was cracked up to be.

"Care to watch?" she asked Shane, never taking her eyes off of Xander.

"Depends." Shane grinned like a fool. "As much as I'd love to see you beat his ass, I'm waiting for someone. She should be here any minute. If you can wait a few minutes, I'd be happy to watch. Or even participate."

Xander was going to put a serious hurt on the man if he didn't shut the fuck up.

"We'd like to watch." The voice came from behind Xander, and he did his best not to turn around, but he knew without looking who it was.

Samantha McCoy.

Lord, kill him now.

"Is that right?" Mercedes asked, turning to address Samantha with a stunning smile on her lovely face. From what Xander could tell, she definitely liked the idea of Sam watching whatever she had in store for him tonight.

"If that's all right with you, of course," Sam amended.

Xander edged around, trying to stay one step behind Mercedes as instructed. He wanted to see Sam as she addressed Mercedes, wondering whether she'd even noticed the drastic role switch they'd done for the night.

"I've reserved room three," Mercedes informed Sam, her hand lifting in the direction of the glass rooms that stood proudly in the center of the main floor. "If you'd like, you can have a front-row seat."

Room three? Fucking hell. He'd been hoping for a private room, but he shouldn't have expected any less.

"We'll be in a private room upstairs," another voice claimed from behind him, and this time Xander turned around. He knew that voice.

Shit.

Elijah Penn.

Fuck. Could this night get any worse?

Xander watched as Sam turned to face Elijah, her eyes widening with obvious appreciation as he moved in closer.

"A private room?" Samantha asked.

"That's right," the Brit said, his hands in his pockets as he watched her intently. "That is, if you're game."

Samantha turned to look at Logan, who nodded his head in response. Okay, so clearly these three had something going on between them. Xander was curious as to what, but it wasn't his business, so he kept his mouth shut.

"There's my date now," Shane said, and everyone's attention was drawn to him.

Son of a fucking bitch.

Clarissa Tinsley.

When the woman approached, she smirked at Xander before placing a quick kiss on Shane's lips in greeting.

"Clarissa," Mercedes greeted the woman, moving toward her and embracing her gently. "I'm so glad you're here."

"Me, too," Clarissa offered, her gaze once again landing on Xander.

Fuck.

Tonight was going to be the worst night of his life; he could feel it.

Clarissa Tinsley, former assistant to a wannabe submissive Realtor, current attorney-at-law. And one of Mercedes's best friends, to boot. Ever since that very first night at dinner, when Clarissa had sparked Mercedes's attention with her submissive admission, the two had become rather good friends.

The same couldn't be said for old Tim Johnson. The wannabe submissive had crossed Mercedes one time too many, and she'd kicked him to the curb. That was about the same time Clarissa was finishing up law school. The timing had been perfect.

But Clarissa wasn't just a friend of Mercedes. She was also a trainee at Kink — a submissive trainee — and for the longest time, Shane had shown a great deal of interest in the woman. Clearly, he was still interested in her if he'd thought to invite her to Devotion.

Fucking hell.

"Well, we'll likely catch up with you later," Logan offered, obviously catching the vibe that was now coursing between the four of them. Xander nodded toward Logan, a silent thank you.

He was going to have a difficult enough time dealing with Clarissa and Shane being there; the last thing he needed was for Logan and Samantha to be witnesses to this.

"We look forward to watching your scene, as well," Mercedes said to Logan, her attention divided between him and Elijah.

With that, Logan took Sam's hand and turned away. Xander couldn't hide his amazement when Elijah took her other hand, leading her away.

Oh, fuck. That was definitely going to be interesting.

When Mercedes moved closer to Clarissa, Xander moved behind her, trying to keep that one-step-behind rule in mind. The move allowed him to keep Shane and Clarissa in his sights, as well.

"So, you're interested in joining us tonight?" Mercedes asked Shane and Clarissa directly.

"If you'll have us," Clarissa said sweetly, her eyes darting up to Shane and then back to Mercedes. She seemed to be ignoring Xander.

Not that he cared. In fact, it would be great if he could be invisible.

"We'd love to," Shane tacked on, wrapping his arm around Clarissa's shoulder and pulling her to his side. "What did you have in mind?"

Clarissa was pretty, not mouthwatering like Mercedes, but she wasn't hard on the eyes by any means. The emerald-green silk sheath she wore clung to her body, accentuating her voluptuous breasts and her flared hips. The woman was small. Much smaller than Mercedes, and Xander wasn't quite sure how he felt about that.

He was a big man. Not just tall, either. Weighing in at two seventy-five, Xander worked diligently to build muscle and to maintain it. Based on how slight Clarissa appeared standing before Mercedes, he had to wonder whether she'd even be able to handle him if things headed that direction.

And he got a sinking feeling that was exactly what Mercedes intended to do tonight. It might not have been her initial plan, but it was something she would do.

Mercedes turned her attention to Clarissa directly. "Do you understand what's going on here tonight?"

"I'm sorry?" Clarissa asked, clearly confused by Mercedes's question.

"Tonight isn't what you think," Mercedes stated clearly. "I know that you've always known Xander to be a Dom."

"Two Doms?" Clarissa looked incredibly curious, and maybe a little confused.

"Not tonight, no. Tonight Xander belongs to me."

"I'm not sure I understand."

"We've been" — Mercedes looked up at Xander with a mischievous gleam in her eyes — "experimenting lately."

Yeah, experimenting, his ass. The woman was submissive, even if she was in denial.

He kept his mouth shut.

"What does that mean?" Clarissa asked, biting her lower lip as she glanced between him and Mercedes.

"It means that, tonight, I'm in charge."

"Oh."

"But I'm all for having you participate if it's something you think you can handle."

Clarissa stared at Mercedes as though she'd just been tossed down a rabbit hole, and she had no idea what was reality and what was fantasy.

"Can you handle it, Rissa?"

Clarissa glanced over at Shane, who was clearly amused by the situation. Xander did his best not to fist his hands at his sides. He was here to play along. That was the agreement, and by God, if it fucking killed him, he would play along.

"I think I can handle it," she said, her attention back on Mercedes.

Xander shook his head to let her know that was not the answer Mercedes would want, but at this point, it didn't matter. The statement was out there, and Mercedes would likely inform her of her mistake.

"I'm going to be lenient with you tonight, Rissa. Only because you're not used to seeing Xander like this. For tonight, you'll address me as your Domme."

Clarissa looked up at Shane, who nodded in response. So the man was willing to play along. He'd loan out his temporary submissive just to watch Xander squirm.

And Xander knew without a doubt that whatever was going on between Shane and Clarissa was temporary. There was no way in hell Shane would share a sub if he'd staked a claim on her.

But then again, the woman Shane wanted wasn't a sub, which meant for the time being, he was still pretending he didn't care.

"When I ask a question, I expect a straight answer," Mercedes continued. "Yes or no would suffice. So, which will it be?"

Clarissa looked completely taken aback by the stern tone of Mercedes's voice. Yep, that was her Domme side coming out in full force, something Clarissa probably wasn't at all used to. At least not having it directed at her. However, Xander was familiar with it, even if he wasn't used to being on the receiving end.

To his astonishment, Clarissa responded. "Yes. I think I can handle it," she said, her voice quavering slightly.

Wrong answer again. Xander fought the urge to smile.

"You can refer to me as Mistress M or Ma'am. Say it, Rissa. Say 'yes, Mistress M.'"

"Yes, Mistress M," Clarissa repeated, her eyes glued to the woman in front of her. Thankfully Mercedes was facing away from him, because he did grin.

He found it amusing, the easy way Clarissa submitted. She was a natural. Even if she was a little too agreeable most of the time. That was one of the main things that drove him crazy about some of the trainees at Kink, they acted like whipping posts. Then again, there were some on the opposite end of the spectrum who wouldn't know how to submit if they spent a year in the role.

Clarissa was a natural submissive, one who enjoyed the role. Xander figured it had a lot to do with her high-powered career. She was always in control in the courtroom, so in the bedroom, she'd easily hand over the reins, letting someone take over.

To each his own and all that.

Xander noticed the way Shane's hand tightened on Clarissa's hip, his eyes on Mercedes. It surprised Xander somewhat. The man didn't seem to have a problem handling Clarissa, but it didn't appear he was quite as excited as he let on about letting Mercedes take control.

Welcome to my world, Gibson.

Xander couldn't wait to see how that was going to work out.

MERCEDES WATCHED CLARISSA, NOTICED THE WAY HER eyes dilated as the woman stood motionless in front of her. This was her good friend. A woman she knew to be submissive because she'd seen her interact with Shane and a couple of other Doms at Kink in the years since she'd met her, but never had she been a part of a scene with her.

Then again, Mercedes didn't act out scenes with female submissives. At least not unless they'd done something that would earn them a punishment from her. And that was very rare.

But this... It was going to be interesting to say the least.

There was excitement banked in Clarissa's light brown eyes, but there was something else, as well. Trepidation, maybe? Figuring she'd leave Clarissa in suspense for a minute, she turned her attention to Shane, who stood rigidly behind her.

"Do you think you can handle this tonight?" She directed the question at him this time.

If his posture was anything to go by, the man was going to take his sub and run as fast as he possibly could away from her.

And that was all right, too. She wasn't going to push them. Sometimes it was easier to think that men could wield the power better than a woman. Then again, Shane had seen her in action, which, quite possibly, might be the cause for his uneasiness.

"If Rissa is open to the idea, I'm game," he answered easily, his tone belying the tension she could see in his shoulders beneath that black button-down.

Mercedes hadn't planned for this. After all, Xander was supposed to be her quest for the night, but she had to admit, the idea of dominating Clarissa had a lot of merit. For one, it would give her a chance to express her dominating side, which had lain dormant for too many days now. But it would ensure she didn't have to see that void she feared she would see in Xander's eyes if she looked too closely.

Not to mention, it might help to put a little distance between her and the inconvenient feelings she was beginning to develop for Xander. The ones that continued to grow stronger with each passing minute.

Just like Xander, Shane wasn't in the least bit submissive, and the worst part of all of this, she knew at some point, she was probably going to have to hand over the reins to him — at least where Clarissa was concerned. Mercedes wasn't all that fond of co-topping. She preferred to keep everything within her realm of control.

But then again, she hadn't expected to enjoy being Xander's submissive. And she did, even if she wouldn't admit it out loud. So maybe she would learn something else about herself tonight.

Glancing back at Clarissa, Mercedes decided right then and there that she was going to keep an open mind about tonight. This was playtime. It was fun. She refused to let her emotions lead her. Not tonight. To see this woman bend to her will was going to be something. It was a challenge that she would grab hold of with both hands.

A scene from a few years ago came back to her. One she'd witnessed at Kink. Shane and another Dom had dominated a sub — per the sub's request. They'd sandwiched her between them and made her come so loudly Mercedes was surprised the windows hadn't rattled. At the time, she had been impressed.

The thought gave her pause.

No, she wouldn't allow things to go that far. She certainly wasn't going to share Xander with Clarissa. Not like that, anyway. A little touching, a little oral ... yeah, she could handle that.

So, sure, maybe she was having doubts about her ability to dominate Xander, or even her desire to, but she damn sure liked the idea of blowing Xander's mind.

It would be a true test — both hers and his.

Tonight appeared to have taken on a new agenda, and Mercedes was okay with that. This was no longer about dominating Xander; it was about showing Clarissa exactly what it meant to obey a Mistress, not just a Master. Mercedes had earned the respect of her peers, and although Xander had effectively stripped her of her control on more than one occasion, she needed a reminder that she was still in charge.

"X, please take Rissa to the room, and Shane and I will be there shortly," she instructed, her eyes still fixated on Clarissa.

Her friend nodded slightly, her utter and complete submission apparent. She was a willing participant, which amped up Mercedes's excitement. If nothing else, she was going to have fun tonight.

When the two of them walked away a moment later, Clarissa's arm linked in Xander's much larger one, Mercedes turned her attention to Shane but kept her eyes trained on the couple as they retreated.

"Well, this is a surprise," Shane said with a gruff chuckle, sounding much more relaxed than he had a moment ago.

Mercedes smiled at him as she turned back to face him fully. "Not what you expected, I take it?"

"In more ways than one." Shane laughed, a sexy rumble that made Mercedes understand just what Clarissa saw in the man.

Although she'd never had a personal attraction to him, she wouldn't deny that he was one damn fine-looking man. Blond hair, blue eyes, great body. He was definitely attractive. Way better than average, in her opinion. And he clearly enjoyed playtime with his submissives, which told her a lot.

"How the hell did this come about?" Shane asked.

"It's just temporary," she explained, not sure how much she should share with him. She wasn't sure how much Xander had shared with him. "If you know Xander, you know he's always up for a challenge. Apparently this was his way of rattling the cage, if you will."

"I'd say he succeeded. I had no idea." Shane laughed again.

"Does that mean you're good with this? You're open to whatever I want to do?"

"If Clarissa is, I'm game. I think she's open to a lot of things. She wants to learn more, to explore what all of this means."

"Well, if you don't mind me saying, she couldn't have better teachers. I'm sure you've taught her plenty, but you have to admit, Xander's something else," Mercedes told him. "But tonight, she'll get to see it from two separate points of view."

"Shit, I'm interested in seeing it from your point of view."

"Just remember, tonight Xander is a full-fledged submissive, which means he'll be relinquishing all of his decision-making to me. Don't look to him as the Dom."

"No worries there," he grinned. "Dressed like that, I'd never take him for anything other than a submissive."

Mercedes smiled. Xander did look damn fine with her collar around his neck. "Trust me, I don't think it'll be easy, but I assure you, I've got a plan. If everyone can remember that this is all about pleasure, we won't have any problems."

"I don't think Rissa will have a problem understanding that."

"Well, if the look in her eyes is anything to go by, I think she's going to do just fine. And trust me, Shane, I'm going to go easy on her." She didn't bother to tell him she was going to go light because she knew Xander wasn't eager to participate, or that she was beginning to doubt her desire to top him.

Shane laughed, nodding his head as he peered over his shoulder to the glass room where Xander and Clarissa now stood talking. Neither of them turned to look their way, and Mercedes could only guess that Xander was offering Clarissa some guidance of his own. Smart boy.

"Consider this an experiment, if you will. I'd like to see how she responds to him, as well as to me," Mercedes said seriously as she looked directly at Shane. "I think it might be just what we all need."

What *she* needed was to put some space between her and Xander, but Mercedes didn't add that part.

Shane nodded as though he understood, but his eyes didn't reflect even a hint of concern.

"Does she have any issues with doing things in public?"

Shane laughed. "No, no issues. Sometimes I wonder whether all of her inhibitions have been destroyed."

Mercedes laughed, thinking about Clarissa and all of the ways she would be able to push the other woman's boundaries. "All right, then I say we give them a few minutes to think this over. You're welcome to join me, but I need to talk to someone for a few minutes."

"Go ahead. I've got someone to catch up with, and then I'll meet you back in the room," Shane said with a grin.

Mercedes walked away with a smile on her face that matched Shane's. This was definitely going to get very, very interesting before the night was over.

CHAPTER THIRTY-TWO

"WHAT IS SHE GOING TO DO?" CLARISSA asked Xander as they stood patiently — okay, *not* so patiently — in the room while Mercedes and Shane talked on the other side of the club. Clarissa tried to keep her eyes from roaming over there, but she was having a hard time.

"I wouldn't worry about it," Xander replied, looking calm and cool and completely unconcerned.

The exact opposite of what she was feeling at the moment.

"Not worry about it?" *Was this guy serious?* Clarissa watched Xander as he stood rigidly straight in front of her, his enormous chest rising and falling steadily as he peered down at her.

This man intimidated her. He always had. He was a Dom, one all of the submissives admired but few had the gall to interact with.

Next to Shane, Clarissa always felt small, but next to Xander she felt like a mouse beside an elephant. He was massive. Like a Mack truck. Or a freight train.

"Exactly what I said."

Okay, so he wasn't going to be much help. Clarissa suddenly wished Shane were there. Just his presence would give her more courage.

"This is part of the plan, you know that, right?" Xander asked as he stepped to the other side of the room, his hulking shoulders and chest blocking her view of where Shane had disappeared.

"What plan?" Clarissa asked, not really hearing the question because she was suddenly feeling a little intimidated. No. No, she was feeling *a lot* intimidated.

"The plan for you to sit here and fret over what's about to happen. It's as much mental as it is physical."

Clarissa jerked her eyes to meet his, her mouth hanging open. "She's not going to do something to me, is she?"

Clarissa had been friends with Mercedes for a long time. But they were just that — friends. Outside of the club, they rarely talked about things that happened at the club. Probably because Mercedes was a Domme and Clarissa was a submissive. Instead, they usually talked about work and shopping. Girl things.

Certainly not about Mercedes dominating her.

Holy crap. Had she really agreed to this?

Xander's grin was quite sexy, but Clarissa's nerves were on edge, and she couldn't find it in herself to admire him for long.

"Probably not, little girl."

"*Little girl?*" Clarissa retorted, her hands flying to her hips as she faced off with the behemoth. Her inner bitch was making its presence known.

"You're pretty fucking hot when you're pissed, you know that?"

He was doing this on purpose. Clarissa took a deep breath, exhaled. Another. She continued the pattern until she regained some of her composure. He was purposely riling her up.

"Don't worry, little girl. I'm sure all of the aggression will be directed at me tonight."

The words didn't make her feel any better. Part of her hoped she'd get to be a participant in this; the other part of her was scared senseless.

"And I'm not little," she murmured under her breath. *And damn sure not a girl*, she thought to herself.

The enormous laugh that erupted from Xander reverberated through the room; his deep, dark voice shook her to her core. Clarissa stared at him, his well-sculpted back to her as he paced across the small space.

"Little girl, compared to me, you're tiny."

Okay, so he had her there.

When he turned to face her again, his face was serious, and Clarissa found herself holding her breath.

"Can you do this, Rissa?" His voice was much lower than before, and his bright green eyes were so intently focused on her, Clarissa shuddered.

"Can *you*?" she countered. "I thought you were a big, bad Dom. How the hell does that happen? Are you a switch or something?"

Xander laughed again. "Been reading up on terminology, I see."

Clarissa smiled at him then. Yes, during her time as a trainee — which hadn't been all that long — she had been doing her homework, thank you very much.

"And no, I'm not a switch. In fact, if you want the honest truth, this is making me fucking insane."

Clarissa was startled by his candidness. She didn't know him well, and yet here he was, letting her know that he wasn't all that fond of this situation.

"I can do this," she finally told him, adding as much steel into her tone as she could muster. She figured if he could do this, be in a position that he clearly wasn't all that comfortable with, then she could, too.

"Good," he said with a small smile. "I'm looking forward to seeing how this all plays out."

Well, that made two of them.

Clarissa forced a smile, mentally asking the butterflies in her tummy to quiet down a bit. She could feel the echo of her nerves deep in her chest, and she wasn't all that fond of the feeling.

Xander moved past her again, this time going toward the wall that looked out over the club, and Clarissa followed the path of his gaze. She saw Mercedes talking to a man, a very attractive man. He looked really familiar, but she knew she had never met him before.

"Who is that?" The question came out, sounding every bit as nosy as it was. She'd have to learn to keep her mouth shut.

"Trent Ramsey," Xander answered, clearly amused.

Trent Ramsey. Trent Ramsey. Why did she know that name?

"Oh, my God! *The* Trent Ramsey? Like, from the *Dillon Chronicles*?" Trent Ramsey, the famous and incredibly handsome actor of one of the most popular movie series of her generation.

"That'd be him," Xander confirmed with a rumbling chuckle.

Clarissa was grateful that Xander didn't explain more. She had too much going on in her brain to even worry about having a famous actor in the same building she was in. No, she was more worried about what Mercedes had in store for her. And how in the world she was going to remember to refer to the woman as Mistress M or Ma'am. Holy crap. This wasn't going to be easy.

Not that Clarissa needed easy, but she felt like a jumbled mess when she was around the woman. There was definitely something intimidating about her.

And to think Clarissa had been completely convinced that Xander was a Dom. Before tonight, anyway. Yet here he was, about to be dominated by Mercedes Bryant. Good grief, this was confusing.

Needless to say, since the very first time she'd met Mercedes years ago, Clarissa found herself both in awe of her and terrified of her at the same time. And now this. If she could dominate a man like Xander, there was no way she'd stand a chance against the woman. But deep down, she knew without a doubt that Mercedes wouldn't hurt her. At least not on purpose.

She didn't know Xander as well as she knew Shane and Mercedes, mainly because she hadn't had the opportunity to see him on a more casual level outside of the club very often. However, she did know that Mercedes was incredibly good friends with both Xander and Shane. Always had been. She could sense there was a level of trust between the three of them.

And she knew without a doubt that Mercedes trusted Xander. She had always suspected the two of them had a thing for one another, even if they wanted to pretend that their dominant natures would be in direct opposition — yes, Clarissa had called Mercedes on it once, and that was the answer she'd received.

All in all, it shouldn't matter who was the Dom and who was the sub, or if they were interested in switching. They still trusted one another. That was all that mattered.

But she could definitely tell something was up with Xander. His usual easygoing air seemed to be disturbed, something more turbulent in his eyes. Based on the way he was staring at Mercedes, Clarissa knew it had to be because of the situation.

"Is it really that hard for you to give up control?" she asked when the silence and her own thoughts got to be too much.

Xander peered over at her, a sinister grin on his face that made her body tremble strangely. "I don't know. I've never done it before."

Oh. Well. Clarissa had no idea what to say to that.

And then coming up with a response was the last thing on her mind because Shane stepped through the door, a smile on his handsome face as he glanced back and forth between Clarissa and Xander. She had the urge to run into his arms, but she didn't want to give him the impression that she was scared. She wasn't.

Nervous, yes. Scared, no.

Okay, so she was petrified.

She was grateful when Shane walked over and wrapped her in his arms, his lips pressing against her forehead. He smelled good, and she liked the easy way he folded her against him. They were friends. It would never be anything more because neither of them was looking for serious, but it was comfortable. And most importantly, they had both accepted that.

"You good with this?"

Why did everyone keep asking her that? Surely Mercedes wasn't as bad as they were making her out to be. She'd seen her play at Kink, had heard a few of the male subs talk about her. No one ever said anything bad about her. Ever.

Looking up, Clarissa met his gaze and nodded confidently.

"That's good, pet. Is there anything you're not willing to do tonight?"

Wait … what?

Anything *she* wouldn't do? Holy hell. What did Mercedes have planned for her? Her hands started to tremble, but she clenched them into fists to still them. She could do this. Anything they wanted from her.

Glancing around Shane, she looked up at Xander's ruggedly attractive face. Yes, she could do this. As long as Shane was there with her, she could definitely do this. Her body was responding to the idea nicely, warming from the inside out. Shane must've noticed, too, because he reached around behind her and palmed her butt with both of his hands.

"Mmm, I like when you get turned on," he whispered in her ear although Clarissa knew Xander could hear every word.

She was just starting to relax when the door opened and in walked Mercedes.

Okay, so much for her confidence. Now she just needed to focus on not letting the other woman make her cry.

XANDER COULD SENSE HOW TENSE CLARISSA WAS. He also sensed the same about Mercedes when she finally arrived.

And not only was he in tune with the emotions pouring from Mercedes, he also connected with her the moment she walked in the room. She looked perfectly controlled on the outside, but he could tell she was hesitant, as well.

He wasn't sure whether it was because of him or if it had everything to do with Clarissa.

He had noticed Mercedes and Shane talking, although he'd made a point not to look directly at them. Whatever they had been talking about, Mercedes had been entirely relaxed. The two of them were working together on this, and what that meant for him and Clarissa, he had no idea. But he was more than ready to get on with it.

He was already tense from having to mentally prepare for this little experiment. He wasn't interested in playing head games with any of them. And if truth be told, he didn't have any desire to be part of this game with Clarissa, either. The idea of the woman's touch didn't do it for him. And it had nothing to do with the little brunette and everything to do with his feelings for Mercedes.

"X," Mercedes said softly, pulling him from his thoughts as his eyes darted to hers. "Over here."

Moving slowly, he approached where she stood on the other side of the room. Letting his thoughts flee, he fell into his role, reminding himself what this was about. And yes, he fully considered it an experiment. He was putting himself in her shoes for a minute. Trying to see things from her perspective. It would only strengthen what they were building, and for him, that was the most important thing.

So, for now, he would hand himself off to her and not worry about anything other than the pleasure that was about to come. Sure, he expected there'd be some pain associated, but he craved anything she was willing to dish out. She'd worked hard to keep him in suspense tonight, and it had worked.

Standing directly in front of her, he let his hands hang at his sides, forcing himself to remain relaxed. He'd already defied her once, and she was probably looking for more, something to shore up her nerve. She couldn't hide from him, even if she wanted to. He could see it in her eyes. There was hesitation he had never seen from Mercedes the Domme before, and he knew it had everything to do with him.

It only made it that much easier to go along with this. Tonight.

From this point on, she wouldn't get that from him. She had enough to worry about with Clarissa and her inexperience. It wasn't necessary for him to do anything more than endure tonight.

"Rissa."

Xander didn't turn around to see where Clarissa was, but he felt her moving in the small room. When she came up beside him, her arm brushed his, and he fought the urge to smile. She was nervous, too. So much so that she was trembling.

Yes, he'd tried to help her out earlier by getting her riled up. She was a strong woman; he knew that much about her. But she seemed utterly unsure of herself when it came to this side of Mercedes. Why that was, he had no idea. He was sure he'd find out soon enough.

"Do you have a safe word, Rissa?" Mercedes asked, and this time Xander did look down at her.

"Yes, Ma'am," she said promptly.

Xander was impressed. She hadn't followed up her answer with a bunch of rambling, which he knew Mercedes would appreciate. As a Dom, he expected it.

"Good girl," Mercedes responded, taking a step closer and cupping Clarissa's face gently with her long, slender fingers. "What is your safe word?"

"Magnolia," Clarissa whispered.

Mercedes smiled. "I like it. Will you have trouble remembering it?"

"No, Mistress," Clarissa said, her voice husky.

Most of the subs at Kink used the house safe word, which was red. Obviously Clarissa had some experience if she came readily prepared with her own safe word. And from the way she'd answered, Clarissa hadn't just come up with it, either.

"Very good." Mercedes turned to look at Xander, and he suddenly ached for her to touch him. He didn't care how she did it; he just wanted her hands on him. "And you?"

His safe word was much simpler. He went with the norm like Mercedes. Because Mercedes didn't ask him what his safe word was directly, he just stared down at her, locking his eyes with hers as he waited for her next question.

"What is your safe word, Xander?" There was a hint of exasperation in her tone.

He knew she was asking more for Clarissa's benefit than anything else. "Red," he answered easily.

"Good boy," Mercedes answered, but she didn't touch him, which was somewhat of a disappointment.

Then again, he made a mental note to punish her later for calling him boy. Especially after Shane chuckled from the corner.

"Tonight, I'm going to introduce you to Xander," Mercedes explained to Clarissa. "I'm not going to push your boundaries yet."

Introduce her? Holy fuck. He doubted Clarissa understood just what that meant, but he damn sure did. And it surprised him on all counts.

Xander noticed the relief on Clarissa's face.

Just wait, little girl.

"If, at any time, you're uncomfortable, use your safe word. Everything will stop at that time, and you and Shane will be free to leave."

Xander watched Clarissa's face closely, which was why he saw her immediate reaction. Concern?

"Talk to me, Rissa," Mercedes encouraged.

"If I have to use my safe word, does that mean we will never engage with the two of you again?"

That was a good question. In his experience, when a sub used a safe word, he would end the scene and let it end there. Due to his expectations, which he admitted were quite high, he expected his subs to endure what he would give them. He fully respected them if they couldn't, but he often found that, given a repeat opportunity, that same sub would safe word out again. He was more than willing to teach a sub how to endure what she needed, but those were discussions he had up front.

He knew with Mercedes, she wasn't quite as cut-and-dried as he was. She was strict, not leaving much room for error, but she would generally allow second chances if a sub opted to use their safe word. Sometimes a third. So, needless to say, he was quite interested in knowing, as well.

Although she would always respect a sub's reason for safe wording, Mercedes usually wasn't a forgiving Domme. If something didn't go the way she felt it should, she'd be the first to shut things down, and she'd move on. He'd seen her do it before.

"No, it doesn't mean we can't pick up in the future at some point," Mercedes explained, gripping Clarissa's chin more forcefully this time. "But I want you to know who I am, Rissa. You have to understand that I'm not a pushover, and it's my job to push my subs as far as they can handle and then some."

"I understand, Mistress M," Clarissa answered, her eyes locked on Mercedes, her tongue darting out to lick her lower lip.

"I will say this," Mercedes began, inching just a little closer to Clarissa. "If I feel as though you're holding back, not using your safe word if it is too much for you, then that'll be the end. I won't engage with you ever again like this. This is something I take very seriously. Do you understand?"

"I understand, Mistress M."

"Very good," Mercedes said, her head tilted slightly as though she was trying to read something in Clarissa's gaze.

Xander hoped like hell she found what she was looking for, because he was rapidly losing his patience. His mind was already halfway home and Mercedes was naked. Beneath him.

"I want you to undress Xander," Mercedes instructed Clarissa, and Xander's gaze slammed into Mercedes's.

Really?

She was going there?

Instead of speaking out, he swallowed his retort.

If Mercedes thought she could put distance between them by using Clarissa, the woman had another thing coming.

CHAPTER THIRTY-THREE

SHANE STOOD NEAR ONE CORNER OF THE room, trying to stay out of the way as Mercedes took control of the scene that would play out before him. It was harder than it looked, especially being a bystander while a Domme directed Clarissa.

He liked where Mercedes was taking this, though. He definitely agreed with introducing Clarissa to Xander. It was a nice visual. Xander with his overbearing personality and his massive body, Clarissa so petite and sweet-looking... Definitely hot.

It did not, however, look like Xander was fully on board with the idea. But Shane would give the man credit — at least he kept his mouth shut.

For now.

It was rather intriguing to see Mercedes direct Clarissa, to instruct the woman to put her hands on Xander. But he noticed that Mercedes did not instruct Xander to touch Clarissa.

And that wasn't an accident, he knew.

Although, personally, he wasn't as impressed with Clarissa's hands on Xander as he would be if Xander were touching Clarissa at the same time. More so if he were the one doing the directing of the two of them. Hell, just the thought of it made his dick hard.

God, the woman was so fucking hot. And he knew she was generally game for anything. But he hadn't played with her much. It had been recent when they had started down this path. Friends with benefits, they had agreed. Multiple benefits.

As he watched the three people across the room, Shane was impressed that Clarissa didn't say anything, nor did she look his way. She just turned to face Xander more fully, staring up at him. Way up.

Having played with Clarissa multiple times at Kink, Shane knew what to expect from her. Being that she probably felt incredibly safe with the three of them because they were all friends, although Clarissa had the least amount of interaction with Xander, she was likely going to go with the flow easily.

That was one thing about her that he had a love/hate relationship with. Although she was nervous, Clarissa tended to do exactly as she was told. She had no problems handing over the reins completely. If he said crawl, she'd crawl. And he had definitely pushed her limits a time or two.

But for tonight, Shane had zero expectations. He truly hadn't anticipated engaging with Mercedes and Xander. And damn sure not with Xander as a fucking sub. Shit, just looking at him was difficult. Even if, as a sub, he still exuded that overwhelming presence that people strayed to.

The man was *not* a sub. You could dress him up and make him do whatever, but he still wasn't a fucking sub.

Shane wondered just how long Xander was going to play along tonight.

Turning his attention back on Clarissa, Shane watched as she moved closer to Xander. Even with her heels on, Xander was significantly taller. And probably at least twice her width.

The man was built like a brick shithouse. Granted, Shane wasn't a pushover in the size department, but he'd be the first to admit, he had never broken six feet. But he did have a muscular build, not even remotely close to what Xander was packed with, although he wasn't a lightweight, either. But truthfully, Shane wasn't sure he'd ever met anyone quite as big as Xander.

When Clarissa's hands flattened against Xander's stomach, Shane's dick pulsed again. Her pale fingers against Xander's tan skin were a vibrant contrast. The dim lights in the room helped to accentuate the planes of Xander's chest and stomach as Clarissa roamed up and over the ripples of muscle.

Considering Xander wasn't wearing anything from the waist up, Shane figured Clarissa was just getting comfortable with Xander's body. Watching her was a fucking turn-on like no other. He loved to watch her when she touched him, as well. To see the wonder in her expression and the heat in her honey-brown eyes. There were times when she still seemed so damned innocent, even if she was getting down and dirty.

And she certainly was a dirty girl. One of the main reasons he liked playing with her. That and she wasn't looking for a relationship. Shane would admit that he cared about Clarissa as a friend, but he could never see anything more than that between them.

No, unfortunately, there was only one woman who'd caught his attention and held it all these years, but she was completely off-limits to him.

Clarissa's hands moved up, her fingers stopping on the bars through Xander's nipples. *Did those hurt?* They fucking looked like they would hurt. He'd asked Xander that more than once, but the big bastard had eluded his question every single time. The closest he'd gotten to an answer was, "Go get yours pierced and find out for yourself."

Yeah, no fucking thank you.

Shane glanced at Xander's face, noticing how the man was staring back at Clarissa, his expression one of complete and total satisfaction, even if it did look somewhat forced. Apparently, they didn't hurt. Or maybe they did, and that's what he liked about them. Either way, Xander seemed content to have her touching him.

Shane suddenly wished he were the one she was touching. Clarissa was incredibly sensual, a truly giving lover, and any time she turned her total focus on him, he knew he was a goner.

Much like Xander at the moment.

When her hands slid back down Xander's rigid stomach, she continued until she found the button on his leather pants. Since Shane was behind her, he couldn't see her face, but by the way her back stayed ramrod straight, he figured she was still nervous.

Shane wanted to touch her, to run his hands along her sides, to press her between him and Xander until she was moaning and writhing. He wanted to drive his cock deep in Clarissa's ass while Xander fucked her pussy until she couldn't take anymore. Until she was screaming their names.

Fuck.

But even he knew there wasn't a chance in hell that Mercedes would ever let that happen. She might think she put on a strong front, but he saw right through the facade. She wanted Xander. Hell, he'd go so far as to say she'd fallen in love with him. Without a doubt, this wasn't easy for her, which was why he suspected she had involved him and Clarissa in the first place.

The sound of a zipper brought Shane's attention back to Xander and Clarissa. Glancing down, Shane realized Xander had on those great big black boots with the laces, which meant Clarissa was going to have to go to her knees to remove them. The mental image that formed in his mind of Clarissa on her knees with Xander's enormous cock in her mouth was like a punch to the solar plexus, nearly driving the air from his body and making his cock thicken.

Shit.

Maybe Mercedes didn't like the idea of Clarissa touching Xander, but Shane certainly did.

Mercedes moved, and Shane's attention was drawn to her. She walked around the couple, riding crop in her hand as she slid the flat end over Xander's skin. She was smiling, but she was looking at Clarissa and not Xander.

"Naked, Rissa. He needs to be completely naked," Mercedes instructed, her tone soothing and calm, yet unyielding.

Clarissa nodded, and she must've realized her mistake, because her eyes were wide as she stared back at Mercedes. And true to her dominating nature, Mercedes gave her no room for error. As soon as her head nodded in response, Mercedes was up against Clarissa's front, the hand wielding the crop buried in Clarissa's long, chestnut hair, tilting her head back so that Clarissa was looking up into her eyes.

"What did I say about responding?" Mercedes asked, her tone still quiet and easy. Not at all what Shane had expected based on her rather aggressive stance.

"Yes, Mistress M," Clarissa whispered.

Mercedes slid her thumb over Clarissa's bottom lip but didn't release her. Their noses were practically touching, and from where Shane stood, he could see Clarissa's chest rising and falling rapidly. She was turned on by this.

Hell, Shane was turned on by this. He wanted Mercedes to move just an inch closer and press her mouth…

Son of a fucking bitch!

Shane's entire body went hard as Mercedes lowered her mouth to Clarissa's ever so gently. Clarissa didn't respond, but Mercedes apparently didn't need her to. The Domme glided her lips gently over Clarissa's, her tongue sneaking out slowly to slide over the seam, and Shane was convinced he might just be reduced to a teenage boy if they kept this up.

Never had he imagined Mercedes or Clarissa kissing another woman, but holy fuck, this was hotter than he could've imagined.

Forcing himself to look away, he glanced at Xander, noticing how the man was tensing right beside them, his face tilted down as he watched them. Lucky bastard. He had a much better view than Shane did.

"And how do you plan to respond next time?" Mercedes asked as she pulled her mouth away slowly.

Shit, if Shane had anything to say about it, Clarissa would be defying Mercedes at every turn. Especially if he had that to look forward to.

CLARISSA WASN'T SURE SHE WAS BREATHING. SHE was overwhelmed by the wondrous scent of Mercedes and the way her soft lips had felt against her own. Oh, God, she'd just been kissed by a woman.

A freaking woman.

And yet, she'd enjoyed it.

She wanted more. She wanted to know what Mercedes's tongue would feel like in her mouth, her hands on her body. *Holy shit.* This was so not good. She wasn't supposed to lust after a woman, but she was. Oh, God, she was.

She truly had no idea how she felt about that, aside from it being way more than she'd expected. She wanted to attribute the strange sensation in her belly to her shock, but she wasn't quite so sure.

Mercedes was beautifully breathtaking. Her flawless alabaster skin, her long, silky black hair, and her soft gray eyes had always filled Clarissa with a strange envy. Not that she wanted to *be* Mercedes, but she certainly didn't mind admiring her. Then, as though her beauty weren't enough, the woman exuded confidence from her pores. It was evident in the way she walked, moved, spoke.

"Yes, Mistress M," Clarissa said softly, remembering that Mercedes had asked her a question.

Apparently her answer was the appropriate one, because Mercedes leaned in once more and pressed another kiss to her lips. Clarissa wanted to open her mouth, to allow Mercedes in, to explore her with her tongue…

"Good girl," Mercedes said with a sexy grin as she pulled away.

Clarissa was breathless, and Mercedes's eyes glittered with what Clarissa hoped was approval. Was this part of the deal? Was Mercedes going to be with her? Like, *with her* with her? Was that even something Clarissa wanted? Based on the way her insides were smoking from the flames that had ignited down low, she was beginning to think the answer was yes.

Or was this some sort of a test to see how much she could take? Or how far Xander could be pushed?

Based on the expression on Mercedes's beautiful face, she had to assume the latter. Mercedes seemed very much interested in Xander, not her. Not to mention, she knew for a fact that Mercedes wasn't into women.

"Very nice," Mercedes said, letting her soft, delicate thumb graze over Clarissa's lower lip once more before she released her.

When Mercedes looked up at Xander, Clarissa saw the way their eyes met. It was a challenge, and she seemed to be in the middle of it. Not that she was complaining because well… Shit. She wasn't sure why it didn't bother her.

Rather than dwell on it, she kept that in mind as she listened for Mercedes's next instruction.

"Now, I want Xander naked," Mercedes instructed more firmly, and this time Clarissa responded with a confident, "Yes, Ma'am," before proceeding to undress Xander.

She was having difficulty removing his leather pants, but it wasn't because they were tight or even all that difficult to remove. Clarissa was just too busy admiring his gorgeous physique. Where Shane was lean and sleekly muscled, Xander was thick and bulky. She knew for a fact that she wouldn't be able to circle Xander's bicep with both hands. He was that freaking big.

And his legs were larger than her own waist, although they weren't bodybuilder bulky like she would've expected. Instead, they were stout like tree trunks and incredibly nice to look at.

Trying to keep her excitement reined in, Clarissa slowly lowered his leathers, carefully freeing his cock as she went. Once again, she was transfixed by the sight of him. His cock was long and thick and slightly curved to the left. In one word, he was … gorgeous.

The urge to lick her lips was too great to pass up, so she did, not bothering to look up at Xander, nor did she look behind her to see where Shane was. She knew he was watching. She could feel his eyes on her, the heat of his gaze searing every inch of her skin. She just wished he'd move around for a better view. For some reason, she needed to see him, to feel that connection with him.

This was a learning experience for her, as well, and she was finding that she much preferred Shane's dominance to anyone else's. Shane made her feel safe. In ways that other Doms didn't. Sometimes she feared she would never respond to another Dom the same way again.

Although what had happened between her and Mercedes had certainly sent a bolt of heat through her. Unlike anything she'd ever experienced before.

Focus, she reminded herself. She couldn't afford to get distracted.

With Shane there with her, she was willing to continue because she was incredibly turned on, and she knew before it was over, she'd be right where she wanted to be. Safely in Shane's arms.

When Clarissa glanced down, she realized that Xander had on boots. With laces. Which meant…

Aww, crap.

This time she did look up at him, her face hot with embarrassment because she knew what she was going to have to do to get him naked. As it was, she'd ignored the fact that they were in a glass-enclosed room, and she knew, if she were to look out at the club, she'd see they'd already drawn an audience. Xander alone would draw a crowd, and him naked was a sight any red-blooded woman wouldn't want to miss.

Lowering herself to her knees, Clarissa slid her fingernails down the front of Xander's thighs, not touching his erect cock as she did. Once she was on the floor, she realized she was eye level with his heavy balls, and she instinctively observed them briefly before remembering what she was doing.

Quickly untying the laces and helping Xander to remove his boots, Clarissa prayed no one else could see how she was blushing from the top of her head to the tips of her toes.

Clarissa jumped when she felt something cool against the back of her thigh, and she fought the urge to turn around and see what it was. She could see Mercedes's boots in her peripheral vision, and she figured it was that leather crop she'd been wielding earlier. As it was, her dress had been pushed up high on her thighs so she could lean over to work on Xander's boots, but whatever Mercedes was doing behind her was raising the silk even higher.

"No panties," Mercedes said approvingly. "Very nice."

Another rush of heat infused Clarissa's face. Damn Shane. He'd insisted that tonight she leave her panties at home. He'd told her she wouldn't be needing them. Shane had decided a while back that he much preferred her to go without panties when they went to the club — it'd been an official rule he'd implemented back when they'd started playing together. That meant that anyone standing outside the room would be able to see her bare butt and probably a whole lot more.

She breathed a sigh of relief when she managed to get Xander completely naked a few minutes later. Returning to her feet, she didn't move away, but she wasn't able to look him in the eye, either. Which meant she had to close her eyes, or she was going to get an eyeful of glorious, sexy male.

And right now, she was so wet she wasn't sure just how much more of him she could handle.

"Go stand by Shane," Mercedes instructed, and Clarissa met her gaze to ensure she was speaking to her.

"Yes, Mistress M," Clarissa said breathlessly. She managed to make her way across the room without running, although the urge to escape was intense. So much so, she was shaking when she reached Shane.

He grinned down at her, his eyes gleaming with that heat she was so familiar with. She wished he would touch her. He did, but not in the way she had hoped. Instead, Shane turned her so that her back was flush against his stomach, the evidence of his arousal pressing into her lower back, and she was facing Xander and Mercedes once more.

But before she viewed the scene directly in front of her, Clarissa made the mistake of glancing out through the glass. And right there, standing front and center, was none other than Trent Ramsey.

He was looking at her, his shockingly handsome face and his intoxicatingly pretty eyes focused on her. *Her.* Of all people. But for some reason, his stardom wasn't even a fleeting thought. No, it wasn't who he was but rather how he was looking at her that had Clarissa feeling a little light-headed.

That was spine-tingling heat she saw reflected back at her. And it did something crazy to her insides, making her body heat another twenty degrees. No man had ever looked at her like that.

Ever.

Now, if she could just get her knees to lock, she wouldn't risk turning into a puddle of lust-induced hormones right there on the tiled floor.

CHAPTER THIRTY-FOUR

"Isn't he beautiful?" Mercedes asked, directing her question at Clarissa as she slid the riding crop over Xander's pecs, pausing briefly to flick his left nipple bar once before trailing lower.

"Yes, Mistress M," Clarissa replied from her spot near Shane.

Good girl.

Mercedes had no doubt that Clarissa was a true submissive. The woman was born to submit, but she also seemed very aware of that. And the way she blushed so prettily was a bonus. She easily understood why Shane enjoyed playing with her. She was extremely responsive.

Mercedes nodded toward the only solid wall in the room, the one directly behind Xander, as she said, "Move back until you touch the wall."

"Yes, Mistress," Xander responded easily, his cock bobbing freely in front of him.

He was hard as steel, his cock darkened from the blood pumping through it, but he was doing well to ignore it. Just as she would expect him to do. He was fairly good at playing the part of a submissive. Then again, just like her, he knew exactly what was expected.

As she admired his physical beauty, she allowed herself to remember the day she'd met him all those years ago.

He hadn't been quite as built as he was now, but he'd been just as beautiful, and intensely confident, yet lacking that annoying arrogance that she would've expected.

Just like then, his tanned skin stretched taut over bulging muscles. His nipples had been pierced even then, but he'd had rings in them. Granted, she hadn't known that when she'd first met him. Back then, the only opportunity she would've ever had to see Xander in any state of undress was at the club, because any other time they were together, he was immaculately dressed.

It had been a couple of months after they'd met when she'd first had the pleasure of checking out his distinct attributes. Back when she had taken Tim Johnson, Clarissa's boss at the time, to Kink as an introduction for them both.

Mercedes studied the titanium bars in Xander's nipples, strangely glad he'd kept them all this time. She remembered asking him years ago why he'd had them done. His explanation had been simply because he wanted to.

Mercedes trailed the crop over his chest and then slid down the narrow line that bisected his well-defined abs before outlining the V that protruded and angled right to his proud cock. Just beneath that rigid stalk of flesh, his balls hung loosely, a heavy sac that she would enjoy teasing very shortly.

Once he was against the wall, Mercedes set the riding crop down on a stand in the corner and then proceeded to connect Xander to the loose chains that had been installed in the walls. It was an intricate system that Xander had bragged about. It came in handy for what she had in mind, especially when this man was a solid seven inches taller than she was in her heels.

After hooking one of the chains to his left wrist cuff — which happened to be designed for this type of activity — she moved in front of him, letting her fingernail graze the full length of his cock until he hissed out a breath. She met his eyes and smiled. He didn't smile back, but she hadn't expected him to. Aside from that little expulsion of air, no one would've been able to detect a reaction from him.

Very nice.

After she got his right wrist attached to the chain in the wall, she moved over to the control box that was hidden in a narrow panel that ran from floor to ceiling. It required a frequently changed master code to access, and she'd had to jump through hoops just to be allowed access for one night. And she'd only gotten it then because she knew Luke, thanks to the sale of the warehouse.

Once she had the panel open, she pushed a button, watching as the chains retreated into the wall, lifting Xander's arms up slowly until they were fully extended above his head. By design, they wouldn't retreat all the way thanks to a safety rigging in the chain, which was there to ensure no one would get in a position they couldn't be freed from.

Due to Xander's height, there was no other way for Mercedes to get him secured appropriately unless she had a step stool, so this had been a no-brainer when she'd been considering her options for tonight.

Moving back to Xander, Mercedes reached up and massaged his left bicep slowly, enjoying the feel of his smooth, warm skin against her palms. "Are you comfortable?"

"Yes, Mistress."

"Any pain? Numbness?"

"No, Mistress."

As with any of her subs, Xander's safety was her main priority, and although there was pain associated with the scenes that she performed, it was never due to the equipment that she used. At least that was the goal. Being that his arms were extended above his head, she knew his hands would eventually start to tingle, but by then, she'd be close to finished with him.

If she was lucky.

Glancing at the clock on the wall, she made note of the time. Without a doubt, she had to pay attention to how long she had him chained up in order to avoid any issues. And given that she was finding herself more and more distracted by him being shackled and at her mercy, Mercedes knew that she had to get her mind fully into the scene from this point onward.

"Spread your legs," she told Xander as she moved over and massaged his right bicep out of habit.

"Any pain on this side?" she asked as he widened his stance, keeping his back ramrod straight.

"No, Mistress," he growled, clearly losing his patience.

That only made her want to slow down even more.

"Good."

Placing her right foot next to Xander's, she pushed gently, letting him know that she wanted his legs spread even more. He obliged.

Making sure she touched him constantly, just to keep his senses heightened, Mercedes continued getting things set up. It wasn't until she had him shackled to the chains near his ankles that she was satisfied.

"Can you move?" she asked as she retrieved another toy she'd brought along just for this particular moment and moved to stand directly in front of him.

"Yes. Mistress."

She noticed how he'd tacked on *Mistress*. Almost like he was preparing to defy her.

She pretended not to notice as she checked the slack in the chain. There was minimal give, but his answer was the correct one. She didn't want him completely restrained to the point of discomfort, but she wanted to ensure he couldn't move far.

Taking the Wartenberg wheel, a small metal tool with a rotating spiked wheel on the end, Mercedes moved closer, keeping the tool hidden. She was pretty sure Xander had already noticed, but like a good submissive, he didn't say anything.

Lowering herself to her knees in front of him, she pretended to be checking the ankle cuffs. Instead, she placed the spikes of the wheel against his left ankle and slowly moved upward, applying only gentle pressure as she went. The purpose was to spark sensation, not to hurt him. There were several uses for the tool she was fond of, and in her opinion, it would've been much more useful had he been blindfolded, but she didn't intend to blindfold him.

She continued on her quest up the inside of his left leg, applying a bit more pressure until she reached high up on the inside of his thigh. From there, she slowly rolled the wheel over his balls using even less pressure than before, smiling when he growled. With a slow, sensual trip down his right leg and then back up, Mercedes eased the wheel beneath his balls, rolling ever so gently across his perineum. Her focus turned to his cock, and she looked up to see him watching her, his eyes hooded, his mouth a thin, hard line. He liked it; she knew he did. She could see the chill bumps on his skin.

When she figured he'd had enough, based on the way his breaths became labored, she stopped. Before she got to her feet, she leaned forward and licked his cock from root to tip, keeping her gaze fixed on his. She fully intended to tease him into submission, although he already seemed to be giving in.

Or maybe he was just playing the part.

With that thought in mind, Mercedes retrieved the riding crop and dropped the wheel onto the counter before returning to her place in front of him. She took a moment to admire her handy work.

Xander Boone was magnificent. And it still stole her breath to see such a big, powerful male submit to her like Xander was, even if it was clear he wasn't all that thrilled with the idea.

Mercedes lifted the crop to Xander's cheek and slowly slid it over the light stubble. She continued to trail farther down his body until she was at the inside of his thigh, just beneath his balls. With a flick of her wrist, she delivered a light, stinging tap. Nothing too hard at first. She continued to do this along the insides and outsides of his thighs, over his groin, a couple of barely there taps along his penis, and then she started again.

Rather than deliver pain, Mercedes was more interested in stimulating the blood flow in these areas, making Xander completely aware of every touch, every caress of air over his skin.

His cock was still rock hard and protruding out from his body at an upward angle, which gave Mercedes the perfect view of a bead of pre-cum that developed on the head. As she continued to tap the crop over his outer thigh, she leaned forward and licked the head of his dick like an ice cream cone, eliciting another sharp gasp of air from Xander.

Nice. He was right where she wanted him.

Turning her attention back to Clarissa, Mercedes smiled at the woman. "Come here, Rissa," Mercedes instructed.

"Yes, Ma'am."

Connecting with Shane's gaze over Clarissa's head, Mercedes waited for his nod. She would continue as long as these two were willing participants. She received a subtle nod from Shane, and then she took Clarissa's arm gently, as the two of them moved closer to Xander.

Clarissa looked at her, and Mercedes could see an obvious question in her eyes.

"What's on your mind, Rissa? Do you have a question for me?"

"Yes, Ma'am," Clarissa answered sweetly, her eyes never wavering from Mercedes's face.

"Ask."

"This might be a dumb question, but I won't be required to hurt him, will I?"

"There is never a dumb question when it comes to BDSM," Mercedes offered easily. "The more you ask, the more you learn. That's the key. And to answer your question, no, you will never be asked to deliver pain to X."

"Thank you, Mistress M."

Mercedes wasn't sure whether Clarissa was thanking her for answering her or thanking her for not making it a requirement that she hurt Xander. Either way, Mercedes was impressed with the woman. She seemed eager to learn, nervous as hell, but ultimately, Mercedes got the impression she was longing to continue.

"Confirm for me one more time that you're okay with this," Mercedes told Clarissa, watching her closely.

"Yes, Ma'am. I'm okay with this."

There was still a hint of hesitancy in Clarissa's eyes, but her response appeared genuine. "Good girl. I want you on your knees."

Clarissa's eyes widened briefly, but she didn't balk at the demand. "Yes, Mistress M."

"Wait," Mercedes said when Clarissa began to go to her knees at Mercedes's feet. "I want you over here."

Pulling Clarissa along, Mercedes positioned her directly in front of Xander, and she could see the slight tremble in Clarissa's hands as they moved closer. "Remember your safe word, Rissa. If it's more than you can handle, just say the word and everything will stop. Do you understand?"

"Yes, Mistress M."

Figuring she'd been lenient enough thus far, Mercedes decided it was time to get down to business. More specifically, it was time to watch Xander squirm.

CHAPTER THIRTY-FIVE

XANDER KNEW EXACTLY WHAT WAS ABOUT TO happen, and he was finding it hard to continue to play along.

With Clarissa standing less than a few inches in front of him, he could feel the heat of her body and see the evidence of her arousal in her beaded nipples protruding through the thin silk sheath she wore. He also noticed that, for the last few minutes, she'd started glancing outside into the club.

Who was she looking at?

He had tried to follow her gaze, but there were just enough people to make it futile to try and guess. Xander was having a difficult enough time trying to keep his head in the game, much less trying to find whom Clarissa had just set her sights on.

Clarissa was a beautiful woman, but no matter how hard he tried, the only way he could keep his erection was to think of the things Mercedes had just done to him. The way her soft, smooth hands felt against his skin, the way her eyes met his even briefly, heat and passion lingering there for him to see.

And he didn't have anything against Clarissa. In fact, had it been five days ago, he wouldn't have balked at the idea of a scene such as this one. Well, almost like this one — never would he willingly sign up to be a submissive.

But that wasn't the point.

He just knew that he couldn't go through with this.

He didn't want to play with anyone else. He didn't want to *be* with anyone else.

It was just a damn good thing he was restrained, because he knew without a doubt that he would defy Mercedes if she insisted that he touch Clarissa. He just didn't have it in him.

He tried to keep himself distanced, tried to figure out what Mercedes was up to, but he had a hard time getting into it.

How far was she willing to go before she figured out she'd pushed too far? How far was Clarissa going to go before she realized what Mercedes was up to?

Because, without a doubt, Xander knew that Mercedes was trying to prove something through Clarissa.

And it wasn't fucking working.

"Lift your dress to your hips," Mercedes commanded Clarissa as the two women stood before him.

Holy fuck.

Okay, he was definitely on the right track. Mercedes was in rare form tonight. Maybe because she'd had to repress her dominant side for the last few days, or maybe because she was trying to prove something. Hell, he had no idea.

The brief moment of hesitation was Clarissa's next mistake, and Xander noticed the moment Mercedes decided on her punishment. "Wait. Scratch that. Take the dress *off.*"

Clarissa's eyes widened, and her gaze locked with Mercedes's as her breathing became labored.

"Remember your safe word, Rissa. Unless you intend to use it, I expect you to do as I say."

"Yes, M-ma'am," Clarissa stuttered as she slowly lifted the hem of her short dress up, the emerald silk sliding over her hips, exposing her bare pussy to Xander's gaze and her ass to the group of people who'd gathered outside of the glass-enclosed room.

Movement out of the corner of his eye had Xander briefly looking over to see that Shane was moving. He wasn't moving closer to Clarissa, rather he was staying along the perimeter of the glass wall, but he was obviously getting into a better position.

It was while he had been watching Shane that he noticed exactly who Clarissa had been looking at.

Trent Ramsey.

Shit.

Xander knew for a fact that she didn't know him. Based on her earlier reaction, the two hadn't even been introduced briefly. You wouldn't know it by the heated look on Trent's face. He was watching Clarissa intently. Almost as though he had staked his claim on her in the last few minutes.

As Clarissa's body came into full view, Xander volleyed between watching her and watching Trent. The man was riveted, but he looked pretty damn pissed all the same. It was a fucking strange reaction from a man who had never met this woman.

Glancing back at Clarissa, Xander watched as her flat belly and the pebbled tips of her dusky pink nipples came into view.

Clarissa wasn't a short woman, but she wasn't tall, either. A little less than average probably. Her slender body was outlined with subtle curves that … Trent Ramsey was all but consuming with his eyes.

"Beautiful," Mercedes said approvingly, drawing Xander's attention back to the two women.

Clarissa's nipples hardened even more, the pink tips darkening with arousal, her stomach muscles clenching, and her gaze was now transfixed on Trent again.

Fuck.

This scene was sinking like a ship and fast. When he met Mercedes's gaze, he noticed that even she had realized it.

She was pushing, trying to hold on to the control, but there were too many factors that she wasn't taking into consideration.

"Stand directly in front of X and then lower yourself to your knees," Mercedes instructed in detail.

Xander watched intently as Clarissa took a tentative step closer and then lowered her naked self to her knees in front of him. He noticed that she was careful to keep her legs tightly locked together, but her gaze never travelled outside of the room.

The woman had no idea that she'd just invited Mercedes's own personal brand of torture. The kind he thoroughly enjoyed watching when Mercedes was doing a scene at Kink but that tonight he didn't much care for.

"Spread your legs wide."

Clarissa sucked her bottom lip into her mouth, but she spread her knees. Xander wouldn't consider that wide, but he had to give her props for trying.

From where he stood, even if her legs were spread completely apart, he wouldn't be able to see the glistening folds of her pussy. He also knew that due to the way she was angled, the audience that had now gathered outside the glass window wouldn't be able to see clearly, either. That included Trent. Maybe a couple of people along the side walls, but the majority would be denied that pleasure. Undoubtedly he knew that was Mercedes's intention, but he figured Clarissa hadn't realized it yet.

"Are you wet, Rissa?"

"Yes, Mis-mistress M," Clarissa said, her entire body trembling slightly.

"Show us," Mercedes said, and Xander glanced over at her.

She was standing with her feet apart, those fuck-me boots making her sexy legs look hotter than fucking hell. Her corset was cinched tight enough that her breasts spilled over the top, but her sweet nipples were still hidden from view.

He fully intended to clamp her nipples as punishment for putting him through this. He remembered how much she'd enjoyed both the pleasure and the pain the last time he'd done it.

His dick throbbed at the memory.

Fuck, could they just get on with this?

He wanted out of these fucking restraints. Out of this fucking room. He'd much prefer somewhere that they could be alone and he could get Mercedes naked and beneath him.

Going forward, he was not going to take his eyes off of her. He couldn't. And if he couldn't admire her naked, he'd soothe himself with an eyeful of her glorious ass encased in that sinfully short leather miniskirt. If she bent just right, he'd get a nice glimpse of her smooth cunt because he knew she wasn't wearing panties, either.

"Show us, Clarissa." Mercedes's tone sharpened as she took a step closer to Clarissa, who was kneeling on the floor at Xander's feet.

Xander forced his eyes to Clarissa, wondering if this was the moment she would safe word out. For the first time in his life, he wished like hell a sub would use their safe word.

Please use your fucking safe word.

But no, that's not what happened, because life was just that cruel sometimes. Rather than calling out whatever goddamn flower she had used as her safe word, Clarissa dipped her hand down between her legs and pulled back two fingers glistening with her juices.

"Lick your fingers clean."

Xander glanced out into the club, watching Trent. The man was watching Clarissa, his tongue damn near hanging out of his mouth.

Fuck, maybe Trent would interrupt the scene. The man seemed to have a hard-on for Clarissa. If they were all lucky, maybe the arrogant actor would waltz right in and claim the damsel in distress as his own, just like they did in the movies. If he didn't, Xander wasn't sure he was going to survive this scene.

In all honesty, it wasn't going anything like he'd expected. Well, aside from him being tied up and naked. That was something he would expect from Mercedes. But she wasn't focused on him. Somewhere along the way, she'd made this about Clarissa.

Was she scared?

Knowing she would never admit to it, Xander forced the question away, looking back down at Clarissa kneeling in front of him. She was using her tongue to clean her fingers, and Xander looked up at Shane, noticing the man was on the verge of swallowing his own tongue.

Oh, fuck. That wasn't going to end well. Trent, Clarissa, and Shane.

Right.

"Very nice." Mercedes's voice echoed in the small room. "Now I want to watch you suck X's big, beautiful cock," Mercedes told Clarissa.

Fuck no. No, no, no. This was not going to happen.

Mercedes turned away and retrieved something from the counter behind her. When she came back, she handed a foil packet to Clarissa.

"Put this on him," she instructed. "I think you'll like this one. It tastes like grapes."

At least Mercedes had the good sense to remember protection.

Oh, fuck. Please let her use her safe word.

Clarissa reached for the condom, but her hands were no longer trembling, they were shaking like a leaf in hurricane-force winds. As soon as she plucked the condom from Mercedes's long, slender fingers, Clarissa dropped it on the floor.

Clarissa reached for it, her eyes darting up to Xander and then Mercedes and back once again. He wanted to shake his head, to encourage her not to go through with it. Before he had the option, the end of the riding crop came up to rest beneath his chin, and Xander lifted his eyes to meet Mercedes's glowing gray gaze.

"I want you to watch the pretty little sub's mouth wrapped around your cock."

The only sound that could be heard was Clarissa's rapid gasps and the rustle of Shane's clothing as he moved somewhere in the background.

Xander stared back at Mercedes, praying like hell she'd realize just what was going on here, stop before the damage could be undone. Or maybe that's what she wanted. Maybe she wanted Xander to be with Clarissa so that she could use it against him.

He saw the battle in her eyes, saw that she was just as tormented as he felt, but she wasn't going to cave. She was trying to prove something here, but fuck it all. He didn't give a good goddamn about proving anything.

Not when it came to his love for Mercedes.

The instant she looked away, Xander said, "Red."

Her eyes darted up to meet his.

"What did you say?"

"Red." There was absolutely no mistaking the fact that he was using his safe word.

He saw the relief that flooded her face before she quickly masked it, doing her best to cover it up with something else. But no matter what she wanted him to believe, Xander knew the truth.

Xander didn't see Shane move, but he noticed Clarissa getting to her feet. He looked up at his friend just in time to see the realization on Shane's face.

Yeah, I went there, he thought to himself. *I fucking love her.*

Xander was pretty sure Shane knew everything he was feeling.

Without a sound, Shane helped Clarissa slip back into her dress, and the two of them disappeared out of the room.

When the door closed behind them, Mercedes moved over to the wall. She hit a button that released the chains and then another that flipped the glass from clear to opaque, sealing them somewhat from prying eyes. It wasn't until she hit the button to turn off the microphones that she finally spoke.

"Why?"

"Why what?" he asked, pretending to be oblivious to what she was referring to.

"Why did you use your safe word?"

Xander didn't answer immediately. He waited for her to come over to release him from the chains that still restrained his arms and legs.

He wasn't about to make the biggest admission of his life while he was in a fucking playroom at the club, chained to the wall. Knowing that Mercedes would likely flee the room and leave him there, he decided to wait.

She must've realized it, too.

MERCEDES WAS BARELY BREATHING. THERE WAS A roaring in her ears that had nothing to do with anger and everything to do with relief.

Xander had used his safe word.

Because of her.

For the last few minutes, Mercedes had been praying Clarissa would safe word. Wishing like hell the nervous little sub would save them all from themselves.

But she hadn't, and Mercedes had been terrified of going any further. She didn't want Clarissa touching Xander. Didn't want to watch anyone touching him.

For some unknown reason, her scene had taken a drastic turn somewhere along the way, and it had been all her fault. But right then and there, the scene was the last thing she worried about. She didn't care that Clarissa and Shane would likely think of her as a failure. She didn't care that half of the club would think that, either.

At this point, the only thing she wanted to do was to come with Xander's cock lodged deep inside of her. To feel him against her. Anything to get Xander's hands on her, even if it meant handing over the control to him. He had effectively destroyed her defenses, making her lose her touch, but she really didn't care. Not right then, at least.

Unable to hold back any longer, Mercedes moved to release Xander from his restraints. Neither of them said a word, but the nonverbal communication between them was loud and clear.

The look in Xander's eyes stole the oxygen from her lungs.

For the last half hour, she'd wanted nothing more than to abandon the scene. It was selfish to put her own needs above everyone else's, but for the life of her, she couldn't go through with it.

Even now, she knew Xander would be more than happy to take over from there, because he was a Dom, and she was … an imposter.

She knew she should consider this the ultimate defeat, but it didn't change the fact that she could hardly breathe for wanting him.

Once he was freed, Mercedes stood motionless in front of him, watching, waiting.

"This is still your show," he whispered. "What do you want?"

"What do you mean, 'what do I want'? I failed, Xander. It's done."

"Not even close," he growled. "Tell me what you want me to do."

Mercedes didn't understand what he was doing. Why wasn't he taking over? Why wasn't he forcing her to do what he wanted?

"We aren't walking out of here until we're through here."

"We are—" *through*. Mercedes couldn't say it. She didn't want it to be true. She didn't want what they had to be over, and she knew he was giving her a chance to redeem herself. To take back the scene that had gone horribly wrong.

"Pick up right where we left off," he told her, but he wasn't commanding her. He was making a request.

Mercedes stared at him in disbelief for a long moment before she said, "Sit in that chair with your legs wide."

Xander gripped the chair that was in the corner and set it down beside where they stood before lowering himself into it. Without another word, he spread his legs wide. His thick, heavy cock was like a steel rod standing proudly against his belly, his muscles tense, but he had a smile on his handsome face.

"Come here," he urged. Still not a command.

Mercedes realized then that she wanted him to take over from here. Because for her, it no longer mattered who held the reins. This man owned her. Every piece of her.

Walking around to stand between his spread thighs, Mercedes put his hands on her hips as she looked down at him, still trying to hold on to the last sliver of control that even she knew had disintegrated a long time ago.

"I want to ride your cock. Right here, right now," she told him, trying to play along.

Xander nodded, and Mercedes gripped his dark hair tightly. If she had been thinking like a true Domme, his lack of response would've angered her, but she was long past that. She wasn't able to keep up the perfect Domme routine. Not with him.

Hooking her left leg on the outside of Xander's thick right thigh, Mercedes gripped his erection in her fist and guided him inside of her before sinking down on him slowly.

"Oh, God," she moaned, pressing her cheek against his. "X," she pleaded quietly. "Please."

She allowed her body to adjust to the blunt intrusion, and once she could take him deeper, she relied on Xander's firm grip on her hips to hold her as she raised and hooked her right leg over his left leg until she was straddling his lap, his cock buried to the hilt inside of her.

"Fuck me, X. Please," she moaned, moving her mouth to his, unable to keep from kissing him.

The way Xander gripped her hips, lifting her until only the head of his cock was penetrating her, and then lowering her roughly, Mercedes knew he was right there on the edge with her.

She was in public, even if the audience could only see shadows through the opaque glass, but none of it mattered. As far as she was concerned, they were the only two people in the entire world.

What that said about her, she didn't know, and she no longer cared.

"Fuck me harder," she encouraged, gripping his shoulders as she stared down at him. The intensity in his gaze was her lifeline, and she clung to it.

Xander held her hips tightly, pulling her flush against him and then lifting her, his cock thrusting up into her from below until the friction all but consumed her, his cock nailing her G-spot with every deep stroke. Mercedes was suspended by a thread, hovering on the edge of an orgasm so explosive she wasn't sure she'd survive it.

With her eyes still locked with his, she ran her hands over the chiseled features of his ruggedly beautiful face, desperately holding on to that connection that she knew she would feel lost without.

No matter what she'd originally thought, her pleasure was owned by this one man. Her perception of what she had wanted was clearly skewed, and without Xander, she'd feel lost and helpless. But Xander eased her, gave her strength, made her feel. And nothing else mattered except him.

Her pleasure was in his hands, and she knew she could give herself up to him completely and never have to worry. He'd be there to catch her when she fell.

And she was falling. Desperately. And fast.

Sucking his bottom lip into her mouth, she gently nipped him, his cock pulsing deep inside of her as the pain registered.

"Are you ready to come for me?" This time he was the one to ask, but his words were a mere puff of air against her ear. He was allowing her to save face, even when no one else was in the room to know.

"Yes," she whispered.

"Then come for me, pet," he encouraged. "Come on my cock. Let me feel you."

"Oh, God." That was all she needed. His permission. Not the other way around. One more forceful thrust of his hips and she was flying into orbit, Xander's hands gripping her ass, bracing her.

When she thought she could take no more, he surprised her by pushing to his feet, the chair he had been sitting in falling over and crashing to the floor.

With her arms around his neck, he held her like she weighed nothing as he began pounding up into her while she worked her hips down onto him at the same time.

"God, I love your pussy," he growled. "Come for me again, Mercedes. Come for me now." Xander groaned, and the words sent her flying over the edge, oblivious to her own guttural cries as she came.

She was only aware of the pulse of Xander's cock deep inside of her as he came, his body stone still as he held her until they were both sated completely.

For now, Mercedes was going to enjoy that euphoric feeling.

Later, much, much later, she was going to have to play out the scene in her head just to figure out where things had gone completely awry.

CHAPTER THIRTY-SIX

T minus zero...
Tuesday

"MEET ME FOR DINNER?" XANDER ASKED WHEN Mercedes answered her cell phone the following afternoon.

"Where?" she asked as she clutched the phone in her hand. At the mere sound of his voice, her spirits lifted for the first time all day.

She'd spent way too many hours fretting over the fact that Xander had left her alone for most of the day. That and why he seemed to be putting distance between them.

She listened while he rumbled off the name of the most romantic, not to mention the most expensive restaurant in downtown Dallas. It wasn't his favorite place, but he knew that she liked it.

"What time?"

"Seven thirty."

Mercedes knew she probably paused a little too long, because Xander followed up with, "Logan and Sam will be meeting us there, as well."

Okay, so clearly this wasn't meant to be a romantic evening out. Not that she had expected it to be.

She'd only hoped.

"I'll meet you there."

"Oh, and Mercedes…"

Mercedes waited for Xander to finish, but he didn't. Unable to bear the silence any longer, she asked, "Is something wrong?"

"Nothing at all. I just… I think we need to talk. See you at seven thirty."

With that, the call disconnected, and Mercedes fumbled her phone. They needed to talk?

Shit. Shit. Shit.

That couldn't be good.

Was he still pissed at her for disappearing before he'd gotten out of bed that morning? He'd certainly appeared angry when he'd showed up at her door partially dressed, but she'd thought he was fine when he'd left a short while later.

In her defense, their five days were up as of that morning. She probably could've argued that point last night and spent the entire night alone in her own bed. But she'd chickened out, wanting — no, needing — one last night with him.

Great.

Now she was rattled as well as out of sorts. Her mind was coming up with a myriad of things that could be wrong, including Xander's disappointment in her. She'd failed last night; she knew that. The scene had gotten completely out of hand. She'd pushed both Clarissa and Xander hard; harder than she'd intended.

Seriously. It had all been done in fear. Fear of what she was beginning to feel for Xander. Fear for what she wanted from him. And she had almost pushed them to the point of no return. Had it not been for him, that's exactly where they would be right then. And there wouldn't be a dinner invitation. Business or otherwise.

Placing her phone into the cup holder, Mercedes gripped the wheel with both hands, trying to keep her hands from shaking.

This was it. Xander was going tell her thanks for the memories, but he preferred that they go back to just being friends. Or worse, maybe he was going to tell her that he couldn't even be friends anymore.

Breathe.

Mercedes took a deep breath as she came to a stop at a red light. She was overreacting. She had to be. Xander hadn't seemed at all upset when he'd left her alone in her condo after their heated discussion. It wasn't quite an argument because Xander hadn't pressed the issue and he'd never once raised his voice.

Even though they hadn't kissed and made up — but why would they if their time was officially over? — he had wrapped her in his arms and held her before he'd turned and walked out the same way he'd come in. He wouldn't have done that if he was going to tell her he didn't want to at least be friends, would he?

No. Xander wasn't made that way. He was as straightforward as they came. He would've called her to the carpet, addressed the issue at the time.

So what did he want to talk about?

Putting her foot on the gas pedal, Mercedes focused on the drive to the restaurant.

Although she hadn't eaten anything all day, she wasn't sure she could eat now if she was forced to.

He wanted to talk.

They *needed* to talk.

And so what if he did let her down easily? It wouldn't matter. She had known from the start that this wasn't going to work.

Keep telling yourself that.

It didn't matter that he'd made her feel things she'd never expected. It didn't matter that she'd let herself fall just a little bit in love with him. None of it mattered because it was just a deal. An experiment. And she'd known from the beginning that it would come to an end.

So why did she suddenly want to cry?

XANDER WAITED AT THE BAR OF ONE of Mercedes's favorite restaurants for her to arrive. He'd spent the better part of the day traveling — a trip he hadn't been able to put off — and when his jet had landed just an hour before, he had called her and asked her to meet him for dinner.

She had graciously accepted, although he had sensed reluctance in her tone. It wasn't until he'd informed her that they'd be meeting with Logan and Samantha McCoy that she'd seemed to relax. What that was about, he had no idea, but he hadn't asked, either.

He should probably thank Logan for calling him with the last-minute dinner request, because otherwise, he'd probably be drinking at home.

Alone.

"Another," he told the bartender when the man made his way over.

"Yes, sir."

Xander was tired. He was stressed. And he was anxious to see Mercedes even if he did have to spend dinner discussing business with Logan. Mercedes's presence would make it all worth it.

Although it had technically been five days since they'd embarked on this adventure, Xander wasn't ready for it to be over. He found that he enjoyed Mercedes's company, and being away from her, even for a few short hours, hadn't been the highlight of his day.

A soft hand touched his back, and Xander turned to see Mercedes standing beside him. "Hey," she greeted. "You okay?"

Better now, he thought to himself. But he said, "Hungry. You?"

"Starving, actually." It was a lie, he could tell, but he didn't call her on it. "Are Logan and Samantha here yet?"

Yes, he had definitely come to the right conclusion. Mercedes was happy to have Logan and Sam along tonight. Probably because she was looking to put some distance between them, and Logan and Sam would act as a nice buffer.

Not that he blamed her. After last night, he wasn't sure how she would respond to him today. That was partially why he'd given her some space by informing her he'd had to go out of town. What he had wanted to do was invite her, but he knew she had needed some time to herself.

So he had graciously given her the entire day in the hopes that the time she had to herself would allow her to realize... Hell, he wasn't even sure what he hoped she would realize. That he loved her? That she loved him? That being with her was exactly where he wanted to be, regardless of who was dominating whom?

Apparently a full day to herself didn't seem to be long enough if the way she was glancing around the room was any indication.

"They're on the way," he informed her. "I asked them to meet us at eight." It was only half past seven, so they still had some time. He'd done that on purpose also. "Have a seat," he said, keeping his tone firm as he pulled out the high-back barstool beside him.

Mercedes gracefully took a seat next to him, and when the bartender returned with his drink, Xander allowed her to order for herself. Although he could've easily made the selection for her. She ordered white wine, her usual M.O. at this particular establishment.

"How did things go today?" Mercedes asked the question, but she didn't look at him.

"Could've been better." He had no intention of going into detail about his day. He wanted to talk, but not about business. As it was, he would have to delve into business with Logan shortly.

Ever since last night, when they'd arrived back at his condo, Mercedes had been avoiding him. Well, not entirely, because they had spent more time together, mostly in the bath, where he'd enjoyed running his hands over her curvy, wet body. But even as he'd made her come with his fingers, he had felt her retreating from him.

She'd probably hoped he wouldn't notice.

He'd noticed.

It was hard not to when he had woken up that morning at five o'clock — about an hour later than normal — to find Mercedes gone from his bed.

Needless to say, he hadn't been happy. His mood had darkened even more when he'd found that she wasn't even in his condo. Rather than calling her, Xander had pulled on a pair of shorts, hadn't bothered with a shirt or shoes, which was very unlike him, and made his way down to her floor and beat on her front door until she answered.

She'd opened the door, her hair wet, her face scrubbed clean. Yes, she'd gone back to her place to shower, and that had been like a kick in the nuts. Mercedes had made the message very clear. Their time together had come to an end.

And after the scene they'd shared at Devotion … that bothered him more than anything.

He knew she wouldn't want to talk about what had happened last night when he had used his safe word to call a halt to the nightmare that they were venturing closer and closer to. But he had wanted to talk about it.

Not just about that, though. There were some other things he needed to say to her. Important things. Things he wasn't willing to keep in any longer.

But he didn't address the elephant in the room. There would be time later, and he intended to address the issue, but he also planned to do so in private. For now, he simply asked, "What did you do today?"

"I took a client out for a few hours."

That wasn't much of an explanation, but he hadn't expected much more than that, either. She wasn't looking at him, seemingly fascinated with her wineglass and the people sitting around them. He ached to put his arms around her, to pull her close, and to assure her that there was no reason for her to be freaked out.

If only it would help.

Knowing Mercedes, she would come up with another excuse to disappear on him, and right now, he just wanted her to be close. It was enough.

For the moment.

"Your table is ready, sir." A young man dressed in a suit, sans the jacket, stood to his left as he spoke.

Xander nodded his head and pushed to his feet, waiting for Mercedes to join him. When she did, he placed his hand low on her back and guided her toward the back of the restaurant.

To his surprise, Logan and Samantha arrived just a few minutes later. After a quick round of greetings, the four of them took their seats and proceeded to order drinks when the waiter approached.

A drink was all Xander cared about. His mind was elsewhere — namely back at Devotion, still chained to the wall while Mercedes did whatever she could to get a rise out of him. It had worked. Just not necessarily the way she thought it had.

What she didn't seem to understand was that he had no interest in those scenes anymore. More importantly, he had connected with Mercedes in a way he hadn't even known possible, and as far as he was concerned, there was no one but her for him.

A woman's submission was something he craved like a drug. He couldn't explain it. Didn't necessarily care to, either, but what had transpired between him and Mercedes last night had defied reason. It had gone so far beyond submission Xander didn't even have a name for it.

He feared that's what scared Mercedes the most. She'd been anticipating topping him from the very beginning. And yet, it'd seemed as though she had turned her sights on Clarissa after she had successfully secured him to the wall.

And then he had ended it all with one single word.

"You said you had a business proposition for me." Logan's deep voice broke through Xander's thoughts, pulling him back to the moment.

He glanced over at Mercedes to see whether she was aware he'd been thinking about her. She still wasn't looking at him, but her interest had been piqued when Logan had spoken up, so he knew she was paying attention.

"I do," he told him, tossing back what was left of his drink. It was time to focus on the task at hand. There'd be time to address Mercedes later.

He hoped.

MERCEDES SPENT TWO HOURS OF HER LIFE hanging on to every word Xander, Logan, and Samantha spoke while she picked at the food on her plate. She had purposely not made eye contact, hoping Samantha would catch on that she wasn't in a particularly chatty mood.

While the three of them had chatted it up, Mercedes had only partially heard what they were saying, not because she wasn't interested in the new business venture that Xander had proposed. No, she was having trouble focusing because she was doing her best to keep her thoughts from getting away from her. If that happened, she was pretty sure she would break down and cry.

The thought pissed her off.

She didn't cry. Ever. It was easier to keep things bottled up, to never get her hopes up, to never anticipate anything other than what she could do for herself. Yet here she was, wishing like hell Xander would tell her he wanted more than five days. That he'd realized in that short amount of time that she was the one he wanted.

No, she didn't like what that said about her. But she couldn't deny the hope that had flared deep inside of her when he'd used his safe word, saving them all from disaster.

But he hadn't wanted to talk about it.

Sneaking out of Xander's condo before dawn wasn't the best idea; she had known that at the time. When he had arrived at her front door, insisting that she talk to him, she'd pushed him away yet again. It had been a test of sorts. One he'd failed miserably.

Or maybe she was the one who had failed.

Rather than stay and talk, rather than push her to open up to him, Xander had given in and walked away. Giving her the space she had asked for.

But why not? Their time was over. He didn't owe her anything and vice versa.

After he'd left, she had spent the better part of the morning in her home office and the afternoon with a new client who seemed genuinely interested in purchasing one of the luxurious downtown condos she'd shown him. Even now, Mercedes had a hard time remembering which places she'd shown him.

Considering her state of mind after what had happened last night, Mercedes was grateful her client had been so agreeable. Had he not been, she wasn't sure what she might've done.

Aside from that brief reprieve from her overwhelming thoughts, Mercedes had spent the day in a fog.

She blamed Xander.

The man had left her completely out of sorts. Especially after he'd taken her home from Devotion and cared for her so sweetly. They'd shared a bath, and to her surprise, he hadn't questioned her about what had happened during their scene. She'd appreciated that more than him soaping her up and then using his skilled fingers to make her come apart twice more before they finally fell into bed.

At least she hadn't had the dream last night. The one that included the shell of a man she'd come to care about more than she was willing to admit. The same man who she had set out to dominate, to prove to both of them just who she was, and failed.

She figured she wouldn't be having the dream again because she feared Xander had worn her down and her need to dominate was fading like print on old newspaper.

She was a fucking submissive. Wait. Scratch that.

She was *his* fucking submissive.

The notion was like a slap in the face, and Mercedes wasn't at all happy. Up until last night, she'd been able to tell herself that she just needed the opportunity to dominate Xander. To prove to him that she was merely acting when she submitted to him.

Yeah, well, they'd both learned the cold, hard truth, hadn't they?

Mercedes *had* submitted to him. Not just once but many times. Including one time without any provocation on his part.

In fact, last night at Devotion, she had focused more of her attention on Clarissa and less on Xander. Because she knew deep in her heart that she didn't want to dominate him.

She was in love with Xander Boone.

Head over heels in love with him.

Never in her life would she have thought herself capable of falling in love for real. And definitely not with a Dom.

Then again, it did explain the series of bad relationships she'd had over the years. She'd obviously been going about it all wrong for her entire life.

During the day, when she had been showing one condo after another to a man who had more money than sense, she had come to realize that she had been working diligently to be something she wasn't. A Domme. She had wasted years of her life trying to dominate men because that kept them at a distance; it prevented them from having any power over her.

The way her father had when she was a child.

And now she had no power whatsoever.

But worse than that, she feared that Xander thought less of her for it. If he were as interested in her as he'd acted, he was probably rethinking now that he knew she was weak.

Mercedes knew the type of women he dated. They were all strong-willed, even if they submitted to him sexually. They weren't the meek submissives he tended to play with from time to time at Kink. The women who held his interest wouldn't just roll over and give up.

God, she hated this pity party she'd thrown herself. She wanted to get out of her funk, but the day had only continued to get worse when she'd realized Xander had never called. At least not until he'd needed a date to a business dinner with Logan and Samantha.

Oh, sure, she had tried to sound relieved, but the truth was, she had been disappointed. Xander hadn't been planning a romantic dinner for just the two of them. He hadn't had any intention of spending time with her.

Or maybe this was his way of letting her down gently. Moving their relationship back to a platonic — *slash* — business friendship. He probably hoped she wouldn't even realize it.

"What do you think?"

Mercedes focused on the faces around her and realized Samantha had asked her a direct question. Since she had absolutely no idea what they were talking about, she felt like a fool sitting there staring at her.

"I'm sorry. If you'll excuse me," she muttered, reaching for her clutch and rising from her chair.

At the exact same time, both men stood, neither of them reclaiming their seats until she was several feet away.

Rather than run to the bathroom and break down in tears like she'd first intended, Mercedes did something worse.

She took off out of the restaurant and straight to her car. And as soon as she was safely inside, the tears broke free and didn't stop, even when she walked through her front door.

CHAPTER THIRTY-SEVEN

XANDER HAD KNOWN THE MOMENT MERCEDES EXCUSED herself that she was going to bolt from the restaurant and not look back. No, he hadn't gone after her. He had wanted to; he just hadn't done it. But that was because he was hoping against hope that she would decide to come back on her own.

When he'd realized the inevitable had happened, and Mercedes had been gone for fifteen minutes, Xander had kindly asked Sam if she would go check on her. A few minutes after that, Sam had returned to inform him that she wasn't in the restroom but that she had inquired with the hostess, and the woman had seen Mercedes leave the restaurant a short while ago.

Not surprising.

Without hesitating, Xander had excused himself with a quick apology to Logan and Samantha, who'd politely waved him off, encouraging him to go after her. On his way out, he'd left his credit card number with the waiter and headed for his car. The drive home had taken half the time it should have, but he was a man on a mission.

Once he made it to Mercedes's front door, he didn't even bother knocking. Instead, he used the key he had and waltzed right in.

That was when his heart had lurched right into his throat.

Following the sound coming from the back of the condo, Xander had slowly made his way, his heart racing as he closed the distance between himself and the woman he loved.

Just as he'd thought, she was in her bedroom. With one foot inside the room, he came to a halt when he saw her standing in front of the floor-to-ceiling windows, silhouetted by the bright lights of the city in the distance.

But she wasn't admiring the view.

She was crying.

Rooted in place by the sight, he tried desperately to find his voice but couldn't. He cleared his throat in an attempt to dislodge the giant knot of emotion that had formed upon hearing her soft sobs, and to alert her to his presence.

In a move that was very unlike Mercedes, she turned to face him, not bothering to try and wipe the tears he knew were streaming down her face. Although she was in shadow, he could still see her face. She didn't smile, and she didn't offer any excuses as to what she was upset about.

He already knew.

He was the reason for the tears, and the thought made his gut churn.

Knowing Mercedes, she had spent the better part of the day trying to come to terms with what had happened last night. But she wasn't coming to the same conclusion Xander had.

No, Mercedes wasn't thinking that the reason he'd ended their scene so abruptly had anything to do with the fact that he had fallen in love with her. She wasn't the glass-half-full type of woman.

He would take the blame for that. It wasn't like he'd made a full-fledged effort to try and talk to her about it. Quite the opposite. Instead of telling her how he felt last night when they'd come back to his place, Xander had, for lack of a better term, chickened out.

And to make matters worse, Xander had convinced himself that she had needed some time and distance to sort through what she was feeling. So he'd left her alone.

"Why didn't you say something?" she whispered.

He could barely make out her words, but he heard enough to process the question, but for the life of him, he wasn't sure what exactly she was referring to. Surely she wasn't asking why he hadn't just come out and told her that he loved her and that he wanted to spend the rest of his life with her. Not after what had transpired at Devotion.

She must've realized he was at a loss, because she continued. "Did you not even think to question what happened between us last night?"

Last night?

Maybe it was the alcohol, or maybe it was the sight of her tears, but Xander wasn't functioning on all cylinders. He knew it wasn't the alcohol because he hadn't had enough to even get buzzed, much less enough to jumble his thoughts.

But seeing Mercedes cry… That was enough to tear him up inside. In all the time he'd known her, never once had he seen her cry.

"I didn't have a reason to question last night," he told her now, trying to put two and two together but still coming up short. Sure, there were other nights he had thought to question, like the first time they'd made love, or every time after that.

"No? You used your safe word, Xander. You backed out of the scene, but you didn't ask any questions."

Xander stared at her. "Me? What about you? Did you think to question me? Did you think to ask why I couldn't go through with it?"

"I did ask you why!" she countered. "You didn't answer me."

She was right. He hadn't answered her. And for very good reason. The last damn thing he had wanted was to profess his love for her in a glass room at a fetish club. He had more class than that. "I didn't want to say it then," he admitted, realizing he was being vague.

"Why? Because I failed?" she asked on a sob. "Because I pushed too hard? I don't blame you, Xander. I know I failed. I tried to manipulate the scene because I was invested, but I was too attached to see clearly."

"That's not why I used my safe word. I used it because I didn't want to go any further. I didn't want another woman, Mercedes. Don't you understand that?" Xander moved closer because he couldn't stand to be so far away from her.

"Stop," she snapped, wiping her tears with the back of her hand. "I don't need your pity, Xander. I know what you think of me. I know you're trying to find a way to let me down easily, but I'm here to tell you not to bother. Our five days are over. You win."

"*Win?*" Xander couldn't control his outrage. As his heart rate doubled, fear digging its talons deep into his soul, he swallowed, then bit out, "How the fuck do I win if you walk away?"

"You did what you set out to do. You proved that I'm submissive. I don't hold a candle to you, Xander. I'm not built the way you are. I gave up too easily. So, yes, you were right."

"I wasn't out to prove anything," Xander growled, ignoring her request for him to stay back. He moved until he was practically up against her. He tipped her chin with his finger, forcing her to look up at him. "I wanted to be close to you. You gave me that. So, if you want to think I won, then yes, maybe so. But only because I had *you* with me.

"You know me, Mercedes. You know how I think. I didn't just come up with this out of the fucking blue. I found an opportunity, and I exploited it. That's what I do. I go after what I want. And I want you. I've *always* wanted you."

Mercedes looked shocked by his admission. Xander inhaled deeply, lowered his voice, and continued, "And after that first night at Devotion, I knew for a fact that what I felt for you was real. There was — no, there *is* — something between us, Mercedes. I'm not willing to ignore it any longer. That was the reason for this. Not because I wanted to prove something. I don't give a damn about any of the rest of it. I care about you." *I love you*, he thought to himself. He didn't say the words because he knew she wouldn't hear him. She didn't *want* to hear him right now; he could see it in her eyes.

"But now you know how easy it was to get me to submit to you," Mercedes responded, confusion riddling her words.

"*Easy?*" Xander laughed, but there wasn't an ounce of humor in it. "Honey, there hasn't been anything easy about you. Not since the day I met you. And definitely not in the last few days." Xander gave her a small smile. "You're one of the most hard-headed women I've ever met. You're strong. Confident. Independent. And you fucking make my blood boil." Cupping her face with his hand, he leaned in closer. "Last night, you made me burn for you. I was willing to do damn near anything to just be near you. But only you. No one else. Don't you see that?"

Mercedes stared back at him, tears glistening on her long lashes. "I'm weak."

"The hell you are," he argued. "And if you keep this up, I'm going to bend you over my knee, Mercedes. This isn't who you are."

"It is. I'm a submissive, Xander. This is exactly who I am."

"Is that what you think? That submitting to someone means you're weak?" He knew she did, but he wanted to force her to think it through. "Is it? Do you truly believe that being a Domme gives you all the power? Have you learned absolutely nothing in the last few days?"

Mercedes tried to push away from him, obviously pissed at his accusations. He didn't let her go.

"Being a Dom doesn't define *me*. And being a submissive doesn't define *you*."

"Oh, but it does," she argued, anger burning bright in her eyes.

"It's about perception, Mercedes. You see what you want to see. Everyone sees what they want to see. When we were at Devotion, and I had you strapped to that bench, do you think I was in control? No, pet, you were." Xander wiped away a tear that slid down her cheek, lowering his voice. "You've been in control since the moment I met you. Since the very first time I laid eyes on you. It didn't matter whether you were submitting to me or not."

"I don't feel in control. I hate this, Xander. I don't want to roll over and give up. I spent too many years doing just that."

"I don't want you to give up, either. I want you to fight. Fight for this. Fight for … us."

"But you want me to submit to you."

"Yes, I did. I still do. Because I want you. I want to take care of you, Mercedes. I want to give you what you need. I want to bind you to me, to know that I mean as much to you as you mean to me. But I want so much more than your submission."

"I grew up submitting. He broke me. He broke my mother. All of my choices were taken away. He ruled everything."

By "he," Xander knew she was referring to her father. The son of a bitch didn't deserve to be walking.

"You weren't submitting, Mercedes. You were reacting. It wasn't submission; it was self-preservation. He was a bastard for what he did to you and your mother. Don't ever compare the two. It isn't the same."

"What's the difference?" she asked, her lips trembling.

"Love," he said easily.

Mercedes tried to step back again, looking as though he'd slapped her when he said the single word that he had a feeling scared her the most.

"I love you, Mercedes," he told her as he wrapped his arms around her waist, not letting her get away from him. "I have always loved you. I loved you before you submitted, and I love you just as much, if not more, now."

Her eyes widened, but she stopped trying to get away.

He had absolutely no idea what she was thinking, but at least, for the moment, she was right where he wanted her. In his arms.

MERCEDES WAS PRETTY SURE SHE WAS HEARING things.

Xander loved her? That's what she thought she'd heard him say, but it couldn't be true. Could it?

Before she had the chance to ask him to repeat what he'd said, Xander kissed her.

It was gentle and sweet, and it made her skin tingle from the inside out. His lips whispered over hers, and her heart felt like it tumbled in her chest. It was a kiss, but it was so much more.

"I love you," he said again. "And I'm not saying that as a Dom to a submissive. I'm saying that as a man to a woman."

This time, Mercedes heard him loud and clear. Taking a moment to study him, she peered into his eyes, trying to read between the lines.

But that was the problem. There weren't any lines. This was Xander. He didn't play games, and he damn sure didn't say things that he didn't mean.

"You love me?" she asked incredulously, her voice hoarse from her tears.

"More than anything."

Xander pressed his lips to hers once again, but not quite as gently. She could taste the bourbon on his tongue, but not only that. There was something else. Passion. Love. Acceptance. That's what she tasted.

He wanted her.

He *loved* her.

Mercedes wrapped her arms around him and held him close, the tears breaking free as he continued to kiss her.

Never in her life had she felt like this. Like her entire being was made up of air, and she was going to float away if she didn't hang on. God, if this was what love felt like, then she knew for a fact that she'd never even come close to loving someone in all of her life. Not like this.

Long minutes passed before Xander pulled back. When he did, Mercedes was scared to let him go. She didn't want to wake up to find herself alone in her bed — to find out that this had all been a dream.

Xander chuckled as he pulled her arms from around him, taking her hands in his and leading her toward her bed.

"I want to make love to you," he told her, his eyes mysteriously shiny. "Just you and me. No Doms or submissives. Just the two of us tonight. Understand?"

Mercedes nodded, lacing her fingers with his and allowing him to pull her closer as he sat on the edge of the bed.

This time when he pulled her against him, she gave in. She allowed herself to feel everything he was offering her. Allowed herself to love and be loved at the same time. Something she had always been too scared to do.

Her Domme armor crumbled into dust just from his touch. She knew there was no going back. Not at this point. But Mercedes didn't want to go back. He'd stripped her emotionally and built her back up all within a breath. With just three words that she had longed to hear, longed to feel.

I love you.

Another rush of tears filled her eyes, but she let them fall.

It didn't take long before they were naked, their bodies in perfect tune with one another as Xander hovered above her on the bed. He was still kissing her, and she was still hanging on for dear life. In fact, Mercedes wasn't sure she was ever going to let him go.

Not today. Not tomorrow. Not ever.

"Love me, Mercedes," Xander whispered against her mouth as he slid inside of her.

Wrapping her legs around his waist, she urged him closer, trying to feel the full length of his body against hers. But Xander was on to her because he shifted positions, lifting her right leg up, which changed the angle, and he penetrated her deeper, making her moan.

He stopped kissing her, his eyes locked with hers as he slowly thrust forward, pausing. "You're my everything, Mercedes," Xander whispered.

Mercedes couldn't stop the next wave of tears. But he must've realized they weren't from fear or pain. They were tears of hope and love. Tears she'd never expected to cry, but for this man, she realized anything was possible.

Mercedes still couldn't speak, her heart lodged in her throat. The best she could do was breathe and fight to keep her gaze locked with his. She wanted him to see everything she felt, to know exactly what he meant to her. Dom or sub, it didn't matter. Just like he'd said.

"Mercedes," Xander growled softly, his hips moving, his strokes deepening until she felt all of him. "Baby."

When his eyes closed, Mercedes reached up and cupped his face. "Look at me," she begged. Although she'd meant it as a command, it came out more as a plea, but Xander opened his eyes. "I love you," she whispered to him and Xander stilled. Right there, lodged deep inside of her, he went stone still.

"Aww, hell," he growled. "Say it again, Mercedes. Tell me you love me."

Mercedes thrust her hips upward, trying to drive him deeper. The movement elicited another groan from him, but then he was moving again, never looking away from her face.

"I love you, Xander Boone. I love you so much."

"I can't hold back, baby. I need you too much."

Xander growled, his release clearly taking him by surprise. And her, too, because as soon as he came, Mercedes saw everything she'd been hoping to see right there in his beautiful eyes.

And that's when she tipped right over the edge with him.

CHAPTER THIRTY-EIGHT

Six months later, January…
At the grand opening of Alluring Indulgence Resort

"I HOPE YOU KNOW WHAT YOU'RE DOING," Mercedes said, a pretty pout on her lips.

"I always know what I'm doing," he assured her. Granted, this time he wasn't quite as confident. He'd already attempted this once, and he wasn't exactly sure what made them think it would work a second time, but here they were.

Acting as Mercedes's submissive for this one last scene was going to take a certain set of skills he didn't think he possessed. It wasn't all that much different than the night at Devotion, but he remembered clearly how that had turned out. A total fucking disaster.

And to make it worse, the Walker brothers were hanging around, which didn't make him at all eager to take those stairs down to the first floor.

In truth, after the way that night had turned out, he hadn't expected Mercedes to follow through with the second request, but it had inadvertently come up in conversation just a week ago. At first, he'd thought she was going to try to talk herself out of it, but Xander had insisted.

It didn't mean he was at all happy or that he didn't hate that he would have to pretend to submit once more. But he did know, with absolute certainty, that he could not go back on his word. They'd had an agreement. She would submit to him if he submitted to her.

It didn't seem to matter that she'd submitted to him completely for all these months, either. A deal was a deal.

However, he was glad to see that there was a significant difference between this scene and the one they'd done at Devotion, when she had successfully restrained him and blown his mind with her dominance, even though she had considered that night a failure.

First, he wasn't wearing a collar.

Second, he wasn't weighed down by wrist shackles.

And third, they'd talked and come up with a plan ahead of time so there wouldn't be any surprises.

He'd appreciated all of those points considering they were at Alluring Indulgence, and the Walkers would be present. Based on what they had predetermined, if things went accordingly, he wasn't even sure people would realize what they were seeing. He knew what they would *expect* to see, though, so it would probably work out in both of their favors.

It was all about perception.

His.

Hers.

And everyone else's.

It was true, people only saw what they wanted to see. In this case, it didn't matter whether they believed the man was always the Dom, or that the Dom wielded all the power. There was a drastic difference between what they wanted to see and what reality was.

"Since you're so confident, then what are we waiting for?" Mercedes asked him — he knew it was rhetorical — as she turned toward the sweeping staircase that would take them to the main area on the first floor.

It wasn't like it was a death march, but Xander preferred to pretend not to think about what they were doing or where they were going. Instead, he busied himself with checking out the beautiful woman who was now leading the way. He was supposed to be playing a part, keeping his eyes forward, not ogling her, but the woman was absolutely breathtaking, and he found himself devoid of any and all willpower where she was concerned.

They were in costume, as Mercedes had put it. He wore nothing more than a pair of leather pants, his shitkickers, and sterling silver hoops in his nipples. He'd traded the titanium bars for the hoops at the last minute, and the way Mercedes had eyed him had given him the courage to go through with this.

No one ever said you had to be submissive to seek approval from the person you loved. Xander was certainly no exception. To know that she was going to enjoy this as much as he was made it all worthwhile.

Then again, he wasn't the main attraction. Mercedes was. It wasn't what he was wearing that would catch people's attention, anyway. Especially not with a tall, willowy, curvy-in-all-the-right places, incredibly beautiful woman at his side.

Tonight, Mercedes's body was showcased in a ruby-red baby-doll nighty that did little to hide the stunning body beneath. Her nipples were visible through the sheer material, and her long legs were accentuated by fishnet stockings with those sexy fuck-me heels on her feet.

But when she turned away from him, that's when Xander's mouth went dry. Her luscious ass was on full display, a tiny G-string doing nothing whatsoever to shield her glorious backside.

It was an outfit very similar to the one he'd had her put on the very first night she'd submitted to him at Devotion. He couldn't help but wonder whether that was intentional on her part.

The view definitely made what was about to happen a little easier.

Apparently someone had been thinking ahead, because, as they began to descend the stairs, "Erotica" by Madonna began playing on the overhead speakers.

Interesting choice.

Doing his best to stay focused, Xander allowed Mercedes to lead him to the center of the main room, straight to the oversized, black leather, circular sofa that was the focal point of the open space. Luckily no one stopped them to chat. Xander could tolerate a lot, but tonight, he had no intention of making small talk.

At least not until this was over.

When they stopped at the sofa, Mercedes mumbled, "I hope you're ready for this."

Taking his seat, he looked up at her, met her beautiful gray gaze, and said, "Baby, you have no idea. But just wait until later. I fully intend to make your pretty ass blush with my hand."

His words seemed to have taken Mercedes by surprise, but to her credit, she didn't show any outward reaction. Rather than waiting to see what she'd come back with, Xander got into position on the couch, lying flat on his back. Because of his height, he stretched from one side to the other, but nothing was hanging off, which was good.

He couldn't help it, he looked over, tracking her with his eyes as she came around the sofa to stand near his head.

"Eyes above you. Not on me," she commanded.

His cock jerked in response. He might not submit to her by choice, but he did enjoy her demanding side from time to time.

As the song continued, Xander freed his cock from the confining leather, stroking himself ever so slowly as he waited for Mercedes to get into position. She had strictly instructed that he was to tempt her, but he wasn't allowed to come. For a scene, this one was incredibly tame, especially for Mercedes, but again, he hadn't complained.

It sure beat the alternative.

When she kneeled over him, one knee on each side of his head, he sucked in a sharp breath, praying he would be able to control himself. As with anytime he was with her, the rest of the world receded. The only person who mattered was her, and this time wasn't any different.

Knowing that she was intimately watching him, Xander continued to jack his cock with one hand, the tension in his balls intensifying as her sweet scent flooded his senses. Keeping his other hand resting at his side and not touching her the way he wanted was the hardest thing about tonight. But somehow he managed.

That's when Mercedes blew his fucking mind. She reached one hand between her legs, sliding her thong to the side as she lowered her pussy to his mouth.

He could imagine what people saw when they looked at them. A wonton woman sprawled over him, ready to ride his face for all she was worth. While her obedient sub focused solely on her, his one and only goal was to make her come. With his mouth.

With her orgasm his full priority, Xander licked her.

Slowly at first, teasing gently before sucking her clit. It wasn't long before she was grinding her pussy against his mouth, her soft moans vibrating through her body, not heard over the sound of the music.

His cock was throbbing, his balls drawing up against his body as he continued to stroke himself, wishing like fuck that her mouth was on him, but that wasn't the way it was planned. Instead, he fought the urge to come while he ate her pussy, relishing the way she was riding his face.

It wasn't until she came, her body shuddering above him, that Xander realized just what he'd do to make the woman come undone.

Even if it meant she would withhold his release from him. Which she evidently intended to do.

Once she was sated — even if it was just the beginning of their night together — Mercedes crawled down him, making her way to the opposite end. When she paused, grinding her hot cunt against his straining erection, he sucked in air. Even with her panties acting as a barrier between them, he felt the wet heat, and it was enough to make him nearly come in his hand.

"Not yet," she demanded as she glanced back over her shoulder. He could barely hear her over the music from the loudspeakers and the people talking around them, but he knew what she said.

With a dangerous choke hold on his cock, an attempt to keep from losing it right then and there, Xander started counting slowly to himself. It was the only alternative to grabbing her hips and pulling her down on top of him.

She surprised him when she stood up. Instead of asking him to get up, like they had planned in advance, Mercedes offered him a wicked grin. One that spoke of promises and retribution.

Figured.

He was in a position that he couldn't very well get out of because he'd agreed well in advance, but that didn't mean he didn't want to.

No, Xander reached deep inside and latched on to his control, while Mercedes came around near his head once more. He was looking up at her; she was looking down at him. When she knelt on the floor, he couldn't imagine what the hell she was doing, but he waited.

"Put your cock away," she told him.

Yeah, that wasn't going to be quite as easy as it looked. But she probably knew that. His dick was throbbing, and the leather pants were going to cause a significant amount of discomfort. But he did it anyway.

Managing to tuck himself back in his pants, he still didn't move.

"This is for you," she whispered near his ear, and she retrieved something from beneath the sofa.

Son of a bitch.

He wanted to laugh, but he didn't. It wasn't part of the scene. None of this was.

"Raise your head."

He did.

Mercedes proceeded to buckle that goddamn collar around his neck once more.

"Sit up."

Xander sat up, swinging his legs around and over the side of the sofa, his painfully hard cock causing a tremendous amount of discomfort, but he didn't say a word.

"Stand up."

Rising to his feet, he kept his gaze fixed on her.

Mercedes stood, coming to stand directly in front of him, and that was when he realized she was holding something else.

It wasn't until she reached up and buckled it to the D ring on the collar that he figured out just what it was.

The wicked woman had leashed him. She'd actually clipped a fucking leash to the fucking collar around his fucking neck.

He took a deep breath. Let it out.

Mercedes stepped closer, went up on her toes, and brushed her mouth to his. "I'm just making sure there is absolutely no doubt in anyone's mind exactly who you belong to."

He nodded, still not saying a word. He was supposed to be playing a part. And he had to hand it to himself … he was doing a damn fine job.

Because, in less than five minutes, he was going to have the collar off, and the leash would be used to redden her backside nicely.

Right before he fucked her until she didn't remember her own name.

EPILOGUE

The day after the opening of Alluring Indulgence Resort

"WHAT DID YOU THINK OF AI?" XANDER asked Mercedes as they stepped onto the private jet that would take them from Austin to Dallas.

"I thought it was rather impressive," Mercedes answered with her one-thousand-megawatt smile, the one that made his blood run hot. "Almost as impressive as you were."

Xander smiled, stepping back out of the way and motioning for Mercedes to take a seat in one of the cushioned leather chairs on the five-person jet that they had used for both business and pleasure on quite a few occasions in recent months.

Once she was seated, he moved to the chair across from her, a small table holding a vase of fresh flowers between them. He knew that Mercedes had a fascination for flowers, and for the last six months, Xander had ensured there were fresh ones on the jet whenever they took a trip, as well as in her office every morning.

"Was that sarcasm I detected?" he asked, looking over at her.

"What would give you that idea?" she retorted, a mischievous grin on her pretty lips. "What about you? What did you think of AI?" Mercedes asked, staring back at him as he relaxed into the chair, his long legs stretching out into the aisle.

Their short visit to the newly opened resort in Coyote Ridge was officially over. Not a moment too soon, as far as Xander was concerned.

Having been personally invited by Travis Walker to check out the Alluring Indulgence Resort at the official grand opening, they'd spent the first few hours after their arrival talking business with Travis, his husband, Gage, and two of his brothers, as well as Luke and Logan McCoy.

A higher power must've been looking out for him, though, because, much to his relief, that had been the extent of the business discussions.

From that point on, it'd been an all-out free-for-all, and as intense as it had been, Xander was anxious to get home. They'd spent the morning having breakfast with the owners and other investors of Alluring Indulgence, without spending any time talking business. Not an easy feat with so many Type A's in one room, but as they'd learned, it was possible.

In just a few minutes, they would be heading back to Dallas.

"I don't have any complaints," he told Mercedes. "The turnout was definitely impressive."

Travis obviously had a long list of acquaintances who'd been foaming at the mouth, eagerly anticipating this event. No one would be going home disappointed.

Considering what the Walker brothers were striving for, Xander and Mercedes had taken the opportunity to talk to Travis Walker about future events at the resort, including some demonstrations and classes related to the diversified selection of sexual kinks. As it turned out, that was one of the main reasons he had been invited, aside from the fact that he held a hefty financial investment in the place.

Apparently, Travis Walker had been rather impressed with the BDSM theme nights that had become quite popular at Devotion. It looked as though Travis was looking to implement some of the themed nights for the resort, as well.

To Xander's surprise, Mercedes seemed more than willing to help by giving them her ideas. The look on Travis's face when he'd realized that Mercedes was a Domme *in her former life*, as she liked to tell it, had been rather amusing.

"Well, I look forward to going back in a few months," Mercedes said, her eyes darting toward the flowers. "Thank you. These are beautiful."

"My pleasure," Xander said, meeting her gaze before glancing over at the pilot, who had stepped out of the cockpit looking for a thumbs-up. Since no one else would be joining them on the short flight back to Dallas, Xander merely nodded his head in agreement.

"Did you talk to Logan while we were there?" Mercedes asked.

"About something specific?" She'd been with him during the brief conversations he'd shared with the man, so he knew she was looking for details about something.

Mercedes raised one perfectly groomed eyebrow.

Yes, he knew her well. She was fishing.

"Do you know if something is going on between Sam, Logan, and … what was his name? Elijah something," Mercedes asked, crossing one sexy long leg over the other, her extremely short skirt rising higher on her thigh and catching Xander's attention. She enjoyed doing that to him. Got off on it. And truthfully, he didn't mind at all.

Shit, what red-blooded man wouldn't enjoy being teased by the most gorgeous woman to grace the face of the planet?

"Why do you ask?" Letting his gaze linger on her long, sexy legs for a little longer than necessary, Xander took his time before meeting Mercedes's eyes once more.

"I don't know. Something just seems … different about her, I guess," Mercedes said as the engines on the plane fired up.

"There's something going on, but I don't know any details," he explained, hoping she wouldn't ask him to elaborate, because truthfully, he didn't know what was going on. He didn't want to know, either. "I did talk to Logan briefly about my proposition. I'm still waiting for him to make a decision."

"About your corporate takeover?"

Xander laughed. He wouldn't go so far as to say it was a corporate takeover, but yeah. "He's content working for XTX. I don't blame the guy, and Xavier Thomas is lucky to have someone so loyal. But I would like his help, if he's willing."

"What about Trent? Did you talk to him any more?"

"A little." Trent had reached out to him several months ago, digging deeper into Xander's new business venture. It wasn't so much a corporate takeover as it was a capital investment. One that he was currently moving forward with. Trent had expressed an interest, as well, which meant he and Xander would be working together a little more in the future.

"So, they're a thing now?"

"Who?" Xander asked, caught off guard by the random question. Hadn't they just been talking about business?

"Pay attention," she scolded him with a grin. "Logan, Sam, and Elijah?" Mercedes asked. "I thought he would've been at the opening of AI, but I didn't see him."

"He wasn't there. Logan mentioned he was away on business, I think." Xander had no idea. He didn't make a habit of getting involved in other people's love lives. Especially now that he had his own to focus on.

"I'd say that Travis was happy with the turnout."

"He had every reason to be. Hell, I was rather impressed. They've worked hard to get to where they are."

And he'd heard all about the design, the plans, and what the future held within the first few hours after their arrival. He ensured Travis that he had no worries. The man knew what he was doing, and Xander had told him as much.

And after the reassurances were made, they'd all moved on to the real reason they were there at the resort designed specifically for the naughty.

The pleasure.

And the activities that had ensued from that point forward had been intense. It had almost been enough to keep his mind off of other things.

For the last twenty-four hours, Xander had been beside himself. Anxious. Mercedes had even noticed, calling him out when she found him fidgeting. Something that definitely wasn't like him.

If she only knew.

But she didn't. Mercedes had no idea that he'd been counting down the minutes for the last six months. And now the time had come. Finally.

For months, the two of them had been acting as a couple. Not only had Mercedes officially moved in with him, she'd also put her condo on the market a month ago. She had relocated her office to the extra one he had at his place. They'd tossed around the idea of buying a local storefront to relocate their businesses, but after a lot of discussion, they found that working out of their home was just way too convenient.

Especially when they wanted to take a trip to his dungeon in the middle of the afternoon, which they did on a frequent basis.

But more importantly, for the last six months, Mercedes had begun to open up to him in so many ways. They'd shared many conversations about their childhoods, and he'd been shocked that Mercedes had lowered her guard enough to let him in. That, as much as the words, spoke volumes as far as Xander was concerned. He didn't doubt her love for him, and because she was willing to share the hard details of her life, he knew she didn't doubt him, either. Trust. That's exactly what they'd found together.

As each day passed, Xander became more and more anxious while Mercedes became less and less defiant. Sure, there were times when her submission awed him, other times when he knew she needed a little encouragement — otherwise known as punishment. But no matter what, she always kept him on his toes.

Of course, there were those times when she called him Master, and the sound still did something to him. It made him feel things he'd never imagined possible.

He loved her. That was all there was to it.

They were making frequent visits to Devotion, and both of them had cancelled their memberships at Kink. It was no longer necessary since neither of them was interested in playing with others, and their reputations still held rather firm in that circle. So, it was just easier to engage at Devotion.

As for Clarissa and Shane, they'd sat down and talked to them both separately. As it turned out, their good friends had stopped seeing each other shortly after that debacle. Xander knew it had nothing to do with that particular scene and everything to do with Trent Ramsey. He wasn't quite sure whether Shane realized that or not, though. But regardless of the reason, if the playboy actor had put the moves on Clarissa, no one was admitting to it. At least not yet.

Needless to say, Xander wasn't sure he was up to speed on anyone else's relationship at the moment because he was too busy trying to move his to the next level.

Mercedes still made his head spin, each and every day. He found that he woke up in the morning to thoughts of her and he fell asleep at night with her in his arms. He wasn't sure he could ever go back to living any other way. Falling in love with her had been the single most profound moment of his entire life. Which was why he'd been working to get to this point.

The timing hadn't been exactly what he wanted, but he had felt the need to fulfill his end of their deal before he popped the question.

As the plane took off, Xander thumbed the ring in his pocket, remembering what had happened in recent days during their trip to AI. Specifically the night Xander had fulfilled his end of the deal they had made all those months ago.

He'd thought the day would never come.

Xander loved Mercedes. With everything in him. If it meant he had to pretend to submit to her on occasion, so fucking be it. There was no question in his mind that he would move heaven and earth to make her happy.

He loved her that much.

She made his fucking blood boil, and as he'd proven, he was willing to go to damn near any length just to get close to her. It was the reason she'd given him a chance in the beginning. Giving himself up to her as her submissive for two nights over the course of six months had been proof. It was something he'd never done before, didn't have any desire to do again, but all in all, it had been worth it.

Totally fucking worth it.

"You said you had a meeting this afternoon?" Mercedes asked, reaching for a bottle of water.

"I do." It wasn't the type of meeting she was probably thinking, but it was a meeting all the same.

A naked meeting.

Right here on his private jet.

"Where?"

Okay, so clearly this conversation was moving in a direction he wasn't quite prepared for. Why he'd thought he'd have more time to fidget and let his mind stumble over what he wanted to say, he didn't know.

"Wait, before we get into what the rest of the day entails," Mercedes said as she stood from her chair, moving toward him. Xander had to quickly pull his hand out of his pocket as she straddled his lap. "I just want to say that I had fun last night."

"I'm not sure I'd go so far as to say that was fun," he said with a smirk, "but I enjoyed the hell out of it." He enjoyed what had happened once they were back in their room, for sure. Just like he'd envisioned all those months ago, he had put that damn collar to good use. And the leash.

"I don't think anyone noticed."

"I'm sure someone did." No one had said anything, but Xander hadn't tried to encourage discussion, either.

"I happen to like when you dominate me," she whispered, leaning her head down. "It's fucking hot."

Yeah. Understatement of the century. "Not gonna argue there."

"So what are you waiting for now?"

What the hell *was* he waiting for?

"Do you want me naked? Right here?"

"I want you naked all the time." Xander's body hardened as he realized she was pushing him to dominate her. Not that she had to push hard.

Sliding his hands up her arms, her shoulders, her neck, Xander gathered her hair in his hand and pulled it over her shoulder. He reached for the top button on her shirt and unhooked it easily.

Wanting to kiss her more than he wanted anything, Xander slid his hands back up to cup her face, but as he did, he felt something beneath his fingers. Pulling the collar of her shirt open, he stared in disbelief at the diamond-encrusted rose that settled at her throat.

Her collar. The one he had given her all those months ago but she'd never worn again. After all they'd been through during those first few days, Xander hadn't found the courage to push her, either.

"Did I mention that I really like it when you dominate me?" she asked him softly.

Yeah, she had mentioned that.

Xander's throat was suddenly dry.

Realizing there was no better time than right now, Xander slid his hand into his pocket and pulled out the ring he'd been carrying around with him for the last three months.

Yes, for three months he'd contemplated popping the question but hadn't been able to do so because he felt as though he owed her. He'd made a deal, and now that he had followed through, he knew there was nothing stopping him.

He reached for her left hand, lifted it to his mouth, and placed a kiss on her fingers. When he lowered it, he didn't let go. Instead, he stared into her eyes, holding her gaze for long moments before he managed to get the words past his parched tongue.

"Marry me."

Mercedes's eyes widened. "What?"

"Marry me, Mercedes. You're already my soul mate. And now I want you to be my wife."

"I—"

"Wait. I'm not finished," he told her as he slid the ring over the first knuckle, pausing. "I crave your submission. I crave your love. But nothing in this world is more important to me than to know that you'll be by my side for the rest of my life. I love you, Mercedes."

A tear trickled down her cheek, and for a brief moment, Xander's heart stopped beating. He was sure he was going to suffocate from lack of oxygen since he'd actually stopped breathing. "Tell me that you'll marry me."

But then she resuscitated him with the sweetest words he would ever hear. "Yes," she whispered. "Absolutely yes."

"God, I love you. So damn much," he whispered, sliding the ring all the way on.

"I love you, too," she whispered against his lips. "*Master.*"

And just like any regular business day, Xander and Mercedes moved on to their next meeting.

The naked meeting.

Where they sealed their deal once and for all.

Acknowledgments

As you may have heard, Xander's book was rather difficult for me to write. It had nothing to do with the subject matter, but more so because Xander is a rather difficult man to please. I actually started writing *Perception* in mid-2013. Let's just say, this book was written several times before Xander finally got with the program. Or maybe it was me who finally got with the program. Either way, I am so happy that his story has finally been told. Xander and Mercedes are a couple that I will love until the end of time.

And I have plenty of people to thank for helping me to get the story written.

First and foremost, I have to thank my family. My husband and my children are by far my biggest fans and I know that. They make sure I know that and it means more to me than they will probably ever know. So, thank you. I love you with all that I am and all that I ever will be.

I definitely can't leave out my mom and dad and my brothers. Your support and love mean everything to me. When you tell me that you are proud of me, I'm not sure you even realize how much that means. I love you guys!

Denise and Chancy, I hope the two of you know how much you mean to me. I could never ask for better beta readers, but more importantly, I could never ask for better friends. If it weren't for you questioning me and pointing things out, I wouldn't have been able to finish this book. I love you both!

I also need to thank Nicole-Nation. As always, you ladies keep me going. Although I had to hide out in my cave for quite some time these last few months, your emails and your comments have spurred me on, kept me going. I love you all from the bottom of my heart.

To every single person who has taken the time to message me…
YOU inspire me to keep going. Whether you send me a sentence,
a paragraph, or a several page email, I read every word. If I
haven't responded to you, please note that I will. I promise. I
haven't forgotten you. You can blame Xander if you'd like. He
won't mind.

To the blogs… Gosh, I'm not sure you even realize how much
you mean to me. Your unwavering support is humbling. I've said
this before and I'll say it again, if it weren't for all of you, I
wouldn't be here today. I would list them out, but there are so
many and I couldn't live with myself if I left someone off.

ABOUT NICOLE EDWARDS

New York Times and *USA Today* bestselling author Nicole Edwards lives in the suburbs of Austin, Texas with her husband and their youngest of three children. The two older ones have flown the coup, while the youngest is in high school. When Nicole is not writing about sexy alpha males and sassy, independent women, she can often be found with a book in hand or attempting to keep the dogs happy. You can find her hanging out on social media and interacting with her readers - even when she's supposed to be writing.

CONNECT WITH NICOLE

I hope you're as eager to get the information as I am to give it. Any one of these things is worth signing up for, or feel free to sign up for all. I promise to keep each one unique and interesting.

NIC NEWS: If you haven't signed up for my newsletter and you want to get notifications regarding preorders, new releases, giveaways, sales, etc., then you'll want to sign up. I promise not to spam your email, just get you the most important updates.

NICOLE'S HOT SHEET: A couple of years ago I produced a weekly hot sheet that gave a summary of what I'd done and what I had in the works, and I have decided to bring it back. This is a more personal newsletter that I send out for those who are curious about me, my family, my dogs, and all that goes along with the daily author life.

NICOLE'S BLOG: My blog is used for writer ramblings, which I am known to do from time to time. I will keep these separate from the newsletter updates or what I post in the Hot Sheet so that I don't duplicate in your inbox.

NICOLE NATION: I created Nicole Nation on my website to provide exclusive content to my readers including, First Look notifications, sneak peeks, A Day in the Life character stories, exclusive giveaways, cards from Nicole, Join Nicole's review team. It's free and gets you access to exclusive content you won't find anywhere else!

NN ON FACEBOOK: Join my reader group to interact with other readers, ask me questions, play fun weekly games, celebrate during release week, and enter exclusive giveaways!

INSTAGRAM: Basically, Instagram is where I post pictures of my dogs, so if you want to see epic cuteness, you should follow me.

TEXT: Want a simple, fast way to get updates on new releases? Sign up for text messaging. If you are in the U.S. simply text NICOLE to 64600. I promise not to spam your phone. This is just my way of letting you know what's happening because I know you're busy, but if you're anything like me, you always have your phone on you.

Website:	NicoleEdwardsAuthor.com
Facebook:	/Author.Nicole.Edwards
Instagram:	NicoleEdwardsAuthor
BookBub:	/NicoleEdwardsAuthor

By Nicole Edwards

The Walkers

Alluring Indulgence
Kaleb
Zane
Travis
Holidays with The Walker Brothers
Ethan
Braydon
Sawyer
Brendon

The Walkers Of Coyote Ridge
Curtis
Jared
Hard to Hold
Hard to Handle
Beau
Rex
A Coyote Ridge Christmas
Mack
Kaden & Keegan

Brantley Walker: Off The Books
All In
Without A Trace
Hide & Seek

PIER 70
Reckless
Fearless
Speechless
Harmless
Clueless

SNIPER 1 SECURITY
Wait for Morning
Never Say Never
Tomorrow's Too Late

SOUTHERN BOY MAFIA/DEVIL'S PLAYGROUND
Beautifully Brutal
Without Regret
Beautifully Loyal
Without Restraint

STANDALONE NOVELS
Unhinged Trilogy
A Million Tiny Pieces
Inked on Paper
Bad Reputation
Bad Business

NAUGHTY HOLIDAY EDITIONS
2015
2016